THE ORIGINAL CROWD

TIJAN

PROLOGUE

I never knew who my parents were; all I know is they gave me up and walked away. I grew up feeling unwanted. I filtered from foster home to foster home, spent some time in group homes here and there. I had to grow up quickly; I never had time for a childhood. I had to learn to take care of myself, because I was the only one I could count on.

But I survived.

I learned how to survive on my own and some lessons were hard—fucking hard.

One of the skills I picked up early on was figuring out what role people took in cliques or groups—I learned who was who by watching people. I could tell who had the power in any dynamic. I tapped into that system; I made myself invaluable to them. I completely manipulated everyone, but it's what I had to do. And I was damn good at it.

When I was in the fourth grade, I started hanging out with Brian Lanser. He was gorgeous (okay, he was cute; fourth graders aren't gorgeous). I know in that when you're in the fourth grade you're not supposed to even know that the opposite sex exists, but I did. I was always boy crazy and in the fourth grade, I had a crush on Brian Lanser. He introduced me to cigarettes, beer, condoms (not that they were ever used, I wasn't like that), and I picked up my addiction—stealing.

In the fifth grade, I switched foster homes again and left town. I noticed that there were the same cliques everywhere I went. The same kids. The same habits. The same behaviors. You had the God blessed ones—the rich and spoiled; the nondescript—the bland and invisible; and then my crew—the kids who all the other kids were scared of.

By the time I was in the sixth grade, I learned how to steal. I was addicted to it. During a heist, I felt invincible; I was stronger, my senses were sharper, and it made me feel alive. After each theft, I fell more in love with it. I could get into anywhere, undetected, in the blink of an eye.

I made friends fast by showing off my skills: pickpocketing a teacher, stealing from the popular dick or too-peppy cheerleader that everyone hated. It was a talent that everyone loved and it made me valuable in return. Plus—the guys liked me. I had a body they wanted (yes, boys were already getting horny at that age), but none had touched me, not then anyway.

By the time I got to eighth grade, I had circled back and found myself in the same school as Brian Lanser and he remembered me. He reacquainted me with cigarettes, beer, and condoms (these still held some mystery to me).

And I taught him how to steal.

We were a match made in heaven. He was my first boyfriend, my first love. We were each other's family.

Then something happened. I was adopted in the beginning of my junior year. I had to leave the only family I'd ever known.

And it all stopped.

CHAPTER ONE

"Taryn."

Yep, that's my name. I just rolled my eyes, not pausing as I made my way down the school's hallway. My sister could screech all she wanted—I wasn't going to help her. Ever. At least not in the way she wanted me to.

"Taryn," Mandy shouted again, pitter-pattering her way to me. No one should run when wearing high heels, at least those high heels—they arched halfway up to her calves. That was my sister—she wore high heels, clingy tank tops, miniskirts, and on some days, a cheerleading outfit.

My new sister was a cheerleader. I had been adopted into a family that raised *those* kinds of kids—the God blessed, rich kids. And Mandy was the epitome of the golden child. At least she thought so—blonde, petite, smart and popular by all accounts. She wasn't the head of her clique, but she was one of them. You know the crowd. The highest of the high. The crowd where only a handful actually hold the power. The rest of the popular crowd just drooled to get into their circle.

"Taryn, for God's sake—stop!"

I ignored her, opening my locker as I heard her stumble to a halt, panting slightly beside me.

Eyebrows arched, I whistled. "Thought you were in shape there, sister. All those late night activities with Devon, right?"

"I'm not here to talk about Devon," she snapped. Ooh, Mandy was on a mission. I knew what she wanted, which meant I needed to distract her.

"I heard Devon hooked up with Stephanie Markswith at Brent's party," I commented casually, grabbing my calculus book.

"Not gonna work, sister dear," she said scathingly, but it had. I saw the twitch in her eye. Oh yeah, she knew I was trying to distract her, but she couldn't let it go. "There's no chance in hell that he would hook up with her. No way in hell!"

"Not what I heard."

"She's not suicidal."

"She was drunk. Don't think she was thinking all that clearly," I remarked, shutting my locker and moving away.

Mandy latched to my side and I could see she was seething from the corner of my eye. "The girl's dead!" she said.

"Better tell *her* that."

I saw Stephanie turn the corner up ahead, along with her mini-Stephanie-wanna-be friends tagging behind: Jackie, Slappy, and Curlie. Of course those weren't their real names, that's just what I called them. They were little anorexic bubbles with air inside. They had no personalities and their only mission in life was to get popular. Stephanie was their first rung on the ladder so that's where they started.

Stephanie wasn't quite where my sister was in the social status, but she was almost there.

Mandy saw her at the same time I did. She immediately veered off in her direction.

I couldn't stop a faint grin. Stephanie was about to be knocked down from whatever standing she had achieved and it was all because of me. I'm such a bitch, but the thing is, I had a reason to sic my sister on Stephanie.

Yeah. I had lied. Stephanie hadn't hooked up with Devon. I have no idea who she had hooked up with, but there was without a doubt something—note that I said something, not someone, she was just that nasty. I smiled knowing she was about to be knocked down; she deserved it. The first week of school—my new life in place with my new resolutions firmly in place—she spread a rumor that I stole our biology exam. She only spread that rumor because her boyfriend hit on me.

Yeah, it might've been something that I'd have done in the past, but this time I was innocent. All of my history had been pulled up, making me look guilty as hell and didn't help my innocence in the situation. They couldn't prove it was me, but it didn't matter.

Instead of being suspended, I received detention for two months. But Stephanie had tarnished my name and all my intents and purposes to be a 'good' kid had gone down the drain.

So I served my sentence, got pretty close with Mr. Hollings, the unlucky teacher who had pulled the detention straw, and I set about trying to reclaim my 'good' name again.

After that incident, I declared war on Stephanie, but for the past few months things have been quiet...guess that's over now.

I could still hear Mandy's screech as I ducked inside my classroom. I couldn't help but chuckle.

Glancing up from my lunch tray, I saw Tray Evans drop into the seat opposite mine. Grinning, so self-assured, he drawled, "Your sis preaches about some of your skills."

"Skills that are firmly stocked and locked. Go away," I said coolly. I didn't care who he was, I wasn't going back to my old habits. No way in hell.

"Come on. Why are you so hard-pressed? A girl like you could get laid, *easily*."

I fixed him with a steely glare. I knew who he was. He was the resident god of the school. Captain of the soccer team.

Heartiest partier. He had his own personal supply of kegs, and, if you were really nice and kissed his ass, he'd even rent a few out to you. Tray Evans was the kind of kid that I hated the most—one of the God blessed. He had the family, the looks, the personality, and the money. He could charm his way anywhere and he did. He was so goddamned lucky because he had everything, but he took it for granted. He chose to spend his days optimizing his level of fun.

He was lazy. Pure and simple.

I hate anyone who's advantaged and takes it for granted—Mandy now excluded because she's my sister.

"A girl like me? And who do you think I am?" I asked coolly.

There was a flicker of alarm in his hazel eyes. Yeah, he was back-pedaling a little now. "Chill. Didn't mean anything by it—it's just that...any guy would be with you. That's it. Didn't mean anything derogatory."

"Right." It didn't set right, the guy was lying. "What do you want?"

Yeah, he was firmly reassessing me. I knew this wasn't the girl that he had been told about. I hadn't pulled out my confrontational bitchiness—yet. I'd played in the background, doing passive aggressive stunts (like with Stephanie), but right now...that wouldn't fly. Not with Tray Evans. He ate those girls for breakfast and came back for seconds.

"Taryn!" Mandy cheerfully greeted, landing in the seat next to mine. "Tray, hey!"

"Matthews," he greeted smoothly.

"Is it true?" Mandy asked. "Is the party at your place?"

"Thinking about it."

Catching me studying her intently, Mandy asked warily, "What?"

"Why are you here?" I asked pointedly. She didn't ever sit by me at lunch. I sat alone. It was my rule.

She sighed. "Come on, Taryn. We need your help."

"That's what this is about? Both of you coming to double-team me?"

"Well...yeah," she said simply.

Tray leaned forward, propping his gorgeous muscled arms on the table, teasing me with a view of a tattoo peeking out from underneath his polo sleeve. I had a thing for tattoos. "Mandy says that you're good at stealing stuff. We need something swiped."

"No."

"Taryn, why are you being so unbelievably difficult? Come on, you're like a legend at this stuff. Mom and Dad had to attend conferences about this stuff just to prepare the family for you."

I went cold.

Gasping, Mandy realized what she'd said.

Coolly, I murmured, "Sorry that *your* family had to learn how to thief-proof their home before their new defected adoptee moved in."

"I didn't mean it that way," she scrambled, "I really didn't, I'm sorry. Taryn—"

But I wasn't listening. I had already stood and crossed swiftly out the door and down the hallway. Without thinking, I found myself in the parking lot, my car keys dangling from my fingers, but as I got inside and put the key in the ignition, I stopped myself. What was I doing? It was times like these—when I felt so alone—that I missed Brian Lanser.

The passenger door opened and Tray got inside. Shutting it, he leaned against it, his arms relaxed, hanging on the seat. "Going somewhere?"

"Get out," I clipped out.

"Where we going?" he counted, grinning.

I couldn't help it. I found myself checking him out. He really was gorgeous—he had startling hazel eyes, eyelashes that girls would kill for, and full plump lips.

He was a God blessed version of Brian Lanser. The difference was that Brian Lansers never got away with anything. They were hated just because they were associated with criminals. The Tray Evanses of the world pulled the exact same stunts and were worshiped. They were the most dangerous in my mind.

"Like what you see."

"Oh, you got the package. We both know that, but you have shit for quality," I drawled back, smirking.

"You think so?"

"All my life, I've dealt with boys like you. There's no surprise there; you're all the same."

Leaning forward, his face slowly getting closer to mine, his breath teasing my skin, he whispered, "You think so." Tilting his head slightly, his cheek grazed against mine.

I held firm. I had to, but I hated that I had to ignore the heat that spread through my body. I hated how I had to hold my breath so I wouldn't jump across the seat and attack him.

I whispered back, "I know so."

"Bet I could change your mind."

"Bet you could...if I wanted you to. But," I pulled away and said flatly, "I don't."

His eyes were laughing and the hazel color had darkened to an almost amber color.

"So get out," I delivered smoothly.

He chuckled softly as he leaned against the door once again. "Listen...business only, okay?"

I was silent, regarding him suspiciously.

He continued, "Next week is homecoming and we play the Panthers from Pedlam." Judging from my silence, he proceeded, "Anyway, last year they stole our game book and we got screwed. This year, it's our turn."

"You want me to steal their game book?"

"Mandy says you used to do this stuff. I respect that you don't want to do it anymore, but we know that they've already been sniffing around campus. We caught a few of 'em Friday night, they were trying to take our state championship flag from last year."

"You won the state championship?"

"Yeah."

"So the one loss didn't hurt that bad," I said sardonically.

"It hurt enough. They had to revise an entire new game book." I could hear the acid dripping from his voice.

"You don't even play football. Why do you care?"

"Because this is my school. I take care of what's mine," he promised firmly.

But this wasn't my school. I didn't have a school. Wait—Pedlam?

"I know people at Pedlam."

"What? You go to school there or something?"

"Yeah...a few times."

"So—"

"So...I don't know if I want to help you screw with a school that I'm probably more welcome at than I am here."

Tray sighed, rolling his eyes. "You're Mandy's sister. This is your school too, Taryn."

That was the first time I'd ever heard him say my name. In fact, until lunch, he'd never spoken to me.

"Get out. I'm not helping you."

"What? Come on."

"Out!" I snapped, glaring fiercely.

"Fine," he clipped out, getting out and slamming the door behind him before stalking off.

Watching him, I narrowed my eyes. Well, if I ever had hopes of climbing the social ladder, it just walked away with him.

As I let myself inside the house—correction—the mansion where my new family lived, I dropped my keys in the bowl beside the coat-rack. The place was just massive. I already knew no one was home. My parents—it was hard to think of them as parents, I had to keep reminding myself not to call them Shelley and Kevin in my mind—were gone on a business trip. Kevin was either on-call at the hospital, or, like this weekend, he was at a conference and he always took Shelley with him, leaving me, Mandy, and Austin home alone. Austin, my new brother, was a fourteen year old brat, but I could beat him up so he left me alone for the most part. Our bonding was a work in progress.

Grabbing a pop, I landed on the couch in the media room. I was having a hard time immersing myself in the movie I had put on when I heard the sound of voices coming from the kitchen. Groaning, I could make out Mandy's friends' voices.

The gods of the gods.

Ugh.

"She's down here," Mandy called out, bouncing down the stairs. "Hey," she exclaimed, plopping down beside me.

"Hey."

"So, Tray said you said no. A big fat no actually."

"No, Mandy."

"Come on...why not?" she whined with a pout, looking at me with big puppy dog eyes.

"What's going on?" Jasmine Kent asked, laughing as she sat on the couch opposite us. Tray, Bryce Sethlers, Grant

Lancaster, and Devon Hedley trailing behind. The only person missing was Grant's sister, Amber.

I knew some about them—there were enough rumors swirling about every single one of them. Amber and Grant were twins. Grant had hated Tray at one point because he screwed Amber a few times—apparently, Amber had been panting after Tray for years until he finally succumbed. And Jasmine had a brief stint with him too—but it only lasted six months according to my science partner who wore microscope glasses. (I could never remember her name.)

I had also heard that even though Mandy was hot and steady with Devon, it didn't mean that she had snuffed out the torch she had for Tray since the sixth grade. However, Devon and Mandy were the longest running couple in the school—I think they have been together for four years now. Bryce and Jasmine merely sleep together every now and then; you could usually see them at parties panting and grinding with each other. Most people would take bets on how long it took before they'd either be found in a corner or some closet. The more I think about it, I don't remember hearing a whole lot about Grant's love life...maybe he just had more class.

Yep. The social elite were in my living room. Well, Mandy's living room.

"Leave her alone, Mandy. The girl's frigid. She said no," Tray said in a low tone.

I rounded on him. "Excuse me?"

"You heard me." He smirked.

"Got your little knickers all wrapped in a bunch, huh? Rejection must really get you if you gotta resort to name-calling. Kinda superficial, don't you think?" I taunted.

"Oh, they're not little." He grinned, completely at ease.

Bastard.

"Says you."

"Says me." Jasmine giggled.

Mandy had fallen uncharacteristically silent.

"And you're pretty experienced, huh?"

"Taryn!" Mandy hissed.

"Whatever," I mumbled, standing and moving towards the door.

"Oh, come on," Mandy called out, "Taryn, come hang out. These are my friends and you're my sister."

I turned around. Tray was watching, amused by the scene. Jasmine had turned to glaring at me—guess she didn't like what I implied. The guys were—well, guys. They were snickering, apparently they thought my comment about Jasmine was funny.

This was a game to them, even to Jasmine as she let a smile slip out after being nudged from Grant.

But it wasn't a game to me. It used to be, my whole life had been just a game, but the stakes were too high now that I had a family I actually wanted to stay with.

"I'm not doing it. Whatever you want me to take, I'm not doing it."

"We're not asking anymore," Tray remarked, sounding bored.

"Yeah," Mandy agreed. "We'll figure something else out, okay? So just chill, alright?"

They were all watching me and I knew whatever I did next would seal my position in the school. Logically I knew that my placement was firm, finalized, because Mandy was my sister, but...that's not what I felt. I went against what my instincts were screaming at me and I slowly sat back down and resumed watching the movie.

Mandy squeezed my arm slightly before she started chatting to Jasmine over my head.

I was silent throughout the rest of the evening. I think they were a little cautious around me; I kept a low profile at school and I was pretty quiet every time Mandy invited them over the few months they've known me. It was the first time anyone had seen the confrontational side of me.

Everyone meandered to the kitchen where Mandy put a pizza in the oven. I had followed and perched on a stool, my hands wrapped around my pop. Tray had been watching me the entire evening, and it was pissing me off. I didn't like letting people read me—call me paranoid, but I was guarded for a reason—but I knew what he was doing. He was trying to figure me out; figure out my weaknesses and so forth. He didn't like having someone so unpredictable in his group.

When the phone rang, Mandy handed it over saying, "It's for you. Dunno know who it is."

Frowning, I asked, "Hello?"

"Babe."

Brian.

I jumped off the stool and scooted out through the patio doors, shutting them behind me. "What are you doing calling me?"

"Babe, come on."

"Brian, leave me alone."

"Come on," he said silkily. "After all we've been through? You and me? You're just going to write us off?"

"There's no us. I made that loud and clear." But God, it was good to hear his voice. The longer I was away from him, I remembered more of the good times we had together than the bad.

"Let me come over. Let's talk about this."

"No."

"Babe."

"Brian, no. Go and screw Liza, I know she's probably panting right behind you."

"She's not you, Tar. There's no one like you, that's what's fucked up. I want *you*. I miss *you*." He sighed.

I couldn't say anything that I hadn't already said and I wasn't about to tell him the truth—that I missed him. He'd be relentless.

"Babe, you can't tell me you don't miss me. I'm your family, Tar. I've been your family for the last XX years. You can't just dismiss me. You know that. I know you know that."

"Yeah, well..." What I said next was harsh, but I had to, "I have a new family now." I hung up. Breathing heavily, I leaned against the wall, hidden from inside where I knew there were at least a few pairs of eyes on me, I tried to pull myself together.

Mandy came to the patio door and opened it a crack as she stuck her head outside. "You okay?"

"Yeah," I said shakily, trying to paste a grin on my face.

"You don't look okay. Who was that?"

"Just...someone from my past."

"An old boyfriend?"

"Guess you could call him that."

"He sounded hot over the phone. Is he hot?"

"Oh yeah, and he knows it." I chuckled. He was different from Tray. Tray's looks could mesmerize people. Brian's almost scared people away—he has the cliché bad boy look and everyone saw that when they looked at him. They'd be correct in stereotyping him; he *is* a bad boy—he's spent more than his fair share of time in juvie.

The phone rang in my hands. I saw Mandy reach for it, ready to do my dirty work, but I shook my head. "No. I have to do this." Clicking the button, I murmured, "What?"

"Babe."

Yep, he was relentless.

"You call me again and I'll get a restraining order on your ass. You know I'll do it," I snapped as I turned away from Mandy.

"You don't mean that. You don't really want me out of your life."

That pissed me off. I'd lived my life not letting anyone tell me what I wanted or didn't want, and Brian knew that—he just screwed up. "Just watch me."

"Babe, you don't really want to do that."

"Oh really? Why? You think I don't know all about your shit you got going on? About your little deal with Carmen Rizzo or about the drugs you always keep at Christian's house? Oh wait, no...here's the best one—how about the videos of that bank you robbed. I have those, I know where they are."

Maybe I'd gone too far because Brian was quiet on his end. I couldn't let it get to me though, I had to be a stone cold bitch to get him to let go of me.

"You mean the robbery you were an accomplice in? The vids you're on too?" he countered.

I laughed. "Oh please. I'm the professional. You think I'd be reckless enough to get caught on video? Oh no, those vids have you and you alone on them. I was nowhere near those cameras; not even my shadow came close to being videoed. Remember who taught who."

"You threatening me, Taryn?"

"It's Taryn now? Not Tar? Not babe? Is Liza crawling all over your lap?"

"You're pushing me," he warned.

"Then stay away from me, Brian. I mean it or else I'll get my hands on that shit and hang you out to dry. Don't think I won't and don't you dare think I can't, because you know more than anyone exactly what I'm capable of doing."

He knew I was right. Brian had watched in amazement as I could slip through any crack, and make my way under any security program. By the time I was reunited with Brian, I was already at a professional level.

"Fine. I'd forgotten how much of a bitch you are," he bit out.

"Oh no, baby. I was your equal. That makes you a bitch just as much as me," I said smoothly and hung up.

Oh my God. I'd burned one of the sturdiest bridges I had ever had in my life and I didn't know if it was worth it. I was still gambling with how this new family would work out.

"Holy hell," Jasmine breathed out.

Whirling, I paled seeing the entire gang on the patio. Amber had shown up at some point and looked shocked.

Tray was staring at me with an unnamed emotion, one (I shivered) I didn't know if I wanted to identify.

Mandy looked like she wasn't breathing.

"Mandy," I said, faltering self-consciously. "I—"

"Mom and Dad told me some stuff, but they don't know about any of that. That's some...that's like some serious stuff."

"It wasn't me. Most of it was...Brian."

"Yeah, I remember hearing Mom talking about him to a parole officer."

"Look," I let the parole officer slide by, I wasn't really surprised at her lack of knowledge, "it's why I don't want to steal whatever it is you want for you. This life, with you guys, is a fresh start for me. Yeah, I'm good at stealing stuff, but I don't want to do that anymore."

Everyone was quietly processing what they'd heard; when I looked at their faces I saw their emotions range from disgust, fear, and awe. When I looked into Tray's eyes, I saw condemnation.

He knew I was lying.

CHAPTER TWO

At school the next day, all of them gave me a wide berth—not that that was different from before, but even Mandy held back when she normally would invade my space time and time again. I caught Tray watching me when I glanced over my shoulder in lit class. As I walked out to my car, I glanced to the side and saw him walking beside me, eyeing me but he passed by swiftly, not saying a word to me as he got into Grant's car, the passenger door already open with Bryce and Jasmine in the back.

The rest of the week passed that way and the rest of the school took notice. Apparently any social graces I had been given because Mandy was my sister had been stripped away. Even some of the nerdy girls looked at me sympathetically.

Friday I found myself walking, alone (what a surprise), to my car when I felt someone fall in line beside me.

Tray.

"Oh, you guys are actually speaking to me now? Not like you used to before." I couldn't help myself, but sarcasm seemed to have returned to my voice. It had always been there, I just stuffed it down in an attempt to be the new me.

"It's not like that. Come on."

"So what? This a pity talk? Pick me up, make sure people see you talking to me?" I had had enough with this bullshit. I didn't need anyone's help, or their pity.

"It's not—God—you're a bitch."

"And we both know it makes you hot."

Tray narrowed his eyes at that, not in shock, but lust...his eyes were amber. Raking his eyes over my body, he murmured softly, "So what are you going to do about it?"

I sucked in a sharp breath. I hadn't fully expected that, but he leaned closer and whispered, "Because I know it makes you hot too."

"Get off."

"I'd love too."

I shrugged him away. "You know what I mean."

He must have had enough because he grabbed my arm and yanked me into a hidden alcove at the corner of the parking lot.

"What are you doing?" I made it sound like I was bored. I was anything but.

Crowding me towards the back, until I couldn't go any further without falling inside the foliage surrounding us, he said smoothly, "You lied."

"What are you talking about?" I already knew, I had seen the condemnation in his eyes that night on the patio.

He stood so close that I could feel the heat radiating off his body. Oh, God. I noticed I was holding my breath.

"You said you don't want to steal anymore, but you lied. You get an adrenalin rush every time you take something—you're addicted to it. It's like a dare...isn't it? And you always win."

"So?" I shoved him back. "I'm not a criminal anymore; I don't want that life anymore."

"I'm not asking you to."

"Right."

"I'm not...I'm asking you to take one thing. One thing, Taryn."

"What is it? What is so goddamn righteous that it'll screw Pedlam?"

"They have some tight security. We need you to get the master. All the codes and everything are kept on this device, it's called a PRS-500. It's top of the line. You get that for us, and you don't have to do anything else, swear to God."

"You just want me to hand over the keys to the school, and probably the security codes for all the other schools and buildings in Pedlam?"

"We only want to get in and do some damage the night before our game. That's all."

And I was pure and innocent.

I snorted in disbelief. "I'm not stupid."

I was blinded by Tray's smile. Oh, whoa. I was suddenly burning up and, judging from the look in his eyes, he noticed my reaction because the amber was back in his eyes. Oh God...

"Oh...no, I know you're not," he said huskily, moving closer to wrap a hand around my neck. He bent forward slightly, his mouth just to the side of mine. I could feel his breath kissing my skin. Without thinking, I closed my eyes and leaned into him, bringing our bodies in contact. His other hand slid from my arm and down my back, ending just on the small of my back as he applied just enough pressure, tipping my hips against his.

Without realizing it, I had slipped my arm around his shoulder, curving it around his neck as I moved my head towards his, our lips touching tenderly; just resting against each other's. Neither of us moved, we were at a standstill. Both of were breathing deeply now. I slipped a finger inside the front loop of his pants and pulled, then Tray's mouth opened roughly over mine.

Opening my mouth, I dipped my head back, granting him better access. As his tongue swept inside, I moved mine against his, my hands now clenched in fists on the front of his shirt. Groaning, I slid my foot around his leg and he immediately grasped it, raising it and pulling my body almost on top of his.

Whipping away, both of us were silent, breathing heavily for a moment. I shook my head, clearing the cloud of lust.

"Just think about it. Alright?" he suggested, his voice husky.

I didn't trust myself to speak so I just nodded dumbly.

"Fine. Fine," he murmured, eyeing my lips intently.

I licked them.

Moaning, he came back, drawing a hand around my neck as I stood up on my toes to meet him halfway. Our mouths fused, he had my leg twisted around him again as his hand slid up and around to my stomach, resting there a moment, his thumb caressing in a rhythmic motion.

Sliding his hand inside my front pocket he pulled out my ringing cell phone and handed it to me, chuckling wryly. I didn't comprehend what he handed me for a moment. Blushing, I snapped it open. "Hello?"

"Babe."

Turning around, my back to Tray, I snapped, "Brian, I swear to God, if you don't—"

"Don't what?" he snapped back. "Give up on the one person who's been there for me my entire life? I'm not doing it, Tar. I don't give a shit what you throw at me."

Without realizing, I had softened my voice. "Brian, I'd do it for you," I said hoarsely. "And you know it. I'd back off if you had this chance."

"No, baby, I'd bring you with me."

"It's not the same."

"Yes, it is. I'd make it work someway."

He would. We both knew it, but I wasn't him. "Fine, but we both know I would've done anything to make it right, and if that meant giving up the fun, I would've done it. You can't do that for me."

"That's what this is about? You think I won't give up the 'fun' for you?" he asked bitterly.

"We both know you won't. You're in too deep, Brian."

"Baby."

"Don't," I said firmly, unconsciously standing straighter.

"Tar."

"I said no." I've rarely told him no and he'd learned to listen when I said it.

Brian was silent on the other end. I knew he'd listen this time too.

"Goodbye," I whispered, closing my phone before he could say I was fighting back tears because I knew he'd listen to me this time.

"You love him," Tray murmured, watching me intently as I turned back around.

"I loved him. He was my...he was my family when everyone else didn't want me."

"I get it." He nodded solemnly. "What you're doing, I get it. I do."

"And yet you still want me to steal the PRS-500," I stated.

Grinning, he shrugged. "Yeah...I gotta take care of the school."

I made my decision. I looked him straight in the eyes and said, "If you're looking to turn me into one of those girls that'll bow down to you—it won't work. I'm not going to pant after you, hoping you'll pay attention to me."

He waited. He saw the decision in my eyes.

"But I'll get the PRS-500," seeing his triumph flare quickly, I continued, "after I have a friend of mine take a look at it."

"What?"

"I'm your best shot of getting it and that's the deal. Take it or leave it. I won't lose any sleep over it."

Narrowing his eyes, he shook my hand. "You're an operator. I should've guessed," he said soothingly.

I smirked, turning around and crossing to my car. As I pulled out of the parking lot, I caught a glimpse of Tray leaning against his, watching me.

Mandy had asked me if I wanted to go to Tray's party that night, but I had declined, instead choosing to slip out of the house and head to an old friend's. As my car slid to a halt outside the ratty old house, I grinned, hearing the music blaring from inside.

Same old Geezer.

Chuckling, I approached it and swept through the door, knowing he'd never hear my knock. I found him where I always find him—his skinny ass stoned on the couch, a half grin on his face, his hair looking even shaggier than the last time I saw him.

Crossing over to him, I swiftly kicked the couch. I watched him stumble off, jolted from the bump. As his eyes lighted on me, a full grin spread over his face and he threw himself at me.

"Tartar!"

Laughing, I disentangled his arms and cut the music. "Geez, you don't ever change, do you?"

"Never ever. Never ever," he babbled, bouncing up and down in place.

Shaking my head, I replied, "It's good to see you, Charles." Using his real name, I saw a small tear slip from his eye. His smile vanished immediately and he threw himself at me again, wrapping his bony arms around me tightly, squeezing the life out of me.

After a moment, I kicked him away. "Okay, that's enough."

He was bouncing again.

Tilting my head to the side, I asked, "Can I ask you for a favor?"

"Yeah. Sure. Anything."

"Brian been around?"

"No," he said seriously. "He's been off, like *off* off, if you know what I mean, ever since you left. I used to think he was scary, but man, he's really scary now."

"Yeah...he's been calling me."

"I think he never thought you'd leave him."

"Yeah." I sighed, rubbing a hand over my forehead. "Uh...I have a favor to ask."

"Sure. Anything. You know that." He beamed up at me.

"I need you to make a device look like it's been wiped."

"Any certain type of device? And I'm guessing you don't really want it to be wiped?"

"Yeah. It's a PRS-500. I only want one code to show up, one set of numbers. Everything else, I want it to look clean, but not actually clean. Got it?"

He saluted. "Yes, ma'am. Whatever you want."

"Okay. Okay." It was good to see him. Really good. Wrapping my arms around him, I hugged him back this time, something that I'd never done before. Brian was the only one I ever hugged. Geezer and the others, I let them hug me, but I never hugged them.

Geezer knew the significance. He was sniffling when I pulled away and swept out the door.

Getting in the car, I quickly started it and peeled out of there, flicking the tears away as they peeked at the corner of my eyes.

It wasn't a long drive, from Pedlam to Rawley, but it was long enough to get my thoughts in order. If I was going to do this, I needed layouts, blueprints, and security parameters. Everything. If Tray wanted this device to get inside Pedlam before the homecoming game, I needed to steal it just before that evening. At the last possible minute so they wouldn't change all the codes. That meant I needed to get it by Thursday night. I had six days to get this assignment perfected. I would need Geezer on standby, preferably away from Tray and the others. They didn't need to mix.

I didn't want to acknowledge it, but I had missed this. The old rush was building and I couldn't stop the grin on my face.

Pulling onto the highway leading into Rawley, I pulled into the town's diner. Normally it was the hangout, but since Tray was having his party it was empty. Everyone, invited or not, wanted to be at his party. Apparently, they were legendary.

So I was surprised when I saw Tray, Bryce, and Grant sitting in a booth in the corner. Before I could duck out, not sure if I wanted to stay or go home, Grant saw me and let out a whistle.

I blushed. I forgot I was wearing my old attire when I went to see Geezer; he wouldn't have recognized me if I wore what I normally did now. I had on tight black pants and a black tank top that dipped low, highlighting the swell of my breasts.

Approaching them, fully aware of the heat in Tray's scrutiny, I murmured, "Hey, guys."

"We thought we'd see you at the party, but you must have had other plans," Bryce called out, grinning wolfishly.

"Nah, just business," I drawled, holding Tray's gaze intently for a moment. "But that's done so I thought I'd stop in for a Diet Coke. Thought you guys would be at the party, since—you know—Tray, you're hosting it."

He grinned, leaning back, relaxed and in control. "Nah, those parties can run themselves."

"Hmm," I murmured, abruptly turning and heading to the counter. As I ordered my Diet Coke, I saw them leave. I heard their car squealing as they pulled out of the parking lot. Grabbing my Coke, I headed towards my car, then slowed seeing Tray leaning against my car, his arms crossed, waiting patiently for me.

Drawing closer, I stopped just in front of him. Neither of us spoke.

"You go see that guy?" he finally asked, the epitome of self-control.

"No, I went to see a friend, the guy who's going to check out the device before I hand it to you."

"You move fast."

"Yeah, well...this job needs a lot of planning. I gotta start early."

"So I was thinking, if you get the device, we'd need to have it by Thursday night."

"I know. The last possible moment so they don't change the codes. I'm on it."

"You're very...professional about this."

"Yeah, well...I used to go to Pedlam. There's a reason why their security is so tight. It's going to be a challenge."

"And that's the only part of this that's a challenge?" he drawled, pushing off from the car so he was right in front of me, almost touching, but not quite.

Tipping my head back, I held his eyes. "It's the only part that gives me a rush."

He grinned. "Somehow I don't believe you."

"You're not the challenge if that's what you're thinking," I said softly, grinning at him.

"But I give you a rush," he murmured, bending so his mouth was against my neck. I closed my eyes, I couldn't help it. I was slowly losing the capability of thinking when I felt his mouth kiss and linger on me, sliding around to the other side. My hand twisted itself in his hair, holding it like an anchor, as my other hand slid down his chest, finding its way underneath his shirt and sliding a finger on the inside of his jeans—just an inch inside. I grinned hearing his sudden intake of breath as I moved my finger slightly, rubbing it back and forth. Then his hand moved and slipped underneath my tank top, and slid upwards, inching up slowly resting just around the swell of my breast.

Remembering where we were, I ripped away from him breathing heavily.

"Shit..." he breathed, his eyes raking my face.

"Go to your party. There's a girl there you can fuck," I snapped, climbing inside and ripping out of the parking lot.

The next day passed uneventfully. Mandy came in my room Saturday evening feeling better after nursing her hangover away the entire day, and filled me in on everything that had happened at the party. Who hooked up with whom; who broke up; who fought; who barfed. It was an awesome party supposedly.

Watching me intently, she asked if I wanted to go out that night with the gang. I declined and continued folding my clothes, showing no reaction.

At her silence, I almost flinched. The rumors had already circulated—someone must've seen Tray and I outside the diner, because I knew he wouldn't say anything and I sure as hell didn't. Then again, maybe he would tell; I didn't really know him that well.

She didn't push it. Instead she launched into a rant about how she thinks Devon might be cheating on her.

Frowning, I turned back to her. "Are you serious? Devon? We're talking about Devon?"

"Yeah." She swung her legs around and sat up, still on my bed. "He was...weird last night. I don't know. Maybe he really did hook up with Stephanie."

"I lied about that."

"I know you did, but...maybe she's going after you through me and she's trying to do it through Devon because she knows that would hurt me.

"Nah," I dismissed easily," Stephanie's pretty direct. She'll come straight after me, not you."

Laughing, she murmured, softly, "You know, after that phone call the other night, you're different. It's like you're a whole different person."

"No. I just wasn't me before. Now the old me is starting to come back out."

"Why'd you hide?"

I wasn't ready to unburden my soul. I didn't care if she was my new sister.

I shrugged. "Getting to know people. Nothing dramatic."

"Oh." She sounded disappointed.

"So are you going to talk to Devon tonight? About your hunch?"

"About Stephanie? No, but I am going to ask him if he's cheating on me."

"Come on, Mandy. The sooner you talk to him, the sooner you'll know what's really going on and be back to being lovebirds again," I murmured, folding my last shirt. Leaning against the wall, I took in her frown and said, "Whoa. You're actually serious."

"Yeah," she said sarcastically, standing up she started to pace. "He's really off and it's getting to me, you know? He's been like this for a while, but last night...it creeped me out."

"Well..." I murmured softly, feeling sad for her. I know what it felt like, Brian had cheated on me a few times too. "Do you stay like this, not knowing, or do you push him and find out?"

Sighing, she replied, "I can't stay like this. No way. It's been...God...like seven months of this already. I didn't want to admit it, but this feeling has been there, you know?"

"Yeah..."

"Yeah..."

"So where are you guys going tonight? And who's all going?"

"The gang and some others." That meant the elite and the crowd that gathered around them, including Stephanie and her wannabes. "We're going to a party at Rickets' House."

Great. I felt a knot in my stomach. Rickets' House was a great big white mansion near Pedlam. It was where a lot of parties were thrown because it was situated deep in the woods. Kids could scatter easily if the cops showed up and it was notorious for being a mating ground for other schools. Brian wouldn't be there, he hated that place, but there'd definitely be some others there from Pedlam.

On the other hand...

"I'm in."

I didn't care about Mandy's abrupt startled gaze.

Devon and Jasmine were driving with us. They'd arrived a few minutes ago and it had been awkward...to say the least. Jasmine had obviously heard the rumors because she gave my outfit a second glance. But, I might run into other Pedlam students and they needed to see me. Not the new me—the quiet, boring, saintly me. They'd just laugh.

So I dressed how I used to. I wore a leather miniskirt and a lacey black tank top that hugged my curves with a diamond necklace that was looped twice around my neck, resting just above my belly-button. Even Mandy had been slightly taken aback and she'd seen the old me a few times.

I could tell that she was distracted by Devon's behavior. He'd been standoffish the entire evening. He arrived and gave her a chaste kiss on the cheek and that had been it. After we traipsed into the car, he'd been silent, just focused on driving. Jasmine sat in the back with me, chatting to Mandy, who was glancing at Devon every few seconds, trying to appear nonchalant. I was staring out the window tuning the conversation out.

Until I heard Jasmine murmur, "...he was with Aidrian last night. God, Tray just pisses me off at times."

I looked over and caught a furtive glance from Mandy under her eyelashes. "What?"

"Didn't say anything."

Jasmine turned to me. "I was just telling Mandy that sometimes I'm embarrassed by Tray. God, especially when he fucks girls like Aidrian Casners. She's white trash. Seriously."

"That's probably why he fucked her," I drawled, leaning back.

Jasmine and Mandy were both watching me intently. Even Devon had glanced in the rear-view mirror.

"What?"

"Nothing," Mandy squeaked.

Jasmine turned to face me. "We heard an interesting tidbit last night...about you and Tray," Jasmine said, trying to bait me. "Care to elaborate?"

"If it's anything short than us screwing on the hood of my car, it's not worth addressing." I grinned, a dry chuckle in my voice. "How long till we get there?"

"We're meeting up with Tray and the rest of the gang at his place first," Devon said tightly, turning into a driveway.

I had to admit, the place was impressive. It was gorgeous. The mansion had two massive pillars right before the front door with a large patio extending off to the side. The living room could be seen through three large windows and inside there was a flat screen TV highlighting one entire wall. It looked like a movie theater with black leather couches gracing the sides of the room. Through the house you could see the pool shimmering through the glass patio doors on the other side of the mansion.

Yes. It was impressive.

Fuck that.

Walking inside we were met with a chandelier—an *actual* chandelier in the foyer with a spiral staircase leading off to the right. There was an open doorway just before the steps and it led to an expansive kitchen, complete with an island in the middle. Even the kitchen looked like a masterpiece.

Most of the 'cool' crowd were lounging around, all drinking, chatting, or in the process of making their drinks for the ride.

I saw Grant and Bryce right away. They were at the table talking with some girls I didn't recognize. Amber was sitting on the island, dangling her feet, talking with a guy that I thought was Brent...Garrett? Basketball team...I think. I didn't really care.

Tray was nowhere to be found.

I felt Mandy nudge me and whisper, "Tray just got here."

I couldn't see him.

"What are you talking about?" I asked in a seemingly bored, low tone.

"I just talked to Erin and she said Tray just ran in. He's getting dressed and then we're all heading out."

"I don't get why we're all meeting here? Why don't we just go to the party?"

"Because Tray and Grant are the only ones who know where Rickets' House is...and...there's probably Pedlam students there. It's not like we all want to show up alone."

I grinned. "What? Strength in numbers? Can't handle a few Pedlamites?"

"You probably could, but I'm secure enough to admit that I wouldn't want to do it. Trust me, we want Tray there with us when we show. He can handle Crispin Gentley."

I scoffed, "Gentley's a baby."

Jasmine had been listening and asked, "You know Crispin Gentley?"

"Yeah and he's nothing to be scared of."

Bryce had crossed the room without me noticing. He asked, "How do you know Gentley?"

"I went to Pedlam a few times."

"A few times?" I didn't recognize this girl, but she was already annoying me. She had platinum blond hair and boobs that shouted 'screw me' every time your eyes skimmed across them. She could've been the poster-girl for Hooters.

I clamped down on my instant irritation. "Yeah. What about it?"

"She didn't mean anything, Matthews," Tray soothed, walking up behind me and wrapping an arm around my waist, pulling me into his side. To everyone else, he said, "Let's head out." He pulled me with him and said, "You can ride with me."

I glared at him, but noticed that Mandy was looking cautiously at Devon. I saw Jasmine pair off with Grant, so I said lightly, "Fine." It would be the perfect time for Mandy to talk to Devon anyway.

Two other guys were walking behind us as we walked to Tray's SUV. I ignored the heat from Tray's hand as it spread, open palm, on my stomach. Brushing him off, I rounded the SUV and climbed into the passenger seat. The other two got in the back.

As Tray started it up, he introduced us, "Helms, Mitch, this is Matthews. Matthews—the guys."

"My name's Taryn, not Matthews," I informed them dryly, seeing each nod in an easygoing way. I recalled that they were both on the basketball team. They fit the description—tall and lanky. They were both wearing Abercrombie & Fitch. Preppy boys.

If I had been worried about having to converse with Tray the entire time, I would've been relieved. For the most part, he ignored me and seemed content making small talk with Helms and Michael.

I tuned them out as I speculated on the night ahead.

Crispin Gently would probably be there. He seemed to always be at Rickets' House. I had only heard stories about the parties there. They were notorious just because kids from other towns showed up. Rickets' House wasn't Pedlam Territory. It was in the middle of four towns. Four territories. I'd been there a few times, enough to know how to get there myself if I was asked, but Brian wanted me to stay away from it when we were together. Cops seemed to always show up and, of course, they always went after Brian first.

Crispin knew my rep though. He'd hit on me enough in the past. Something about the fact that I could steal anything seemed to fascinate him. He and Brian were constantly getting in shoving fights—usually over me. I think I was just an excuse, though. Gentley hit on me because I was Brian's girl. Everyone knew it, so he used me to get a rise out of Brian—and it worked.

Of course, I think Gentley was just entertained by me. I had noticed, on a few occasions, there had been amusement in his eyes when he had hit on me, even when Brian wasn't anywhere around. He enjoyed baiting me and seeing how I handled it. Normally I handled it with grace, but one time, he'd gone too far. That night, Gentley received thirteen stiches and spent the night in the hospital.

Without realizing it, we were already there. I blinked. That hadn't taken as much time as I thought. As Tray drove through the back winding roads, I glanced uneasily at the forest on both sides. The woods always unnerved me. I don't know why but they just...freaked me out. It was something I'd never told anyone; not even Brian. Snapping back to the present, Tray was already pulling into the long driveway around the hill that led its way to Rickets' House, its lights already blinding from the party going on inside. There was a good amount of cars loitering the driveway as we passed them by.

"Dude, where we going to park?" I think it was Mitch who asked.

"Forget that. Look at all these people. Holy fucks! We're going to get trashed tonight." That must've been Helms then?

I grinned, catching sight of Grayley's fender. He'd think it's a riot, me showing up with the crème de la crème from Rawley's royalty. No doubt he'd double over in laughter when he saw us make our entrance.

"Something funny?" Tray asked silkily, watching me from the corner of his eye.

I looked at him. I had to admit, he looked good; he looked more than good. If I were to create the perfect guy, I have to admit, he'd looked like Tray. His knowing eyes were still resting on me as he paused briefly for Helms and Mitch to jump out.

"I just recognized a few of the cars back there," I said lightly, moving to open the door.

"Walk with me," he requested. Anyone else would've taken it as a command, but I heard the questioning lilt to his voice.

So I sat back and waited as he moved the SUV forward. The rest of our train did the same thing; each car paused for the passengers to hop out and the cars all followed the others, parking side by side on the opposite end of the hill.

As we got outside, Tray didn't move to draw me against his side. I was grateful, but at the same time I was seething at myself—I had kind of hoped he would have. We walked easily beside each other, making our way up to the house. Turning back, I saw Devon walking alone, looking lost in thought. Jasmine was walking with some guy—I couldn't place his name.

When he neared the door, we saw that everyone had already gone inside. There were quite a few drinking and lounging on the patio in front of the door. I recognized one or two from Pedlam.

"Holy shit!"

Whirling around, I paled at seeing Veronica Teedz teetering unsteadily on her high heels, beer sloshing over her yellow cup, her eyes transfixed on my face. "Holy shit," she exclaimed again, drawing nearer. "Taryn! How the hell are you!? I can't believe it's you...it is you or am I that drunk?"

I was taken aback. Veronica Teedz had never acknowledged my presence before, why now? Coolly, I replied, "You're that drunk." And I moved past her, catching an amused look in Tray's eyes.

I failed to see her pull out her phone as our group moved inside.

Inside there were people everywhere; each room was packed tight. A few tables were set up in the corners for some card playing. I knew from previous experience that the dance floor was in the basement, but the bass of the music pounded throughout the entire house. The second, third, and fourth floors were the bedrooms—hookups and smaller parties usually congregated there.

Apparently tonight was different because the main floor had been turned into a dance floor, along with the patio outside.

I felt Tray grab my hand and pull me towards the kitchen area. He shelled out some money for our cups. After they had been filled from a keg, he gave one to me. Pulling me closer, he murmured in my ear, "You here to work?"

I tilted my head back, my lips brushing against his ear, a hand braced on his chest. "Yeah. Some of my old crew is here, they might be willing to help me out."

He nodded and turned into the crowd, leaving me alone.

I didn't notice how some of the crowd stopped to watch us.

Pushing through the room, I worked my way through the crowd, smiling in return to a few greetings, some from those who recognized me from Pedlam, some just from drunken pervs.

Finally, I pushed my way into a backroom. I saw that Tray had taken root against the wall off to the side. He was swamped on both sides by people. Some were Rawley students, I recognized Tamira Case from another school I briefly attended—from what I remember, Tray was exactly her type—there were others that I didn't recognize. Tray had an atmosphere around him that told the world that he didn't give a damn about anyone or anything; it made him all the more appealing.

On the other side of the room, was Crispin Gentley, also surrounded by bimbos—okay, to be fair they were cheerleaders—and jocks—okay, to be fair they were cheerleaders. I saw Tracy Hardkins and Kimberly Ringsworld. They were at the top of the food chain in

Pedlam. I groaned softly. I saw Crispin's eyes grow wide, falling on me at the same time I saw the person I had been searching the entire house for: Grayley.

Grayley fit in with anyone—it was one of his gifts. He was a pretty likeable guy and pretty popular. He had become friends with me and Brian years ago; he was also Geezer's best friend so I knew I could trust him. I knew he wouldn't say anything to Brian or Crispin, but as I took a step in his direction, I gritted my teeth, finding myself blocked by the Crispin Gentley.

"Well, well, well," was all he said, in a tone like I was a mouse caught in a cat's paw.

It set my teeth on edge and I knew that Tray was watching intently.

I didn't say anything, but just waited for him to finish.

"Looking good, Rosette."

"It's Matthews now," I stated.

"Oh right. I heard that you'd gotten adopted. Good family, I hope?" He chuckled.

He didn't give one damn. We both knew it.

"Get lost, Gentley. I'm not here for you."

He laughed outright at that one, tipping his head back, his perfect teeth blinding. "I've forgotten this. You and me. Our little...foreplay—"

I smirked, moving closer a step. "Oh, honey, when it's foreplay, you'll know. You've never gotten close."

Grayley had finally noticed us and I saw him starting to push his way through the crowd towards me, a look of panic on his face. That made me frown slightly...

"Come now, Rosette...now that you're free from Lanser, we don't have to continue this little game," he coaxed.

Grayley was almost to us and the pale color on his face was more distracting than Gentley's repulsive comments.

I struck out without thinking, taunting him, "Oh, little Crispin, just a poor neglected boy. Always hiding in the closet, his little G.I. Joe clasped tightly in his hands, afraid his abusive, drunk daddy will find out his secret...he wet the bed last night in a long run of nights." I stepped back. "It explains a lot."

Crispin had fallen silent, just watching me, not letting any emotion show.

So I continued, "At least that's what your file says about how you developed your over-compensatory behaviors, pretending you're Mr. Sex God—so full of sexual prowess, when in fact—"

But I was cut off as Grayley flung himself in between us, pushing me back, facing Crispin and saying urgently, "She's drunk, Gentley. She doesn't know what she's talking about."

Crispin was seething in a tightly controlled rage as his eyes flickered over mine, leaving me cold. "She better remember where to step, Grayley."

I leaned over Grayley's shoulder. "It's not the only thing I read in your file. Want me to share your other secrets?"

"Goddamn, you little—" He was cut off as someone launched himself around us and shoved Crispin against the wall, raining punch after punch against his face and stomach.

It was Brian and I was shocked to see my ex-boyfriend so livid and uncontrollable as he assaulted Crispin savagely.

"Oh fuck!" Grayley bit out, before launching himself at Brian, desperately trying to get him off Crispin.

I couldn't help it, I looked at Tray, pleading.

Tray had straightened, hearing the exchange, but he saw my look and hesitated for a moment. Watching the two guys fighting, Grayley and a few others tried to get between Crispin and Brian, but then Tray nodded and the rest of his crew rushed the fight and pulled them apart. Tray crossed to stand behind me. He leaned close, one hand splayed on my hip, and murmured in my ear, "This part of your plan?"

"It was until Brian showed up."

"That's your ex?"

"Yeah," I said tightly, unconsciously hugging myself.

"You want out of here?"

"I—" I faltered. I did, but I didn't.

Tray decided for me. "Let's go." He grasped my hand and led the way, weaving through the crowd. We were out the door when Veronica Teedz stopped us again, if possible, even more unsteady on her high heels. "I called him, you know, Taryn. Brian's been miserable and we all know it's because of you. He wanted to know if you were here."

"You called him?" I demanded through clenched teeth.

"Yeah...I did. He loves you. It was the two of you. You guys were so...you guys are perfect together."

"Yeah, except that I've changed," I said tightly, following behind Tray as he pulled me down the steps and down the driveway. Walking side by side, in silence, I hugged myself, suddenly feeling cold.

Tray didn't say anything. He just glanced at me once before he resumed walking by my side. When we got to the SUV, I climbed inside after Tray unlocked the doors, huddling against the window.

As we drove past the house, I saw Grayley standing outside, frantically searching the parking lot.

"Stop," I said, rolling my window down as Tray paused in front of the house.

Grayley saw us and approached the car looking relieved. "Holy fuck, Tar!" He groaned, shaking his head. "Holy hell for fuck's sake."

"Sorry," I said weakly. "I'm...sorry. I didn't realize that was going to happen."

Grayley was eyeing Tray, but he murmured, "Yeah, well, for what it's worth, I think Gentley forgot that you go for the jugular. He'll remember next time."

"I didn't know Brian was there."

"Yeah."

"Is he okay?"

"He'll...Brian bounces back. He's looking for you, you know. He's convinced you're still inside."

"Oh, God, Grayley, he's going to do something stupid."

"I know."

"Can you watch him? For me?"

Grayley's grey eyes pinned me down. "And when he asks why I'm around? If he asks if I'm doing it for you? What then? He'll get the message that you still care."

"I..." I was lost—I didn't know what to say or so. "I don't know..."

"Look," he sighed, running a hand over his buzz-cut, "Geeze told me what you're up to. That why you're here?"

"Yeah. I was looking for you."

"Alright." He nodded, glancing around. "I know what you're going to ask and the answer is, of course, stupid. Just...get out of here. Brian's already boiling over, he doesn't need anything else to cause him to explode."

"Thanks, Grayley, I miss you, for what it's worth. I'll need the blueprints to Pedlam High; I gotta get in there."

"Yeah." A rueful smile graced his features, his grey eyes solemn. "Now get out of here."

"Okay." I nodded, sitting back holding Grayley's gaze as Tray pulled forward. When he was out of sight, I rolled the window back up and huddled against the door, my forehead pressed against the glass.

We drove in silence except when Tray's phone would go off.

"Yeah," I heard him say. Then a moment later, he responded, "Nah. Have fun. Grant knows the way back."

His phone rang quite a few times and he had the same conversation.

Sighing, I turned over and murmured, "A lot of people want you to go back to the party, huh?"

He glanced sideways at me, but didn't say anything.

Then he said quietly, "You get what you wanted back there?"

"Hmm...I guess. It'll do."

My phone rang, interrupting anything else he might've said. I realized, rolling my eyes at my own stupidity, that I was flustered. Flustered because of Tray. How old am I? Thirteen? I flipped my phone open without checking to see who it was first. "What?"

"Where are you?"

I realized two things at once. It was Brian and he was furious.

"I got a ride home."

"With Evans?" he demanded harshly.

I looked at Tray—he'd heard. He could hear the entire conversation. Great.

"What of it?"

"God, you're such a bitch!"

"I'm the bitch!? Me? I am? What about you, Brian? If anyone's a bitch, it's you. Going off on Gentley like that. What are you thinking?"

"Please. Gentley's got nothing on me."

"He'll retaliate, Brian. What were you thinking?"

"And if he retaliates, trust me—he'll be the one hurting, not me."

"Oh my God, you're delusional. This is how it's always been, Bri. The two of you put me in the middle every time. Well, I'm out. Okay? I'm done."

"The fucker was all over you. He was two inches from—"

"From hitting me, not raping me. I was handling him," I hissed, fully aware that Tray had pulled over and was watching me, seemingly content to sit back and listen.

"You were handling him? You're the one who's delusional, Tar. He needs to know that you're still my property. He fucks with me if he even goes near you."

That was it. I hung up on him and looked at Tray. Coldly, I asked, "Wanna have some fun?"

"What kind of fun?" he asked, smirking.

"My kind of fun." I grinned. I hadn't felt like this in a long, long time and it was about time Brian learned once and for all we were done.

"Where to?" Tray merely asked, a faint grin on his face.

CHAPTER THREE

Staring across the road, Tray asked guardedly, "Am I going to get killed in there?"

I laughed, I couldn't help it. He was warily eyeing the nightclub. The Seven8 was home to Jace Lanser, Brian's older brother, and his gang. He led the Panthers, a gang that had the cops running around with their hands tied. Brian and Jace had a love/hate relationship, but Jace had something that Brian didn't: discipline. Jace was smart, he had to be to lead the Panthers at his young age and still come out on top after the police had issued war against them. Brian was smart, but Jace was smarter and ruthless. Jace took care of me; he always had.

"Come on. You'll be fine," I reassured him, climbing out of the SUV. Rounding to his door, I murmured, "Just...don't say anything."

Tray didn't look appeased, but he followed anyway.

Approaching the club, I saw Ben, one of the bouncers, outside, manning the door. I called out, "Ben."

"Taryn," he said reservedly, studying Tray intently. "He going to be a problem?"

"I'm just here to talk to Jace, then we're out. Promise. No trouble."

"Hmm."

"Brian's not in there, is he?"

"No."

Ben had actually majored in communications. With his muscular built and tattoos circling his bald head, he could get anyone to tell him anything with the right look. He was

Jace's number three man and I think his noncommittal answers were one of the reasons why Jace trusted him.

"Is Jace in?"

"He's in. He's with Cammy."

I grinned. "Those two back on again?"

"Don't care. She's either here or she's not."

"Right." I snorted in disbelief. "You going to let us in or do I go in my way?"

Ben glared at that one. One night he refused to let me inside, Brian and I had had a huge fight and he didn't want it to escalate. I got in anyway, from the roof. Ben didn't like to be reminded that there was someone who existed that could get around him and I loved to remind him every chance I got.

"He's in the back. Take the small hallway."

Tray followed me as we circled around the front entrance, the pounding music already blaring in our ears. Catching Casey's gaze, the front bartender nodded in greeting as we slipped behind him and trailed into the hallway that let its way around the club to the back offices.

At the closed office door, I rapped briskly and waited. . A second later, it was opened as Cammy slipped outside, sliding the strap from her halter-top onto her shoulder. Blinking in surprise, she stumbled slightly when she saw me.

"Oh! Uh...Taryn, I didn't know—"

"Let her in, Cammy!" Jace ordered from inside.

Flushing, she rolled her eyes and slipped around us.

Inside, we were greeted with the sight of a shirtless Jace, with his pants unbuttoned, hanging low on his lean hips. Raking a hand through his tousled hair, he grinned ruefully at me, his abdominal muscles starkly highlighted against the neon lighting inside.

"Heya, Terry," he murmured, buttoning his jeans as he moved to give me a hug.

Jace was the only one who could get away with calling me that. Brian had tried once and I'd kneed him in the balls. He'd never done it again, although he always sneered every time Jace said it, so of course it made Jace say it anytime he could.

"Jace," I greeted. "You and Cammy back on?"

"For the night," he said easily, raking his eyes over Tray who had stayed by the door, leaning lazily against the wall. "Who's he?"

"Not important," I said smoothly, but Jace was frowning staring intently at Tray. "Wait—" he murmured.

A light of recognition sparked in his eyes and he stated, "Evans."

Tray straightened and moved to stand beside me.

As he looked at me, I blurted out, "Oh my God, you can talk."

He grinned lazily before turning to Jace. "Yeah. I'm Evans. You're Lanser."

I glanced between the two, feeling uneasy.

Jace was regarding him cautiously while Tray informed me, "We had a business meeting a while back."

"Business?" I didn't like that, but then again, I didn't know Tray all that well.

"Yeah. Rawley controls the highway intersection on the state line. Panthers really like to use that highway." It was all Tray would say and looking at Jace, he wasn't going to expand on that at all.

Fine. This wasn't why I was here.

"I can give you the codes to Corrigan's safe," I stated bluntly.

Jace looked startled, but he recovered instantly. "What do you want in return?"

"I want Brian to know that I'm the one who gave them to you."

It was enough said—Jace got the message. Knowing that I had given that information to him and not Brian, would burn Brian. It had been the focus of a crap load of arguments between us. Both brothers wanted to know the information because both wanted what was inside. They'd both asked me to get the information and I had, but I had yet to choose who would get them. At first I'd refused to give them to Brian, just because I didn't want him to get caught trying to get to the safe and because I knew the contents were probably drugs. I didn't want Brian getting in any deeper than he had to. If anyone could handle the codes, it was Jace. He'd get around the security, somehow, he always did—he was already immersed in the business. It would force a wedge between Brian and me if I gave the codes over to Jace.

I was forcing it now.

"You're a cold bitch, Taryn," Jace stated, tilting his head to one side. "Probably why you're family."

"Yeah," I said quietly.

"Brian hasn't been leaving you alone, has he?"

"You mean he was supposed to be?" I scoffed.

"Yeah, well...my little brother's always been obsessed when it came to you. Give him time, he'll come around."

"Yeah, well...that's not good enough for me."

Jace nudged me slightly, rocking back on his heels. "Wanna tell me the sudden change of heart?"

"Brian called me his property."

Jace burst out laughing. "My little brother can be an idiot, that's for damn sure."

"I know," I said dryly.

Glancing between me and Tray, Jace asked, "There a reason you couldn't have done this over the phone? Or did you just want to see my handsome face? I'm favoring there's another reason, because you're not one to look back."

There was another reason, but I wasn't going to tell him. I grinned easily. "Just keep Brian away, okay?"

When Tray and I got back into his SUV, I said briskly, "Drive around the corner." With only a quick look, he did as I said. When he stopped, I murmured, "I'll be right back. Keep the engine running."

Tray didn't say anything as I ran across the street, this time heading towards the alley. Quickly scaling up the side of the building, I threw my leg around one of the windowsills and pulled my body up. Feeling just underneath the frame, I pulled out two pieces of wire and nudged them underneath the window, crisscrossing them. Then I jerked them out, neatly dislocating the window off its frame, just slightly but enough for my finger to get underneath and nudge it upwards. It was one of my tricks. Climbing through, I was in Brian's room that he kept at the Seven8. Quickly moving to his computer, I booted it up. Working my way through his files, I closed them and shut it down. When Brian would try to get into his computer, he'd find all his files frozen and protected by three passwords.

It was petty. I knew that, but I couldn't help it. Geeze had shown me once how to do it in case I ever wanted to piss someone off. Of course, I knew Brian would have Geezer figure out what was wrong with it and, of course, Geeze would automatically know it was me, but I didn't care.

I've never been anyone's damn property.

Stopping just before the window, I froze, catching sight of a bracelet. The moonlight hit it just right, because only a small corner was actually visible. It was hidden underneath a pillow on one of his couches. Taking it out, I saw that it was made of diamonds.

Holy...Where the hell did he get this? I wanted to take it. I knew I shouldn't, but...holy hell, I wanted to.

I placed it back underneath the pillow.

Before I climbed out the window, I wedged the wires back underneath the frame and climbed out. Shutting the window, I scaled back down.

Darting back across the alley, making sure Ben was currently inside the door, I climbed in the SUV finding Tray sitting patiently.

"We ready to go?" he asked, sounding almost bored.

"Yeah," I said breathless, thinking back on that bracelet.

His phone kept ringing as we drove back to Rawley.

"Why aren't you answering?"

He kept his eyes on the road. "Because they're drunk."

Taking his phone, I looked at it, the name Aidrian was displayed as the phone rang once again. Flipping it open, I answered sweetly, "Hello?"

On the other end was shocked silence, before she yelled, "Who the hell are you?"

"Tray can't talk right now. He's too busy fucking me," I said, grinning. Looking at Tray, I saw him staring at me, showing no reaction other than a slight flicker of amusement in his eyes. "And he's sooo good," I moaned into the phone.

There was a twitch at the corner of his mouth.

Aidrian was quiet, but I could hear screeching in the background. "Who is this?" she demanded.

I laughed. "The girl that took your place apparently." Before I could say anything more, my own phone went off. Hanging up, I answered mine, "Yeah?"

"Girl." It was Crispin Gentley.

"What do you want, Gentley?" I asked coolly, seeing Tray glance at me intently.

There was a laughing note in his voice when he answered, "You always surprise me, you know."

"Really?"

"I thought that I missed our little run-ins, now I'm reminded why we kept having those."

"I took a sneak peek at your file before I left," I remarked casually. "Imagine my surprise at all your little secrets."

"And you are such a bitch!"

"I've been called worse, Gentley," I taunted. "Piss me off and I'm sure I can get a look at your daddy's file. In fact, I'm fairly positive your momma hired a P.I. to get some dirt on daddy dearest...wanna know how I know? You'll love the irony." Waiting a moment, hearing silence, I pressed on, "Because he asked me to get your file and his requests didn't stop there. Oh no, he wanted me to bug your home, your bedroom, your Jeep, and get all of your computer files. Wow, I can see why Stephanie Markus is your Girl Friday. She's a screamer."

"Thought you might want to know that I'm going to put your boyfriend in the hospital," Gentley said harshly.

"Brian's not my boyfriend and if you do, you deal with his brother."

"Wasn't talking about your ex-boyfriend. I'm talking about Evans. The guy you're sitting next to."

Hanging up swiftly, I cried out, "He's behind us." Just then a pair of car lights turned on, blinding us from behind.

Tray seemed fine, no reaction showed as he looked in the rearview mirror. He pulled over.

"What are you doing?" I cried. "He's going to kill you."

Tray said calmly, "Get out of the car. We'll be fine."

"Do you even know Gentley? He said he's going to put you in the hospital."

With amusement in his voice, Tray replied, "No, he won't. He wants to deal, that's all. He was just getting a rise out of you."

Seeing that I had no intention of getting out of the car, he said again, "We'll be fine."

Reluctantly climbing out, I saw Crispin walking towards us with his two friends, Brent and Hayden right behind him. They were infamous in Pedlam. Tray walked around to the back of his SUV and leaned back casually. I stood beside him fidgeting nervously. I felt Tray grab my arm and pull me against his side. "Relax," he soothed, stroking my arm with his thumb.

"Evans," Gentley greeted icily. His eyes raked over my form. "Bitch."

Before I responded, Tray squeezed my arm and said, "Tsk, tsk, Gentley. You're insulting one of mine. Not a good beginning for our partnership."

"What partnership? You took off before we could even strike a deal," Crispin sneered, rumpling his Ralph Lauren polo as he hunched forward.

"Lanser's presence wasn't foreseeable. It added complications," Tray said smoothly.

God, Tray was hot.

What the hell was he talking about?

"I don't want her here. Why'd you bring her?"

"Hey," I said indignantly.

"She's one of them. She'll go running to them."

"She's one of mine," Tray promised, a hard glint in his eyes. "So she stays."

"Whatever. This isn't how I do business."

"This is how it's going to have to be or we won't deal."

Crispin stared long and hard at both of us. Jerking a hand out, he ordered Brent, "Give it to him."

"Dude."

"I said give it to him," Crispin snapped, kicking some gravel away.

Brent produced a brown bag and passed it to Tray, then backed away.

"This is the last of it?" Tray asked, looking inside and passing it to me. I held it, slightly unnerved. I didn't like surprises and whatever this deal was—was a surprise. I didn't like it one bit. I really didn't like it that Tray had done a business meeting with Jace, much less Crispin Gentley.

I didn't look inside, but I really, really wanted to.

"She'll probably swipe it. That's what she does, you know. She steals shit for them. She can steal anything. Just ask her what she's stolen for them."

I gritted my teeth and snapped, "I wasn't lying about your daddy's file."

"It was good doing business with you," Tray said clearly, pulling me around the SUV to the door.

"You can't trust her, man. She'll go running to Lanser. You don't know the two of them. They're like freaking Bonnie and Clyde."

"I heard your first warning," Tray said, a warning note in his voice. Opening my door, he ordered me to get in.

Walking back around, Tray got in on the driver's side, started the car and moved back onto the highway.

I waited a whole minute before saying anything. Then I shrieked, "What kind of business deals are you doing with Gentley? And how exactly do you know Jace? What is it? Something illegal?"

Tray skimmed my figure, seeing the barely contained rage, and said lightly, "It's not as bad as robbing banks."

"What is it...steroids?

"How the hell—?" Tray gazed at me in surprise. "How did you know?"

"If it were drugs, you'd know Jace a lot more than the little bit he could remember you and it's the only thing I could think Crispin dealing."

"You're a nightmare, you know," he suddenly growled. "You're in deep with both of the Lansers. You got guys like Gentley avidly hating you. And...you got me driving around and waiting like a good little lapdog for you while you're off doing God knows what."

I sat back in my seat, arms crossed. "I wasn't doing anything illegal. Well, I was, but it isn't anything that's going to get reported, trust me."

Tray snorted in disbelief. "The way you walk is illegal."

"It is not. Shut up."

"Just...be quiet," he shot back.

I sat back, mystified. I couldn't stop a smile from growing. I hadn't this much fun since...since I'd broken into a car dealership with Brian. *That* had been fun.

As my phone rang again, I sighed. "For the love—" I mumbled, but seeing Mandy's name I quickly answered, "Hey."

"Devon and I broke up," she said rushed. "I was right. He's been sleeping with Jasmine. Jasmine of all people! God, and the way she acted tonight, like she didn't even know who he was. I caught 'em in one of the bedrooms. I hate that bitch!"

"Mandy, I'm so sorry." I could sympathize. After I caught Brian cheating on me—twice—I could've murdered both of them.

"Oh my God...I hate her, I hate her so damn much. What am I going to do? It's going to be all over school!"

"Fuck school. You don't let her get away with this," I bit out. I was feeling for my sister here.

"I know, but what can I do? I'll get caught whatever I do and then I'll probably get suspended. I can't do that, Mom and Dad would be furious with me. Not to mention, I might lose my scholarship to Brown next year."

"Mandy," I said sharply, "are you forgetting your resident criminal newly adopted sister, here?"

"I wouldn't want you to get in trouble. That'd be much worse than me, they might send you back to juvie or something..."

"Meet me at Tray's, we're almost there."

"You're still with Tray?"

"Yeah."

"I hate Devon. I absolutely hate Devon. I'm going to...I'm going to key his car, that's what I'm going to do."

"I'm hating him for you and keying his car is juvenile. Trust me, there are much classier ways to get back on a cheating bastard. I've perfected ways to get back on cheating bastards."

"Brian cheated on you?"

"Twice, but my revenge was so good I actually got paid to help other girls when their boyfriends cheated," I said smugly.

I ceased caring that Tray was still in the car. He was a bastard just like everyone else.

Noticing the SUV had turned into his driveway, I murmured, "Okay, we're here."

"I'll be there in a little bit. Thanks, sis. Love you."

I was shocked. Mandy was my sister. I knew this, but the words seemed different just then. They weren't forced, it wasn't just a phrase. There was meaning behind them.

"Hey," Tray interrupted my haze.

"What?"

"We're here. You coming in or waiting for your man-hating sister out here? Or is an hour in my house with another—*man*—going to dissolve your bond," he teased.

I gasped. "You have humor. You actually know what comedy is. I never would have guessed."

"Fuck off," he growled before slamming the door, but not before I caught the small grin that flitted across his features.

The place was eerily vacant compared to the mob that had been in his home earlier. Following Tray as he strolled lazily inside, I shivered a little from the breeze that wafted through the rooms.

"Want a drink?" he asked, opening the fridge and rummaging inside.

"You have beer?"

"Is that meant to be an insult?" He smirked, pulling out a bottle and sliding it towards me over the counter.

I didn't reply, but tipped my head back and took a long drink.

Leaning against the counter, his arms crossed over his chest, he regarded me. "So Devon and Jasmine, huh?"

I narrowed my eyes. The bastard knew.

"You knew," I stated.

He shrugged, crossing the room towards me. Grabbing my beer, he took a drink. "Yeah."

"And said nothing," I condemned.

He merely smirked, rounding the counter to come up beside me. Setting the beer in front of me, he kept both his arms on either side of me, effectively trapping me in place. Nudging the barstool I sat on with his knee, he twirled me around until I was facing him; he was so close I could feel his breath on my face.

"I'm not a narc," he replied, studying me.

I hated that word. I really did. I hated narcs. The thing was, I understood him. There had been a few times I'd known some of my friends had cheated on their boyfriends or girlfriends. I'd said something only once, and immediately hated my decision when the girl flew into a hysterical rage. She'd turned on me since I was the one there. Kill the messenger and all that shit. Ever since then, I'd stayed away from all that drama. I had enough drama in my own life.

"How long has it been going on?"

"What? Dev and Jaz?"

"How long?"

"Uh huh. Nope," Tray said, pulling away. "That answer will not help Mandy at all."

"She said seven months...was it seven months?" I persisted, grabbing his arm as he straightened.

Glancing at my hand, he lifted his eyes to my face. "No, I'm not telling you."

I pulled him closer. "How long?"

"Why are you pushing this?"

"Because Mandy's my sister and because the girl has to know how long it's gone on for. Don't ask me why, but we just have to know. Besides, I'm getting the PRS-500 for you, it's the least you can do."

"Fuck that. No. That's for Mandy to ask Dev, not you to ask me," he said firmly.

I needed a new tactic, so I pulled him closer and slid a leg around his and twined it around his waist, bringing him into full contact against me. I could feel him through my clothes and I slid one hand up his chest to curl around his neck. He had both arms around me, one tilted my neck back and the other was on my butt, grinding me against him, our mouths inches apart.

"I want to know how long," I breathed against him, my lips grazing his as I spoke.

"And my response is, fuck you."

His hand left my neck to grasp my other leg and twine it around his waist, both legs now wrapped around him. I fell against the counter slightly as he arched me against him. I gasped from feeling him and the heat that seared through my body. He slid his hand to the front of my pants and moved underneath my shirt. I panted silently as his fingers caressed me, moving upwards to softly flick against one of my nipples.

"I'm going to get you off," I said silkily, seeing his eyes darken at my words and his body's response. "And you're going to tell me what I want."

"And my response will be the same, I want to fuck you," he promised, his intent glittering in his amber eyes as he slammed his mouth against mine. It wasn't exactly rough, but it was fiery.

I tilted my head back and opened my mouth, feeling his tongue sweep inside where it met with mine. As I felt him lift me from the barstool and plant me higher on the counter, I heard a soft moan and realized it had come from me. One of his hands was keeping my leg firmly wrapped around him as the other was exploring underneath my shirt, moving to the other breast. I slid one of my hands underneath his shirt and explored him in return, the other was wrapped firmly around his taut shoulders.

And then he ripped himself away from me, both of us breathing hard.

"What—" I murmured, dazed.

Tray ran a hand through his hair. "Fuck."

Then I saw the headlights through the window. Mandy or someone had arrived.

I don't think I even cared if they had seen us or not.

"Bathroom," I choked out.

Jerking his head, he clipped out, "Second door on your right."

After I'd composed myself, I emerged from the bathroom and could hear Mandy's shrill voice yelling. Rounding the corner, I saw Tray leaning against the counter again, his eyes unreadable as he watched the scene before him. Mandy, eyes wild, hands gesturing in the air, was ranting about Devon and Jasmine. Seeing Grant lounging in the doorway, I figured he was her sober-cab since it was obvious Mandy was very drunk. Her speech was slurring, but everyone could make out exactly who she was damning to hell, the cheating bastard.

Spotting me, she exclaimed, "I know now, Taryn! I know now. God, I want to kill that bastard. I thought she was a friend, but Jasmine's nothing more than a back-stabbing bitch slut."

I was at a loss. Mandy was beyond control right now. Tray and Grant both looked detached, as if this were a common occurrence, one they'd grown immune to. And maybe it was.

"Huh," I faltered, shaking my head, "so you walked in on them?"

That was the wrong thing to say because Mandy launched into a screech, painting a vivid picture of what she saw when she caught them: what clothes were missing, what position they were in, and the grunting noises they were making.

"Okay," I said quickly, "that's good, I get the picture."

Mandy let out a sob, you could hear the catch in her throat when she said, "It's been going on for a year."

I met Tray's eyes, he was bemused, remembering my promise.

"That slut has been going behind my back for a year. It started last year at homecoming. At Bryce's party. I was in New York with student council so I missed it and I guess Devon got lonely," she said bitterly, hiccupping on a sob. "I fucking hate them!"

I moved beside her, but stayed a few feet away.

"Oh my God, Taryn!" she wailed. "What am I going to do? Everyone's going to know. And...I'm...I loved him. He was my first, you know...how could she do this to me? What am I thinking, of course she would've. Jasmine's screwed every guy in our grade. They all just run to her, the only guy who's sent her packing was Tray," she scoffed, gesturing carelessly in Tray's direction. "Guess she had to move onto a new target. Bryce wasn't enough for her."

"You get even," I said coldly, "and you keep your head high at school. Fuck whoever knows or talks about it."

"I don't know if I can," she sniffed, her eyes glued to mine, "I'm...I'm not like you."

"That's bullshit," I said firmly, not blinking. "You just haven't gone through what I have."

"Yeah, but—"

"No, Mandy. First thing first though," I glanced to Grant, "can you give us a ride home? Devon was our ride here."

"Yeah, sure," he said in surprise.

"I want to get even. Tonight," Mandy cried. "I want to—".

"Mandy," I interrupted, "you need a shower. You need to calm down—slightly—and then we'll figure out what we're going to do."

She stared at me, seemingly enraptured by whatever she saw in my eyes, before she nodded slowly. "Okay." She sniffed, moving to follow Grant as he was already walking outside.

As I moved to follow, Tray pulled me back and asked quietly, "What are you planning?"

"Why?" I shot back. "You want to get involved?"

"No, but Devon's a good guy even though he cheated on her. He doesn't deserve whatever you might be dishing out."

"That is just like you to say he's still a good guy. He's a cheater. He'll always be a cheater."

"Look, just don't...paralyze the guy or something. He's our best linebacker."

I wrenched my arm away, fixing him with a cold stare. "And we're back to the precious football team...with their new game book."

His eyes went cold as he stepped back. "Whatever."

I walked out, letting the door slam shut behind me.

We didn't end up doing anything that night. Mandy cried the entire ride back to our house. After she showered, she curled up on my bed and cried herself to sleep. I wasn't sure what to do, so I slept on the couch in my room. I figured Mandy didn't want to be alone and she probably wouldn't want me to sleep in her room. The next morning, she cried again—through breakfast, lunch, and dinner. She didn't once ask about getting revenge on Jasmine or Bryce. After she went to bed early that night, around eight, I dressed in some black work-out clothes, and slipped outside to my car.

Mandy might have cooled off, but I hadn't. I knew what she would probably meet in school the next day, so it was in my hands; I needed to do something to help take the heat off of her tomorrow.

Driving to school, I parked on the road by the football field. It was far enough away from the normal parking lots that no one would look at it suspiciously and, if need be, I could easily run through the football stadium and evade anyone in the trees that outlined the perimeters if I got caught.

Coming up to the school, I circled around to the janitor's office and hooked a leg onto the fire escape. Darting up, I pulled myself onto the roof and crossed to one of the heating fans. Seeing it had been turned off, I unscrewed the shaft and lifted it clear off. Then I went to work on the fan—wedging a rock between the blades, just in case it turned on, I slipped my hands through and found the bolts. After they had been unscrewed, I lifted the fan up and then slipped through. My feet touching the ceiling, I ran my hands around the flooring until I found the hatch that led to the venting shafts. Again, I lowered my body down, and then crawled through the vents until I measured the distance in my mind, counting every inch I moved forward. When I thought I was in the main office, I lightly kicked the screen out and quickly caught it before it fell to the ground. My estimation had been correct—I was in the main office. Climbing out, I went to P.A. system where it was located by the principal's office. Turning it on, I went to work, changing the alarm timings and preferences. I programmed it to play some rap music (left on the desktop from when the student council had persuaded the administration to let them play music at the end of the day) around the clock. Then I protected that command with a password, followed by a second password.

It paid to have criminal friends sometimes.

The music should work first, and hopefully they won't be able to shut it off for a few hours, and then after that, the alarm system should kick in, making the alarms ring every five minutes. The last command, I protected it with another three passwords. The only way they would be able to stop them immediately is if they shut off the electricity, completely. And they won't do that, not until they were desperate.

That should cause enough chaos.

Hoisting my body back through the venting shafts, my only thought was that I needed to remember to bring some ear-plugs tomorrow. I'd make sure they got passed around to the students; maybe put them in a bag on one of the lunch tables.

Mandy drove separate from me the next morning. She barely said a word at breakfast, but I could tell she was terrified because she was completely white in the face—she looked like death warmed over. When I asked if she wanted to ride with me, she'd said that she had cheer practice and then a student council meeting after school.

And me, my plans for after school, entailed meeting up with Grayley and getting the blueprints to the new school Pedlam had built last summer. They'd had tight security when I went there so I didn't know if they would've kept it up or loosened it since I no longer attended. I needed to find out what I was walking into Thursday night. Grayley would get me everything I needed.

The parking lot was already full so I had to park on the street. I saw students talking on the lawn, which wasn't unusual but normally it was only a third of the students. Today the number had tripled, guess the music had deterred people from hearing their gossip inside. I could still hear the music blaring through the open doors. Walking inside, I passed the office and saw the entire faculty jammed inside, well, probably not all the faculty, but enough. They all looked pissed.

As I drew near my locker, I saw students running through the halls. The stoners had taken the opportunity to get high in the hallways; no one was paying attention to them. Putting my backpack in my locker, I passed my classroom and found it empty. I followed the hallway to the parking lot where I saw the remaining student body loitering on the lawn or standing around their cars. Spotting Mandy, I saw her head bent in a group of cheerleaders—who knows what they were talking about. I saw Devon sitting on the back of his truck, Jasmine was hanging on him with the rest of their crowd lounging around. Tray leaned against the pickup, his arms crossed over his chest as he seemed to be listening to whatever story Amber was telling. Bryce and Grant were both grinning.

Dropping to the grass, I leaned against a tree, pulling out my iPod, but I didn't press play right away. I was listening to a conversation between some sophomores (I think) behind me. They were talking about the music and what the school was going to do, wondering if classes were going to be cancelled or not. I couldn't stop the grin on my face; there was no word about Mandy, Devon, or Jasmine. That's all I cared about. Then I pressed play.

They ended up canceling school. They couldn't get around my passwords, which surprised me. Pedlam usually blasted through my passwords within an hour. As I walked through the hallways to my car, my science partner (with the microscope glasses) ran up to me and told me excitedly that the school had to call in a specialist; that whoever had done the prank was a god and it was the coolest thing that had happened to Rawley, ever!

Told you I was a legend at my skill.

However, I didn't like that they called in a specialist. When I pulled a similar prank at Pedlam, they had to call in a specialist too. If it was the same specialist, I was in deep shit. I hadn't even thought of that. Hopefully they won't put two and two together. As a shiver ran down my back, I veered away from her (I still hadn't caught her name) and got inside my car quickly. Starting it, I pulled into traffic and drove home.

As usual, it was empty. Shelly and Kevin had called last night telling us they wouldn't be home till later this week. Austin had let out a whoop of joy as he bounded up to his room.

Grabbing a soda, I went to my room and turned my computer on, telling myself that I was going to do some research for one of my papers, but I found myself clicking on eBay, checking out wire-trimmers and pick handlers—marketing tools for breaking and entering...

Hearing voices downstairs, I clicked out of the website and closed my laptop. Making my way downstairs, I heard Mandy giggling, exclaiming, "We can get so much done now that we have the whole day off. I heard it was Mark Jenkins and his gang that did the prank."

"I heard it was Tyler Justins."

"Whatever, we all know who was behind it. He might not have done it, but I bet he knows who did: Tray Evans."

"Ooh, did you see him today? Tray Evans is seriously hot," another girl moaned.

Great. She'd brought the entire cheerleading squad to her house—our house—which meant I needed to leave. Now. I didn't mix well with cheerleaders.

"Taryn!" Mandy yelled excitedly, seeing me turning around on the stairs.

Busted.

Plastering on a fake smile, I turned back and said warmly, "Hey." I was met with varying reactions: hostile, curious, and/or clueless.

"We're gonna have practice here since school and all...and I'm going to have our student council meeting this afternoon, okay?"

"Uh...what do you want me to do?"

"Nothing." Mandy shook her head, a dazzling smile on her face. "Just letting you know...in case..."

"I want to cut and run," I finished for her dryly.

"Yeah..." The hesitation was enough. Mandy didn't want me to leave, so that meant that Devon must have been on the student council. Devon would be heading over to the house and she was nervous about it.

"What time is your student council meeting?"

Relief flashed in her eyes as Mandy responded, "At 2:30."

Nodding, I murmured, "I'll be back after lunch."

Darting back up to my room, I quickly changed clothes, putting on a white halter top and some tight blue jeans. I slipped on some sandals and grabbed my purse. When I walked back downstairs, the cheerleaders had gone out to our backyard—thank goodness—and I left through the front door, crossing to my car. Climbing in, my phone went off. Seeing Brian's name flash across my screen, I put it away, silencing the ringer as I drove off.

Returning at two, I was surprised to see ten or more cars in our driveway and on the street. Apparently the meeting had started early or they'd come early to gossip. Probably the latter. Walking inside I was met with the same reaction as the cheerleaders: hostility, curiosity, and/or cluelessness.

Fuck them. I shrugged it off as I zeroed in on where Mandy was. I found her in the kitchen, busying herself with drinks and food. Making my way through the crowd, I stared at one of the girls in the kitchen and said flatly, "Leave."

She ran.

Mandy choked on a laugh. "Taryn, seriously. Friends are a good thing to have."

"I have friends," I said coolly, hopping onto the counter. "So, where is he?"

She sighed. "He's on the patio with Grant and Amber."

"And where are you at?"

"In a land of denial, telling myself everything is perfect except that my boyfriend cheated on me and is no longer my boyfriend." She turned to me, her eyes misty. "Did you see them this morning? She was all over him."

"Anyone say anything?"

"No, thank God. Everyone's been talking about that stupid prank—and it couldn't have come at a better time—but Amber hasn't even talked to me. I think she's on Jasmine's side."

"Has she talked to Jasmine today?"

"I don't know, but Jasmine backstabbed me. You'd think Amber would say something to me, right? She's my best friend."

"Yeah...friends have a way of not being your friends when they're needed the most. I learned to take people with a grain of salt," I murmured. "So, you want me to hang out for moral support?"

"Yeah...and because the gang is having dinner here tonight."

"What? Mandy!"

"I know, I know," she groaned. "I couldn't stop myself. Devon was talking to Grant and Amber in the dining room and everyone was watching. Next thing I know, I'm inviting them for dinner. I don't know why—"

"You did it because you don't want them to know that you're suffering. Makes perfect sense to me. Stupid though."

Mandy grinned. "I know. So...you have to be here tonight."

"It's your whole crowd, right? Grant, Bryce, Amber, Devon, Jasmine, and Tray?"

"Yeah. And Carter."

"Who's Carter?"

"Bryce's cousin. He's in town, he moved last year to Southington but he's friends with all of us. Carter's hilarious. You'll love him, well...maybe."

A girl popped her head in the kitchen and said cheerfully, "Mandy! Guess what? Tray Evans is here with Carter Sethlers. How cool is that? Tray Evans isn't even on student council and Carter Sethlers doesn't even go to our school anymore. I'm so happy you had the meeting here."

"Anyone else with them, Shelley?" Mandy asked guardedly.

"Nope. Just those two."

"Can you tell them that Grant, Devon, and Amber are on the patio?"

"Sure." Shelley flashed her a blinding smile, which matched her blonde highlights. "I think Patrice already did, but I'll check anyway. Gives me an excuse to chat up Tray, hmmm?"

When she left, Mandy sighed in relief. "Thank God Carter's here."

"He's pretty cool, huh?"

"Yeah," she murmured, her eyes vacant. She was thinking hard about something.

"Look," I spoke up, jumping off the counter, "student council and socializing isn't my thing. I'm gonna camp out in my room. Keep your cellphone with you and call me if you need me down here ASAP."

"Okay. Thanks, Taryn." Mandy sounded grateful as she wiped at some tears that were in the corner of her eyes. "Thanks."

I escaped, breathing lighter when I shut my bedroom door a second later. Falling on my bed, I turned my iPod on again, but felt my phone buzzing next to me. Lifting it up, I saw Geezer's name on the screen. Flipping it open, I greeted warmly, "Hey, Geeze."

"Brian's on his way to your place."

"What?!" I cried out in alarm, sitting up.

"Yeah, he and Jace had a huge fight this morning. Like the cops were called even. Brian split before they showed up, but Grayley called and said Brian said something about sorting stuff out with you once and for all. Brent called from the gas station and said Brian was heading towards Rawley on the highway. Two plus two plus two equals six, babe."

"Geeze, don't call me that."

"Hot stuff," he said instead.

I peeked through my window-blinds, but didn't see his car. Great. Just great.

"Okay." I sighed. "Thanks for giving me the heads-up."

"Oh and Grayley told me to tell you that he's got your stuff."

"Good. I'll head over tonight."

"I'll tell Grayley to bring it all here. Brian doesn't ever show up here anymore."

"Okay. Thanks again, Geezer. I'll see you tonight."

"Good luck, hot stuff."

"You can try all you like, Geeze, but your seduction is wasted on me," I teased before hanging up.

This day was turning out to suck more than I had imagined and most of it was my fault—cheerleaders, student council and now the ex-factor. Great.

I dialed Jace's number.

"Hey, Terry," he greeted wearily.

"I heard." It's all I had to say. We both knew what the fight had been about and why—I'd asked him for this purpose.

"Hey, ah...look, my little brother's on his way to your place. You might make sure there are people around. I had some guys follow him, but—"

"This is my fight," I finished tiredly and I *was* tired. I've been gone for months now and Brian was still making me exhausted. "Are you...I heard the cops were called?"

"I handled it, you know me and the authorities—we have a hate-hate relationship. But I'm good. If you need the guys to step in, just let them know."

"Got it," I said faintly, hanging up. We both knew the conversation was over, it was pointless to say goodbye. Arming myself with a taser—for my own strength—I headed back down the stairs, but I slipped through the window of the bathroom rather than passing through the entire student body council which I could hear in the kitchen, living room, and dining room—they were everywhere. Rounding the house, I sat on the stoop by the street. Waiting...

I didn't have to wait long. I heard Brian's car screech around a corner and slam to a stop right in front of mine.

Part of me wanted to hop in and tell him to go to a park, where we could hash it out there, but Jace's guys were coming to the house and wouldn't know to go to the park. So I stood wearily, bracing myself when Brian slammed his door shut and strode angrily to me.

Oh yeah. He was in a rage.

"You bitch!" he snarled, still crossing the street.

"And what's new?" I shot back, standing my ground.

"You gave him the fucking codes. Him!"

"Yeah. I did."

He reached out and grabbed my shoulders, shaking me.

Grunting, I twisted out of his arms and kneed him in the balls. As he doubled over, I said coolly, "You don't get to touch me. Ever again."

"It's not going to work," Brian grunted. "You bitch."

"We're over. I have no loyalty to you anymore."

"You love me, baby, you just want this future so desperately. When it doesn't work out, you'll be grateful that I didn't give up on us."

"I'm not your girlfriend, I'm not your accomplice, and I'm not your fuck buddy anymore. I'm out—get that in your head—before I do something to keep you away from me permanently," I growled. I was beyond pissed now. "And I'm not your property. I have never been your property or anyone else's. Got it?!"

"That's what this was about? You gave Jace the codes because I said you were my property?" Brian asked incredulously, straightening slightly.

I didn't respond, but glared frostily.

"You're so damn gorgeous when you're furious." He grinned, still in pain.

Oh I hated him. I especially hated the melting that started in my heart at that grin. It always worked on me, always, and he knew it. The bastard.

"I hate you," I seethed, my hands balled into fists.

And the bastard laughed. "No, you don't, baby. You could never hate me because you'd be hating the one person that's been there for you through everything. Thick and thin, Tar."

Fully straightening, he grabbed my hand and tugged me closer. I dug my feet in and ended up being dragged awkwardly across the space, my arms acting as a barrier since I had them crossed over my chest, as he tried to hug me. I was stiff in his embrace. I felt him nuzzle my ear, which made the melting intensify and spread.

"You still love me, Tar, and no matter how much you push me away, I always know you're pushing yourself just as much," he whispered, kissing my ear. "You want this new life so much and you're willing to cut us all out in order to do it, but it's not going to work. I'm a part of you, you can't push yourself away."

Hearing a few car doors slam, I looked up and saw Ben watching from a few feet away. I recognized the rest of Jace's guys, one must've been new because I didn't recognize him.

Brian shouted across the street, "We're good. You don't need to come and protect little '*Terry*.' You can report back to big brother that no cops need to be called."

"Taryn?" Ben questioned, intent.

"Taryn?" Oh God, that was Mandy. Turning around my eyes widened in horror, seeing Mandy standing with the rest just outside the front door of my house. I saw Tray, Grant, and another guy slowly walk down the driveway.

My house.

Shoving Brian away, I said quietly, "Get out of here. Now."

"Tar?"

"Get lost."

"You don't mean that," he soothed, self-assured.

I snapped. It was the only thing that could explain the sudden change inside of me, but I'd had it being placated by him.

I slapped him and then yelled, "I don't mean that? I don't mean that? I'm sick and goddamn tired of being told, by you, what I do and do not mean! I'm not a child whose parent's know what's best for her. I'm not anything to you, Brian! Not anymore. Not to you!"

Brian frowned, and I saw his resolve set in.

"You want to know why Jace looks out for me so much?" I was such a bitch. A cold, heartless bitch. So I said, "Because I fucked him on your birthday. Your birthday last year when I walked in on you and Liza. You couldn't find me that night, because I was with your brother. And holy hell, did he make me scream that night."

"You're lying," Brian seethed, white around his mouth, his jaw firm. "You'd never do that. Jace would—"

"We did," I said smoothly, "And the next morning, we did it all over again." Gesturing to Ben, I suggested, "Ask Ben. He was there. He saw me leave the next morning, hell—he probably heard us the whole night."

Brian looked over at Ben stiffly, not saying a word.

Studying me, Ben nodded, tightly.

It was enough because Brian started yelling, "You fucking bitch. You're nothing but a slut. A whore who gets her rush stealing crap. How pathetic is that? I wasn't only with Liza, baby, you want to know all the other girls I fucked—"

I used my taser on him and it worked because he shut up and fell unconscious to the ground.

Huh.

I looked up as a shadow fell across the ground near us. Ben. "You can take him now," I said coolly.

Ben gestured to the rest and his guys swooped in and picked up Brian and carried him to his car. One of the guys, I think his name was Carl, got in the driver's seat of Brian's car.

"He'll leave you alone," Ben spoke. "I'll make sure of it, even if Jace doesn't, and we both know Jace will now...now that..."

"That I've told," I murmured softly, hugging myself. "Thanks Ben."

"Hey," he called out, turning back around. "Whatever he just said, the boy was infatuated with you. Those two times—they were only the two times. I'd have known otherwise, so I'm telling you...he only had those two fuck-ups. Don't let that filth nag at you, alright, girl?"

It was stupid, but it comforted me. Because it would've eaten at me, in the back of my mind, thinking about who else Brian had been with. As their two cars slid away, I glanced behind me and saw everyone was still there. Still watching. Some of the girls were gaping at me. Tray and the other two had lingered at the end of our driveway, just a few yards away from me.

I met Tray's gaze and let him see the plea in my eyes. I needed to get out of here.

Nodding, he walked to his SUV and got inside while I ran around to the passenger door and climbed in. I huddled against the door as he looked at me once before starting the car and pulling down the street.

Away from everyone.

I closed my eyes and saw Brian's face flash across my mind, screaming at me, hearing his words lash against me. Over and over again.

I was barely keeping it together. Lifting my hands I saw a trickle of blood in my palms where my nails had dug through the skin. I hadn't even noticed.

A little while later, the car came to a stop and I looked up, seeing we were at Tray's home.

Following him inside, neither of us had yet to speak. I saw a little more of his palace as he led the way to the back, outside to the pool house. Apparently this was where he lived. Once we were inside, he shut the door, and nudged me into his little kitchen area.

Without asking, he took out a bottle of tequila and poured us both a shot. I tipped my head back and downed it. Tray filled it again.

It felt good. It burned my throat, but that's what I wanted. I wanted anything to take my mind away from Brian.

I set my glass down for a third shot and Tray filled it. He took out a beer for himself as he lounged against the counter, watching me.

I was never one for talk, so I closed the distance between us and tilted my mouth to meet his.

It was better than the tequila because a fire exploded inside of me. He answered my demand with his own. I felt his arms pick me up and place me on the counter, my legs automatically wrapped around him.

Tray must've carried me to his bedroom because pretty soon we had tumbled on his bed. Tray moved his mouth to my neck, and had me groaning as I worked at his shirt to come off. Rearing up, he threw his shirt off and then met my eyes as his hands slid underneath mine and pulled it off, followed my bra, then his pants, then my pants. I was panting heavily when he slipped two fingers inside my thong and slid it down, slowly.

Taking charge, I flipped him over and straddled him, kissing my way down his chest, lingering on his stomach, then moving further down before I took him in my mouth. I grinned when I heard his own groan.

Before long, I found myself on my back again, Tray leaning over me, kissing my mouth, my neck, and worked his way down. I arched my back when his mouth found me and went to work.

I frantically pulled him back up to meet my mouth and I entwined my legs around his hips.

Panting, he pulled away and grabbed a condom from his nightstand. I took it from him and put it on, my eyes holding his the entire time. He paused and I grabbed him to bring his mouth down to mine. It was all he needed and he slid inside. He went deep with each thrust and I nearly screamed with the first one.

Neither of us had spoken one word. Not throughout the entire thing. Not before our first time, our second, or the third—much later. We'd spent the entire day in his bed, without saying one word.

I loved it.

After showering and a fourth round, we got dressed before we silently walked to his SUV and drove back to my house.

I breathed easier seeing only a handful of cars still in the driveway. Turning my phone on, I hadn't realized I'd turn it off, but six messages were waiting for me.

I turned it back off.

I caught a flash of amusement in Tray's eyes.

When he turned the engine off, both of us sat there for a moment.

I couldn't help it, but my eyes trailed to where I had stood with Brian a few hours earlier.

"If he really loved you, selflessly, he'd have respected your wishes a long time ago." It was the only thing Tray had said before we both unclasped our seat belts and walked up to the house. Inside we were met with hysterical shouting. Great...Mandy and Jasmine.

"You're a fucking tramp, you bitch!" That was Mandy, I could recognize her screech if I were deaf; the vibrations in the floorboards were a dead giveaway.

"Oh please." Jasmine huffed. "What do you expect from me? An apology? You're never around and when you are it's all cheerleading this, student council that, not to mention yearbook crap and your perfect little family with your perfect little GPA and your precious scholarship to Brown. No, you're a great girlfriend. You're a perfect girlfriend, except you don't give a shit where your man is or how he feels."

There was shocked silence when Tray and I made our appearance. Devon was anxiously watching Mandy, Jasmine was staring indignantly with Amber in the corner by her brother, her eyes skirting between the two girls. Bryce and Carter were lounging on the couches looking amused.

"I can't believe you just said that!" Mandy yelled, leaping towards Jasmine.

Devon moved to intercept her, but Carter beat him to it, leaping from the couch. Grabbing her shoulders, he held her back as Mandy tried to get around him. "Get off me!"

"Mandy," he urged soothingly.

Alarmed, Jasmine had taken a step back. Devon stood in the middle, arms half raised between them, uncertain of what he should do.

I saw Amber staring determinedly at us before she sneered, "Where have you two been?"

Tray shot her an amused look. "We had business."

"What kind of business?"

"None of yours," Tray said firmly, settling against the wall near the door.

"Mandy," I spoke up, walking to her side, "go to your room."

"Taryn—"

"Mandy," I interrupted sharply, "go."

"Fine," she cried out, shoving Carter aside as she swept out of the room.

Turning on my heels, I faced Jasmine squarely. An icy calm had taken over me and all the rage I had from Brian, Jace, everything—all of it erupted inside of me as I saw a fitting target for my outlet.

"You're a pathetic, little, insecure, selfish, bitch with narcissistic tendencies. You have no empathy and no compassion in your bones. If you did, you wouldn't be screwing your best friend's boyfriend." I was seething. Stepping closer, I hissed, "And if you had done it to me—trust me, you'd find yourself in a psych ward by the end of the month and you'd have no idea how and where exactly you got fucked along the ride."

"And who are—" she sputtered, taking another step back.

"I'm not done," I cut in ruthlessly. "You will stay away from Mandy. You will not speak to her, you will not speak about her, and you better be clear across the room every time you're in the same vicinity. Because if I get wind of any rumors, any nasty little things your pathetic mind could think up, you'll deal with me. You won't deal with Mandy, I'll be coming straight for you. And trust me, you don't want to be my enemy. There's a few bitches in lock-up who can attest to that."

Everyone was silent. Jasmine had grown pale, shrinking away.

"Now get out," I finished.

Devon grabbed her arm and hauled her behind him, out the door.

Amber slipped away after them, dragging Grant with her.

Bryce, Carter, and Tray all remained behind.

A moment of silence filled the air between us before I heard a deep laugh coming from Carter, who had thrown his head back. "Oh, I like you. I really like you." Passing by, he thumped Tray on his chest and chuckled. "She's a cold hearted bitch."

I took it at as a compliment. I heard him walk up the stairs and knock on Mandy's door.

Bryce stood up, stretching. "Evans, let's go get a burger."

Tray, who'd been staring at me steadily, nodded before turning and following him out.

Mandy knocked on my door that night, around eleven-thirty, so I was pretty surprised when she told me I had a guest downstairs. Swinging my legs off the bed, I asked, "Who is it?"

She shrugged. "I don't know, but he's hot. Like really, really hot."

Before she turned, I saw the shadows underneath her eyes. "You okay?"

"Carter's staying over," she said, walking into her room and shutting the door.

I frowned at her bedroom door a moment, seeing the light turn off from underneath the door.

Walking down the stairs, I halted abruptly seeing Jace casually leaning in the doorway, looking like he owned the place.

"Hey," I said softly, crossing over to him, stopping a few feet away, uncertain.

"Hey." He attempted a grin, but it came out more a frown.

"So..."

"You told him, huh," he stated.

"Uh..." It wasn't often when I was short for words, but Jace had effectively made me speechless. He'd had the effect on me for a long time, ever since Brian and I first became friends in the fourth grade. He'd already been famous in the eighth grade, he was the Lanser that everyone knew was either in detention or skipping school. He was the number one hated student by all faculty in middle school and high school. I'd always had a crush on him, but Jace was just too much, at least for me. He was too much for anyone, even the cops.

"He's on a rampage, Taryn." He sighed, looking exhausted. He sighed, looking exhausted.

"I should've called. I'm sorry."

"Ben called, but a little warning would've helped," he said dryly.

"It was the only..."

"I know." He sighed. "And the shit of it is that I don't even know if this will do it. He'll be back in a few months, doing all the same shit again. He'll compartmentalize it somehow, make a way where you and me together doesn't affect him, had nothing to do with him...I don't know. He'll be back."

"I'm sorry, Jace," I said softly, meaning it.

"He and I—that's been broken for a long time. And we're done, there's no going back with us, but hell...there hasn't been for a long while."

"You don't know that..." I said half-heartedly, because we both knew it was true.

"Come on, Tar, Bri's hated me all my life. He grew up hating me. Our dad made sure of that."

"What happened tonight?"

"Threw a few punches, that's it really. Cam got in the middle, had to take her to the hospital."

"Oh God. Is she okay?"

"She'll be fine." He shrugged. "More worked up about you and me. Heads up, by the way, she's gunning for you."

It was ironic really. I had to watch my back because I was a cheating bitch while I was protecting Mandy from the same thing. I had to appreciate the irony, for a moment anyway.

"I'll handle her..."

"I'll smooth things over, she always comes back, but with you...she's always wanted a reason to hate you. I can't fix that." He gave me a faint grin. "I think she always wondered...about..."

"I can handle myself." I grinned, trying to be cocky, but looking away.

Jace chuckled, running a hand through his tousled hair.

"Nice of you to dress up to see me." I couldn't help myself, lightly punching him on the chest, feeling the cement wall of muscle beneath his bleached t-shirt.

"Yeah." He chuckled again. "How do you know Evans?"

My mood sobered instantly. "He goes to my school."

"He runs your school," Jace pointed out.

"Yeah...I know what he's got going on."

"Then you know he's not a guy to take lightly."

My eyebrows arched. "That's high praise coming from the likes of you."

"We've had a business deal going on. Only met him once though, but...he's got this town nicely locked together."

"What do you mean?"

"None of my business comes in or out of Rawley."

Thank God. I'd never spoke up against Jace, against what he did, but...I cared about him. Bottom line, I cared. And that meant there were many nights I had wished fervently for a different world. A different world for me, Brian, and Jace. But Jace most of all—because he'd never get out. And if he did, it'd be a bloodbath. Blood got you in, blood got you. So I just never said anything, he was in too far.

"How'd he manage that?"

"I don't know, I've already said too much. He's not like Brian, Taryn. Remember that."

"Meaning that my obsessive ex is the lesser of the two evils."

He grinned at that. "If the shoe fits, bitch."

I punched him for real this time and I probably hurt my hand more than him. "Hey."

He grabbed my hand, laughing softly. Raising it, he kissed the knuckles tenderly and said huskily, "You know I say it lovingly."

I pulled my hand away and smirked. "Right."

He turned to the door, opening it, but paused in the doorframe. He looked serious. "Listen, don't worry about Brian. If you want him gone, which you must, I'll make sure he stays away."

This was it. We both knew once that door closed, the line was drawn for us. No going back. No more crossing it, from either side. And a part of me wanted to crumble up and cry for the rest of the night. A part of me wanted to go with him. He was family, no matter what happened between me, him, or Brian. The three of us had been family.

"Hey, Jace," I called out, stopping him.

Our eyes met. And held. We'd had that one night and like I'd said before, it brought up stuff that neither of us had ever admitted. Much less to ourselves than each other. But, this might be the last time...so...I walked over to him and kissed him. Tenderly. I didn't stop the feelings this time.

Jace put his arms around me, drawing me closer, as he returned my kiss.

It felt just like it had before—for a moment, the world stopped. Because this wasn't a cheated night taken in revenge. This was goodbye, so nothing was held back.

And then I pulled away. Our eyes held again as he walked out.

I shut the door. Returning to my room, I flicked a tear away from the corner of my eye and then curled underneath my blanket.

Mandy had left early for school. Through my open window, I'd heard Carter say goodbye as he got into his car. A second later I heard Austin pad by my doorway on his way to the kitchen. Moments later, I heard his friends pull up and honk their car horn.

"Hey, dude. Hurry your ass up!" One of his friends must've called because Austin slammed the door shut and yelled back, "Shut the hell up. I'm moving."

I stayed put. Another second later there was silence.

I rolled over, pulling my blanket over me.

It was a few hours later when I got out of bed. I saw my phone blinking, knowing there were probably a few messages, but I just didn't care. I didn't care about school. Not today.

After showering and grabbing a bite to eat, I dressed and walked out to my car. Getting in, I turned it in the direction of Geezer's, knowing I'd forgotten to go to his place last night, but knowing he probably didn't even noticed.

An hour later, I looked at the old house again. This time the music wasn't blaring from inside and it was quiet—almost too quiet. It was eerie.

Walking inside, I sighed, smelling the ever-present aroma of his favorite substance and I found him curled on the couch...again. Greeting him like I always do, I dropped kicked the end of the couch and he fell off.

Blinking in a drug filled haze, he croaked, "Tarter?"

"You got something for me?"

Frowning, he ran a hand through his hair, making it even shaggier. "Uh...like what?"

"Like some plans that Grayley was supposed to give you."

"Oh."

He had no idea. Grayley might've just dropped them off and taken off. He dropped out of school the second it was possible and spends the majority of his time not on our realm of reality. Geezer wasn't known for his ambition, but then again—who would be with a father who stopped caring about him at the age of three and a mother who was in jail for selling meth. His parents stopped caring a long time ago, so why would Geezer? At least that was his motto.

Sighing, I moved into his kitchen and found the blueprints placed on the counter with my name written at the top of them.

I heard a crash behind me and whirled around, breathless for a moment. I saw Geezer on the floor, his blanket wrapped around his feet.

Helping him up, I asked, "You trying to walk like us adults? You should know better."

He laughed, a hand balancing on my shoulder as I helped him unwrap the blanket. "Oh, Tartar. What are we going to do without you?"

"What have you been doing?"

"Smoking up." he answered.

I laughed. "That's the truth, but it's no different from before."

"It's different," he said quietly, stumbling back to the couch. Curling back up, he said again, "It's a lot different."

Then he fell asleep.

Standing there, I frowned down at his form, seeing the innocence that's only present when asleep.

I moved into the kitchen and dialed Grayley's number.

"Yo," he greeted. I could hear sound in the background.

"You're at school?"

"Yep. Aren't you?"

"I'm at Geezer's, got your present."

"Oh. Hey, I got all I thought you'd want. You know, tried to be comprehensive."

"Comprehensive?" I grinned, leaning a hip against the counter. "The English teacher must be hot this year."

"It's the T.A." he said, actually serious.

"Geezer's in rare form."

"Yeah."

That was it. Not that I'd expected more. Grayley was pretty tight-lipped about his best friend, the bond between them had always been there, since they were kids. I felt that Grayley had taken the protective older brother role.

"Anything I should know about?" I asked lightly.

"Nah. I got it covered. Go do your own thing, we'll manage." I think he meant it jokingly, but I heard an edge in his voice.

"Alright—" I faltered, hearing him hang up abruptly.

Leaving, I made sure there was some food in Geezer's kitchen and was surprised to see it full. Moving back out, I took a last look at him before crossing out to my car. By the time I got back to Rawley, I could make my last class: psychology. Guess I might as well. It would give me a chance to check on how Mandy's doing.

Moving through the hallways, I ducked around a group of giggling girls and jocks who decided the hallway was a perfect place for wrestling. Dropping my bag in my locker, I grabbed my books and headed towards my classroom. Mandy was already seated at a table with Sophie—I think??—I recognized her from the student council meeting at the house the other day. And Jasmine was across the room, laughing with Bryce, her hands lingering on his arm.

Hmm.

Mandy was avidly glaring at them.

Dropping into a chair at one of the back tables, I was surprised when I recognized my science lab partner in the other seat.

She gave me a tentative smile.

Oh hell.

Sticking out my hand, I said, "I don't know if we've actually ever been introduced. My name is Taryn Matthews."

A squeal escaped her mouth as she extended her hand. "Molly Keeley. I'm your—"

"Science lab partner. I know that."

"Yeah, and I'm in your health class."

Wait. "I'm in health?"

"You skip for study hall."

"I thought I had study hall."

"You should probably tell your teacher that."

"Oh." I sat back, surprised. "Thanks."

"No problem. We're playing volleyball next week, so it should be fun."

"You play volleyball?"

"Only with my family. I can't wear contacts and the glasses—they don't help."

"Right. Your microscope glasses."

My eyes widened as I realized what I'd just said. "Oh, Molly, I didn't mean—"

Shrugging, she grinned. "They do look like microscopes, but my mom won't let me get new ones. They're not cost-effective."

"Whatever. They save your social graces," I cut in. Again not thinking. "Oh my God, I'm so sorr—"

This time she laughed whole-heartedly. "You're not what the rumors say you are."

"That I'm a stone cold bitch."

"Yeah, that. And that you screwed Tray Evans."

"Where?" Could I not think before I talked? What was wrong with me?

She listed them off with her fingers, "In the school parking lot, in the parking lot at the diner, at one of his parties, at Rickets' House, and in his car."

"Oh. I've been busy."

She giggled, ducking her head suddenly.

I looked over and saw Tray staring back, kneeling down beside me.

"What?" I asked.

"Two days," was all he said."

I flushed in annoyance. "Yeah. So?"

"You going to be ready in two days?" he demanded. And now I remembered detested him—I still did, no matter how amazing he was in bed.

I snapped testily, "Ask again and I won't be."

He smirked. Yep, he was still detestable. "Don't get all worked up. We had a deal, a business deal. I need to know if you can deliver your end of the deal."

"I'm ready to go on my end."

"Whatever." He stood up. "Saw Jace Lanser leaving town last night. Stopped at the diner for a burger."

I stood also. "Yeah. So?"

He backed off, taking his own seat across the room, the entire class now listening avidly. "Nothing. The guy's a loser."

"Spoken like a true horse's ass," I shot back. Jace was family. No one talked bad about my family.

Mandy gasped, "Taryn."

Jasmine smirked, but there was still a note of fear in her eyes.

"Spoken like a true bitch's ass," he retorted, sitting back, looking relaxed and arrogant.

"One that you're hot for," I said coolly, seeing him draw his breath in at my words. Before he could reply the teacher strode in frantically. "Sorry, class, so sorry I'm late."

I sat back down and the rest of the class reluctantly turned their attention to the teacher.

Molly leaned over and whispered, "You are officially my idol. Just thought I'd share my reverence from this day on." I cracked a grin at the litany. Microscope girl had a sense of humor.

After class, Molly walked with me out the door and towards my locker. I shot her a glance, wondering what was up, but she stayed at my side and even waited while I grabbed my bag.

"Something up?" I finally asked, noticing glances from the other students.

She shifted nervously on her feet. "Uh...well—"

"Out with it."

"There's a party this weekend. I think Justin Travers is throwing it and I was wondering—"

I had no idea who Justin Travers was. Pretty sure I couldn't help her.

She continued, "You seem really, really nice, no matter what they say, and I was wondering...would you go with me? Or get me an invite?"

"Why?"

"Because Justin Travers is gorgeous and I've had the hugest crush on him since the third grade. One time he gave me his lunch. It was awesome."

"I don't know who he is."

"He plays soccer and he's on student council and he's super gorgeous. He knows your sister, Mandy."

"I still don't know who he is."

"Yeah, but I'm sure you'll be invited to his party. You're one of them, but you're cool and nice. You can introduce us."

I'd had enough. The girl was going to get crushed.

Shutting my locker, I said bluntly, "Listen. I'm not saying this to be mean, but if he's what you make him sound—he's not interested. In you at least. He's going to go after little cheerleaders who give it up to be popular and have the IQ of a poodle. That's not you."

She was stunned and through her microscope glasses, I could tell she wasn't even blinking.

I didn't know what else to say, so I turned and walked outside towards my car. I might have crushed her, but it was nothing compared to what he would've done.

"That was pretty cruel."

Turning I saw a skinny guy with waxy hair glaring at me.

"Who are you?"

"You can't just treat people like that. It's...It's," he sputtered, "inhumane."

"She's not a dog and what I did was save her from being humiliated," I remarked.

"You really are the bitch everyone's saying you are," he called after me as I passed him.

I shrugged and gave him the finger, grinning as I walked to my car.

Wednesday passed without incident. Mandy acted like nothing was wrong, sitting with students on student council and some of the cheerleaders. Jasmine sat at a different table with Amber, Grant, and Devon. Bryce and Tray were missing. And me, I sat alone like normal. Molly chose a different seat in psychology and the guy who'd spoken up for her had glared at me as I left school.

I loved being popular—and hated.

But I was happy. I hadn't heard any rumors about Mandy and Devon's break-up. I didn't even know if it was known at school. Monday the halls had been buzzing about the cancellation, alarms, and unending music. I'd missed Tuesday, so I didn't know what the rumors were. But Wednesday had two themes. The first was my retort to Tray in last period and the other focused on Justin Travers' party.

Nothing was spoken about Jasmine and Mandy. That's all I cared about.

Wednesday night I was packing my bag, double-checking everything for the heist tomorrow. I was planning on going after school and waiting it out until eight o'clock that evening. That was usually when the faculty and staff finally left. The students should be gone by six or so—at least. I just needed to make sure that Geezer was sober and at my side to work on the device before I handed it over to Tray.

Hearing the doorbell, I sighed and walked from my bedroom towards the stairs. Hearing it again, I yelled, "Coming. Hold on."

Opening up, I saw Carter on the opposite side.

"Hi." He gave me a wide smile, leaning one hand against the doorframe.

"Mandy's not here and I don't know where she's at," I clipped out, moving to shut the door.

"Whoa, whoa." He stopped the door, putting his foot in the doorway. "I'm Carter. We haven't actually met."

"And I'm perfectly fine with that, I'm done with your crowd. I'll stick to my sister."

I kicked his foot out and shut the door.

The whole school was on edge the next day. Amidst the excitement from Monday, it seemed everyone had forgotten that this was homecoming week. The cheerleaders reminded everyone on Thursday and that meant tension. Tension, chaos, and everyone suddenly acting like they're going to get laid. They were playing Pedlam the next night.

At my locker, I grabbed a book, my cellphone tucked between my neck and ear as I called Grayley. Hearing him answer, I said, "Make sure Geezer's sober today. I'll need him tonight."

"Sure thing," Grayley remarked, I could hear laughter in his voice.

"Things crazy over there?"

"Yep."

What's up with the non-answers?

"Brian's standing right there, isn't he?" I asked coolly.

"Sure is," he said cheerfully.

"Okay." I hung up. No point worrying, Grayley knew what to do; he'd helped me numerous times over the years.

"Hey."

Turning around, I saw my sister.

"What's up?"

"Huh," she faltered, shuffling her feet.

"Mandy," I said firmly.

"What?"

"What's up?"

"It's...," she rolled her eyes, her hands resting on her hips, "Carter said you two met and that you were—"

"Less than friendly," I supplied dryly, shutting my locker and moving down the hallway.

"It's just, why? Why do you have to be like that?" she cried out.

"I'm not going to be nice to a guy that's temporary."

"What?"

I stopped in the hallway, facing her squarely. "He's the rebound. I get it, I understand, but he's not my friend. In fact, none of these people are my friends. I'm here because your family adopted me. You're my sister, I'm starting to get that—but everything else—your friends being my friends...it's not how it is, Mandy. It's not how it's going to be."

"It's not like that," she argued. I could hear the hurt in her voice.

"He's the rebound," I stated.

"Look, now's not the place to talk about this. He's having a party tomorrow night and he wants you to come."

"I'm not going."

"Come on, Taryn—"

"No." I shrugged her off, ducking into my classroom. It was fifth period and I had Spanish, but luckily for me, this course is a cakewalk. If you actually wanted to learn, those students chose French. Spanish consisted of learning donde esta el bano, hola me llamo es ____, and zacapuntas. That was about it. Our teacher was usually flying around wearing a sombrero, helping the motivated students make piñatas—no joke.

Sliding into my chair, the only one open was in the front when I first started; therefore, my designated chair for the rest of the year. Just my luck.

Feeling someone tap my shoulder, I turned around and was blinded by the whitest pair of teeth, surrounded by a curly mop of blonde hair, framing piercing blue eyes.

"Hey." When had our nation adopted this as the normal greeting? I think I'm going to start using a simple "hi" from now on.

"Hey," I murmured. Nope, it was already ingrained.

"You're Matthew's new sister, right?"

"Yeah."

"I'm Justin Travers."

The dude Molly liked. I gave him the once over and, yes, I was correct in my assessment. The guy had a cheerleader on his lap.

"And apparently you know me," I said wryly, moving to turn back around.

"I'm having a party tomorrow night. You're coming, right?"

I turned back around and studied him, noting the smirk and cockiness. I looked at the platinum blonde on his lap—the Hooters poster girl from Tray's house—watching me intently. It felt like I was being tested.

I sighed. "Look, if you think there's even a possibility that the rumors about me screwing Evans are true, doesn't mean shit to you. Because one, I am not one of those girls who's suddenly realized how fun sex is and I'm going to start sleeping with anyone remotely popular. Two, if I did screw

Evans then he's probably the only one I'd settle for in the future. And three, I don't have low self-esteem. I am not going to turn into a groupie."

"Why are your panties so twisted?"

God, I'd had enough. Okay, yes, I'd gone on the offensive and he was only shooting back, but seriously. I'm sick and goddamn tired of guys thinking they can reduce everything to sex.

So I grinned coolly and flipped his chair backwards.

"Fuck."

"Ah."

Someone screamed, someone gasped, and a whole lot laughed. I caught the glances of a few people, but they quickly looked the other way.

"You bitch," Travers shot back, slowly standing up.

"Psycho bitch is more like it," said Hooters girl.

And I was hoping we'd be friends.

"Miss Matthews!" Señora Graham, the Spanish teacher, exclaimed, her sombrero falling off in her state of shock. "Principal's office. Now!" Shouldn't she have said that in Espanol?

Leaving the classroom, I realized I had left my books inside. Oh well.

I started getting a funny feeling in my stomach and, as I continued down the hall, it exploded inside me, leaving me gasping in surprise. It took me a moment to recover. This was new. Was this guilt?

I never cared about getting in trouble before I came to Rawley. I've walked down this hallway so many times before—they were all the same, with the same destination. In the old days, Brian would've gotten kicked out beside me, and he'd already be dragging me out to the parking lot by now. I could picture his grin and almost hear his laugh.

But this time, I cared. I cared that Mandy was probably going to get some slack for this, because of something I'd done. And it bothered me.

Turning the corner, walking towards the office at the end of the hall, I saw Mandy standing with six other cheerleaders in the hallway. They were coloring a poster for the game tomorrow night, or at least that was my guess since it said, "Pedlam Sucks."

Mandy was nudged by a girl that was standing beside her when she saw me.

"Taryn? What are you doing here?"

"I'll go to Carter's party."

"You will?" I felt guiltier seeing the smile that stretched across her face.

"Yeah."

"Wait. What are you doing here?"

"I...uh...I'm sorry."

Mandy paled. "What did you do, Taryn?"

"Uh—" I brushed her off, turning and walking back towards my locker.

"Miss Matthews!" The principal had come to look for me. I stopped and looked around, seeing him just behind Mandy, frowning fiercely. His tie flung across his shoulder, as if he'd dashed out of his office.

I didn't say anything. What could I say? So I met Mandy's gaze as I walked steadily past her and through the office door the principal was holding open.

"Miss Matthews, take a seat."

He shut the door and walked around to sit behind his massive mahogany desk. His black leather chair creaked slightly as it tipped backwards under his weight.

"Señora Graham tells me that you assaulted a student," he said coldly.

"It wasn't assault."

"Mr. Travers and Miss Klinnleys have bruises proving otherwise."

"It happened like thirty seconds ago," I pointed out. "The bruises aren't from me. And it wasn't assault, I moved a chair."

"Two students were harmed from your actions. Under my classification, that can be considered a form of assault."

"I didn't even touch 'em," I said calmly.

I sighed, settling back in my chair.

"You have quite a history, don't you, Miss Matthews? I think you should learn what *appropriate* boundaries are and how to implement them in your life."

I smirked, folding my arms. "You have nothing on me. I pushed a chair. That's it."

"There were two students *in* that chair."

"Exactly," I deadpanned. "Two students. In one chair. If anything, you should be hauling my teacher in here and not me. Shouldn't she be supervising such inappropriate behavior? Since when was it school policy that we could sit on laps here? At least in our classrooms."

As he stuttered, I knew it was over. The breakdown was right and I did point out a much more serious issue than my supposed assault. I saw the decision made in his eyes before he even opened his mouth.

"You may go, Miss Matthews, but if I find you sitting across from me again, you won't like the ramifications. You can quote me on that one, Miss Matthews."

Mandy was waiting for me in the hallway and pounced on me as I walked by. "What did you do?!" she hissed.

"It won't happen again, okay?"

Mandy latched onto my arm and pulled me into the bathroom. Checking it, making sure it was empty, she asked, "Are you doing this on purpose?"

"What are you talking about?" I gingerly retracted her hand from my arm.

"All of this. For like attention or something? Are you doing it on purpose? You know, taking attention away from me and Devon?"

"This last incident? No."

"What about you and Tray on Tuesday?"

"No."

"Oh." She was appeased, slightly, but I saw the wheels turning in her head. She'd put two and two together eventually. I hadn't actually answered her question, but it was an evade that I was quite proud of. And she knew it wasn't out of my character to do something.

"Has Jasmine left you alone?" I asked softly, stepping closer as a few girls trailed inside.

"Yeah, but Carter said you threatened her."

"Oh God. Carter again." I moaned, moving to leave.

Mandy followed me. "Are you really coming to the party?"

"I thought Justin Travers was having a party? Why aren't you going to his?"

"Because Jasmine and Devon will be there."

"So your crowd is just going to split, huh?" I noted, walking to my locker as more student filed out of their classes. The bell had rung when I was in the principal's office and I hadn't even noticed. I didn't even think I'd been gone that long.

Mandy trailed behind me. "Well...I guess. Until me and Devon are okay, I guess. Jasmine and I will—breathe each other's air if we have to, eventually. Jasmine and Amber had to do it after the whole fiasco over Tray."

"What fiasco?"

"He dumped Jasmine for Amber. Or...well...*I* think he just dumped Jasmine and Amber happened to be there, you know."

"So who else is going to be at this party?"

"Pretty much everyone else. A lot will go to Justin's party because Carter's is more exclusive, you know. A lot of people will *want* to go to Carter's and they'll probably crash, but the only people who I know won't come are Jas and Dev."

"If they do, then what?"

She shrugged. "Then Carter'll kick 'em out."

I shook my head.

"What?"

"You. You're so sneaky, I almost have to give you credit for it."

"What are you talking about?" Mandy asked, her eyes wide in an attempt to look innocent.

"I threatened Jasmine and now Carter's making sure they don't come to his party. Your back is covered no matter where you go. How'd you work that out?"

She grinned and bumped me with her hip. "Got myself a cool adopted sister, that's what."

"And you put out for Carter."

Mandy stopped. "We didn't have sex," she said seriously. "He just stayed the night. That's all that happened."

The hallways were emptying, so I said quickly, "Gotta go. See you in psych."

I grabbed my seat like always when seventh period rolled around an hour later. A second later someone dropped into the seat next to me, and turning, I was surprised to see Molly. Microscope girl. Huh.

"Thought you hated me," I stated.

"I did." She grinned, pushing her glasses up her nose. "Until I realized you were actually being kind in a very harsh way." Leaning closer, she asked, "Did you really shove Justin Travers and Sasha Klinnleys?"

"No." And I hadn't.

"Oh." She sounded disappointed.

I shrugged and then, gritting my teeth, I remembered Mandy reminding me that friends were a good thing to have.

"I just...I kicked their chair and it fell over. That's all. I swear," I relented, sighing.

I saw the quick smile before she blushed and ducked her head.

Somehow I knew. I didn't know how. I couldn't explain it. But I knew if I turned around, Tray would be watching me.

Turning around, I saw him staring steadily at me.

"What?"

"We need to talk," he spoke, standing up and pulling me out of the classroom with him.

"Our teacher's going to be coming pretty soon," I argued, but followed nonetheless. I knew what this was about: business.

He leaned against a locker in the empty hallway and regarded me. "Our teacher's always twenty minutes late. I think we'll be fine."

"You don't need to get snippy," I huffed.

Tray rolled his eyes, his hands stuffed in his pockets. He looked at ease. A casual confidence radiated off of him.

It irritated me. "So what'd you want to talk to me about?" I asked.

Tray lifted his eyebrows and remained silent. I saw the amusement in their depths.

"What?" I asked again.

He chuckled, leaning to face me. "I didn't realize till now how much I unnerve you." He whistled. "You must hate that."

I moaned, "You're a bit too conceited."

"You came," he remarked, smirking.

I had to take a step back. I was there for business. Business only. The incident with Brian, then saying goodbye to Jace—it must've messed me up even more than I wanted to admit for me to have landed in Tray's bed after the fight with Brian. Right now...I needed to step back. This was just my body remembering the explosive sex. There is no way a relationship with Tray would end well.

"Business," I reminded him.

"Right." He sighed. "Are you ready for tonight?"

"Yeah."

"When do we get in?"

"After I have my guy look at the device."

"Not before? When will that be?"

"How many guys you got coming for this?"

"Enough to get our shit done," he deadpanned.

I studied him for a moment. I didn't know what they really wanted; the PRS-500 could unlock more doors than they even knew existed. I was loathe to give that power to them—there was no way they'd get their hands on it without Geezer working his magic on it first.

"What are you guys going to do again? I don't remember."

He gave me a faint grin. "Good try. No bulls-eye."

"You're just expecting me to give this to you? To give you free-entry into a school that I used to go to? Where my friends go?"

"And your ex?" he asked smoothly.

"This isn't about him."

Tray shifted closer to me, his eyes melting to amber as he whispered, "I kinda like it when he comes into the picture."

I held firm.

As he drew closer, his head bent towards my neck, I felt his lips lightly caressing there, and he breathed, "I'd like another go round."

"Mr. Evans! Miss Matthews!"

Looking up, a bit more dazed than I wanted to admit, I saw our psych teacher hurrying down the hallway, shooing us with her hands. "Get inside. Now," she cried.

As we walked inside, the entire class immediately hushed, watching both of us make our way to our seats.

Molly was in awe. I could tell from the worshipful glaze over her face. Mandy was frowning. Jasmine was glaring. Bryce was just amused, with his head tipped back, a small smile spread on his face.

Molly leaned close and whispered, "I heard that Carter Sethlers is in town."

"Yeah. I guess."

"I heard he's with your sister."

"I don't know," I whispered back.

"And I heard that he's having a party tomorrow night." The girl was relentless.

"So?" I asked, scooting my chair aside. Did the girl have a clue what personal boundaries were?

"Can I come?"

"You hit me up to set you up with Justin Travers and now you're trying to get me to take you to Carter's party? What kind of science nerd are you?"

She giggled, clamping a hand quickly over her mouth, petrified as some of the students glanced over. "Please," she whispered around her hand.

"Why? Why do you want to do this stuff? Be around these people?"

She gave me a dumb-founded stare. "Because I'm a nerd. I'm socially challenged."

"I'm not exactly known as the nice girl from the popular crowd. You know, one of those types that's popular and incredibly sweet so everyone tries to be friends with her because they think she can make them popular. That's not me."

"Exactly," Molly pointed out.

"What happened to you being pissed at me?" I moaned.

"You were right about Justin. I'll always think he's the hottest thing here, but...I don't know." She shrugged, ducking her head, flushing. "I just...I'd like to tell my mom that I went to one party this year. One of those that she'll freak out about and forbid me to go to."

"And there are reasons why you should be forbidden from going to those types of parties." I reasoned.

"You could watch out for me."

I was about to say I wasn't going, but remembered I had already told Mandy I would—out of guilt. Damn.

"And what if I'm too busy? What if I'm going to hook up with a guy?"

Molly looked indignant as she pushed her glasses back on her nose. "You don't strike me as that type of girl."

"Look, I'll let you know tomorrow." I glanced away, uncomfortable.

Mandy wants me to have friends. I can have friends. Just not...her friends.

After the bell rang, I made my way to my locker, evading most of the hallway rush. I probably would've made it to my car without speaking to anyone, if that one guy hadn't stopped me outside on the front lawn. The guy who'd told me I was inhumane.

"Hey, bitch," he called out, loping across the lawn towards me.

I took a harder look at him this time. He'd called me inhumane our first meeting, glared at me the next day, and now he'd called me a bitch. Again. I eyed him up and down and saw nothing significant about him—he was skinny, had shaggy hair, and he looked almost bug eyed (I'll give him credit though, they were a startling green color that demanded more than one look at them).

I smirked, waiting to hear what he had to say.

Drawing closer, he said, "I heard what you did."

I was starting to think back to what he could be talking about...what hadn't I done? Seriously. Why did everyone have to care so goddamn much about what I did or did not do or who I did or did not do?

"And what was that?" I drawled out.

"Travers and that slut Klinnleys."

"So what? Was that inhumane too?"

"No way. That was awesome!"

This guy was killing me.

"Is there a reason why you feel you have the right to continuously interrupt my peaceful walk, three times in a row, and claim your judgment on my behavior?" I bit out. "Because if I made you my judge and jury in some prior life, I'd really like to know so I can correct my stupidity—somehow in this life!"

"Hey, dude, I'm just saying that I was wrong. You're my personal hero. I've been wanting to take Travers down a notch ever since freshman year."

"Oh. A whole five months, huh?" I snapped.

"Whatever." He shrugged. "You might want to think about changing your script. All you do is be a bitch followed by being a bitch and then serve a dessert portion of...being a bitch."

"Yeah, well, it's worked for me so far."

"Doesn't seem like it. You're the one pissed off right now and me," he grinned, backing away, "I'm peachy. Travers got taken down. You made my year."

"Hey," I stopped him as he was turning around, "what's your name?"

"Me?" he asked, surprised.

"Yeah. Your name. What is it?"

"Garrett Larkins."

"You want to go to a party tomorrow night?" I couldn't believe I was doing this, but I already started it.

"Seriously?" He didn't even ask which one.

"Yeah."

"Sure," he rushed out, smiling widely.

"Fine. Find me after school tomorrow."

I watched him a second later, noticing that he had run over to a group of kids playing hackey-sack. It reminded me of Geezer and Grayley. They used to play that game too.

I crossed the street to my car. I'd taken to parking on the opposite side of campus where the parking lot was placed. It was just easier to avoid drama, but, apparently, drama like to single me out because I saw Tray leaning against my car door. His SUV parked just behind, with some of his friends. Mitch and some others that I recognized from the basketball team.

"Hey," I murmured as I pulled my keys out.

He didn't move, but reached to tip my head up as my arms moved to unlock the door, bringing me in contact with his body. "What's the plan tonight?"

I shrugged off his touch. "I'll call you when I have the device."

"And when will that be? Like an approximate time."

"I don't know. Nine? Ten?"

"You can't be any more definite? It's not like we have all the time in the world. We're going to be sitting around, planning on doing something pretty illegal, and you just expect us to sit around on our hands? What are we supposed to do? Twiddle our thumbs?"

Whoa. Evans was mad. Actually, inspecting him closer, I realized he was beyond pissed.

"What are you so pissed about?" I didn't even know if I should ask, but it was already out of my mouth. "This was the deal. I go in, get the device and hand it over to my guy. You get it afterwards."

"It's not good enough. We could get caught."

"And so could I!" I cried, now getting pissed in my own right. "What do you want? I'm not giving you a time-schedule for when I commit my crime. Is that what you want? Got a nice little deal worked out with the cops? You doing this to catch me?"

"Oh please," he groaned.

"Are you? Because I'm starting to think that's what's going on," I said tightly.

"Just get your end done and call me," he said stiffly, pushing off my car and striding to his own. Climbing in, one of the guys smirked at me as Tray gunned the engine and peeled out into traffic.

He was infuriating.

This was my moment. This was my element. Standing atop the roof of my old school, the black night as my backdrop, the wind rushing behind me, I closed my eyes for a moment just enjoying the feeling. It was like nothing I'd ever experienced. I don't know what it was, or how I could describe it, but even the hairs on my fingers were vibrating. I felt so alive.

The drive to Pedlam had been uneventful. Grayley had called and said he had Geezer, sober and on standby. Everything was ready and in place. I had memorized the blueprints and alarm time schedules from the info Grayley had gotten me. He, Geezer, and I had been a team, before I moved to Rawley. Brian had always wanted to be included, but I never let him. Grayley and Geezer were steady; Brian and I were just volatile together. With Grayley and Geezer, there was no drama, they did the job and followed through. I knew I could depend on them, even if they were pissed off or high.

But right now—this was the part where it was just me.

The PRS-500 was nicely tucked away t in the superintendent's locked cabinet, in a locked drawer, behind, of course, his locked office door. His office was situated just inside the main office, which was behind another locked door. Not too hard for me to get to, but not the easiest either.

What was new, since I'd been gone, was a twenty-four seven shift of security guards. This made me wonder what else was inside this building that would need to be guarded around the clock. Obviously, the first thing I needed to take care of was the guards.

So this brings me to where exactly I was standing, or who exactly I was standing above—the guard's office. I knelt at the venting shaft and unscrewed it, slipping inside, with the rope around my waist already secured around a handle outside the shaft. This venting system was different from Rawley because it dipped down, straight down so you aren't able to just find your footing easily, so I had to rappel downwards, counting the distance inch by inch until I felt the ground beneath me.

I had counted a good sixteen feet, which coincided with the blueprints Grayley had gotten for me.

Finding the hatch just to the left of my feet, I unscrewed it and lifted it up. Beneath me, I could hear sounds from a basketball game. Guessing the guards were watching ESPN, I slipped through. I could see them through the door; there were three of them, all sitting with their backs to me, feet propped up on the camera panel. Two of the video screens were on a rotating schedule covering different areas throughout the school. There was one on top that focused only on the main office. And the screen in the middle—ESPN. It wasn't basketball though. Anaheim was losing by two goals.

Seriously. What were they keeping in a school that needed three security guards? Whatever happened to nice locked doors?

I needed to move on. I could get inside without the guards seeing me, but Tray wouldn't be able to.

I slipped past them, moving down the hallway, pausing at each corner before I slipped my mirror around, checking if a camera was up ahead or not. I'd watched the rotation schedule enough to memorize most of the areas, but it didn't hurt to be sure.

Arriving on the second floor, I slipped through the men's bathroom and opened the vent. Pulling myself up, I crawled inside, following it for a count of sixty. I could measure distance by my counts. It was an old system I had down pat.

According to my estimation, I should be just overhead the principal's office. The superintendent's office didn't have a normal size venting shaft over his office. He used one of those tapered off vents, making it impossible for any good-intentioned thief, such as myself, to climb in and out. Pulling through, I stood atop the desk and smoothly moved to the door. From what I saw on the security camera, there was only a slight angle that covered the superintendent's office door, but it was enough of an opening.

Gritting my teeth, I moved quickly and plastered my body as much as I could against the wall while I worked on the door. I used a Wesson steel wire point and jerked upwards with another ballpoint blade. Hearing the door click open, I pushed inside, keeping my head turned away from the camera and shut the door, but not letting it click shut. Moving to the closet, I quickly moved through that locked door.

The cabinet drawer was another challenge in itself. It was keypad lock. Grabbing my ballpoint blade, I worked it underneath the covering panel, dipped inside, and pulled out the black alarm wire. I clipped the wire onto a seventy-three delay wire that I had in my pack and ran it around to the base, as close to it as I could, to place it against the wire just inside the cabinet panel. Then, holding my breath, I made sure the delay wire was in place and clipped the wire close to the base.

And the cabinet lock clicked open with the keypad still showing green. The delay wire had worked wonderfully.

Inside lay the PRS-500. Grabbing it, I sheathed it inside a pack I had clipped around my back, zipping the device just inside the small of my back. My job was almost done.

Shutting the cabinet lock, I unclipped my delay wire and pocketed it quickly. Then I closed the closet door. Slipping out through the office door, I still didn't pull the door completely shut, I closed it just enough so it looked shut from the camera angle. Keeping my head turned away, I entered the principal's office and hoisted myself up through the venting shaft again. I crawled, finding myself outside the security room once again and back up through the hatch. Feeling around the dark, I found my rope and clipped it back on me, then I started hoisting myself back up, pulling the rope back through my karabiner on my waist.

It took longer, but I was back on the roof and screwing the venting shaft in place once again. Then I slipped into the darkness.

I couldn't stop the grin that spread across my face.

CHAPTER FOUR

I found Grayley and Geezer up ahead where they'd parked around a small group of trees. It was where we always parked if we wanted to get high, skip class, or have sex—sometimes all three of them together. It was our little hideaway, which made me smile as I approached the car from behind, through the trees.

"Hey guys," I said softly, directly behind them.

Geezer jumped.

Grayley let loose whatever had been in his hands.

And I laughed. I couldn't help myself.

"Taryn! Holy fuck's sake," Grayley gasped, scowling at me.

Geezer was too busy checking me out. "Looking good, Tartar." He whistled.

I didn't have it in me to blush. I was decked out in all black. It wasn't nylon, but a fabric that was somewhat in the middle between cotton and nylon. It was glued on me, but it was what I needed for my jobs. I'd already ditched my little theft kit in the car, so they didn't get the somewhat dorky look of a little pack hanging around my waist, complete with bungee cord karabiners, ropes, and everything else I needed. All of that needed to be locked tight on me, to save me from making any extra sound. You never knew what you would run into on a job and I liked to be prepared. The only thing I had with me, other than my car keys, and the PRS-500 was my bottle of chloroform. And I wasn't planning on using it.

But I knew the image I made. I'd let my hair down so it shook free around my shoulders.

"You too, Geezer. I especially like the sober look. It's got a certain...mystery...about you." I nudged him with my hip.

He blushed. He never failed to blush from any teasing or from any sort of compliment. It was endearing to watch and I loved seeing that he still did it. Apparently that hadn't changed.

"Hey, not to be an ass or...well...we kind of have some stuff to take care of tonight, so can we hurry this along?" Grayley asked, running a hand through his gelled back hair.

I grinned. "Yeah. I'm sure Geezer's got a lot of plans tonight."

"Whatever," Grayley commented, hunching over as he leaned against his truck.

I handed the PRS-500 to Geezer and gave him my instructions. He climbed inside the truck to use the light for his work.

Studying Grayley, I commented, "You look more preppy than when I left. If I were to notice things like that."

"Preppy?" he asked, surprised at my comment.

"Yeah. Someone who'd hang out with Gentley."

"You mean someone who'd like to stay alive and therefore needs to avoid Brian at all costs? If that's preppy, keeping my neck screwed on, then yeah—I'm preppier. God—if that's even a word, Taryn."

"What are you talking about?"

"Look, I don't know what happened between you and Brian, but he's been a loose cannon this week. I heard that he and Jace had a huge brawl the other night. They both had to go to the hospital and now Brian's been off—doing who the hell knows what. He's dangerous, Taryn and I think you set him off."

"He bothering you at all?"

"No. Not yet. But I've no doubt he's just making his rounds. He roughed up Kerri before his fight with Jace."

"Kerri? Is she okay?"

Kerri and I had been on okay terms. She was one of those girls that was just on the scene and sort of just ended up being accepted in the group. She was just there, you know. I know she'd slept with Geezer a few times. But, one time she'd helped me out with something and ever since then I had grown a soft spot for her. Still...we weren't exactly best buds.

"I think so. Still, it's Kerri. He roughed her up. A girl, Taryn. I didn't know he had it in him—"

I snorted.

He amended, "Okay. I did know, but he's just scary now. He's not stable."

"Well, we're over."

"I know you are."

We fell silent. What else could really be said on that topic.

"So, you're with Gentley's crew now?" I asked.

"I guess. I'm not with Brian anymore. That's for damn sure."

"Still. Gentley?" I asked scornfully.

"Yeah." He sighed. "School's not the same. It's not...I don't know."

"It can't be that different. I mean it's just a school."

"Bri's off his rocker. I heard that the school got a restraining order on him."

"All that happened within one week?"

"Most of it's just rumors," he murmured, jumping to sit on the back of his cab.

Anything else we would have said was interrupted as Geezer slammed his door shut. Brandishing the PRS-500, he exclaimed, "Alrighty, tighty. It's programmed how you want it. Those suckers won't get through my fire walls. If they do, I want to meet 'em. Give 'em some of my weed because I'll be in awe."

Tucking the device back in place, I said warmly, "Thanks, Geezer."

"No prob." He waved me off.

"What can I do to thank you?"

"Oh. Oh!" He grinned, his eyes sparkling. "Oh no. I'd like to live to see next week. Thanks, though."

I laughed. Couldn't help it, but I was still worried. Something seemed off. "You okay, Geeze?"

"Yeah, yeah." He shrugged, jumping in place.

I caught Grayley's eyes and saw the resignation in them. Something was up.

"What's going on?" I asked sharply.

"Nothing. Really. Take off," Geezer joked.

"Charles," I barked this time, "you better tell me what's going on."

"Jeez, Taryn, come on."

"Now," I snapped, folding my arms.

Geezer shuffled his feet self-consciously.

Grayley rolled his eyes and kicked him with his foot. "Just tell her, dude. Maybe she can help."

"I don't know…it's…"

"Geezer, tell her!"

Finally, Geezer lifted his eyes to meet mine. I was surprised to see a sheen of tears in them.

"What's going on, Geezer?"

"It's my dad."

Seeing he had fallen silent, I looked at Grayley.

"He's back in town. He sent him a letter a few weeks back. He wants to stay at the house for a while."

"What's he doing in town?"

"I think—" Grayley started.

"You don't know that. You don't know that at all! It's fucking stupid is what it is. Fucking stupid," Geezer cried out angrily.

It was the second time I'd seen any sort of emotion like that in Geezer. I was taken aback.

Grayley snorted. "Come on. Why else would he be in town?"

"What? What do you think?"

"I think," Grayley announced, waiting for a reaction from Geezer, "that he's in town doing business with Jace."

"Oh." I didn't know what to say. It was probably true. And it'd be just like him to use his son while he was toting up on drugs. "So what do you want me to do?"

Geezer lifted his eyes, but didn't say anything. He went back to shuffling his legs around, still self-conscious.

I looked at Grayley.

He rolled his eyes again. "Can you talk to Jace?"

"Uh huh. No. That door on my life's closed," I said quickly, but already knowing the inevitable. Geezer was one of my best friends. He was family.

"Taryn," Grayley murmured.

Geezer looked up at me with his hazel puppy dog eyes. Seriously. Why can I not be a bitch to those who are certainly condemning me to a further slide in my own pit of pain? But no. These two guys. These two guys—I'd do anything for. Including signing up for another week of wallowing pain.

Ugh.

Fuck.

"Fine," I murmured.

Geezer lit up in a smile, rocking back and forth, his arms hugging himself.

Grayley chuckled, punching me lightly in the arm. "Thanks Tar."

"Yeah. Yeah. Consider it a thank-you for helping me with this job." I raised my eyebrows at Geezer. "But I'd be up for—performing—a more personal thank-you, if you'd like."

And there was that blush I loved so much. Chuckling, I waved goodbye and moved back through the trees, heading to my car. Walking across a back alley, I pulled my phone out and dialed Tray's number.

"About damn time," he bit out in the phone.

"Hey. Chill," I soothed.

"Where are you?"

"I'm coming to you guys. You parked on Bentley, right? Behind the hardware store?"

"How'd you know that?"

"Because it's where I'd parked—if I wanted to break into the school." I hung the phone up, circling around the SUV. Inside I saw it was packed with guys, mostly jocks after further investigation. Not that it mattered, they all ran in the same social circle.

Mandy's. Not mine.

There was another Expedition behind Tray's and it was packed with students also.

What were they planning?

Tray climbed out, along with all the other guys as I approached from behind.

He raked his eyes up and down my figure, a faint grin curling at the corner of his mouth.

I clamped down on the warmth that started to spread through my body at his perusal. The guy could irritate me to no end, but one crook of that tempting mouth and...not going there.

"Got something for me?" he asked, now grinning, but I still saw the irritation in his eyes.

I handed it over. "It's been wiped clean by my guy. You got the codes on there for Pedlam High, that's it."

"No trust, Taryn. No trust," he tsked. "What kind of relationship are we going to have if there's no trust?"

"One where we just fuck?" I smirked back, rolling my eyes.

Tray held my eyes at that statement a moment. Then he grinned, before turning to follow his guys.

"Hey."

Tray turned back. "Hmm?"

"There's three guards on shift."

"Three guards? What?"

"Oh shit," one of the guys moaned.

"What the fuck do they need three guards for?"

"How are we supposed to handle three guards?" another guy asked.

Tray was studying me. "How'd you get by them?"

I smiled, saying smoothly, "It's why I do what I do."

"Taryn, this is wasn't what I do." He shot me a smug grin. His eye fell on the bottle in my hand. Pointing to it, he asked, "That for us?"

I handed it over. "It's for the guards. Don't use too much and don't leave it behind."

He lifted it up. "Thanks."

I sighed. Why the hell was I helping him?

One of the guys hollered, "Thanks, Taryn! You're awesome."

"Shut the fuck up!" Tray snapped.

I turned to leave, but Tray asked, "Where are you going now?"

I turned back, but continued to walk backwards. "I got some more business to take care of."

He frowned. "More?"

"Yep."

"The same sort that you took me on a ride with?"

"Yep."

I didn't know how he knew, but he did. What perturbed me the most was that a part of me was glad he knew. I don't know why. I didn't understand it. But the other part of me...I didn't like being read. Being read meant that I could be predicted. I was known for being unpredictable.

Tray just nodded, not saying anything, watching me walk backwards until I finally turned and disappeared in the darkness.

I could hear their feet shuffling against the street as they headed towards the school, in the opposite direction.

Holy. Shit. I did not want to go into that building.

I was standing across the alley, the Seven8 was pumping in music, sweat, and drugs. I could hear the shouts from the crowd from where I stood. There was a waiting line, trailing around the corner.

The club wasn't normally this crazy, but apparently I had picked the best night to run an errand for Geezer.

And my errand was inside.

Oh God.

I'd rather—sit in jail. Maybe not for a week, but...close enough.

Taking a deep breath, I crossed the road, jumping lightly onto the sidewalk, seeing Ben holding back two screaming girls. He was joined outside the door by Grunt and Moan. Okay, those weren't their real names, but those were the nicknames I'd always given them. Actually, I think Grunt really was his name. Probably not Moan though.

Moving forward, I ducked around a girl who got shoved from the line. It was kill or be killed when getting inside this club.

Drawing closer, I murmured, "Hey, Ben." Seeing a somber look appear in his eyes, I didn't take it as a good sign.

He didn't even say anything. He just watched me guardedly.

"It's that bad?" I asked, a pathetic try for a joke. Anything.

"He was in the hospital, Taryn," he finally said, folding his massive arms over his chest As the door opened, he simply turned back and effectively blocked three girls from darting through. They just bounced off his back. When he turned back around the stared at me gravely.

"That wasn't me. I didn't do that."

"No, but your psycho ex did."

"Way I heard it, both of them visited," I pointed out, standing uncertainly before him.

"And you were the reason they fought."

"Right. Because they've had such a loving relationship all their life," I said sarcastically, starting to get pissed. "Is he in or not?"

"What makes you think you're welcome around here?"

"Jace does," I answered him honestly. Jace would never turn me away. I knew that. Jace knew that. And Ben knew that. "Look, I just gotta ask him a question. One question, that's all."

Ben was unmoving. The door opened again and Grunt allowed two girls to go inside while a couple left. Moan was watching the exchange between me and Ben intently. All three of them were just massive and had tattoos scattered from their shaved heads, necks, to even their fingers. They didn't intimidate me though. What would intimidate me is if Jace didn't want me allowed inside.

"I can get in another way," I finally said. I didn't want to. I didn't want to have to break in, but I was desperate to help Geezer.

Ben sighed, his hand moved to the rope, and he lifted it up, clearing the way for me. Ducking underneath, I held his gaze as I walked inside, seeing the concern in them—

something I've never seen in his eyes before. I'd never even noticed they were a chocolate brown.

Jace was just as excited to see me. Actually, I didn't know. It's just what I felt as I was making my way down the back hallway. Two guards were outside his room and one of them knocked briefly. Instead of Jace, his second in command, Krein, poked his head out. "What?" he asked crossly.

The guard jerked his head towards me.

"Oh," Krein murmured, rubbing a hand over his bald head looking suddenly tired. Stepping out of the room, I saw he was only dressed in jeans that were unbuckled. He was a little stockier than Jace—Jace had a body that was just cut, in every sense of the word, but he was leaner than Krein—still, Krein wasn't exactly hard on the eyes.

"Jace here?" I asked softly.

"Uh..."

"Krein,"Came a moan from inside.

I grinned, rocking back on my heels. "Another playmate of Krein's harem?"

"You know it!" he returned smoothly, smiling at me. "How you been, girl?"

"I'm here on business for a friend. I'm not here to chit chat or to catch up."

"So things are good, huh?" he asked, not breaking a stride.

"Is he here?"

"Yeah. Ah...he's in the club. Hold on. Ducking inside, he emerged a second later, pulling a shirt on and his holster. "I'll show you."

"I've been in the club before," I murmured, but I waited anyway.

He bypassed me, now leading me towards the club. "I know, but tonight's kinda more crazy than normal. Wouldn't want you getting raped or something."

"Shit..." Was all I said, before Krein opened a side door and all sound was drowned out by the pounding music. I could feel the beat through the floors against my feet. Some of the glasses on the counter were vibrating from the music.

I felt Krein grab my arm and pull me behind him.

We both ducked simultaneously as one shirtless guy stumbled backwards, his drink spilling over in his hand.

Krein wrapped a hand around my waist and literally lifted me out of the way and placed me in front of him, protecting me from three sides, a hand in front to ward off anyone.

"Sorry, dude..." the shirtless guy slurred.

Krein shrugged him off, nudging me forward.

We shoved our way through the next tier of people and Krein pointed towards a corner where I got a brief glimpse of Jace standing in a corner, two girls pressed up against him while he was nodding to whatever some guy was telling him.

Krein switched places with me and muscled his way over to them, two guards let us through, both giving me the once-over.

The new guy from Monday nodded in greeting to us as he shifted aside so we could walk through.

Hax, another of Jace's guys, nudged Jace from behind. He nodded in our direction when Jace glanced at him.

When he spotted me, I saw the slight widening around his eyes. The rest of the world would just see the same poker face, but they weren't privy to the storm that was brewing in his eyes. Great. There was the same tight jaw he always got when he was really pissed.

Jace broke away from the group he had been standing with, leaving the two girls disappointed, until they latched onto someone else. One girl managed to send me a glare first.

The next thing I knew, Jace had grabbed my wrist and was pulling me back the way Krein had just brought me.

And just like Krein, at the first drunk who stumbled in our path, Jace simply lifted me up and placed me in front of him, his arms coming around both sides of me to protect from all angles.

Ben must've sent Grunt, because suddenly he materialized in front of us and cleared a trail for us until we set foot in the back hallway.

"Jace," I started.

"Don't," he said harshly, not letting go of my arm as he led me to his office. One of the guards saw us and ducked inside. A second later a scantily dressed girl darted through and ran down the hallway, away from us.

"Greg," Jace ordered, "I don't want her going that way. Get her back."

Greg nodded and left quickly behind the girl.

When we were inside the room, my eyes had to adjust for a moment to the dark lighting.

Jace didn't say anything. He brushed past me and disappeared inside his bathroom. Emerging a second later, he pulled off his shirt and grabbed another one laying on the chair. Pulling it over his head, I diverted my eyes when I saw his stomach muscles ripple from the movement.

Jace regarded me for another moment in silence. "What are you doing here?" he asked smoothly.

I hugged myself, feeling self-conscious all of the sudden. "I came for a friend."

"Oh. So this is business?" he asked coolly.

"My friend, Geezer—"

"You're here about his dad."

"Yeah," I breathed out.

"And you want to know if he's working for me?"

"Yeah." I willed myself to look up and hold his gaze. "Is he?"

"And what right do you have asking that? Why should I tell you? he demanded harshly.

"Because..."

"Because, why, Taryn? Last I know, the only thing you've done in my life is walk out of it and cause more rift between my little brother and I."

I flinched. He was right. I'd been so focused on moving forward, finding a better place in life for me, that I'd left everyone behind. And not gave one shit about who I was hurting or how many times I hurt them.

And Jace and Brian probably had gotten the worst of it.

"I'm—"

"Don't even say it," he interrupted uncaringly. "Don't even think of saying it."

"Is he working for you or isn't he?" I asked instead.

Jace narrowed his eyes, frowning in my direction.

"Is he?"

"And what if I tell you that you have no right to even ask that? That I've killed for less—people wanting to know my business."

"Jace." I choked out, turning away. I couldn't handle his biting words. The hurt and anger I heard in them.

"Because you keep walking, Taryn. You keep giving any right you have, any place you have, away. You keep throwing it away. Like it's trash—like I'm trash." He clipped out.

"What do you want me to say?!" I finally snapped, "I'm sorry, alright. Alright!? I'm trying to make a better life for me. One that's not..."

"Jail, sex, drugs?" Jace supplied.

"Yeah. I'd like to actually have a weekend when I wasn't worried one of you guys would call me from the hospital, with a bullet-hole in you. Or call me from jail, asking me for a

$500 bond. Or hear how some girl O.D.'d from drugs that everyone knows you run through this town. I'd like, for once, to have a weekend where I didn't need to worry that any of that would happen." I breathed, "Can you blame me?"

Jace just stood there, watching me. I couldn't read him. Not any longer.

"So is he working for you or isn't he?" I asked.

"No," Jace said softly, walking closer to me. "I cut him loose when I realized who his son was. He went to another business in town."

"Another business?" I asked, alarmed. That meant Jace was at war and suddenly everything I'd been fighting for vanished. Jace was in a war.

He shook his head. "No. That's all you get."

"Jace," I cried.

"Go home. Go have supper with that family of yours."

"Jace, you can't just... Are you in danger?"

He grinned at that one, his white teeth almost blinding in the dark. "When am I not, Terry?"

"Jace."

Rolling his eyes, he walked to me and grabbed my arm. Pulling me to the door, he pushed me outside and said sternly, "Go. Don't break your way in here. Just...go, okay."

"You can't...not like this."

Reaching up to tuck a lock of hair behind my ear, his eyes held mine as he said softly, "This is what it's like when you try to make a better life. You gotta leave the bad stuff behind."

Then he disappeared inside, locking the door behind him.

None of the guards tried to usher me out. They knew I could slip from their grasp and just find my own way back in.

So I stood there, staring at the door for a while longer until I turned and walked down the hallway.

My footsteps a deafening echo.

CHAPTER FIVE

Parking my car across the street, I glanced up at my school and knew it was going to be a shitty day.

Why you ask? Because it's homecoming, of course.

Duh.

Who else would be capable of making this universe pause mid-rotation?

Cheerleaders. That's who.

Crawling out of my car, I threw my bag over my shoulder and marched across the lawn, a scowl etched on my face.

No sign of Garrett.

I was more relieved than I wanted to give the guy credit for. One less headache to deal with.

However, the second I got inside, the headaches came rushing at me at full speed.

Mandy gasped as she saw me and darted over first.

Grabbing my hand, she hissed, "Did you hear?"

"Uh—"

"Pedlam's coming here to play. Their football field got tilled last night. Can you believe it?"

Oh. Holy. Fuck.

"What did you just say?"

"Yeah. Their football field was tilled. Freaking tilled. Can you believe that? I heard that their gymnasium got tarred, too. Seriously. Who's crazy enough to do that shit?"

"Excuse me," I murmured, my entire body going numb. I pushed past her, past my locker and went right through the hallways, back out to the parking lot.

There. In the back corner, he was just getting out of his SUV, looking freshly showered and tired.

Well. Hell. Was he going to be even more tired after I got through with him.

Marching over to him, unheeding the whispers that followed me, I walked up to him.

"Hey—" Tray murmured, watching me, confused as I reached around him and opened his door. I pushed him inside, closed the door, and then walked around to the passenger seat.

"Drive," I said shortly, folding my arms across my chest to keep myself from lunging at him. If I didn't keep them in place, they'd more than likely be around his throat. "Now!"

Tray closed his mouth and started the car. A little while later, I saw we were parked at a nearby park.

I counted. Breathing in and out. One to twenty. Then I was out the door.

"How could you do that?! Are you insane?" I shouted. I knew full well how enraged I was, but I was past caring.

I didn't give a shit. Not anymore.

"How could you? Or are you just that stupid? Huh?" I cried, knowing full well he saw how enraged I was.

"What are you talking about?"

"Last night. Pedlam. You tilled their football field. You tarred their gymnasium," I clipped out.

"Yeah," he said, looking at me like I'd gone crazy.

"Are you stupid?!"

"What are you so pissed at? You knew we were going in there to do some damage."

"Not this. Not damage that'll launch an entire investigation."

"What are you—"

"I'm on their cameras!" I cried out.

Taken aback, Tray abruptly shut his mouth.

"I'm on their cameras. I mean they didn't get my face, but they might recognize my handiwork."

"You're on their cameras?" he whispered in disbelief.

"Yeah."

"Why didn't you get to those?"

"There was no way. I couldn't take on three guards."

"We destroyed the video surveillance."

"Did you destroy it during the time I was there?"

Tray frowned, thinking.

"No," I cut in, "because you probably didn't think about it. I'm guessing you cut the surveillance that just showed you guys entering the building. Am I right?"

"Yeah," he said reluctantly.

"Yeah."

"Oh...fuck."

"Yeah," I said tightly.

"Taryn," he began.

"Don't." I shot my hand up. "Just don't. Anything you say right now won't help."

"We fucked up."

"We?" I glared up at him.

"I fucked up."

"I knew you were going to do some damage, I mean—I knew it. But I didn't know you were going to do enough damage where the cops are going to get called in. I didn't know...I didn't think you'd go *that* far."

"I wouldn't have told you anyway." He sighed.

"Shit. Shit. Shit." I knew what I would have to do now, but holy hell, I did not want to do it. "Shit!" Catching a look of disgust on a woman, I shook my head and climbed back inside his SUV.

Tray took another moment before he reluctantly climbed in beside me.

He didn't start the engine, but instead looked at me.

"What can we do?"

"You can't do anything. I—me—I have to do something to save my own ass right now," I muttered.

"What are you going to do?"

I sighed. "Might be better if you don't know."

"Taryn," he argued.

"Tray."

"Let me help."

"You want to help? You can get Mandy off my back tonight. I'm supposed to go to Carter's party—an act of good faith that I'm developing friendships here. Oh, and I'm supposed to take these other two kids—Molly and Garrett," I added. "You want to help? Take those two to the party and keep Mandy off my ass."

"Who are the hell are Molly and Garrett?" Tray asked, shifting into drive and pulling out into traffic.

"My science lab partner. Molly sits beside me in psych. class."

"Does she wear magnifying glasses?"

"Yeah." I sighed.

Tray was silent a moment, driving back to school. "Who's Garrett?"

"I'll just tell him to call you. His last name is Larkins."

"Hmm," Tray mused. "How is it that I have no idea who these people are?"

"Because gods don't have to know who the minions are," I retorted, not caring worth a crap how antagonistic my tone was.

Tray just shot me a look as he pulled into the parking lot and into his normal parking space. There wasn't a sign that said it was designated as his, but no one else parked there. Everyone knew it belonged to him.

I slammed my door as I got out and swept inside, not waiting for Tray.

School turned out to be useless. I couldn't concentrate, but I didn't want to skip. That'd probably warrant a phone call to my adoptive parents. I might be getting into enough trouble, anything extra was just not needed. But I had to move quickly. Right now I needed to go into damage control, and get my hands on those tapes—that's what I needed to do.

No matter whose hands they were in.

Or which authorities.

I was already running through plans, past trips to jail, and any information that I might have stored in my not-so-helpful subconscious. Seriously. Information locked up in there should want to come out to help. Subconscious and conscious were both parts of me. If my brain didn't let me have my own information, I'd be stewing in jail. The subconscious would be punished right along with the rest of us. And right now, my id wanted revenge.

Enough with the psychology bullshit.

Fourth period proved semi-interesting. We were dissecting little pigs and I was able to butcher the freakishly cute animal with our tweezers. I kept pretending the little snout was my face.

God. I'd screwed up!

I was too distracted with all this other bullshit drama in my life—Jace, Geezer, Geezer's dad, Brian, and, I hated to even acknowledge this, Tray and the nonexistent communication about the mind shattering sex we had.

"If you don't stop, we're going to a D on our project," Molly spoke up, the tremble in her voice gave her away though.

I sighed and placed the tweezers down. Nice and slowly.

"Sorry," I mumbled, busying myself in our textbook.

I knew she was still watching me. She'd been watching me the entire class. Why the hell was she watching me?

"What?" I exclaimed, whirling around to face her.

"You don't want to take me, do you? I mean, you've been avoiding me all day and you've hardly said one word to me in class. So if this is you, telling me that you regret your decision—break my heart now. Just get the misery over with, alright?!" she cried out.

Holy hell—I could see myself in her microscope glasses. She needed to get a new pair of glasses, or contacts at least. It'd help with her social skills and I wouldn't be needed in the first place.

Fuck.

"Sorry. Me, not talking, has nothing to do with you. Really," I managed to get out.

"Oh?"

"Yeah." I turned away.

"So we're still going, right?"

Great. Fucking great.

I turned back to her, frowning and broke the news, "Actually, Tray Evans is going to take you."

And that's when I learned that you don't deliver news like that to someone as socially challenged as Molly. At least not how I did it anyway.

Molly fainted. In science class. And I just stood there, more annoyed than worried about her as the teacher rushed over.

Tray Evans was not faint-worthy.

Lunch consisted of a pep rally and Mandy was certainly peppy. She'd gushed throughout our entire third period. And she was still gushing, jumping up and down in her cheerleader uniform.

When they brought the football players out wearing cheerleader uniforms, I decided my exit was duly needed.

The hallways were empty. Thank goodness.

At my locker, I looked inside, fully meaning to grab my book, but I found myself just standing there. Lost in thought, I stared down the inside of my locker. Oh yeah—I was winning. That metal in the back was going down.

I'd been there myself on a few occasions, but I never paid attention. I never thought I'd have to break in there and not out.

Yeah—I knew the exits. I didn't know the entries.

Although, exits could be entries...I cannot believe how stupid I am right now.

Hearing people shouting in the background, I turned without thinking and found myself staring into Tray's hazel eyes.

He was walking inside from the parking lot with Mitch, Helms, and Hooters girl—Sasha Klinnleys.

Mandy would be so proud. I remembered two extra people today. Of *those* people, *her* people.

As they drew closer, Sasha was chattering with Mitch and Helms both grinning at her. Tray was watching me.

I busied myself inside my locker, grabbing for anything. As they passed by, I could feel him behind me. He was standing close enough that I could feel his heat. Literally. His after-shave smelled so damn good—that wasn't helping me either.

"What?" I sighed, my back still turned.

"What are you going to do?" he questioned intently.

I shrugged him off, not saying anything.

"Taryn," he insisted, grabbing my arm and whirling me around to face him. He was so close, I could see the perfect shape of his eyes, and I saw they were turning to amber.

Oh God. His thumb was lightly rubbing back and forth on my arm in a soft erotic caress.

Shit.

Without thinking I pressed against him, I closed the small inch of space between us and grinned when I heard his sharp intake of breath.

No one was in the hallway except us; everyone was at the pep rally. I closed my eyes, feeling Tray lean downwards. Then his mouth was on mine kissing me softly. It wasn't what I was expecting; it wasn't how we kissed before. I kissed him back, deepening it.

Tray reached around me and pulled me closer against him, pressing me against the locker.

Opening my mouth, Tray dipped inside and I met him as I reached around and grasped his neck, pulling him closer. Feeling one of his hands around my waist, the other was on my hip and sliding downwards. Slowly.

Tray heard them first. He ripped away from me, turning away from the students now starting to stream out of the gymnasium. We both were breathing hard.

"Oh...wow," I murmured, running a hand through my hair.

Tray grunted, then moved off down the hallway.

I took a deep breath and turned once more to my locker.

Well, if anything, he'd taken my mind off my possible prison sentence.

Fuck.

"Taryn," Someone spoke from behind me.

Molly.

I grinned. "You're not going to faint again, are you?"

"Is," she said hesitantly, inching closer, "is it true? I mean...what you said before?"

"About what?"

"About, you know," I could actually see her gulp, "Tray Evans. Taking me. To the party."

I grinned, closed my locker and leaned against it. "Yeah. He's helping me out with something. He's taking you and Larkins."

"Larkins?!" she asked sharply.

"Garrett Larkins. He plays that ball game, like hopscotch or something. The guy camps out on the lawn."

"Oh God," she moaned.

"What?"

"Why is he coming?"

"Because I invited him and he said yes." What the hell did I just step into?

"Oh." She brightened up. "You mean, you and Larkins. Like together?

"What?" I was confused.

"Like on a date."

"Uh—"

"That's great!" Molly exclaimed, a wide smile on her face. "So, it's like you and Larkins, and me and Tray Evans."

Oh...no. It was all I could muster. I had no idea how to derail her.

"Um," I muttered, unsure of how to stop her.

I looked away from her, and I caught sight of Grayley wandering down the hallway, measuring each face intently before he moved on.

"Hey," I called out.

Grayley saw me and a relieved grin broke out over his face.

"What are you doing here?"

"I have to talk to you," he muttered, not breaking his stride as he grasped my elbow and dragged me behind him, around a corner. Finding an empty room, he pushed me inside and closed the door.

"What?" I asked. "Look, if this is about what happened at Pedlam, I swear—"

"It's not about that," he cut me off.

Taking a closer look, I realized he was slightly white around his lips, giving him a strained look.

"What is it?" I asked, feeling a sense of dread inside.

"You know what you said about Geezer's dad?"

"Yeah..."

"Geezer went to Brian. He wanted to know who Jace's competition was...who his dad was working for...and..."

"Oh no." I already knew where this was going.

"Yeah—Brian wanted to know why Geezer wanted to know. Geezer doesn't give a shit about a lot as long as his supply is stocked, you know."

"Brian hurt him?" I felt a punch to my stomach when I asked.

"Brian was pissed—Geezer's in the hospital. He's got three broken ribs, a punctured lung, and..."

Oh God. What else.

"A broken right arm."

"Oh my God," I moaned, falling against the wall, slowly sliding down until I hit the floor. I wrapped my arms around my knees. Oh God. Brian had hurt Geezer. He'd hurt my best friend. Someone who I considered family. Who I swore to always protect and look out for. Brian had hurt Geezer.

That fucker.

I reached blindly for my cellphone and pressed three on speed dial. Brian's name flashed across my screen.

Standing up, I heard his voice and I said coldly, "You just signed your fucking death warrant. See you in hell."

I hung up and strode from the room.

"Taryn," Tray called out, the hallways now empty again. Everyone had gone in to class, a few stragglers glanced at us in curiosity.

I didn't slow down, but hurried to my locker.

"Taryn," Tray called out again, jogging lightly behind me.

"Taryn." That was Grayley, he had darted out behind me and caught up just as I reached my locker. "What are you doing?"

"It's the last move. He's going down, someone has to take him down. I'm going to have to do it." I choked out, inside raging. How fucking dare he?

Tray was quiet, listening to the exchange.

"I didn't tell you so that you'd go all psycho on me," Grayley reasoned, grabbing my arm and slamming my locker door shut. He had my car keys in his hands. "I told you because you're Geezer's friend. He needs you. At his side."

"What are you talking about? Geezer will heal. He always does."

"He found out who his dad is working for," Grayley said somberly. Gravely.

I froze. The realization suddenly slammed into me...and I came back sputtering curses. I lunged for my keys.

Grayley neatly checked me into place, holding me against the lockers and dangled my keys away from me.

I was so enraged, I didn't care that a few moments ago, Tray had been holding me in the same place. I'd been melting then, now pure fury was coursing through my veins.

"Taryn. You need to stay out of it. You need to let Jace handle Brian. And he will. We both know it. Bri's too stupid and hotheaded to last long in the business. He's going to mess up and Jace will take care of him. He'll do whatever he needs to do."

"He fucked up. He crossed the line," I seethed.

"You need to be Geezer's friend. You're his family. You and me. That's all he's got, okay. You can't go all vengeance on Brian right now, not when Geezer needs you."

"I need to castrate him is what I need to do," I cried out.

"Maybe," Grayley bit out, letting me go, seeing I wasn't reaching for my keys, but he kept a firm hold of them nonetheless.

"So what do you want?" I asked suddenly, rolling my eyes.

He watched me warily. "I came over here to make sure you stay out of it. I know you, Taryn. The second you'd checked any of your voice messages, you'd be going after Brian. You can't do that."

"What's it to you? You're with Gentley now."

"No. I'm with you and Geezer. But neither of you go to my school anymore, so yeah if I have to, I'll side with Gentley to survive. But it's you and Geezer, you know that, Tar," he said quietly, seemingly wounded.

"Ah! I know. Alright. I know, I already got guilt-trip 2000. I've been so busy running away from—everything—that I walked out on you and Geezer."

"We're not Jace and Brian."

"I know."

"We're your best friends."

"I know."

"And as your best friend—Geezer needs you more than Brian needs to be put in his place. It'll happen. Just not by you."

"Who else—" I began to argue.

Grayley rudely interrupted, "It'll be dealt with. But. Not. By. You."

"I'm the one who should do it—I'm the reason—" I argued, heatedly.

But Grayley cut in, uncaring, "No, Taryn. Brian's been a ticking time bomb our entire lives. You're the only thing that reeled him in. He's doing this, he's gone off the deep end. It has nothing to do with you."

"But—"

"Just shut up! Okay."

So I growled. It was the only thing I could do and I didn't care if it was very unfeminine. I needed an outlet.

Tray chose that moment to chuckle.

Grayley slid a wary look towards him. He shifted away. "You're Evans." It wasn't a question.

Tray leaned against my locker, his hands in his pockets, and gave one of those too-cool half-grins. "Yeah."

They studied each other for a good minute—or that's what it seemed like.

"Okay!" I exclaimed. "Stop it."

Tray chuckled again.

Grayley grinned, slightly relaxing.

"I'll...I have something to take care of and then I'll go to the hospital. Promise," I said, holding my hands in mock surrender. "Promise."

He studied me for a good minute, before he gave me back my keys. As I swept them from him, he said lightly, "Cops are watching Brian 24/7 so stay away. You'll just get in trouble."

"Fine," I said tightly. It killed me to say it, but I had to. I had to tell the truth. I didn't lie—well, I did—but I tried not to lie to Grayley. And he knew that.

It was enough because Grayley visibly relaxed. "Okay." He sighed. He glanced at Tray and stuck out his hand. "I'm Grayley. Idiot, here, doesn't have the social skills to do introductions."

"Shut up." I flipped him off.

"Tray." Tray shook his hand, hip-checking me at the same time, which earned him a grin from Grayley.

Searching my face, Grayley said, "Cool?"

"Yeah." I sighed in resignation.

"Good." He turned and walked out.

"I like him," Tray announced, waiting as I opened my locker. Once it was opened, he reached inside for my textbook.

"Excuse me."

"I got it. Let's go." He sent me a blinding smile. There was that instant warmth—fucking hormones.

He dropped me off at my fifth period class. Of course, the teacher lectured me for a good two minutes before she let me slink into the only empty chair. Which, again, was right in front of Justin Travers. Sasha Klinnleys was, luckily, not on his lap this time.

I expected him to say something, but surprisingly, he was quiet.

I was alarmingly disappointed. I'd hoped to be distracted this period.

CHAPTER SIX

Seventh period turned out to be torturous. Molly was blushing every other second, for which I was to blame. She kept glancing at Tray, who in turn was watching us. Or—watching me. But I hadn't had the heart to tell her. How do you burst someone's bubble in the beginning of a possible new friendship? Well, apparently it wasn't going to work out with me and Molly.

Maybe I could help Larkins out. Although, Molly seemed adamant about not wanting Larkins around, until she'd paired him up with me.

Fucking drama.

Luckily, I was saved from further awkwardness when our teacher paired each table with another one. Groups of four for small group discussion. Molly and I got paired off with Sasha Klinnleys and Devon.

No luck on the save from awkwardness.

Devon's smile was so forced I'm surprised Molly missed it with her magnifying glasses.

Even Sasha was glancing uncertainly between us. Of course that might have more to do with me dumping her to the floor.

I had so many friends. How could Mandy think I didn't have friends? Cue the sarcasm.

"Hey, Taryn," Devon muttered, scooting closer to the table.

"Hi!" Molly exclaimed, "Are you guys going to Carter Sethler's party tonight? I heard it's going to be so great! Really."

Kill me now.

"Uh—" Devon started hesitantly, watching me.

But Sasha interjected harshly, "No way in hell."

"Oh. I'm sorry." Molly misunderstood.

Sasha smirked cruelly. "Uh huh. You don't get it. I meant no way in hell are *you* going."

Molly frowned, glancing at me. "Uh..."

Well, hell. I could take care of two birds with one stone.

I grinned. Devon sighed in resignation. He must be learning my looks already. I leaned forward. "Back off, platinum bitch. She's going because I was invited—," oh this is good—three birds, "by his girlfriend, Mandy." I was watching for a reaction, and there it was. Devon completely understood me. "And Tray is helping me out. While I need to take care of a little chore for him, he's giving Molly here a ride to the party." I turned my gaze to Molly to see if she got the message—which she did. I saw a flash of hurt then disappointment in her eyes. I tried to send a silent 'sorry' to her, but I don't know if she got it.

Sasha had shut her mouth. Freaking hallelujah.

"Uh," Devon cleared his throat, "we're supposed to talk about Erickson and his stages of development."

"Let's start with isolation versus intimacy," I interjected. "I'm on the edge between them. How about you?"

Devon held my gaze, both of us trying to read the other. And he sighed, leaning back in his chair, "I was in intimacy—"

"Till you screwed that up," I said lightly, leaning back in my own chair, my gaze challenging him.

He didn't accept the challenge. He muttered, "Trust me. I'm firmly in isolation now."

"I'm not in isolation," Sasha put her two cents in. "I mean, I have a ton of friends. Plus, Justin. Hello."

"Trust me. I don't think what you have with Travers can be qualified as intimacy," I drawled.

"Like you'd know."

"I would, actually," I shot back. "I just got out of a five year relationship." I counted fourth grade. It didn't really count, but I counted it anyway. Sue me.

Sasha grinned. "God. Tray never fails. He screws 'em when they're vulnerable and on the rebound. The guy's a skilled player."

"Sasha," Devon said in surprise.

"What?"

"It's fine, Devon, platinum Hooters girl here seems to think Tray screwed me. Trust me, honey, it was the other way around," I said soothingly.

"Right," she scoffed, rolling her eyes.

"He keeps coming back for more." I grinned. He really hadn't, but the girl had to be put in her place.

She rolled her eyes again and then completely surprised me. "Who was that guy you were talking to before?"

"Who do you mean?"

"That guy. He doesn't go here. I'd know if he went here—he's too hot to miss. I think I've seen him at Rickets' House."

Grayley.

"Why?" I asked tightly.

"Because he's hot."

"And he's unavailable. To you."

"I've got a friend."

"Set her up with someone else."

Sasha smiled, almost maliciously. "So," she leaned forward, "this must be someone you care about. I mean, you won't even tell me his name."

"And you've got a snowball's chance in hell with him."

"Please. He checked me out. I think this snowball might have a chance."

"I'm thinking your chair is a little wobbly. Don't you?" I returned sweetly. Fuck. I wasn't sweet so I said, "If you really want to try, he hangs out at the Seven8."

"Taryn," Tray murmured in my ear, a warning. Glancing over my shoulder, I realized he must've been listening in the whole time, and looking over his entire table, realized that they all had been listening. Including the two tables on our other sides.

Great.

Apparently Tray didn't like the idea of sending one of his 'kind' to the Seven8.

I sighed. "Just kidding. He doesn't go there."

"What's his name?" Sasha tried again.

This had been fun and all, but enough was enough. I fixed her with a piercing glare. "If you want to try and go against me on this, go ahead. You won't be the one standing at the end."

The smug grin had been wiped clean from her face.

I added, "He's family and I'll do *anything* to protect what's mine."

"Okay, class!" the teacher exclaimed, calling us back to attention. "Let's hear what your groups each had to say."

Devon and Sasha turned back to their table while Molly busied herself with her book. I sighed. I actually hadn't wanted to hurt her, but better it's better she find out now, rather than later.

The rest of class passed uneventfully. Devon made up a bunch of shit for our group. It was almost as if he didn't want me to speak. Huh. Wonder why.

As the bell rang, I stood up and moved out the door.

At least I'd been distracted from my legal worries for a while.

But not anymore. Now, I had to save my ass.

I dumped my books in my locker and grabbed my purse.

"Hey," Molly spoke up hesitantly, shifting on her feet.

"Hi."

"Listen—"

"I didn't mean for you to take it that way. I'm sorry."

"No. No. I am. I mean, seriously, like Tray Evans would be remotely interested in me. Really."

"He would be if he were a great guy," I said sincerely.

"Please." She laughed. "We both know what kind of guy goes for me."

"I asked Larkins to come because he chewed my ass for you, when I told you about Travers."

"Really," she murmured, blinking in surprise.

"Yeah. The guy's got backbone. Not many do. Those are the ones worth grabbing."

"So. Tonight...?"

"Be ready by ten. I'll have Tray call you for directions. He really is taking you and Larkins. He owes me."

"Wow."

"What?"

"I mean...still...Tray Evans. The hottest guy in school—he rules this school—and he's going to be picking me up."

I grinned. "Make sure your mom is watching out the windows. Not only are you going to a sin-infested party, but the devil, himself, is picking you up. Think of all the worries that'll go in her head."

"Why aren't you coming with us?"

"I'll show, but I've got something else I need to deal with first," I promised.

"Ok," giving me a piece of paper, she said, "that's my number."

"I'll give it to Tray."

"Put it in your phone too." Molly smiled, suddenly flushing as she turned and darted down the hallway.

Maybe I'll get to keep her as a friend after all.

Crossing the lawn, I stopped and just waited. I saw Garrett break from his hackey-sack (that was the sport!) and jog over to me.

"Ice Bitch," he called out warmly.

I chuckled, I couldn't help it.

"Give me your number," I greeted him, getting straight to business.

He flicked out a business card.

"Nice," I murmured.

"Just tell me when to be ready, baby."

"Be ready at ten. You'll get a call."

"Ready and waiting. Ready and waiting," he taunted, grinning knowingly at me.

Turning my back to him, I smiled widely, anticipating his reaction when he realized who exactly his ride was.

Tray was leaning against my car.

"What do you want?" I called out crossly, reaching around him and unlocking my door. Tray didn't move, so I shoved him aside.

Instead of budging, even a little bit, Tray grabbed my hand and twisted my arm around me, pulling my body fully against his.

Holding my head away from him, the rest of me pressed tightly against him, I asked, "What? I have to go and save my ass, remember?"

Tray studied me intently and I averted my eyes. I didn't need him trying to read me right now.

"Hey," he said firmly, tipping my chin to meet his gaze.

"What?" I snarled.

"You're terrified," he stated, surprised at his realization.

"No, I'm not."

"You've been hot and cold all day. That's how you deal, isn't it. You react and you're scared to death of what you're going to do. What are you going to do?"

"It's a one-woman job."

"Taryn."

"No."

"Taryn."

"I said no," I cried out, trying to get away, but he only pulled me tighter—if that was possible.

But he reasoned again, "Taryn."

So I grabbed his chin and pulled him to me, his mouth meeting mine. It worked because it shut both of us up.

Tray quickly took charge and dipped my head back, giving him more access to my mouth. He whirled around, moving me against the car, with his body pressing me back. God. One of his hands was sliding down my thigh, sliding around to my stomach, sliding up underneath my shirt. His other hand was firmly clamped on the back of my neck, keeping my mouth in place.

I wasn't fighting it. Believe me. I was meeting every one of his moves with one of mine. I had my own hands pressed up under his shirt, one hand moving to circle around his shoulder and the other tracing his abdominal muscles. Then I switched and my hand was sliding around his back, resting on the back of his shoulders, while the other slid to the inside of his pants.

I felt his sharp intake of breath and grinned against his mouth, lightly biting his lower lip.

He groaned and swept his tongue inside my mouth roughly.

Holy...

One of his hands traced upwards, softly against the swell of my breast, hidden from view, and lightly cupped me.

I groaned this time and could feel him grin.

Then I shoved him away, breathing raggedly.

"Not. Here," I choked out.

"I know," he said hoarsely, trying to steady his breathing, leaning his elbows on my car's roof.

"I have to go."

"I know."

Getting in my car, I remembered and shoved my hand out through the open door. "Here."

"What are these?"

"Molly and Larkins' phone numbers. I told them to be ready by ten."

"Can't they just show up at my house?"

"I told them you'd call and get directions. Make Larkins come to your palace, I don't care, but you need to pick Molly up at her house."

"Why?" he asked, perplexed. He hadn't reacted to my terms. Figured.

"Just because."

"Nice." He sighed.

"Whatever." I shut my door and glared one last time at him, of which he answered with a earth-shattering grin. That annoyed me even more so I gunned the engine and shot into traffic.

Driving myself to Pedlam's police headquarters.

Parking my car in the parking ramp, across from the hospital, which was just a block down from the police headquarters, I rounded to my trunk. Grabbing my theft pack, I took what smaller items I'd probably need. I'd love to go in with my rope, pulley, well—everything. But I couldn't.

So I needed to improvise, and that meant only taking the barest essentials.

I hated it.

I pulled on a blonde wig and added a sweatshirt underneath my jacket. It had to be enough. They couldn't recognize me when they'd look over their surveillance videos later.

Walking in through the front-door, I spotted the cameras first. I approached the front desk, and positioned my back to the cameras, a put a wide smile on my face. "Hi. I heard you guys have an opening for a secretary here? Could I get an application?"

"Sure," the officer replied, sliding an application from underneath the counter. "Here you go. Pencils, pens, clipboard. You can sit there to fill it out."

"Uh." More help than I expected. "Thanks."

"Yep." Then he was back to chatting with his buddy.

Fuck. This place was busy for a Friday afternoon.

So I sat—hunching over so my face wasn't visible—and filled out the paperwork. I did it as slowly as I could, reminding myself that some people could take up to hours to fill out paperwork.

Every few seconds, I'd glance up and watch. Just to observe what was going on around me. I noticed the cops who loitered around the pop machines, around the kitchen area in the back. I saw the one who remained in a group in the back, laughing. Then I noticed a lot people in plain clothes were wandering in and through the back hallway.

Shift change.

Or at least I was hoping.

I hated this. I had to go in blind. And in a freaking police headquarters at that. To make matters worse, they've rebuilt it since the last time I was here.

Fuck. Fuck. Fuck.

Good news, the cop behind the counter had apparently taken pity on me—probably thought I was too stupid to get the job anyway—and stopped watching me like a hawk about an hour ago.

Another hour later, I noticed a routine. Every twenty minutes, the counter-guy would disappear for a moment. A bunch of females would slip around the second left corner, disappear for a few minutes, and then come back, splitting into their respective directions.

Female bathroom.

Bingo.

So I waited. And the second the counter-guy took off again, I slipped around the counter and walked, as if I purposely knew where I was going—and was rewarded with a bathroom sign. I slipped inside and into a stall.

And waited it out. There were enough stalls so no one noticed when my door stayed closed.

Another hour. And another routine. Every thirty five minutes there'd be a rush for the bathroom, followed by another rush twenty minutes later. Don't ask me why. My only guess is that maybe they were in different meetings that would either start or end at the same time. Either that, or everyone drank their coffee at the same time.

As the last twenty-minute rush exited, I slipped onto the counter in the window-frame and tipped open the vent.

Pulling myself up, I crawled inside and hoisted the vent closed behind me. Thank God this one wasn't screwed in place. It was a Seal-Loc, and it worked perfectly because the damn vacuum was pulling me backwards—just slightly though.

This is where I stayed—for another freaking four hours.

My adrenalin was rushing so much, my body failed to recognize that I had to pee or eat.

In some ways—that was the nice thing about jobs like this—the long-ass ones. They were also the ones that had the best rush at the end.

This hasn't been my first time doing a job like this. One time I'd stayed in the venting shafts for a good day. My legs had barely been able to hold me upright when I set foot on ground again. But that night...that might have been one of the best nights of my life. That's when I'd gotten the codes to Corrigan's account. I never mentioned the account was in a bank...with maximum security.

Funny. You'd think the police would have better security, but no...they were probably equal.

I just hoped I didn't have to stay here a full twenty-four hours.

Four hours later, I heard the day-shift investigators leave, shutting off their computers, saying goodnight. All their offices were pulled shut, with their lights off, and doors locked.

There are two areas in police headquarters. The office area—where the detectives worked and the hub—where criminals were booked and charged, where the interrogation rooms were, and where the activity would be throughout the rest of the weekend.

If my guess was right, one of these offices would belong to the detective that had been given the Pedlam case.

And, from my bank of knowledge, it was probably the 'Small Crimes' office.

Now, given that this building had been newly renovated and built—I'm hoping against hope that they've put the offices according to name. Which meant 'Burglary and Theft' would be the first office.

So, I took a peek in the first office I came to, which was the 'Special Investigations' office. That meant the offices were now in reverse order, by name.

The desk was right underneath the vent, so my feet touched lightly before I gracefully dropped to the floor. As I studied the office, I swiftly cursed as my eyes fell on a freaking map.

Grabbing it, I raked my eyes over it, absorbing every freaking detail. And, spotting the office I needed, I estimated the distance. Sixty counts, with two right turns.

So I went back up in the vent, pulling it shut behind me, and I was off. Working my way, using my system.

Same layout, which was perfect for me. Stupid for the developers. I found the office I needed and I grinned, so damn smugly, when I saw a box of evidence left in a chair by the door. Grabbing it, I riffled through, skimming the desk at the same time. I saw one note scribbled on a pad—Pedlam tapes. And at the same time, my hand found two DVDs; they each had 'Pedlam' scrawled across in big black marker.

I looked through the rest. Just to make sure.

I found a few witness accounts. Huh. None on me, but they saw two trucks parked behind the hardware store. No license plate numbers; therefore, no credible information.

I shredded the witness accounts. Spying a candle on the desk, I opened the drawers, searching for a lighter. Flicking it on, I burned the bottoms of both the DVDs.

And I left the same way I got in.

Arriving at my car, an hour later, I first put everything back in my trunk, and then slid into my seat where I let out a deep breath. Holy shit.

My blood was pumping. My heart was racing. And my whole body was thrumming with energy.

I'd just broken into Pedlam's police headquarters and destroyed evidence.

Checking my watch, I saw it was close to midnight. Carter's party should be in full-swing by now. I had switched on the radio and heard Rawley had won, 28-14. Close enough to be a good game, but enough of a lead for bragging rights.

As I drove into Rawley, I turned my phone on and saw that Mandy had called three times. Grayley had called once.

Geezer.

Visiting hours were over, that wasn't even a question. I didn't really feel like breaking into a hospital in the same night. So that meant I needed to hold up another promise.

Listening to Mandy's first voice message, I could hear the anger in her voice; she was pissed, accusing me of purposely skipping the game. In the second one, she'd been happy—must have been right after the win. And by the third one, she was drunk.

What a shocker.

I would've known where the party was from a mile away if she hadn't left directions. Okay. Not really, but seriously—the music was blaring so freaking loud, I finally chose to turn my own radio off. The house was another palace, just like Tray's. Lights were streaming out through walls that were just consisted of windows. Seriously. There were little wooden frames every now and then, but the entire house—just windows.

Parking at the end of the lane, I walked closer and saw groups of kids in the front yard.

Fuck. I recognized some Pedlam students. What the hell? They were supposed to wallow in their own parties. In Pedlam. Not here.

And apparently, seeing more and more, they'd all taken root on the front lawn. So the rest of the kids inside were probably Rawley students.

I hugged myself, suddenly chilled, and almost wished I'd kept my sweatshirt on, but to no avail, I was dressed in a sheer sweater, a black tank top underneath, and a pair of jeans.

"Yo." Came a holler, followed by a whistle.

"Hey. Hey. It's Lanser's bitch." That just had to be Gentley. Of course, he had to be here. None of the parties I'd been to in Pedlam had ever come to this proportion. Makes perfect sense now why so many Pedlam students were here, including Crispin Gentley.

I hated him. Really. Really. Hated him.

I rolled my eyes and kept walking.

"Hey," he said again, grabbing my elbow just as I was about to pass by.

"Let me go!" I snarled, wrenching my arm out of his grasp.

"Whoa. Calm, bitch."

My nerves were shot. I was too wired—my blood was still pumping from the job and my heart rate hadn't slowed down, so I didn't want to deal with him. I didn't know what I would do or say. I didn't feel in complete control of myself.

"Whatever," I muttered, darting past him and inside.

"Hey!" he shouted, turning to follow me, but I quickly got lost in the crowd.

I was a bit surprised that people were actually saying hello to me. What the hell?

I searched the living room. The dining room. The second living room. The upstairs—cringing at every door I listened to—and then moved down into the basement, where I was more amazed to find an additional two living rooms. They were complete with an entire game room, exercise room, and whirlpool—which was full to the max.

Huh.

So I walked back upstairs and wandered outside, where I found Mandy. She was on the opposite side of the pool, situated on one of the five patios, in the corner with the volleyball courts to one side and a pool-house on the other.

How could people live in homes like these? How could they remember to be people?

She was sitting on Carter's lap, his hand underneath her shirt, laughing and drunk. I was more stunned to find Tray at the same table, an amused grin on his face with Molly and Larkins in seats next to him.

What the hell?

Carter spotted me first. "Hey, you made it," he said warmly.

"Taryn!" Mandy screeched, stumbling over to me, throwing her arms around me. "I love you so much, do you know that? You came. I'm so happy. I didn't think you would."

I hugged her back and patted her on the back. "I know. I had to take care of something."

"You're always taking care of something. I...I worry about you. But you came! So yay!"

"Yeah."

"You're the best sister I've ever had."

I couldn't say anything. I was still racing from my job and now this—a knot had formed in my throat. So I contented myself with patting her again.

Carter rescued me. Laughing, he said, "Leave her alone. You're suffocating her, Mandy."

Mandy giggled, pulling away and finding her way back to his lap. "I know," she murmured, curling her arms around his neck again, "but I really do love her so much."

Tray kicked a free chair out for me.

"Thanks," I murmured gratefully as I dropped into the chair.

I needed to calm down.

Tray frowned, studying me. "You okay?"

"Yeah," I said quickly. Looking over at Molly, I asked her, "You having fun?"

"Oh my God. My mom freaked when Tray pulled up. Then he came in—I swear my mom was going to have a heart attack," Molly gushed, smiling widely. Realizing what she'd just said, she ducked her head but not before everyone at the table saw a blush explode over her face.

Carter grinned at me. "Your friends are pretty cool. Larks has been entertaining us with stories about his pot-smoking buddies. Something about a goat."

Molly let out a shriek, laughing, and then ducked her head again.

Molly was drunk.

So was Larkins. I saw it in his eyes as he was openly staring, with lust, at Molly.

Tray leaned closer and asked, "You want a drink?"

"Yeah. Maybe one."

"Be right back."

As he left, I commented to Carter, "You're one of the few around here who doesn't seem drunk."

He smiled, his thumb rubbing against Mandy's thigh. "Yeah. It's turned out to be a good party."

"A lot of crashers."

"Yeah. But what can you do?"

"Having Pedlam and Rawley together, that means there's going to be some fights."

"I know," he shrugged, "but we've got our crew. We can handle ourselves."

"Taryn."

Turning around, I grinned, seeing Grayley standing just behind the patio gate.

"Hey," I said warmly.

Jumping lightly over the gate, he sat in Tray's deserted seat.

"Pedlam student," Carter pointed out.

"My best friend," I pointed right back. To Grayley, I remarked, "How you handling the loss?"

He snorted, running a hand through his hair. "Please. As long as we can drink, we're happy."

I laughed, feeling myself calm down a little. Grayley always had that effect on me.

"Uh—" he started.

"I haven't gone to see him yet, but I will. First thing in the morning," I promised.

"Okay." He relaxed visibly. "You weren't at the game. I knew you had something to take care of, but I didn't think it would—oh."

"Yeah." I grinned.

"Oh!" Understanding finally dawned on him as he sat straighter in his chair. "Holy—Taryn!"

"Just...shut up, okay?"

"But—holy fuck's sake, Taryn. You—"

"Yeah."

"Oh my fucking—you didn't get caught," he stated, sitting back a little dazed.

I hated it. Grayley always figured everything out. It was why I'd only have to say that I needed to get in somewhere and he had everything for me. He'd think of everything. And he knew I needed to get into Pedlam, he knew I had stolen the PRS-500, and he knew Pedlam's football field and gymnasium had been destroyed the same night. If I had to do something tonight—something that took a long time—he'd figure it out. Which he just did. He knew a job after a job meant saving your ass. And he knew the security, he knew there were videos...and he fully realized where I had just spent a good six or seven hours at.

"Just shut up about it," I said heatedly.

"I will. You know I will," he murmured. "But, fuck, Taryn. I mean—"

"Shut up!" I said sharply, kicking his chair.

Grayley chuckled, grabbing my foot and shoving it away.

"Who are you?"

Stupid me. Mandy and the rest had been watching the entire conversation. And Mandy had never met Grayley.

Not good.

"Uh…this is Grayley," I murmured. "He's one of my best friends."

"And I'm just hearing about him now? I knew about Brian, but seriously, Taryn." Mandy was now shouting. People in the crowd were starting to watch.

And of course, Tray chose that moment to return, two cups in hand. He gave Grayley one brief nod in greeting as he placed the drinks on the table and promptly pulled up a chair to sit between us.

Mandy's mouth fell open.

"Tray knows him!" Mandy exclaimed. "Tray knows him and I don't!"

Oh, for the fucking love of all things holy. "Mandy, it's not that big of a deal. Tray met him today at school. It's not like—"

"He was at school and you didn't even think of introducing him to your sister?"

Grayley sized up the situation and leaned closer to me. "This info doesn't need to be broadcasted."

"I know," I hissed. "I'm trying."

Tray stepped in and asked Carter, "You going to Italy this summer?"

It worked like a charm because Mandy's eyes lit up.

As she turned back to Carter, gushing over the news, I let out a breath of relief.

"Thanks," I said quietly, my eyes holding Tray's as I took a sip.

He just nodded and drank his.

And we sat there—Grayley, me, and Tray—silent and perfectly content with it.

Molly and Larkins were flirting. Drunk and flirting.

Carter and Mandy were now kissing, his hand was slipping further up her shirt.

I liked everything else except that. I could do without seeing that.

A few minutes later, Grayley asked," You calm yet?"

I loved that he knew me so well. He knew I couldn't handle a lot, not right after a job. And he knew, from the size of the job I just pulled, that I was probably still climbing Mount Everest inside.

"Almost," I said back, drinking the rest of my cup.

He grinned back at me. His eyes trailing over my shoulders, he spoke, "I gotta go. I'll see you tomorrow."

And he was gone. Probably after some girl.

"I like him," Tray said again.

"Me too." I grinned, my head falling back against the back of the lounger. "He's a like brother to me."

"I know."

"Yeah."

We held each other's gaze.

Hearing Molly shriek in laughter, I sighed.

"Come on," Tray murmured in my ear, standing up.

I didn't have to ask what he wanted, so I said instead, "What about them?"

He pulled me behind him, through the crowd. "I gave Larkins cash for a taxi and programmed 'cab' in his phone. I told 'em both they weren't getting a ride home with me."

"Hey." I dug my feet in, pulling him to a stop.

"What?"

"Let's," glancing to the front door, I suggested, "is there any way we can avoid the front lawn? Gentley's out there and I'm not up for a fight."

He tugged me after him. "You'll be fine."

He was right. Gentley took one look, saw I was with Tray, and turned back to his group.

A part of me loved it. The other part of me felt my stomach form knots.

We walked to his SUV and saw that it was blocked in by other cars.

I climbed inside while Tray took his phone out and called someone. A little while later, three guys came out with keys and moved the cars. I had no idea how they did it, but they did. And Tray climbed in beside me and backed out onto the road.

We drove in silence, just like before.

Except he broke it once. "Whatever you had to do—you're okay, right?"

"Yeah." I sighed, relaxing against my seat.

And that was it until he pulled up to his palace and cut the engine. We walked side by side around the house and towards his pool-house. Tray didn't turn on the lights, and grabbed my hand and led me towards the bedroom. Once inside, I was in his arms, his mouth on mine, pressing me against the door, his hands already in my hair. I lifted my legs around his waist, hoisting myself up, my arms around his shoulder.

As we tumbled onto his bed, Tray above me, he moved his mouth down my throat, until it reached my stomach where he lifted my sweater. My tank top followed next. I slipped my hands underneath his shirt, and Tray promptly pulled it off. Taking his time, gazing at me, he slowly leaned down to kiss me. His lips meeting mine. I wrapped my legs around his waist, pulling him against me, as tight as I could get. Hearing him groan, I grinned, tilting my head as he moved back to my neck.

And the night progressed like that. Each move he made, I met him, full force. The first time was slower than before. It wasn't rough. It was slow and sensual. Throughout the night Tray reached for me again and this time I straddled him, our hands interlocked throughout.

Just before early morning, I felt his arms tighten around me and I felt his lips skim my shoulder. I closed my eyes and fell asleep.

CHAPTER SEVEN

I woke when Tray got up and padded into the bathroom. When I heard the shower turn on, I rolled over and checked my phone. Four calls from Mandy. And...holy shit...one from home. That meant Austin. And that meant—fuck—something was wrong.

Calling Mandy, I braced myself, hearing her answer in a panicked voice, "Oh my God. Where have you been? Where'd you go last night?"

"I'm at Tray's," I said, waiting for the bomb to drop.

"Well get your ass home. Mom and Dad are showing up in an hour."

"Oh...fuck."

Mandy hung up.

Just then the shower cut off, and a moment later, Tray strolled into the room, a towel around his lean hips.

"What?" he asked, stopping in mid-reach for some pants.

"My parents are heading home." I groaned, falling back on the bed.

"Alright." He grabbed the rest of his clothes and dressed in front of me.

Glancing at me, he asked, "You going to get ready? We gotta get over to Carter's to pick up your car."

I'd forgotten about my car. I was still reeling, thinking of all the illegal acts I've been committing since my adoptive parents had been out of town. If they knew—holy shit—they'd either give me back or never let me leave the house again.

Tray sat beside me and nudged me with his leg. "Hey, you okay?"

Numbly, I said, "I broke into the police headquarters yesterday."

"What?" Tray choked, turning to me, one hand bracing himself up on the bed.

I started to ramble, "I broke in and I destroyed evidence. I broke into their high school and stole their controller for all their security. My ex-boyfriend put my best friend in the hospital. I've got another best friend who's pretending to be friends with a guy like Gentley, so he can make it through high school. God, he's just faking it. Everyone thinks he's this happy, carefree, likeable guy who's just interested in a piece of ass—and he is—but that's not all he is, and no one over there knows. Except me and Geezer. And Geezer's got a punctured lung and three broken ribs. From my ex-boyfriend who I thought I loved and would always love. Me and Bri. That's how it was supposed to be and now..." I took a deep breath, biting my lip, the tears just there, teasing my eyes. "Oh fuck. Let's go."

"Wait." Tray turned and neatly trapped me on the bed, between his arms as he peered down at me.

I fell back against the bed, watching him above me.

"What?" I asked. He was just staring at me.

"I don't know," he said lamely. "You broke into a cop shop?"

"Yeah."

"Holy hell, Taryn. I can't believe you." He shifted and fell beside me, he rubbed one hand over his face. "Wow."

"Yeah," I said dryly. "Sorry I laid all that on you like that."

"No. It's...wow. I'm just...I just slept with a chick that broke into a police station."

I let a laugh escape. Couldn't help it. But when it's put like that—yeah, it was funny. And I slept with a guy who had tarred a high school's gymnasium and tilled their football field. All to get revenge because they had their game book stolen. At least he wasn't in the drug trade.

Wait.

"How frequent is your steroid business?" I asked.

"Uh..." he mused. "It's not really something I talk about."

"I just told you I broke into the police station. You can humor me," I said shortly.

"It's...it maintains itself, mostly."

"Jace warned me about you."

Tray didn't say anything, but I could feel his body stiffen.

"He said you were the lesser of two evils."

"Between him and me?"

"You and Brian."

"Fuck, Taryn, we're just messing around. It's not like we're in some relationship," he cursed, shoving off the bed.

I stood up, uncaring that I was naked. "Hey," I stopped him, grabbing one of his arms, and swinging him back to me, "that's not even where I'm going with this."

He took in the fierceness in my eyes and then slowly slid down my body, a faint grin coming to his mouth. Those lips—I tore my lustful thoughts away. "I'm just saying, we both have some shit on each other. That's all it has to go—nowhere else. Alright?"

Slipping one arm around me and pulling me against him, he murmured, "I seem to remember a few of your threats to Gentley."

"You're not immune," I shot back, melting into him as one of his hands came to my neck, already tipping my head back as his mouth descended, slowly to mine. "You leak anything I just spilled—we're at war."

He kissed me and murmured against my lips, "I don't really want to piss off a girl who can break into a police station."

When you put it like that, I could see his point.

I deepened the kiss and then pushed him away. "I should probably be at the house when my parents show up." Bending over, I grabbed my clothes and quickly dressed.

Tray ran a hand through his hair. "You want to shower?"

"We don't have time."

He chuckled. "I'll stay out. Just thought you might want to be all fresh and clean when you see the parents."

"I'll open my windows in the car," I said dryly, snagging my purse and already heading out the door. "Come on."

As Tray drove, I called Pedlam Hospital.

"Charles Josephson's room, please."

The phone rang twice before I heard a female's voice answer, "Geezer's room."

"I'm a friend of his. Can I talk to him?"

"Sure." The phone was transferred and I heard Geezer croak, "What's up?"

"Hey, Geeze," I said softly.

"Tartar!"

"You hangin' in there?"

"Oh yeah. Yeah, yeah. I'm not high, so it's total suck-age, but other than that, hospitals are awesome for picking up chicks."

"You getting frisky with your nurses?"

"Some of 'em. Some of 'em." I could hear the laughter in his voice, but I heard him hiss in pain the next second.

"How long you going to be in the hospital?"

"Oh. Not sure. They want to keep me for observation, something about my lung."

"My parents showed up today so I gotta go play 'nice daughter,' but then I'm all yours, okay."

"Good. Good. I'll see you then, Tartar."

I hung up and relaxed in my seat, hearing Tray on his own phone.

"Hey," he spoke monosyllabic. From the other end, I could hear someone talking. "Yeah. Meet me at the diner in about twenty."

Seeing Carter's house come into view, I was amazed again. The place was just not meant for one person should live in. Seriously. A movie star would buy a place like that.

"Carter's parents live in Europe. A lot of it's just guilt," Tray murmured. He must've read my thoughts.

"And yours?"

"My parents live in South America." He flashed a grin, pulling beside my parked car. Mine wasn't the only one there. There were at least a good dozen cars, scattered up and down the road.

Must've been one hell of a party.

I unclipped my seat belt and opened the door.

"Hey," Tray called out.

Pausing in the door, I looked back at him and waited for him quietly. .

"Call me tonight. If you want to, I don't know, come over and watch a movie or something." He rolled his eyes.

"Thought we were just messing around."

"Precisely." Tray grinned, one might classify that grin as wicked, but not me. That was just him. There was a little bit danger mixed in with him. It was there. I'd gotten glimpses of it, just little flashes though—but I saw it again. And it made me wonder, as I closed the door and climbed into my car, when I'd see the full face of what was just simmering underneath his façade.

But I didn't dwell on it too much. As soon I pulled up outside my home, I breathed a quick sigh of relief—the parents weren't home yet. Hurrying, I swept inside and up to my room where I grabbed my robe before heading into the bathroom. I could hear Mandy in her room, probably on the phone because she was talking to someone, and Austin was probably hibernating in his room—anywhere to keep away from us.

After showering and changing clothes, I wandered down into the kitchen, now more relaxed. Austin was poking around in the fridge, his lanky form wearing basketball shorts and a Rawley jersey.

"Hey, kid," I spoke up, reaching around him and grabbing a yogurt.

He raked his eyes over my form. "Showering doesn't hide your recent lay."

"Excuse me?" I muttered, startled. The kid was in eighth grade.

"Mom and Dad are going to know."

"Hey," I shot my leg out and blocked his exit from the kitchen, "what the hell's your problem?"

"Nothing. I'm just telling you—you look like you got laid last night and showering isn't going to hide it."

I tipped my head to the side, eyes speculative, "You get laid last night?"

He snorted, "I'm fourteen. Mom and Dad would skin me alive."

Whatever. I asked instead, "So what's her name?"

Austin shoved my leg off the counter and walked out of the room with a plate of pizza. A second later I heard the TV blaring.

I shook my head. The fourteen year old had an attitude. Looked like we were a match made in heaven. I'd need to pay more attention to him.

"When did you leave last night?" Mandy asked, coming down the stairs.

"When you and Carter decided to start a make-out session at the table."

"Everyone saw you and Tray leave together. Seriously. It was so sweet—Jasmine and Devon showed up with Grant at the party. Jaz still has it for Tray and I guess they showed up just when you guys were taking off. I seriously loved it! It's the perfect revenge." she chatted happily, grabbing a Pop-Tart.

"Except it has nothing to do with you, Jasmine, or Devon," I remarked, jumping on top the counter, swinging my legs, watching Mandy rush back and forth in the kitchen. "What are you doing?"

"Trying to make some food for when Mom and Dad get home. They should be here any minute." She expelled a deep breath.

Huh. I'm fine with what I had to eat.

"So you and Carter," I mused.

She shrugged and, if possible started to busy herself even more. She remarked, "I don't know. We just...I guess so."

"You were all for it before. Carter specifically asked me to come to his party, remember? And he stayed the night."

"Nothing happened."

"Something did. You progressed," I pointed out.

"Yeah..."

I narrowed my eyes, studying her. Something had happened. Something...oh shit. I announced, "You talked to Devon last night."

Mandy jumped, spilling the milk.

"You did. And you're thinking of taking him back," I pressed on, my eyes wide in shock.

"I did not. I mean...maybe...I don't know."

"When'd you talk to him? After your make-out session with Carter and before the two of you had sex?"

"We didn't...well...shut up about it, alright?" she snapped.

My sister. All blonde. Cheerleader. On student council. And flustered right now. I loved her.

"Mandy. It's fine if you did. You guys were together for like, four years."

"What?" She whirled to me. "Oh. You mean me and Devon."

"So that's it." Understanding was now dawning. "You had sex with Carter last night and now you're feeling guilty about it because of Devon."

"Shut up," she hissed.

"It's not like you have to call Devon, begging for forgiveness—"Catching that her hands froze at my words, I swore, "Holy crap, you did, didn't you? Mandy!"

"What?" she exclaimed, and I saw the despair in her eyes. "It's not like...I still love him, you know? Me and Dev. We were together for four years. Four years, Taryn. I can't just...wash that out of my system."

I cringed at every word; it was like a dagger stabbing me with each word. I could relate. Trust me. I gritted my teeth and slammed a steel wall on the emotions that were boiling inside me.

Tuning back in, Mandy was still talking, I heard her say, "And Carter...he's...I used to have such a crush on him, but he was dating Sabrina Lyles...and what Devon did."

"Devon cheated on you," I said flatly. "For an entire year. He fucked around behind your back, with your best friend. He's not a guy you want with you."

Mandy went pale at my words and I didn't care.

I pressed harshly, "He'll do it again because he's weak, Mandy. You need a guy that's going to put you first and not let some little tramp seduce him—over and over and over again. He went behind your back for over a fucking year. And I bet it wasn't Jasmine doing the seducing, I'd bet you a million bucks Devon was the one doing most of the calling."

"Shut the fuck up!" Austin cried out behind me. He'd heard every word and had probably been listening the entire time. "Just because you stayed with some loser, doesn't mean Mandy's like you."

"No, she's not. But she's about to make the same mistake I did." Brian hadn't continued to cheat on me, but those two times—they'd been enough to rip my heart out.

I'd had enough of this conversation. Hopping off the counter, I said, "I'm going to visit a friend in the hospital. Tell your parents I'll be home tonight."

Mandy and Austin both froze, registering my words, before I swept out the door.

It wasn't until I was in my car that I cursed, realizing what I'd just said, *Tell your parents I'll be home tonight.*

I hated hospitals. I'd always hated hospitals. I'd been coming to them my entire life. It always seemed someone was in an accident, someone had tried to kill themselves, or now—someone had been beaten close to death. I know Geezer wasn't dying, but he could have. I watched Brian put a few people in the hospital over the years, and they'd stayed a lot longer than just for observation. One of them had been in a coma for a few days.

Brian had spent that time in jail, followed by a short stint in prison.

And I stayed with him. I had been terrified, yes, but...he was all I had. He'd been there, through thick and thin with me. But now—some of that love was starting to give way to my right, my fury.

The son of a bitch had twisted so much from me over the years. He'd convinced me that only he cared and I believed him. I still do in some way.

I don't care what Grayley said. I knew, deep down, it had to be me who'd put Brian in his place. Only I could. I just had to figure a way around my promise to him—somehow.

But not today. Today was for Geezer.

I absent-mindedly wiped away a tear as it slipped down my cheek as I parked and walked down the parking ramp, towards the hospital.

Checking in at the front desk, I pinned my visitor's pass to my shirt and took the stairs.

Again. I'd been here many times and knew my way around.

I could hear voices in the room as I slowed down, approaching it.

The door was open so I knocked with the back of my hand, pausing in the doorway.

Geezer's face lit up in a smile—or it would've—if the bruises had allowed it.

God.

"Tartar!" he said, his voice still weak.

"Hey." I forced a smile, moving to his side. Bending down, I kissed his cheek. "The other guy better be in the morgue," I teased.

Geezer looked at me gratefully.

Noticing who was in the room, I blinked, seeing a lot of our old crew. Kerri, I frowned, seeing her own bruises. Liza, her waif-life figure swamped in a Cowboys sweater. Grayley was there, he'd hopped up on the windowsill, making room for me. I sent him a small smile. He winked back at me in understanding. And, to my surprise, I saw Trent Gardner, tipping back in his chair, one hand on Geezer's bedrail.

"Hey," I said, sweeping my eyes over them all.

Kerri greeted warmly, "About time you got here."

And that was it—I'd been welcomed back.

"Hey, chick," Trent drawled, "about fucking time you showed your face around these parts."

I grinned, sitting in Grayley's vacated seat. "Shut up," I retorted back playfully.

Trent rolled his eyes and launched back into his story, apparently about a party last night where he'd tapped some form of ass. Hearing a familiar name, I interrupted, "What party were you at last night?"

Trent looked at Grayley. "What party, dude?"

"Same party as you, Taryn. That one guy's. No idea what his name is," Grayley informed me.

"Who'd you tap?" I asked Trent.

"I dunno. I think her name was...fuck, I don't know."

"Sasha." Grayley helped out. "Looked like a Hooters girl."

I groaned, "You fucked Sasha Klinnleys? From my new school?"

"What of her?" Trent asked. Of course Trent would ask that. He didn't give a shit that I knew her or wasn't happy that he'd screwed her. No. This was Trent. He was unmoving, laidback in the face of death, antagonistically cool—Trent.

I didn't know how to describe Trent. He'd always been around in our circle, but he could be placed in a lot of other groups. He and Liza had been an item for a little bit, but that'd ended when she slept with Brian. Trent was probably the only guy in Pedlam who could tell Crispin Gentley to fuck off and then just walk away—unharmed. I didn't know how Trent did it, but he did. Every damn time. He was just...nonplussed. Down to the bone. He'd hang out with the popular kids one week. The potheads the next. The Goths the following weeks. And even the preppies liked him.

But he'd taken a liking to Geezer. I'd forgotten that. Since he was here with Geezer, that meant he'd taken a stand against Brian. Guess Brian had violated some code or something otherwise Trent would've shown up at the house or something. Or just asked Grayley how the Geeze was doing, if he was still limping and smoking. Something like that. Not be in the hospital. With his ex and all of Geezer's friends.

"Nothing. I don't like her." I rolled my eyes.

Liza laughed. "Like I'm surprised that you wouldn't like someone."

"What's that supposed to mean?"

"You're not the easiest person to get along with," she said shrugging.

"Leave Taryn alone," Kerri spoke up. "She's got a lot of stuff going on—like her new family. How is your new family going?"

"It's alright. Got a cool sister and brother. I just realized today that my new fourteen year old brother has an attitude like mine."

"Sounds perfect. You dealing with a mini version of you." Kerri sighed.

I looked at Geezer and saw he was just watching all of us. I could tell he was happy from the sparkle in his eyes. It was nice seeing a sober Geezer looking back at me. Too bad I knew he wouldn't say that way for long. He'd be back smoking as soon as he got in the car of whoever picked him up.

Grayley must've recognized my look because he coughed and spoke up, "Geeze's sleepy. Let's head out."

"No..." Geezer argued weakly. "Stay."

"Nope," Grayley said firmly. "Let's head out. We'll be back in a while so you can get some sleep."

No one said a word when they saw I stayed in place. That's probably why Grayley made the comment, so I could talk to Geezer alone. As soon as the door was pulled shut behind them, I grabbed Geezer's hand and whispered, "I am so, so sorry."

Geezer shook his head quickly. "No," he choked out hoarsely.

"I promised Grayley I wouldn't do anything to Brian, but...he can't get away with this."

"He won't," Geezer murmured. "Grayley's freezing him out. He and Trent."

"What do you mean?"

"No one. No one will talk to him." Geezer coughed.

"Oh God. I'm sorry. I'll talk to Grayley. Don't worry about it." I smiled softly, brushing his hair behind his ears. "You rest and heal, okay."

Geezer squeezed my hand tightly. I saw the tears at his eyes and bent to kiss his forehead again. Resting my cheek against his forehead, I whispered, "Just get better. Heal."

Geezer knew I wasn't talking about just physical healing. I meant it in every other way possible. I was tired of seeing my best friend high 24/7. I was tired of not having him around me anymore. He needed to grow up with me, not stay the same age.

I curled up in the lounger beside his chair and closed my eyes. Pulling my knees against my chest, I wrapped my arms around them and promptly fell asleep, Geezer snoring right beside me.

Grayley woke me up an hour later. The nurse needed to do her checks and they needed privacy for Geezer. Whispering goodbye to Geezer, I pressed a kiss to his forehead again and moved out the door.

Grayley was waiting for me in the hallway.

"Hey."

"Hey." He gave me a half-grin back, leaning against the wall, his hands stuffed in his pockets.

"He's...um..."

Grayley shrugged.

I left it alone. I didn't have the energy right now anyway.

"I took off before my parents got home. They're probably pissed at me." I sighed.

Grayley nodded.

"Gardner, huh," I murmured, finding myself staying in place instead. The door wasn't coming to me.

He nodded again.

"Geezer said you guys are freezing Brian out."

Grayley shrugged.

"Could you talk, maybe?" I shot out, starting to get irritated.

"I told you. Leave it alone." Was all he said.

"You're pissing me off."

"I can handle it," he said smoothly.

"Fucker."

"Bitch."

I rolled my eyes, chuckling.

"Go. Pacify your parents. We'll be here." He nudged me with his shoulder.

"Okay. Okay. I'm going." I started walking backwards. "But I'll call for a report later in the week."

"You can stop by for a report," Grayley pointed out. "But I'll give you one anyway."

"Alright. Tell him..."

"He knows," Grayley finished, turning and leaning one shoulder against the wall, just watching me walk backwards.

When I found the door behind me, I hit the button, asking for it to be unlocked. When it buzzed, I pushed through and it closed. I saw through the window that Grayley turned back and entered the room as the nurse left.

I hit the elevator button and waited.

And found myself staring in shock when the doors slid open, revealing Brian's startled eyes.

"Taryn!" he cried out, slapping the elevator door shut as he moved to follow me.

I blinked, realizing I had instinctually taken a step backwards.

"No," I said, and shoved him away. "Fuck no!"

"Taryn," he said again.

I slapped him, uncaring where we were or if I set him off. I slapped him again. "You put my best friend in the hospital, you asshole!"

"Taryn," he pleaded, trying to grab my arm.

I slapped him a third time. "You hit Kerri."

"Come on..." He was starting to get pissed, but I didn't care. Hell, I wanted him mad. I wanted to see that side of him. I wanted to remember it so I could have that picture in my mind when I hated him for the rest of my life.

I hit the elevator again and shoved him inside.

When the door shut, I hit the emergency button, halting the elevator and full-out punched him. The funny thing is that I decked him using the moves he'd taught me. I grabbed his head and brought my knee up.

Now. Fighting is wrong. Assault is wrong and I could get arrested for this, but I rarely stopped to think about the consequences before I did something illegal. Right now, all I cared about was hurting Brian as much as he'd hurt me and those I loved.

So I whirled and kicked him again. My heel neatly clipping him in the face.

Asshole.

"Stop, Taryn," Brian hissed, grabbing my arms.

I wrenched my arms up and wrapped them around his. As his eyes widened at my hold, I brought my knees up, hard. In the groin.

Brian toppled to the ground.

I released the emergency hatch.

"You fucking stay away from my friends. You stay out of my life."

Brian groaned, "Bitch."

I knelt beside him and tapped him on the forehead. "You bet and this bitch can get you hauled off to prison if you keep pushing me. You touch my friends—I'll send what I got to the cops. And trust me, if I have to, I'll go searching. Whatever I need to get you in prison."

Feeling the elevator come to a halt, I brought out my taser and grinned in satisfaction as it crackled against his chest.

Then I pocketed it and stepped out from the elevator, leaving Brian on the ground in the fetal position.

I'm a cold bitch and Brian knew it.

I heard gasps from behind me as I walked through the circling doors, feeling the sunlight hit me as I stepped out onto the sidewalk.

As I strolled up the parking ramp's stairs, I called home and heard Shelley answer.

"Hi, Shelley. It's Taryn."

"Taryn!" she gasped. "Where are you? Mandy said a friend of yours is in the hospital."

"Yeah. One of my friends from Pedlam. He's got a punctured lung and a few broken ribs."

"Oh my gosh, Taryn. Well, you stay as long as you need to," she rushed out.

"Um...thanks, Shelley. I might sleep over at a friend's tonight.""

"That is totally okay with your father and myself. I think Mandy will be relieved. She was talking about a party with some of her friends anyway. We'll just have a nice quiet dinner tonight."

"Okay," I said, lamely.

"Alright. I'll tell your father what's going on and we'll see you tomorrow then."

"Okay," I repeated, hearing the dial tone as I sat, dumbly, in my car. The keys still held in my hand.

I put the keys in the ignition and started my car, turning down the ramp.

An hour later, I pulled up to Tray's house and walked around to his pool-house.

What the hell was I doing here?

But I kept walking.

I heard music and laughter coming from the main house so I steered that way. Opening the back door, I followed the noise, finding myself going down to the basement and—whoa—saw the largest media room in my life.

The screen looked like it belonged in a movie theater.

Grant, Bryce, Carter, and Tray were lounging on the couch, beer bottles opened in front of them, the Spurs game on the screen.

Grant saw me first. "Hey, Taryn."

Everyone else looked over at me.

"Hi," I said awkwardly, feeling out of place.

Tray stood up and approached me. "Hey."

"Sorry," I said softly. "I...don't know why I'm here, really."

He frowned, studying me and then grabbed my hand and pulled me upstairs. Leading me into the kitchen, he opened the fridge. "Want something to drink?"

"I'm sorry. I...I shouldn't be here." I moved to leave, but Tray was there, pressing me against the counter.

"Hey," he said quietly, tipping my head back to meet his eyes, "you want a pop?"

"Uh..." I faltered, feeling my cellphone buzzing, I pulled it out and saw Grayley's name flash on the screen. When I didn't answer it, Tray's eyes shot to my face, seeing the hesitation. I don't know what else he saw because he steered me to a stool and took my phone out of my hands. Watching me, he pocketed my phone and then grabbed a Diet Coke from the fridge and poured it into a glass.

Grabbing my hand, he led me downstairs. He let go when we reached the media room and wandered over to the couch. I followed uncertainly and curled up on the couch beside him, a little space between the guys and me. Tray put my Diet Coke on the table in front of me and grinned, grabbing his beer as Bryce cursed at the screen.

I watched the game with the guys.

Devon showed up an hour after I did and he paused, only for a few seconds when he saw me, then sat on the other couch after helping himself to some mysterious supply of beer bottles in another room.

The guys didn't talk about girls. It was kind of nice. When I hung out with Geezer, Grayley, and whoever else chose to show up, they always talked about girls. They treated me as one of the guys half the time. Notice how I said half the time.

These guys watched the game, drank, and laughed about who got into what fight at Carter's party.

It was a nice...break.

I didn't partake in the conversation. For one, I didn't watch the Spurs enough to have any form of opinion. And two, I was content to curl up quietly beside Tray. When Tray didn't press me, the rest followed suit. Listening to their conversation, I could hear how Tray was the leader. Of course, I'd always known that. But...there was this steel respect each of them had for him.

Sometimes Tray didn't even speak up in the conversation, but the other guys were constantly asking what he thought about so and so. What he'd do, etc. If someone ventured onto a conversation Tray didn't want covered, he'd look over and the topic would instantly be dropped.

It was nice. Brian would've growled, cursed, threatened and finally the topic would've been changed. Hell, sometimes he would've just hauled off and thrown the person into the wall or off their chair.

Tray respected the guys back.

Another hour later I finally realized what I was hearing. It wasn't just respect. But loyalty.

These guys were loyal to each other. To Tray, first and foremost.

Brian hadn't been stable enough to even demand loyalty. Well, he'd demanded it, but he'd forced it. It hadn't been given out of free will.

Tray did that. He got loyalty because it was freely given away. He was loyal back.

Brian was anything, but loyal.

I must've dozed off or stopped listening because I blinked, startled when Tray spoke up, "It's Mandy, Taryn."

Looking up, I saw Tray regarding me, waiting for my decision. The rest of the guys were watching too, with questions in their eyes as they saw Tray holding my phone.

"Uh—"

I saw Carter and Devon glance at each other, but neither spoke.

Then again, apparently it was the rule for these guys. No talk about girls—too much drama. I don't know if that was really the case, but I could see it being the reason.

I shook my head and stood up, wandering upstairs and into the pool-house. I curled up in Tray's bed and closed my eyes, falling asleep within seconds.

I woke up sometime later when I felt Tray slip in beside me and wrap his arms around me, pulling me against his chest.

I didn't say anything, but he knew I was awake. I felt his hand rub against my stomach, slowly, and I closed my eyes, feeling the warmth spread at his touch. Falling to my back, I felt his hand wander down, slipping underneath my pants and inside my underwear.

Feeling his hand down there, I gasped when his lips found my neck.

Arching into his hand, I reached for him and met his lips.

As he brought me to the edge, I groaned against his mouth, feeling his tongue sweep inside and then I spilled over, gasping.

Tray laughed softly against my mouth when he rolled me underneath him, both of us still fully clothed.

I wrapped my legs around his waist and let my head fall against the pillow. Tray laid there, his mouth now moving to my neck, one hand resting underneath my shirt entwined under my arm, by my shoulder. The other resting on one of my legs, caressing it lazily.

Tray let his full weight rest on me, which I liked and swept a hand down his back, and we stayed like that, neither pushing to go any further.

After a little while, Tray lifted his head and moved to the side, half his body resting on top of mine.

He murmured, "I get a distinct impression that you're hiding out here."

"Your distinct impression would be correct."

He chuckled softly. "Because I actually came in to tell you that Mandy's here."

"What?" I cried out, sitting up.

"Relax. Thc door's locked."

"I don't want to talk to her. Not yet. She thinks I'm staying at a friend's in Pedlam tonight."

"You told her that?"

"No. I told our mother that."

Tray chuckled, sitting up. "Mandy's not one to narc."

"Is it awkward in there?" I couldn't help asking, biting my lip as I met his sardonic gaze.

"Between her, Dev, and Carter?" He chuckled again. "It's a roll in the fucking hay."

"Fuck." I sighed, as Tray got up from the bed and moved into the bathroom. A moment later, he came back out and murmured, "Come on. Otherwise Mandy's gonna come in here and I don't want Mandy in my bedroom."

I laughed, couldn't help it. But I let him grab my hand and hoist me out of the bed. The guy was strong, holy hell.

When Tray cut down into the basement, I grabbed a Diet Coke out of his fridge before reluctantly wandering down the stairs.

I gritted my teeth, prepared for whatever Mandy was going to throw my way when I entered the room.

But all she said was, sitting on the farthest corner from Devon's couch, "Your friend Grayley's called the house, like three times."

"I figured he would," I remarked, sitting on a lounger and placing the Diet Coke on the stand beside it.

"You're avoiding his calls?" she asked in surprise. "Way you guys acted last night, it was as if he was your brother or something."

I sighed. "Leave it alone, Mandy."

"Why?" she asked sharply. God. She was pissed and probably not because of me, but she'd chosen me as her whipping lamb.

"Because some shit's going on that you have no idea about and I don't want to deal with it right now," I snapped, running a hand over my face.

"Like what?" she asked, pouting.

Anything I would've shot back at her was interrupted when Jasmine and Amber called out, from the top of the stairs, "Hey, hey. We're coming down."

I sat back, unable to suppress a grimace as their giggling got louder.

"Oh!" They blinked in surprise, seeing that everyone was already there. "Hey, guys," Amber murmured, sitting down hesitantly, between Mandy and Devon. Jasmine wavered, not saying anything, as she looked around for a place to sit. She finally chose the floor, in front of Grant.

And they hadn't been alone. I suppressed another grimace when Sasha popped her head out from the doorway, a Coke in hand.

Sasha called out, sickeningly sweet, "Hey ya'll." She perched on the corner of the couch by Bryce's arm.

Carter let out a laugh, the sound breaking the frozen silence that had taken hold of the room.

I glanced at Tray and saw him watching the game, my phone was beside him and flashing. I must've had a dozen calls by now.

"Tray, I didn't see you at Carter's last night," Amber spoke up nervously.

"I was there," Tray murmured lazily.

"He left early," Mandy said flatly.

Carter laughed again.

"So," Grant spoke up, "Sasha, I heard you and Travers broke up last night."

"Hmm mmm." She giggled, taking a sip of her Coke.

"Ask Sasha who she hooked up with last night." Amber giggled, as if it were hysterical.

No one asked, but Sasha piped in, "This guy from Pedlam who's freaking hot!"

"Who?" Devon asked, probably just to be polite. And probably grateful the attention wasn't on him.

"Uh...Trent...Standley?"

"Trent Gardner," I supplied.

Sasha looked over at me in surprise. "How do you know? Were you even there?"

"He's a friend of mine," I said coolly.

"Oh!" She smiled, flashing a Cheshire smile. "I need to make a point of getting to know him. Again."

"Good luck," I said dryly. "At least you knew his first name. Can't say the same for him."

That wiped the grin off her face. "You're such a bitch."

This was a distraction I could handle.

I grinned back and it seemed everyone else braced themselves for what I would say next. "At least I can count the number of guys I've been with on one hand—with a couple of fingers left over. Can you?"

Mandy groaned, burying her head in her hands.

I swore I heard the rest of the group take a deep breath.

"Are you calling me a slut?" Sasha demanded sharply.

"You gotta expect it when you swing shit my way," I merely retorted, curling my feet underneath me, getting more comfortable.

Sasha rolled her eyes and—surprisingly—stayed quiet.

Carter swore, "Fucking hell. He could've made that shot." Referring to the game.

"Fuck that," Bryce added, taking a drink of his beer.

Just then the buzzer rang, Spurs losing by four points. Tray switched the channel to some music videos.

No one knew what to say, so the guys complained about the game some more.

Jasmine stood up and went into a room. A second later, she returned with a beer in hand and perched on the arm of the couch by Devon, where she started talking to Sasha. Amber stood up and circled to stand by them. Mandy was watching Carter, glancing to Devon every now and then.

Looking over, I saw Tray gazing at my phone.

He looked up at me and held it out to me, "The guy's called you like seventeen times."

I sighed and took the phone, standing up and moved up the stairs.

I dialed Grayley's number and heard him exclaim, "About fucking time, Taryn!"

"Sorry. I just—didn't want to deal with anything—Brian related."

"You did a good job on him."

"So you know."

"Yeah, I know."

"What do you want? I'm not sorry. Is that what you want? Brian put Geezer in the hospital."

"Is it helping?" Grayley asked, quietly.

"Is what helping?" I didn't want to play mind games with him. He always thought he knew me better than I knew myself. "Stop it, Grayley."

"Is it helping you? Remembering all the shit-poor stuff he does so that you can get over him?"

"What?" I choked out in disbelief. I couldn't believe he was playing this card. "Are you kidding me?"

"No, Taryn, I'm not. If you want to hate Brian, you can hate him. Just don't use Geezer as your excuse, because he doesn't deserve to be used like that. And if you think he doesn't know what you're doing, you're pretty dumb."

I wanted to scream. Grayley was fucking right (somewhat), but...fuck him. I wasn't going to admit it.

"I'm not using Geezer as an excuse. Trust me. I'm hating Brian all on my own. And what I did to him...that was all me. Yeah—Geezer was *a* reason, but he wasn't the only reason. And I'm *not* using him." I repeated.

"Whatever you keep telling yourself," he said smoothly.

"Why are you on my ass about this?" I asked, irritated.

"Because Geezer's now blaming himself for the entire break-up between you and Brian. And it's not right. He thinks it's all his fault."

"Geezer went to Brian about his dad."

"And who sent him there? You. Through Jace."

"Grayley—what are you on? Are you pissed that you weren't the one to take Brian down? I don't get you."

"No. I'm pissed because you didn't think about what you were doing. You're not the one who's going to pay. We are. We always are. The fight's got nothing to do with you, you need to stay out of it. The fight's between us and Brian. We have to deal with it."

"Is that why Trent was there today? You and he are going to take Brian down?"

"Somewhat. Trent's there because he wants to be there. He likes Geezer. Look," I could hear how tired he was, "just stay away from Brian from now on, okay? Let us handle him."

"Fine," I muttered, glowering to an empty room.

"Taryn."

"I said fine."

"Yeah and you said that before, but look what you just did."

"I was pissed and he was there. I couldn't pass it up."

"You tasered him, in an elevator," Grayley pointed out wryly.

I grinned, a chuckle escaping my lips. "Oh. You should've seen him."

"I did," he remarked. "He was taken to the E.R."

"Oh." I blinked, I didn't think I'd done *that* much damage. "Why?"

"Because you beat the shit out of him," Grayley said, exasperated.

"Oh. Uh—"

"He wouldn't file charges so the cops aren't coming after you. But still...you're fucking lucky, Taryn. Brian said it was in self-defense. He said that he grabbed you first and he wouldn't tell them your name."

Fuck that. I was not going to be grateful to Brian. Not for anything.

"I'll stay out of it," I said through gritted teeth. Grayley had gotten what he wanted. That annoying little shit.

"Good. Get rid of that taser."

"Jace gave it to me."

"Exactly," he pointed out, hanging up on me.

I rolled my eyes and put my phone in my pocket.

Mandy spoke up, from behind me, "What did you do this time?!"

Again—fuck.

CHAPTER EIGHT

"I don't—" I began, but stopped short. I didn't know what to say to her. I'm pretty sure Hallmark doesn't make a card for bonding over illegal activities.

"What?" she asked again.

I changed tactics and shifted my hip against the counter. "What are you doing up here?"

"I came to find you."

"Hmm mmm. Why?"

"I...," Mandy wavered, rolling her eyes, "because I can't handle all of them downstairs."

"Oh. You mean the little trio of Pop-Tarts downstairs?" I mocked, sweetly. "How can you not? They're so...sugarlicious"

Mandy chuckled, and then groaned. "Ugh. You'd think I could handle this. This was me, four years ago before Dev and I got together. But now, Jasmine's scared to be in the same room as me, Devon looks like he's going to bolt any second, and Amber, I've realized, has no spine. Plus," she sighed, "I think they've replaced me with Sasha Klinnleys."

"I call her Hooters Bitch."

"I just...I feel like I've lost my place. You know?"

"You're asking me?" I asked skeptically. "Mandy, welcome to my life the past six months."

"What are you doing here, by the way?"

"Hiding," I said without hesitation. I could at least tell her part of the truth.

"From?"

"From my life," I said dryly. "My friends in Pedlam. Shelley and Kevin."

"You mean, Mom and Dad."

"Yeah.I guess."

"Taryn...they're your mom and dad too. You just gotta...let them."

"Not really used to having parents around."

"Well, I was grateful, but now...I'm thinking I should have had a nice dinner at home with Mom and Dad, instead of coming here." Mandy cringed.

Just then Amber walked into the room, a large smile plastered on her face. She halted and placed her hands on her skinny hips. "We're going to get in the pool. You guys want to come?"

"Um," Mandy said uncertainly.

"No swimsuits," I remarked.

"That's okay. Tray's family has a bunch in the changing rooms. Just go and pick one," she said cheerfully, before bouncing back out.

This was not my scene—hanging out with the social elite—but it was Mandy's and she needed my support so I pushed her forward. "Let's go. Pick out a bikini to show off that hot bod. You'll have both Devon and Carter drooling before the night's over."

Mandy didn't look convinced, but she went anyway.

I knew my body and I knew what guys liked. I figured I might as well have some fun. So I picked a black bikini that tied at the sides. The folds accentuated the sweep at my breasts and I knew all the guys would take notice.

Which they did.

Amber, Sasha, and Jasmine were lounging at one end. Mandy was paddling with Carter in the shallow end of the pool. Tray was behind the bar. Bryce, Grant, and Devon were watching me.

Not one to not make a scene, I walked over to Mandy and jumped, completing a clean backflip in the air, over her and Carter. I managed to sweep my arms out in front me just as I hit the water, sending a small splash over my sister.

I kicked my way to Mandy's side before I broke the surface, grinning at her shocked face.

"When did you learn to do that?" Mandy asked.

"I took swimming in the seventh grade at Earlington."

"They're the state champs," Carter remarked.

"If you weren't a swimmer, you were a loser there. I learned to swim." I hauled myself out of the water and then jumped back in, laughing as Mandy scowled, knowing the splash would hit her full-force this time.

"Looks like you kept it up," Carter noted when I swam back over to them.

One hand holding the side, I slicked my hair back and commented, "It was the only place I could get away from my boyfriend. I swam a lot to keep in shape."

"He must've hated that."

"Nah. He never knew." It was true. Brian never knew I could swim. I'd always thought about joining the Pedlam swim team, but it didn't seem the same. Earlington ate, breathed, and slept swimming. Pedlam, they didn't really care. If you swam, you swam. If you didn't, you were just like everyone else. But breaking against the water helped with arm strength. Which helped me when I had to climb—sometimes against the side of a building.

Brian knew I didn't spend that much time lifting his weights. But he'd never ask how I could climb as quickly as I did.

He'd never cared to ask. That had been the bottom line.

"Rawley has a swim team. You should try out," Mandy suggested.

"Maybe," I offered. Climbing out, I crossed to the bar where Tray was talking with Grant and Bryce.

"Drink?" Tray asked, watching me intently, almost like he was trying to read me or something. What the hell?

"Beer."

He grabbed a bottle of Michelob Golden Light and uncapped it.

The beer tasted good. I've never been a fruity drink girl and I'm certainly not a whiskey drinker, but beer made me think of the sun, water and friends. Which either ended with making love, some rough and passionate sex, or a fight.

An unusual calm had been called over the group and I didn't know handle myself. Normally, I was either having sex or fighting with these people. Okay, there was only one person here that I was doing the first with, but the second, is why I'm so uncomfortable. I wasn't under attack and I didn't know how to deal with these people under any other circumstance. Jasmine had retracted her claws long ago and Sasha had either given up or she was just waiting for a better place for another go.

Remember when Stephanie was my biggest headache in this town? Jeez. And her, I'd handled by making up a lie that she hooked up with Devon. Funny how my lie turned to be half-truth. He had hooked up, just not with her.

And Stephanie had fallen, fallen, to the point where she wasn't even a blip on the social radar anymore.

And Mandy? Mandy had zeroed in on her, knowing full well that I'd lied to her. But she'd done it nonetheless.

Wow. It just hit me how much Mandy had changed with this whole Jasmine/Devon thing. She didn't have the old spark in her anymore. But then again, seeing her grinning at whatever Carter had just whispered in her ear, I saw her glance a moment later to Devon. And I saw the hurt that flashed in her depths.

Yeah. My sister was hurting.

And for once, there was nothing I could do. I couldn't go on the attack. I couldn't blackmail anyone. I couldn't break in somewhere and steal all their files, full of little ugly secrets. This—this I needed to sit back. And just let Mandy figure it out for herself.

Not my ammo in life.

"Taryn." I came back to reality, realizing Bryce had spoken my name—and it looked like he'd done it a few times.

"Sorry." I grinned ruefully. "What were you saying?"

"I was asking if you wanted to take a shot with us." He flashed a cocky grin my way.

What the fuck?

"Sure." I shrugged, turning in my place with Grant and Bryce, one on each side of me.

Tray set out the four glasses and filled each one. One by one, we tipped our heads back and slammed the shots.

Tray filled 'em again.

This night might get interesting.

After the third—whoa—Jasmine, Amber, and Sasha had wandered over.

Tray set out some shots for them.

Devon was standing behind Jasmine uncertainly.

Seeing his jaw tighten, I realized he'd been watching Mandy and Carter in the pool. When Mandy let out a shriek of laughter, Devon grabbed Jasmine by the back of her arm.

Bryce nudged me. "We're waiting."

A fourth shot sat before me. Full and waiting.

I tipped it back and watched as Jasmine was listening to whatever Devon was whispering in her ear. I saw the smug look that came on her face and I saw that her hand reached behind him and entwined with his.

Shit.

This night was already getting interesting.

I begged out of the next round of shots. Sasha and Amber were finishing off their—third?—I think.

"Taryn, you aren't done, are you?" Bryce taunted, watching me coolly. He looked smug. Narrowing my eyes, I took another long look at him and saw him wink at Tray. What the fuck?

What the hell was going on in his head?

"Maybe," I said stiffly and shoved away from the group. I plopped down next to Mandy and Carter, dipping my legs in the pool.

"Hey," Mandy murmured, disentangling from Carter as she swam in front of me. "What's going on up there?"

"I don't know. Some confusing shit."

"What do you mean?"

"Pretty sure Bryce is trying to get me drunk," I hesitated and said lamely, "and that's it."

"Bryce probably wants to see if he can get a piece."

"Huh?" I was dumbfounded. Yeah. It made sense. A guy trying to get a girl drunk sometimes would equal getting a piece. Guys always think it's a sure thing. But me? And Bryce?

Carter laughed. "Bryce bet Tray he could get in your pants."

"And Tray agreed?" Okay. Now, I was just pissed. And insulted.

"No. Tray just said good luck, but he didn't take the bet. Bryce probably thinks if he can get you, Tray'll cough up the money."

"What do you think?"

Carter chuckled. "Tray bet me how long before you send Bryce whimpering like a puppy dog."

That made me grin. I'd never admit it to myself, but I was relieved that Tray hadn't played me.

Bryce could come after me all he wanted. Maybe now I'd just have some fun with him.

Suddenly the pool area was flooded with voices. Turning around, I saw a good thirteen people turn the corner. Some were already dressed in bathing suits and vaulted over us into the pool. Others took a seat at the many patio tables.

Mandy murmured, her eyes wide, "Looks like we're having a party."

I glanced over my shoulder and saw Tray was busy hooking up a keg that some guy had wheeled over to him. There were four other guys, all carrying two more kegs.

"Looks like it's going to be a party to remember," I murmured, more to myself.

Devon and Jasmine disappeared into the house, holding hands.

This night was going to be full of drama. I could feel it in my bones.

So far, I was actually having a good time.

This guy, I think his name was Rooters, slapped a two on the deck.

"Fuck."

"You shit."

"Asshole."

Rooters just grinned and flipped his last card on the table, as he announced, "Pres-i-dente!"

We were playing Assholes and Presidents. I was neutral, which really pissed me off.

This other fucker, Aaron, slammed his last card on the deck and shouted, "Vice-President! Vice-President. Oh yeah! Oh Yeah!"

I spotted my turn and slipped in my last pair of sixes.

"Neutral!" I called out, laughing when Helms flicked me off, because I'd skipped him.

Honey and Bits glared at me, which made me laugh even harder. That wasn't their real names, but it was how I kept them apart. They seemed to appreciate the nicknames, since they'd been calling each other those names since I accidentally blurted them out after the last round.

I had been recruited into the game when Bryce had grabbed me and pushed me into the empty chair beside him. It seemed that two others had recently left, after starting their make out session during the game.

Before that, I'd stayed by the water for a while, but moved when it started getting colder out. Mandy and Carter were in the media room, making out. Tray was outside, talking with a group of guys by the kegs. And I'd gone the complete opposite direction when I caught a glimpse of Sasha and Amber, still in their bikinis, sitting on the laps of some guys at a patio table.

"Take that, fuckers!" Bryce hollered, throwing his last card on the pile.

Rooters rolled his eyes and drawled, "You're neutral, dumb-ass."

The table immediately quieted, waiting to see what Bryce would do. Guess the elite didn't get treated that way.

Bryce shrugged and retorted, "Just wait. I'll be Prez pretty soon and then you'll be my beer bitch."

Honey hooted. "Beer bitch, Rooters. That's you all the time, isn't it?"

Bit giggled, her eyes wistful as she skimmed over Bryce. "Yeah, beer bitch."

Bryce fully knew the effect he had on the girl because he winked, grinning smugly at her. Downing the rest of his drink, he turned to me. "How about it, Taryn? Another shot?"

"Right. And give you the chance to drug my drink? I'm not an idiot," I muttered, standing up. "I'll get my own drink."

"I said a shot. Not a drink. There's a big difference," Bryce argued back, following me.

"Whatever." I know. It lacked my usual energy, but really—the guy hadn't pissed me off enough to get the full force of my attitude. I guess I was still playing with him or maybe just playing along until he crossed the line. Then he'd be filleted.

Pushing through the crowd—it had tripled within the past hour—I half stumbled to the keg with Bryce right behind me. He put his hand on the small of my back for a moment. I don't know why he took it away, but it was the only thing that saved him because I was already turning around, ready to kick his ass. I looked at him and saw that he wasn't even looking at me.

Whatever.

I turned back around and saw Tray's amused eyes; he'd seen the whole thing.

I grinned at him, taking the cup that he was extending to me.

Bryce hollered against my ear, "I need two shots. Pronto!"

"Ah!" I yelled. "Back the fuck up, Bryce!"

Bryce grinned, ignoring me as he reached for the two shots.

Miraculously, I found one in my hand and frowned. Was I—never mind—I'd already shot it.

That one was good.

"Five bucks, right?" I knew that voice.

I grinned dumbly, happy seeing Trent give Tray some money."

"Trent!" I shouted.

He looked up, took one look at me, and shook his head, grinning. "Fuck, what are you doing here?"

I made my way to him, pushing two people out of the way. "I'm at a party," I announced stupidly.

Trent sighed.

"What are you doing here?" I asked, moving closer. The music was so loud. Did it have to be that loud?

"That girl I hooked up with last night called. Said this was *the* party to be at." Trent was frowning. Like, really, really frowning.

"Why are you looking like that?" I asked. It was a question that I needed answering. I didn't like frowns, did I?

Trent shook his head again, looking resigned. "Because I brought friends with me."

"That's great," I said warmly, grinning stupidly. Wait. "Who?"

"Not friends of yours," he said bluntly.

"Oh no." I took a step back.

"Yeah." He sighed again.

"Not...Gentley? I can handle Gentley."

"Not like this, Taryn. You can't handle Gentley drunk."

"I'm not drunk." I argued drunkenly.

Whee.

"Is Grayley here?" I asked weakly.

"Yeah. He's here too." He didn't sound happy about that either.

Then it clicked. I'm drunk. Gentley's here. Grayley's my best friend and Grayley's supposedly friends with Gentley now.

Not good.

"Oh." I mouthed the word. Fuck. I was in a shitload of trouble.

"Girl," Trent held my shoulders and said seriously, "you need to get out of sight. Now."

"I'm not one to run, Trent," I replied. I wasn't. Why should I run? This was my turf now, right?

"I know, but right now it's what's in your best interest," he reasoned. Why did sober people always have to sound reasonable? Why couldn't they be drunk like people like me? The universe would be a lot better off. Truly.

Madly.

Deeply.

I always liked that song. I have no idea who sang it.

"Trent, do you know who sang the song—" I was about to ask, but I blinked, finding myself face to face with Crispin Gentley, Tracy Hardkins and Kimberley Ringsworld right behind him, followed by three other football players from Pedlam, and a pale Grayley.

I decided to take the offense and opened my mouth to say the first words in my head, "Why are so many goddamn fucking Pedlam people coming to Rawley parties?"

"Oh my fucking word," Kimberly spouted off. She really hated me. I'd heard once that she'd always had a crush on Brian. They'd gone on two dates and he'd dropped her because the next day I'd come back to Pedlam. That had been in eighth grade—she still hated me to this day because of it. Or at least...I think that's why she hated me.

Tracy was smiling. She looked evil. "You were one of us not long ago, Taryn."

"Oh no," I said horrified, "I was never one of you! Trust me."

Gentley chose that moment to interject, "Heard what you did to your ex. Nice. It was a good reminder why I never dated you."

"That and the fact that you need to have a dick to date me. It's one of my requirements."

Whoa. That was a personal best.

Trent and a few of the other guys were desperately coughing, trying to cover up their laughs, turning away.

Gentley glared at me, full force, as he stalked closer. "Oh, Taryn. Trust me. I've got more than enough dick for you."

I smiled sweetly. "Not really. I've seen pictures."

That pissed him off. Even drunk, I took a step back in self-preservation.

"Maybe I should give you another view," Gentley whispered, suddenly in my face. "Maybe you can get up close and personal to reconsider."

That didn't sound like a good thing to do.

Suddenly, Gentley was wrenched away. Grayley and Trent were both standing between us.

"She's drunk, Crisp. Leave her alone," Grayley was saying, pushing Gentley back another step.

"Are you kidding me?" Gentley laughed, more perplexed. "Are you and Gardner actually protecting that bitch?"

"It's not right, dude," Trent said. "Taryn's not up to par. Anything less cheapens the triumph. We all know that."

"Please," Gentley scoffed, shoving both of them back. "Get off me, Gray. You've been in love with her since the eighth grade. But you, Gardner, I'm surprised."

I narrowed my eyes. Grayley was not in love with me. No fucking way. I was about to say that too when I felt familiar hands grab my arm and pull me backwards.

Tray.

And Bryce. Then, blinking, I saw Devon, Carter, Grant, and about four other guys materialize out of nowhere.

"Out," Tray ordered. "We don't need a brawl right now."

"Excuse me? What the fuck did you just say?"

"I said," Tray said icily, "you can leave. Now."

"Whatever, fucker, we all know it was you who messed up our field and gym," Gentley growled.

Without another word, Tray stepped up and neatly clipped Gentley on the jaw. Crispin fell. Just like that.

Tray stepped in and kicked him. "This is my town and if you go against one of mine, you go against me. Now get the fuck out."

Gentley shoved him back and stood up. "Taryn may have been one of your bitches in bed, but trust me—she's just like any other slut."

That was it.

The fucker was going down. Once and for all. Drunk or not, I could still talk and words were my second favorite weapon.

I shoved through the crowd and shot back, acid dripping from my voice, "Please. Crispin. How long are you going to hold this grudge against me? I rejected you in the ninth grade. Two. Fucking. Years. Ago. I'd figured that Kimberly had been comforting you. I mean, you and her got so much in common since both of you wanted to break Brian and me up." I looked at Kimberly. "You're more than welcome to him, now by the way. He's probably at home since I landed him in the E.R. today. I'm sure he's got to nurse those wounds."

"Shut the fuck up."

I blinked. More in surprise because it hadn't come from Kimberly. Or Gentley.

It came from Grayley.

"Grayley..." I stammered.

"You don't fucking think, Taryn!" he yelled. I could see his rage now. "Yeah. Big fucking deal. You beat Brian up. Guess what? He's not going against you. He never would—he knows you can bury him. No, he's going to go after me or Geezer or Kerri—or anyone else. Maybe even Jace. You ever think of that?"

I paled at his words. Fuck. He was right.

"You and Jace. Bri's known about the two of you since it happened, he just never had proof. Now he does. All he needs is some courage from some fucking empty Jack Daniels bottle and he might actually go after his brother with a 9mm. How'd you like that? Would you just love it if I took you to Jace's funeral? Or Brian's funeral?"

"Grayley..." I tried.

"No," he cut me off, "you just...you never fucking think."

Suddenly, I was sober and was really looking at Grayley. It was plain as day, he was exhausted. Exhausted from fighting on three different sides—mine, Brian's and Gentley's.

"Grayley," I murmured softly, "I'm—"

"You're sorry. You're always sorry, Taryn," he cut off bitterly. "You're so fucking sorry that you don't ever think about what you do. I'm tired of worrying about you. God...what you do sometimes, Taryn. If you ever get caught, do you know what could happen to you? Where you could end up?"

"I stopped."

"No," Grayley shook his head, "you didn't stop. My God, where were you just yesterday? You weren't at the game. Where were you?"

I paled.

"Shut up," I said quickly. "That was..."

"That was stupid. And suicidal. And you better fucking not ever do it again," Grayley finished roughly.

I couldn't say anything. He was right and we both knew it.

"Grayley," Tracy spoke up, moving to stand beside him, curling one hand around his arm, "come on. We're all leaving."

I never would've thought those two would hook up.

That was the last stupid thought in my head when Grayley shot me one more exasperated glare, before he turned and followed everyone else who had left without us realizing.

Trent stayed in place.

"Hey," he shrugged, "that chick invited me. I'm not leaving." And he pushed through the crowd, in search of Sasha.

Looking up, I realized that a lot of people had stopped watching. When Grayley started in on me, the appeal had lessened. Grayley wasn't as fun to watch as Gentley. Or Tray.

Glancing at the keg, I saw Tray was back to talking to the guys at the kegs.

His eyes met mine for a second.

Fun had departed when Pedlam had arrived.

Fuck that.

I'd found sanctuary in Tray's bedroom. After searching the entire place, I'd realized that this was the only room that was off-limits. Everything else—trust me—they'd all been occupied. In some way or other. In some form of dress or another.

"You were supposed to rip Bryce a new one tonight."

I didn't look up from my spot in his bed.

Tray didn't sound like he was about to jump me anyway.

"Oh yeah?" I said back without emotion.

The bed dipped under his weight as he sat beside me.

"Yeah," he murmured, looking down at me, "but you knew about the bet, didn't you?"

"I know," I murmured half-heartedly.

"Which is why you let him think he was playing such a good game all night," Tray mused.

"Look," I breathed out, "I'm not really up for it right now. I'm only here because there's nowhere else I can go where I'll be left alone. And I can't exactly drive yet."

"You're not driving regardless," Tray said smoothly, lying beside me.

"I'm not drunk."

"Oh yeah you are." He laughed. "I counted every drink I gave you. You had seven shots and at *least* eight beers. You might not feel drunk, but you are."

"Like you'd know," I snapped. "I just got yelled at by my best friend."

"Who was about to get the shit beat out of him," Tray noted, dryly.

"Shut up. What do you know?"

"More than you. I'm sober."

"Look. We're not in a relationship and just because we're screwing doesn't mean you need to come and comfort me, you know," I said crossly.

Tray laughed. "Oh, I'm not coming to comfort you."

I looked at him, seeing his grinning face beside mine on the pillow. "What are you doing then?"

"I came in to warn you."

Oh for the love...

"Warn me about...?" I let the question hang between us.

He grinned another moment and then delivered the news, "Mandy found Devon and Jasmine having sex."

Oh fuck.

"Carter wanted me to find you. Mandy's gone psycho," he said bluntly.

I shoved off the bed and led the way. Outside, I could hear her screech over the music and crowd. I pushed through the circle that had formed and found Mandy, looking—psycho—with Devon and Jasmine, both of them half-dressed.

Oh. Fucking shit—they'd been screwing on the couch. In freaking plain eyesight.

Morons.

They deserved whatever Mandy dished out to them.

"You are such a slut!" Mandy shrieked. "I can't believe I ever thought you were my friend!"

"Oh please," Jasmine retorted. "All you give a damn about is your perfect life! It's no wonder that Devon called me four times a week when y'all were together. He was practically begging me for it. You were so fucking frigid, you could have froze his dick off!"

Huh—I needed to remember that one.

"Oh please," Mandy parroted furiously. "How much does it hurt, Jasmine? Knowing that you're the girl the guys go to second. You're just second class," she finished scathingly.

Yep. Mandy needed no help here.

Carter shifted next to me. "Hey," he said, "you going to stop this?"

"Are you kidding me?" I asked, confused. "This is great. I finally get to watch this stuff."

"Mandy will not be happy that you let her go off like this. You know it, Taryn."

Mandy continued, "That's because all you really are is white-trash. You look like it, you smell like it, you sound like it, and you sure as hell—act like it. Just saying it how it is."

I'd missed whatever Jasmine had said before.

This was good. Really good. Mandy needed to do this. Really. If anything, this would help Mandy get back to her old fighting, bitching—popular—social elite self.

I can't believe I just thought that was a good thing.

"Really," Jasmine said in a voice that dripped acid, "if anyone is white trash, it'd be you. I mean...you have the first rate poster child for it right in your own home."

Now I interjected.

"You really want to go there?" I drawled, stepping into the circle, pinning Jasmine down with a glare.

She shut up.

"Go on," I said smoothly, stepping back.

Mandy glared and opened her mouth, delivering another round of insults. I patted Carter on the shoulder and murmured, "She's all yours."

I moved back through the crowd and found Tray at the kegs—where else would he be?

He'd been watching me as I weaved through the crowd.

Most of the people had moved inside, more interested in catching the latest shake-down than waiting in line for more beer.

"Everything okay," Tray stated. ,

"She's good," I murmured, moving closer.

"And you."

"I'm good too." And I was, probably because I wasn't as drunk. I did not like being out of control or stupid. Not when so many people wanted to kick me while I'm down.

Tray was watching me evenly.

"You," I stated.

"I'm always good." He grinned arrogantly.

I wanted him.

Seeing it, his eyes widened a bit. It must've been blatant because he grabbed my hand and swept me into the pool-house.

Locking the main door, he locked the bedroom door.

Our mouths met and clung to each other. I raked my hands through his hair, groaning in frustration. I couldn't get enough of him. Wrapping my arms around him, I felt him lift me and my legs wrapped around his waist. He turned and pressed me against the door.

I gasped, arching up against him as his lips trailed down my throat and neck.

Suddenly, we were on the bed and both of us were blindly pulling at our clothes. A second later, Tray was sliding in, pushing deep and I could only hold on. It was rough, deep, and the best sex I've ever had.

CHAPTER NINE

Groaning, Tray pulled out of me. We'd gone another round before we heard pounding at the door.

Seriously?

"What?" Tray yelled angrily.

"Collins and Helms are going at it," Grant said timidly. He knew full well what he was interrupting.

"For the—," he cursed. "Go and break it up."

"We got another situation."

"What?"

"Um...Mandy's locked herself in your parent's bedroom. She won't let anyone in."

I let out a deep breath of air then started getting dressed. I called out, "I'll be there in a little bit."

Tray yawned widely, grabbing for his clothes.

"Hey," I murmured a little uncertainly, "um...thanks for before. You know, with Gentley's crew."

He shrugged. "It's not like the first time Pedlam's come here and stirred up shit. Gentley's usually harmless, at least with me, but he's got it in him to be nasty, and he had that look tonight."

"Oh."

"Plus, I didn't like how he was looking at you," Tray murmured, leaving the room.

That surprised me. Neither of us had made any comment about...well...about us. The most we had even acknowledged is that we were screwing around—that was it. There were no emotional ties that went with a relationship, but his statement hinted at one—slightly. Then again, Tray was particularly cautious about anyone who didn't live in Rawley. He considered Rawley his and from I've seen—it was.

Which still made me wonder how he'd accomplished that.

Gentley didn't own Pedlam. He might run the school now, but he didn't run the town. Jace ran everything else. And, I guess, Brian was trying to get some of that action. But Gentley never wanted to go against Jace. For one, Crispin was just a high school student. Jace had graduated a couple years back, but Jace got a world-class criminal education.

And Jace was just intelligent as hell. Gentley was not. Neither was Brian. They couldn't match him.

But Tray.

Tray was different. He ran a different game, and I hadn't figured it out yet. Not that I was actively trying to figure out his secrets. I really was trying to get out and live my life.

Which reminded me...Mandy.

It was much later in the night, but the party was still going strong. A lot of people were sitting outside at the patio tables, enjoying the night's warmness. There was a slight breeze in the wind.

I grinned at Trent, seeing him at a table with Sasha on his lap. He flashed a smile at me before commenting to someone at the table they were sitting sat at. Amber was there too, with Bryce. Justin Travers was glaring at Trent, which—of course—didn't even faze Trent.

Devon and Jasmine were there, wrapped around each other. Huh, guess the couple decided to go public.

Slipping through the hallway, I circled to the stairs and climbed upwards.

The place was just huge, which said a lot because it was currently crawling with people. I could just imagine it without people in every inch.

I spotted a large double door at the end of the hallway. They looked extravagant, so I figured I might've gotten the right room.

Plus, Honey was outside the door, speaking into it, "Can I get you anything, Mandy?"

No answer.

I moved to her side.

"Hey." She looked up, standing up from kneeling. "She's been in there for a while now. She won't talk to anyone."

"Where's Carter?"

Honey shrugged, her wheat blonde hair falling off her shoulders. "I have no idea. Bit came and got me before. She went to see if Evans has any pizza. It's worth a try, right?"

I grinned at their names. They'd kept using them.

I was struck by the sincerity in her voice. She was really nice. Like, actual nice. Not fake nice. Or trying to gain something nice.

"Mandy likes Canadian bacon and pineapple. If he doesn't have any, you could just order. I'll pay you back," I offered.

"It's worth a try." Honey grinned shyly.

"What?" I asked, dumbly.

"I just thought it was hilarious. Jasmine's about to go off on you and you just step in, cool. She backs off. It was priceless. I know it made my night." She giggled softly.

So others felt the same way I did about Jasmine and her previous reign at Rawley.

"Mandy," I knocked, "let me in."

We heard sniffling a second later—Mandy must've gotten closer to the door—because she murmured, "Go back and have fun, Taryn. I'm just crying right now. I need some time alone."

Okay, I was much more comfortable verbally sparring with someone than comforting someone. Being soothing?

Nurturing? So not my forte. But I knew this is what Mandy needed and it was a skill that I eventually need to develop, sometime in my life.

"Mandy," I said softly, "Grant came and got me so that means he was worried. I'm betting there's a lot of people who are concerned. So let me in so I can do my sisterly-duty."

"Taryn, seriously. Just go away." She sniffed. Honey and I shared a look. Mandy wasn't fooling us. Mandy needed attention and comfort twenty-four/seven.

Mandy was not a loner. No way in hell.

"Mandy, either let me in or I'll break in. Your choice," I said sweetly, rocking back on my heels.

Honey's eyes went wide at my words, and even wider when the door opened a second later—revealing Mandy, swamped in a terry-cloth robe, her eyes swollen and puffy.

She took one look at me and I saw the break down. I moved in and wrapped my arms around her.

"Hey, hey," I murmured softly, "it's okay."

"No it's not," she sobbed, clinging to me. "It's not okay. It's over. Me and Dev...we're over."

Oh. Understanding finally dawned on me. Mandy got through this past week because she thought she'd get back together with Devon at some point. She was allowed a little revenge fun and then...her and Devon would be okay again.

Okay. I could do this...I think.

I turned to Honey and gestured for her to shut the door. Which she did, with her on the inside, with us.

I was not the girl for this.

Honey must've seen my discomfort because she shifted to sit on the bed with us. She placed a hand to Mandy's shoulder and murmured, "He was yours."

Was that really helping?

Mandy sobbed harder.

Honey continued softly, "But that chapter has to close."

Mandy kept crying.

"For you and him. It's a new chapter. And you'll have someone who'll enter your chapter. But you have to let that last page end. Finish your chapter with Devon."

Wow. This was even making sense to me. Brian and I had an entire set of books between the two of us. Maybe I needed to figure out where my new chapters were—with Pedlam friends, Geezer and Grayley, and with my new life. Shit—maybe Tray even needed to be included.

No. Not yet.

Honey was still murmuring to Mandy, "He was yours."

Mandy turned to hug her instead. Honey wrapped her arms around her and propping her chin on Mandy's shoulder, she whispered, "Four years. You guys were a part of each other. And now...he's not a part of you anymore. It's okay to not be okay with that. She won't replace you. No matter what. She can't go back to those four years and take your place. Those four years were yours."

God. That's what I'd been doing. I was so focused on moving forward, cutting all my ties—I'd just now started mending those with Grayley and Geezer again. But...a part of my identity had been with Brian.

And I'd been floundering because I hadn't even realized it. That a part of me was missing. Or that I needed to figure out who I was again.

I realized my hands were fisting the bedcovers. I was trying to restrain myself to stay there. But every instinct I had in me was screaming for me to get the hell out of there. Just—run and hide.

Yeah. I confronted. I confronted when it was a battle that had to be done. But this stuff—this feeling stuff—I always ran the opposite way.

So I was forcefully keeping myself there. Anyway I could.

Mandy needed me. She, at least, needed my presence there.

So I stayed.

And I felt my insides tearing as I listened to Mandy's suffering.

I was still really uncomfortable, but I hung in there. Mandy had cried—sobbed really—for most of the night. Honey had stayed with her. I'd laid back on the bed, content to say a few words every now and then. But Honey had done most of the heavy-lifting. Bit had even been granted access. At one point she helped Honey out and—of course—Mandy had cried even harder.

I'd persevered.

I probably aged a good twenty years because of it. But I stayed.

"What time is it?" Mandy asked, hoarsely.

"It's, like, four in the morning," Bit replied, sighing happily.

"Four in the morning?" Mandy gasped, sitting up. "I can't believe it's that late."

"Just tell Mom and Dad what you always tell 'em." I suggested tiredly. Mandy usually told 'em she'd crash at a girlfriend's. She didn't want them to be worried about her driving late at night. It always worked.

"Well, I know...and I already did. But still—we spent almost the entire party in here."

"Tray had three kegs. And I'm pretty sure they were carrying in a fourth one when I came up here," I murmured, yawning.

It was the best timing because we heard a knock at the door. A second later, Amber stuck her head in. "Hey." She grinned, cautiously, at Mandy. Her eyes skimmed over Honey, Bit, and myself, but they lingered on Mandy. "Can I come in?"

Mandy took a deep breath and nodded. Soothing her hair back, she said, "Thanks, guys. I'll be...I'll be okay."

I studied Amber intently, trying to figure out if she had intent to harm or foul.

Mandy sighed. "Taryn, leave her alone."

So I did and followed behind Honey and Bit outside the door.

They were sharing a look when I closed the door behind me.

"What?" I asked.

"Nothing," Bit spit out, sounding irritated.

"What?"

"It's just...this is how it always is."

"What do you mean?" Seriously. I was clueless.

"They always get into a fight and one of them spends the entire party crying, locked in a room. We pick up the pieces—"

"Lori," Honey interrupted hastily, looking at me uncomfortably.

"No," Bit—Lori—cried out. "It's so unfair. And then one of them shows up, after the party's almost over, and tomorrow it'll be like nothing ever happened. They'll all be giddy and—"

Ah. Now I got it. These two girls were nice, but the problem is that they were too nice. They were social-climbers, just like Stephanie's wannabes

I could, kind of, sympathize. Bit liked Bryce. I knew that, I could tell from the card game. And Honey—she was just nice and almost—too wholesome. These girls didn't have enough bitch in them to climb that last rung on the ladder.

So they were nice to whichever 'it' girl was down and out. They were kind of—like Band-Aids. They were there to cover the wound, but the 'it' girl needed to show up to make things *really* alright. These two didn't cut it, because...they weren't one of the social elite.

I was pissed off at myself because I was feeling sympathy for these two—because they couldn't get popular.

How trivial and annoying is that.

So, I said flatly, "Try being mean."

"What?" Bit asked, confused. I'd checked out of their conversation a few seconds ago.

I shrugged, moving down the hallway. "You're too nice. Be mean."

I caught sight of Tray outside. He was sitting at the table with the rest. Trent was there with Sasha on his lap—still. I think the girl had to have a new lap to sit on whenever she sat down. She was probably worried her own would get bruised or flattened.

I know it's irrational, but I didn't like her. I could think whatever I wanted.

Jasmine and Devon had left. Thank God.

I caught Tray's eyes for a second. His were unreadable, but I veered to his pool-house where I curled up in his bed, slipping underneath the covers. A second later I was asleep.

Blissfully.

I woke up later and checked the time. It was ten in the morning. I had a good six hours of sleep. Rolling over, I saw Tray asleep beside me, his head was turned my way and he had one hand on my leg.

How had I not noticed that?

I tried to get up without waking him to no avail. Tray's eyes opened to small slits when he saw me moving across him.

He grabbed me and pulled me on top of him. "Hey." He nuzzled my neck.

"Hi," I whispered, inhaling his scent. The guy smelled good, even after a night of drinking. How screwed up is that?

"Where are you going?"

"Shower, breakfast, and then home." I listed my destinations off.

"Okay." He yawned, letting me go.

He flipped onto his stomach when I came back from the shower.

I finished dressing and saw in surprise that Tray had already slipped on a shirt without me knowing.

"Where are you going?" I asked, startled.

"Breakfast. With you," he stated, grabbing a pair of pants.

"Oh." I stood uncertainly as I waited for him to finish. I led the way outside, sighing when I saw a few people sleeping off their drunk on the patio loungers. Inside, they were spread out in the hallways and I caught a glimpse of more in one of the living rooms. The kitchen was already being invaded.

Mandy, Amber, Bryce, and Grant were finishing off a box of doughnuts. Honey was awake, sitting at the table. Alone.

Mandy giggled, trying to hide her doughnut behind her hand.

Amber giggled at that and then they both dissolved into laughter.

Honey and Bit had been right.

"Hey, dude," Grant called out, shoving the box our way. "Carter went for treats."

Tray leaned forward to inspect what was left and I bypassed them to sit down beside Honey.

"Hey," I greeted easily, biting back a yawn.

"Hi," she said gratefully.

"Where'd you sleep last night?"

She shrugged, looking away. But I caught the brief glance she'd sent over my shoulder. Following it, I saw that it landed on Bryce, who was currently devouring his second doughnut, grinning at Tray's curse that they'd taken all the good ones.

Hmmm.

Bit liked Bryce.

I wasn't stupid. She had a guilt-ridden, one-night-stand look. It seems like Honey had hooked up with Bryce after I'd left.

"Where's...Lori? Bit."

Honey flushed, crossing her arms over her chest. "She went home last night."

"Right," I said dryly.

"She did."

Whatever. I was going to push straight through. I leaned forward and asked directly, "She know about you and Bryce?"

Honey paled at my words, seemingly shrinking back into her chair. I guess that would be a no.

"You should come clean. Tell her why you did what you did," I said shortly. "Because next time you're at a party, Bryce is gonna remember that you were the girl he hooked up with once. He'll come sniffing around again and he's not going to care who's around or who's going to hear him. Bit's gonna care and you'll be down one friend."

"What are you...why...?" she faltered, taken aback.

"Look, I'm just trying to save you from a lot of extra drama. If you come clean, Bit will understand. Unlike Mandy, I don't have a case of selective amnesia with whoever's higher in the popularity status...you guys were both there for my sister. That means something to me and I'd hate to have you guys get sucked up in this kind of drama. You guys seem solid as friends. That's a good thing. You need friends—good friends."

"Hey, Taryn," Bryce greeted, plopping down in the chair next to mine, throwing an arm around my shoulder. "Where oh where did you disappear to last night?"

"You're an asshole," I said simply, shrugging his arm off.

"What?" he sputtered, more startled than insulted.

"You're an asshole," I said again, pissed. "Do you not even know that you might end a best friendship? Or did you know and you just don't give a damn?"

"Excuse me?" he huffed, now starting to get pissed. "What the hell are you—?"

"You're trying to get a piece of me last night. That didn't work. You knew this other girl at the game liked you. So what do you do? You hook up with her best friend. All because you think you have some God-given right."

"Hey, it's not on me what she did or if her friend likes me—" he started to argue.

I stood up and said simply, "Yes, it is. It's called being responsible and just being a decent human being."

Sasha and Trent chose that moment to walk into the kitchen. Sasha took one look at us and immediately glared.

Trent took one look and left, heading the opposite way.

I grabbed my purse and left behind him. "Trent," I called out, hurrying to catch up with him.

"Taryn, you deserve half the shit that's thrown your way. You know that, right?" he mused, waiting for me.

"How do you figure?" I grinned.

"You could choose better battles, you know."

"I know. I just...get so mad."

"And that's what usually ends you in deeper shit than you can tread," Trent noted.

"Yeah, but I don't care."

"Yeah, but you care about a few of them." He stopped, staring at me. "And that's why you should pick your battles. All your words, they get washed over them, you know. Don't get me wrong, way I got it, that Evans guy can handle anything you send his way. But your sister, she's just another one of those kids that you claim you hate."

"Alright. Fine. Picking better battles, check," I said cockily, tilting my head. "You going to see Geezer today?"

We'd reached his truck and he opened the door. Climbing in, he murmured, "Maybe. I don't know."

"I was thinking of coming out."

"I think you should stay put," Trent said bluntly.

"Why?"

"Because you're at the end of Grayley's rope. Just give him space." Then he started the engine, shut his door, and roared off down the road.

Not many people could leave me standing speechless with my mouth hanging open.

Trent had that effect.

So did Grayley.

Probably why I considered them friends.

The rest of the day passed without event, thank God. Shelley and Kevin had both politely asked how my friend from Pedlam was doing. I filled them in, for the most part.

Mandy returned home later that afternoon. She showered, changed clothes, grabbed her book bag, and had headed back out.

I had been laying on my bed, listening to my iPod. During a break between songs I heard Amber's voice outside the window. Rolling over, I saw Amber was outside in her car. Bryce and Grant were also with them.

Then Mandy walked down the hallway and was outside in a second. I heard her call out, "See you later, Mom. I'll call later, but I'll probably be out for dinner."

Figures. Mandy was tight with Amber again. She'd want to make sure it stayed that way.

I rolled back over onto my back and thumbed the volume up.

After a little while, I'd gotten up, checked my email, and finished up my homework. Now I was bored—which is sad.

Spying my swimsuit, remembering the feeling of swimming yesterday, I grabbed a bag and packed it. Slipping on some flip-flops, I called out, "I'm going swimming."

"What was that, honey?" Shelley came out, smiling warmly.

"I'm going to go for a swim. I think the school has a pool I can use."

"Oh yes! That'd be wonderful. Hold on, let me grab my own suit. I'll come with you."

What...the...oh hell.

My new mother was coming swimming with me. Not my idea of me time.

Emerging from the hallway, she had a bright smile on, and called out cheerfully, "Okay, honey. Let's go."

Shelley drove and I sat in silence. I didn't know what to say, so I didn't say anything. The nice thing was that she knew where the pool was, where to park, and which doors to take.

Turning the car off, Shelley explained, "I used to be a swimmer. So any excuse I have to slip on the old suit, I'm happy for!"

Nice.

"When'd you learn how to swim, Taryn?" she asked.

"When I went to Earlington."

"Oh, that's right," Shelley exclaimed, "you were on the swim team, weren't you? I remember reading that in your file. I was so excited. I thought for sure you'd try out here, but I didn't want to push you."

"Yeah."

"You were on the varsity team, weren't you?"

"No," I said hastily, "I was on J.V. I didn't make it to varsity."

"Still," she said proudly, "you were in the seventh grade. That's quite an accomplishment. Especially for Earlington. They've been the state championships for the past twenty two years. They have an excellent program. I'm sure you'd have no problem making varsity now. Taryn, you could maybe even get a scholarship for school."

Okay. Too fast.

"Uh...I don't know."

"Okay," Shelley was back-pedaling, "whatever makes you happy, Taryn." She put her hand on my arm. "But I must tell you, I'm extremely excited that we've found this bond between us."

The uneasy feeling disappeared the second I walked out and saw the sparkling Olympic-sized pool.

I chose the second highest diving board and performed a tuck, slicing through the water and smoothly cutting through the water to do it again.

It felt like home. God, I'd missed this.

I didn't notice Shelley at all. She might've been watching for a while, but I caught a glimpse of her later on. She was doing laps in the lanes.

I stayed with the diving board for another good hour before I moved on to swimming laps.

It felt right. I let myself enjoy it and pushed harder through the water.

Pulling myself out of the pool, an hour later, I sighed happily. I had missed that, and pushing through the doors, I vowed that I'd keep at it. Who knows. Maybe I would try out for the team.

Shelley was beaming at me the entire drive home. Pulling into the driveway, she cut the engine, but stayed put.

"What?" I asked, resigned to whatever she had on her mind.

"You blew me away, Taryn. I have to tell you that. You really blew me out of the water," she giggled, "but...I just think it's a waste of talent if you don't try out for the team. You've already missed most of this year, but you could still practice with the team. Get to know them. Train with 'em in the off-season. You could be more than ready to compete by next fall. And we could get some scouts to come and watch you."

"Shelley," I said, "I...I don't know...maybe."

Shelley grinned, just giddy, as we walked through the door and inside.

I stopped, seeing Amber and Jasmine in the kitchen with Mandy. Grant and Bryce were sitting on the counters, each with a bag of chips.

"Hey, guys," Shelley called out, "I've missed seeing the old crew."

I beat a hasty retreat.

Pick my battles. It's what I had to do. Even if it meant biting my lip the entire evening—or staying locked in my room.

Stripping out of my wet clothes, I showered, and dressed.

I felt good, strong, as I fell onto my bed, my hand reaching for my iPod.

A little while later I heard a soft knock at my door, and called out, "Come in."

Mandy poked her head around the door, a small smile on her face. "Hey."

I sat up and leaned against my headboard, "Hi."

She came in and closed the door. She sat at the end of my bed uncertainly. "Mom said you guys went swimming together."

"Yeah."

"That's good. I mean...you could join the team."

"Maybe. I don't know."

"Mom said you're really good. Like, really, really good. You could get a scholarship, maybe."

"Yeah."

Could she stop beating around the bush?

"Um..." Mandy fell silent, glancing around the room.

"I don't get it," I said bluntly. "Amber treated you like shit and now you're friends with her and Jasmine again?"

She sighed, tucking a strand of hair behind her ear. "It's not like that. I mean...I've been friends with Amber and Jaz for—forever." She shrugged. "I have to forgive 'em sometime."

"No," I spoke, "you don't."

"Taryn."

"Mandy, you don't. Look, you and me, we're cool. We have to be, we're sisters. But Amber, Bryce, Jasmine—no. I don't want anything to do with them. They treated my sister like shit."

"Bryce didn't."

"No. He treated a girl that listened to you cry for hours last night like a sex toy and we both know it. He used her and discarded her—knowing full well that her best friend has a thing for him and knowing full well that she'd let him use her because she wants to be popular." I stood up. "I think it's disgusting."

"Like you're any better," Mandy cried, standing up. "You judge—you judge my friends."

"You're right. I left my friends behind when I moved here, but I'm trying to make up for it. So give me a break with that. But I'm not like you guys with how you use people. You take advantage of them."

"And if they were us, they'd do exactly the same thing. They'd be taking advantage of us."

"It doesn't make it right," I clipped out. Standing firm in my belief.

Mandy left and I heard the door click shut, the sound echoing in my head.

Maybe life would be easier if I just avoided it.

CHAPTER TEN

Mandy and I had come to a stand-still. An impasse. That night, Mandy stuck around with the rest of the group. Devon had stayed away. Sasha had been called over. And I heard Tray and Carter's voice downstairs at one point.

I stayed upstairs the entire time.

Shelley had knocked on my door, asking if I wanted any supper, but I declined.

Instead, I'd finished my homework for Monday, Tuesday, and started a paper that was due at the end of the term.

See. Avoiding people does have some benefits.

I'd heard Shelley and Kevin say their goodnights and a moment later, Shelley poked her head back through. "Hey, wanted to say goodnight. And don't forget to just ask the coach tomorrow. It doesn't hurt. If anything you might make some friends you can train with."

I nodded and said goodnight back. Kevin waved over Shelley's shoulder before they both moved on.

About an hour later, I heard another knock before the door swung open and Tray slipped through.

I didn't say anything. Neither did he. But I did move over as he crawled onto the bed, lying beside me.

We stared at each other for a moment. Tray lifted a hand and tucked a strand of hair behind my ear, his fingers smoothed out the rest of my hair before sliding down to my arm, then down to my waist.

I closed my eyes and leaned forward, finding his lips with mine. I felt myself melting into him. He traced my lips with his, then swept inside. I moved my arm around him, and twisted one of my legs around his, pulling him tighter against me. He caressed my leg, keeping it locked around him.

I sighed, moving back as Tray rose above me.

Hearing my phone ring, I groaned, my mouth still fused with his.

"Leave it," he murmured, trailing kisses down the side of my face to my neck. Then farther down, bringing a grin to my face.

Dazed, I numbly grabbed for my phone and raised it to my eyes. I saw a number I didn't recognize. "What the..." I mumbled.

Tray reached for my phone and stuck it inside a drawer in my nightstand as his lips met mine again, more insistent this time.

I complied and wrapped my arms around his neck as he pressed me back into the pillows.

Breathing hard, awhile later, Tray called a halt to our make-out session, sitting up in bed. Staring at me, he said hoarsely, "If we don't stop now, we won't be stopping for the rest of the night."

"I know." I sighed. Everyone was still downstairs, not that that would've put a damper on us, but...the parents, not to mention Austin. He was a smart eighth grader, but he was still an eighth grader. He might think he knows shit, but I'd rather him not learn it from me.

Tray ran a hand through his hair, regarding me wryly.

I chuckled and gasped, feeling him suddenly lift me in the air and settle me against his chest, with him resting against my headboard. He placed me before him, one hand against my stomach.

"This is new," I murmured.

I felt Tray grin into my hair, his face resting against mine. "Yeah. I'm not after sex all the time. Just most the time."

I grinned. "I am."

He chuckled softly. "You also like to hide in my bed."

"The activities make it tempting. It's Pavlonian."

"You're telling me."

Hearing a beeping sound, I remembered my phone and pulled it out. Checking my missed calls, I saw Kerri's name flash across the screen. She hadn't left a message though, so I put it back.

"Not someone you want to talk to," Tray noted.

"More like...just confused as to why she's calling. We're not really close."

"She's one of your friends from Pedlam."

"Yeah. Somewhat."

"You and Mandy are fighting."

I grinned. "And see I was thinking you were coming up to get some quick and easy action. But now...now I know the real reason you came up here. Mandy sent you, didn't she?"

"Guilty. Except she didn't. Believe it or not, I came up for some quick and easy action."

"Mmmm. I always fall for the romantic guys," I mocked with a dreamy look. "They just get me right here." I patted my chest.

"Your breasts."

"My heart, you ass."

Tray chuckled, tightening his arms around me. "Actually, I came up because it was either this or listening to Amber, Jasmine, and Mandy rehash the latest SNL skit that made fun of Paris Hilton."

"I'm touched. You chose me."

"Well, I'd like to think we've started a tradition over the past few nights. It'd be heartless of me not to keep that tradition going."

"And what is that?"

"Me and you. In bed."

I laughed at that one.

"Except tonight," I pointed out. "We will not be progressing as we have in the past."

"Such fond memories." He sighed, resting his cheek against my head.

"I feel like it happened just yesterday. Imagine that," I scoffed, laughing.

Suddenly we heard a knock at my door, followed by Carter's voice, "Dude. You dressed?"

"Oh my—get in here," I called out. "I don't need my parents thinking we wouldn't be dressed in here."

"Sorry." Carter grinned, shrugging as he closed the door behind him. "I figured I'd take my chances on you guys."

"They're still talking about Paris Hilton?" Tray asked, running a hand down my knee, which was resting over his.

"Nah, dude, now they're talking about that witch show. *Charmed* or something."

I grinned. "Carter, I bet you a mil that if I were to look in your computer, you'd have every episode on iTunes."

"Would not," he scoffed uncomfortably.

"Should we go?" Tray saved him, glancing at the clock on my nightstand. "It's midnight."

"Yeah, sure." Carter stood up gratefully. Tray paused, once, to meet my eyes before he left, pulling the door shut behind him. A few minutes later I heard them leave through the front-door and climb into Tray's SUV.

I recognized the sound of its engine.

Monday dawned bright and early. Mandy, as usual, had left for school long before I'd even stepped foot in the kitchen. She was an early bird, and me, I'd like to aspire to be one of them. Someday.

But today I got the joyous opportunity of dropping Austin off at his school. Mom and Dad didn't approve of his little buddies, so I got stuck with a pissed off eighth grader. My 'have a good day' was met with a middle finger.

That made my day.

Parking in my usual spot, I realized school had a different light to it. For some reason, I felt more...comfortable. Don't ask me why.

Larkins met me on the lawn, as usual.

"Hey, Ice Bitch."

There was my God-given name.

"Hey, Larkins. You get some action Friday night?" I teased, but was met with a flush. I raised my eyebrows. "You did, didn't you?"

He shrugged, shoving his hands in his front pockets. "Yeah, well, we had fun. It was a fun party."

"You called her the next day, right?" I asked, watching him intently.

"Huh?" Larkins asked, confused.

"You got action, you should've called her."

"I wouldn't call you."

"I'm not Molly Keeley," I pointed out. "You have to treat her differently than you would me. Or girls like me."

"I didn't call her." He paled.

Well. What'd I expect?

"I'll take care of it," I assured him. "You do want me to take care of it, right?"

"Yeah. Yeah. That would be awesome," he insisted gratefully.

I saw his hackey-sack buddies waiting in the background. "Your buds look impatient."

"Oh," he murmured, nodding again. "Thanks, Ice Bitch. Thanks."

"Larkins."

"Yeah?" He turned back.

"The name's Taryn. Anyone else call me what you do would be in the hospital by now," I murmured, bypassing him into school.

When I entered the school, there were no homecoming signs to greet me. There was a God.

But—hell—I just saw a poster for state championships plastered on the wall. It was decorated with little footballs, pompoms, and each jersey number of the players.

That's right. They won Friday night. That meant—off to play-offs we go.

Whatever. I weaved my way through a crowd of sophomore gawkers. They were, I hate to admit that I even noticed this, staring at Bryce and Grant. Who were in turn, staring at Jasmine and Mandy.

Remember the day when I broke into school and fucked with the alarm system? All to distract my sister from school gossip?

I was a moron.

I opened my locker and reached for my first period textbook when I felt someone beside me.

It was Molly. With brand new microscope glasses.

"Hey. I like the pink," I noted.

"Tray Evans had a party Saturday night and you Did. Not. Call. Me."

Guess she didn't like the pink frames.

"Sorry," I said lamely.

"Or was Friday night you're one charitable moment?" she continued sarcastically.

"Hey, sorry. I had things on my mind," I said softly, moving towards my class.

Molly let out an exasperated breath as she turned the opposite way.

As I walked into first period, I saw Mandy and Amber. Of course. I loved having Mandy in most of my classes, especially when she chose loser traitorous friends over godly loyal ones.

"Morning, class," Mrs. Tationa, our humanities teacher, spoke.

We were reading *Of Mice and Men*. Which I'd already read, and watched the movie.

I couldn't help but glare at Mandy as we pulled our books out.

Talk about friendship and sacrifice.

Amber raised her hand. "Mrs. Tationa, Mandy and I were wondering if we could be excused. We'd like to finish up some posters before the pep rally this week."

"Oh, Amber, of course—" the teacher was about to say, but I interjected, "Are you kidding me?!"

"Taryn," my teacher reprimanded, startled.

I ignored her and turned to Amber. "You're not even on the pep rally committee—and trust me—I know. I live with the president of the pep rally committee. Two, you're not a cheerleader. And three, if anyone should benefit from this discussion—it's you!"

"Taryn!" Mandy screeched, pale. "Shut. Up."

"No," I cried out, pissed—beyond pissed. "I'm sick and tired of you guys running around this school like it's your personal playground. All the teachers just let you guys get away with whatever you want. I'm so tired of it."

Someone snorted behind me. "Aren't you being hypocritical?"

I turned around and saw some guy in a polo shirt glaring at me. "What?"

"You're one of them," he pointed out. "Have *you* ever been in trouble for anything?"

"I got sent to the principal's office for 'assaulting' Sasha Klinnleys and Justin Travers."

"And from what I heard, the teacher got in trouble. Not you," he muttered, disgusted. "Aren't you dating Tray Evans?"

"No," I remarked.

Amber scoffed, "Then whose bed were you in this weekend?"

"We're not dating," I said firmly. We weren't. Hello. Screwing around and dating are totally different.

"Whatever," Amber shot out. "You get on your high horse about us—we don't do half the shit that you do."

I went livid at that one.

"Excuse me?" I asked softly, my eyes narrowed.

"Like it was just 'by chance'," air quotes, "that the Monday after Mandy and Devon break up, our school gets canceled. Just a pure coincidence, I'm sure!" she cried out sarcastically. "And I wonder how Pedlam got broken into. Seriously. Doesn't Pedlam have some tight security? And someone just *happened* to break in and mess up their stuff."

"Amber," Mandy hissed.

But Amber was pissed. "And Friday night. Where were you? Not at the game. Not with your 'boyfriend' who you asked to take two of your 'charitable' cases to Carter's party."

"You got something to say?" I asked, through gritted teeth. I was so holding back. My nails were cutting into my arms, there'd be blood pretty soon.

"We heard some evidence got destroyed. My cousin's a cop in Pedlam," she exclaimed.

I laughed. And I knew it sounded awful, but I was beyond caring. I had started this, yes, but the girl had to go down.

I stood and said tightly, "You've got some fucking nerve."

"Whatever." Amber rolled her eyes, but she'd said her piece. She had nothing else, and we both knew it. Unless she pulled in Brian, which she knew next to nothing. But, then again, I hadn't realized how public the other stuff had become. Tray knew. He was the only one, and if he sang—he'd be singing himself. Not just me.

"Let's talk about you, Amber, and how you parade yourself around this school, like it's for you to pick and choose who to be nice to and who to torture. You sway down these hallways, acting like you're the shit and everyone had better be nice or you'll make their lives hell. Trust me, it's not gonna work on me," I promised, the teacher had lost control a long time ago. "You're a piece of shit just for how you act in this school, but what really gets me—is how two-faced you've been with Mandy. Jasmine screwed Devon—for a fucking year—and you knew, the whole time."

It was a hunch, but I saw it was true.

Mandy gasped. She saw it too, just as everyone else did.

I added, seething, "And where the fuck were you when my sister needed her supposed 'best friend'? Not being her best friend, I can assure you. No, instead you were with Jasmine, supporting her skanky-ass ways. Until Saturday, when you *suddenly* decided to be Mandy's friend again. After she'd been comforted for hours by some really great people—people who, you decide to just walk all over and use then throw away and treat them like they're garbage the next day."

"What Bryce did—" Amber began.

I cut in harshly, "What Bryce did is what each and every one of you do...every goddamn day at this school!" I glanced at the class and noted a lot of affirming nods. "I bet if I asked this class how many of them had been screwed by you guys, I bet half of them would raise their hands. At least. I bet they're all pissed as hell...and hurt. If not more."

Amber glanced around, fearful, seeing similar stares from others.

"You hurt people," I bit out. "You hurt people and you don't care. And it's wrong."

Mandy and Amber were both white, eyes fearful.

"I hurt people," I announced. "But I hurt people like you."

Amber fled the room. Mandy paused, her hand on the doorknob when she turned and took one look at me.

I knew I'd crossed the line, but—fuck—I'd had it with people like them. Even if Mandy wasn't going to stand up for herself, and even if I had to paint her with the same color, this school needed to change.

One way or another.

When they left, I stood uncertainly for a moment, before slumping back into my chair. It was at that time that I realized there were smiles on the other students. Okay, —a few of the 'popular' students—none of the elite—didn't look happy, but I still saw some grudging respect and gratefulness.

And then I remembered—Tray ran this school.

Oh hell.

I didn't have long before I started feeling some of the repercussions. Jasmine glared at me when I left first period. Guess Amber and Mandy had found her. Grant and Bryce were also glaring at me, but not as much as the girls. And Sasha—don't get me started.

When I walked up to my locker, I caught Sasha writing, 'whore' in permanent maker on it.

I grabbed the pen from her hand and smirked. "Your locker's a few down."

"You don't even know what you did. You have no idea," she taunted smugly, grabbing her pen and leaving.

Well—yeah, I did. Because I'd done it at Pedlam too. Yeah. That was the kicker. I'd been the one to cause the two rifts in Pedlam, between Brian's group and Crispin's. Brian had never been the instigator. He'd been the muscle, but the brain—everything else—that was me. And most everyone knew it. Brian was just the mascot.

But I'd been happy letting him stay that way.

Which is probably the real reason why Crispin hates me so much. And why the 'rift' had coincidentally disappeared when I left for Rawley.

The thing was...I hadn't been sleeping with Crispin.

Like I was sleeping with Tray.

This might mess things up—a bit.

"Way to go," Larkins shouted, slapping me on the shoulder as he passed by.

Word did get around fast. I even saw Molly grinning, before ducking behind a locker. I caught a flush in her cheeks—which never happened.

And Honey and Bit. When I turned from my locker, there they were. Smiling. Preening.

"Hey," I greeted half-heartedly.

"We heard," Honey spoke up. "And I told her." She nudged Bit a little. "She's okay. Mad. But we're good. Both of us. And it's only fair if she sleeps with Bryce next time."

I rolled my eyes. That wasn't the point.

I tried to reiterate the point to them, but it was done half-ass. I had to worry about second period and who was in that class.

Wait. I normally went to study hall. Molly told me I actually had health.

"Where's health class?" I asked them.

"Oh." Honey brightened. "We're in health too. Mr. Hauge always says your name in roll call. And of course, someone says you think you have study hall this period. It's turned into this comedy bit actually."

Not today. I followed behind them.

I paused in the doorway before forcing myself to move forward.

Tray was in this class.

And, judging by the look in his eyes, he was angry. Guess he heard about my blow up. And he wasn't happy.

"Miss," Mr. Hauge directed at me, "you are?"

"Taryn Matthews."

"Oh. Miss Matthews, you've finally decided to grace us with your presence. I see someone took it upon themselves to let you know that we are, in fact, not study hall and that you are, if fact, supposed to be here."

"Yeah."

"Good. Good. Take a seat. I see an empty one by Mr. Helms."

I glanced uncertainly at Helms and saw a look of disgust pass over his eyes. Abruptly he stood up and announced, "I'll sit with Tray."

So I got my own table. Yay!

Thank goodness it was behind Honey and Bit.

But before I could sit down, Tray spoke up, "She can sit with me."

Helms froze, about to sit down beside him. He looked at Tray and read something on his face because he didn't say anything when he stood back up and returned to his table.

I met Tray's eyes, saw the fierceness, and figured...probably not a good idea. "I'm good up here."

"Oh no, Taryn," Tray said quickly, "sit with me. Really."

The class was watching, every fricking word, and they loved it. Honey and Bit's eyes were as wide as saucers. Molly squeaked from her seat, which was parallel to Tray's table.

So I sat at Tray's table—reluctantly. Tray flicked his gaze to Mr. Hauge, who must've taken it as a command to start, because he immediately started class then.

Tray sat rigidly next to me. I could feel the tension in his body.

I stole a few glances his way, but was met with a cold, even stare back. Tray was quite fine glaring at me during the entire class. I gave up trying to win the staring contest, mostly because I got weirded out.

I couldn't help but remember Jace's words about Tray.

"He's not another Brian, Taryn. Remember that."

"Meaning that my obsessive ex is the lesser of the two evils." I had joked at the time.

I looked at Tray again. Nope. This was all on me. I didn't have Brian or Jace to hide behind, to protect me. I had to fight this one all on my own.

Mr. Hauge asked the class, "Mrs. Grantlins has asked me to send two volunteers to the counselor's office."

Tray spoke up, "We'll go."

And, of course, that meant me too, because no one else was standing up.

Tray didn't give me time to decide because he simply grabbed my arm and hauled me out of there. Once in the hallway, I wrenched my arm away and snapped, "Ouch."

That's when I was met with the full force of Tray's fury because he grabbed my arm again and yanked me into the empty gymnasium.

"This isn't the way to Mrs. Grantlins' office."

"You don't even know who Mrs. Grantlins' is," Tray snapped, hauling me into the equipment closet. The door was heavy as he slammed it shut. "What the fuck do you think you're doing?!"

"Excuse me?" I asked stiffly. Yeah. The sex had been great, but if it was the price—I'd give it up gladly.

"You know what!" he cut out tensely. "The entire fucking school is going off about you and Amber. You said that we hurt people, that we don't give a shit about them."

"You don't!" I cried out.

Tray shot back, "Neither do you. You are the coldest bitch in this school and now you've decided to be their personal savior?!"

"I care," I yelled back.

"No, you don't. You started caring the second you saw Mandy bending under Amber's influence."

Well...yeah.

"No, I didn't. I'm sick and tired of how—" I started to say.

"Save it for someone who doesn't know you," Tray interrupted rudely, uncaring. "You're pissed because your sister is letting Amber and Jasmine walk all over her. You're trying to fix her problem, like you've always done. You set the alarms to save Mandy from gossip and now—you're covering this by going after all of us."

"Not all of you."

"You said 'people like you.' That means me, my crowd, my people."

"I'm not going after you. This has nothing to do with you."

"Yes, it does," he retorted fiercely. "This is my school, you're messing with my friends."

"No—"

"Mine," he bit out and I remember him saying the exact same thing to Gentley. I remembered feeling the warmth that washed over me at those words. I was his. That's what he implied.

"Look," I spoke a little calmer, "I'm just tired of how Amber seems to get away with everything at this school."

"So do I," he stated.

"I know, but," I faltered, "this isn't about you. About you and me."

"Oh no. You're goddamn right about that one. This has no bearing on you and me."

So he liked the sex too.

Good...I think. I refused to admit that I felt relieved.

"Look, I was just pissed. Amber and Mandy wanted to get out of class for some fucking pep rally posters. I'm tired of how they can do whatever the hell they want. So I said something and then Amber brought my shit up. About the alarms last Monday, about how Pedlam got broken into, and she heard that some evidence got destroyed." I bit my lip. "How'd she know all that?"

"Not from me." Tray sighed, raking a hand through his hair. I hated how, even now, I was feeling the warmth, remembering what it felt like—what he felt like. God, he was freaking gorgeous. And those lips...his shoulders...

"She aired my shit so...I went after her," I finished.

"But—hell!—Taryn. You went after me in the same second."

"I went after Amber, Jasmine, Devon and Bryce. Well...more Amber, Jasmine, and Bryce—because of how they've treated Mandy and how Bryce played with Honey and Bit."

"Who the fuck are Honey and Bit?" he asked wearily.

"I don't know their real names. That's what I call 'em."

"You mean the chick that Bryce screwed at my party?"

"Well...yeah, but how can you condone how they just use people?"

"Are you kidding me?" Tray gave me an exasperated look. "You want me to start making my friends saints?"

"No, I just..."

"What? Only be saintly to Mandy and the people you've befriended?" he asked shrewdly. "Holy hell, do you realize how hypocritical you are? You've got serious history with the biggest drug-runner in Pedlam. You used to date a guy that roughed up a girl."

"I was pissed. I spoke up. What do you want from me?"

"I don't know. A clarification. Who you're condemning? Who you're not," he said sarcastically. "You're sleeping with me and I run steroids, not to mention—the town doesn't let the Lansers do business here."

I sighed, turning away to rest my head against the wall. I didn't know what to say. I'd opened a can of worms, but—hell—I wasn't one to sit back and let stuff slide by. Not if I was pissed enough and could stop it. Or, to be more accurate, if I even wanted to stop it. Tray was right, I let a lot of stuff by because I didn't care about it. But this time, I'd cared. So I'd opened my mouth.

"How do you do that?" I asked, quietly. "Jace told me...he told me to watch out for you."

"Great. That coming from a drug lord." Tray snorted, rolling his eyes.

"He's not a drug lord."

"No, he's a drug dealer. A lot more prestigious," he said sarcastically.

"Jace is—"

"Jace is someone you should stay away from. He might care about you, but he's not going to change. And one day he's going to end up in prison or dead."

That was enough. "And how do you know so goddamn much?" I cried out, frustrated. The guy was insufferable.

"I know. Trust me."

"But how? I don't understand—it's like you're—one of them."

"I am," he remarked.

"You run steroids, but you won't let the drug-runners in town. I don't get it—how can you keep drugs out of Rawley?"

"It's not that." He sighed, raking a hand through his hair. "I just don't let Jace Lanser come in here."

"But how?" I asked dumbly.

"My dad used to be the chief of police here and my older brother's with the DEA. I know both sides, trust me. I know where to step and where not to step." Tray relented, sitting on a roll of wrestling mats against the wall. Bracing his elbows on his knees, he said further, "That's why I won't let Jace Lanser come into Rawley and it's why he stays away."

"Jace said something...that you run the interstate intersection?"

He grinned, resting against the wall behind him. "Yeah, more like I just know which cops to call and which not to. Plus, I've got some buddies that like to rough people up. They're always good for sending after someone."

"I don't know...," I shifted on my feet, confused, "if I understand."

"Do you have to?" he asked me, his eyes piercing mine.

"Why steroids?"

"Because," he sighed, "in the beginning, they pissed my dad off."

I sighed, and moved to sit in front of him. Tray pulled me back against his chest and wrapped his arms around me. I laid my head on his chest.

"So...what now?" I asked, both of us knowing what I referred to.

"I don't know," he murmured.

"I'm not going to be good with Amber and Bryce. Or Jasmine and Devon. Hell no."

"Is it Mandy? Or do you just have to piss off all my friends?"

"I go after those that hurt the ones I love. If Mandy's going to lay down and let them roll over her—fine. But I won't. And if she expects me to act nice, fuck no."

"They're expecting me to put you in your place," he mentioned, one hand caressing my leg.

"So what do you want me to do? I'm not backing down. That's not me."

"I know, but it's going to make things a lot tenser with the group."

"Why? It's not like I'm exactly friends with you guys." I turned to face him, his hands moving to my waist.

"I know. But I like to be with you as much as possible." He grinned.

I rolled my eyes, but I couldn't contain the faint grin that tugged at my lips.

"I just don't like how they treat people."

"And we've covered this already," he said wearily.

"We're supposed to be volunteering at Mrs. Grantlins'," I reminded him. Waiting.

"Mrs. Grantlins asked for volunteers from a bunch of other classes. She's moving furniture in her office. I'm not volunteering for that," he said disgustedly.

"And we're doing exactly what I just lit into Amber about doing," I commented, frustrated.

"No. We're skipping. I'm not asking to get away with it. If I do—which usually happens—then fine. I'm not passing it up." Tray grinned, running his hands up my arms and back down to my waist. He pulled me closer to him and leaned forward, nuzzling my neck.

I melted. I wrapped my arms around his neck. The conversation was officially over.

Tray kissed his way up my neck, along my chin, and found my lips.

I lifted my legs and turned to straddle him. Tray slid a hand down my back, slipping it inside my jeans, then up my back, moving to softly caress my breast, underneath my bra.

"—this place is usually—whoa."

Tray heard them first because he lifted his eyes and said simply, "Out."

I hid my face in his neck. Glad Tray kept his arms around me, otherwise I might've fallen off. I didn't trust my legs to work, not at that moment.

"Dude." It was Bryce, and I could hear the grin in his voice.

A second later the door clicked shut and Tray nuzzled my neck again.

I moved to find his lips and we started kissing again as if nothing had happened.

When the bell rang, I pulled away and stood—unsteadily. Tray held onto my elbow for a little bit.

"I'm good."

"This isn't just for you," he retorted, breathing heavily.

I chuckled, feeling some relief that he was affected just as much as I was. A moment later we left the equipment closet, and once we were in the hallway, we went our separate ways. Tray's locker was near the quad in the senior hallway. It was the best place for a locker because there was a ton of benches over there, and it was the hub where students just hung out. My locker, on the other hand, faced the parking lot entrance. It was almost impossible to relax or talk with anyone because so many students were either walking into school or leaving.

I did notice Amber's heated glare when Tray turned down his hallway. She was leaving the bathroom and saw his hand linger for a moment on my elbow.

At my locker, I found Sasha waiting for me.

"What?" I snapped, ready to go another round with her.

"You think you're so damned better than us. You're not. You're a whore," she delivered without preamble.

I sighed, and gave her a pointed glare. "I'm really good at finding out people's secrets. Want me to find out yours?"

"Are you threatening me?"

"I'm warning you. If you want me to come after you, keep it up. It'll work and when that happens, you'll find out why guys like Crispin Gentley hate me so much."

Sasha just perched her hands on her hips and looked at me with derision. But it worked. She shut up and, after a second huff, she turned and marched down the hallway.

"The only reason you're still breathing." Came from behind me. I turned and saw Amber glaring, she said hotly, "Is because Tray must really like being in your pants. The second he's tired of you, you need to remember th`is time. Because this is me, promising that you'll be begging to change schools when that time comes. Take that as a guarantee."

"You heard me say my deal to Sasha," I remarked, heatedly. "But that was a warning. You, I'm already coming after. So you better remember this day, because this is my promise to you—you're going to learn what a bitch like me can do."

We both knew students were stopping to watch us, but neither of us acknowledged them.

I'd had my say. Amber had her say.

Now neither of us were willing to be the first one to walk away.

Grant saved us because he walked up and merely dragged Amber behind him. But she wasn't protesting at all, she just glared at me until he hauled her around the corner.

Now I realized why I felt comfortable here. It was just like back at Pedlam.

I grabbed my textbook and hurried into third period where I slipped into an empty seat in the back. I'd purposely sat amongst the potheads. They reminded me of Geezer and I drew some strength from that.

Walking through the hallways, so many people had sent greetings my way, I thought I had something plastered on my back, like a target or something. But no. They seemed relieved. Grateful. Fourth period was biology. And Molly was almost squealing from her excitement. Guess she'd always hated Amber. Which, I gotta tell you, was a surprise. I knew that I didn't like Amber, but I never realized how much everyone else hated her, too.

Guess Amber was the reigning bitch in this school. I always thought it had been Jasmine, but I guess not.

Molly filled me in, "No one's wanted to say anything bad about Amber. When Jasmine and Tray broke up, Amber was vicious to Jasmine. Jasmine left school crying a few times and she even quit the cheerleading squad. But that was last year and Amber quit too. I heard that Amber even got Jasmine thrown into a psych ward. She called the police and said she was Jasmine and that she wanted to kill herself. Jasmine's parents didn't believe her, so she got put on a seventy-two hour observation."

"You have to be making some of this up," I murmured.

"And one time, in seventh grade, Amber made Carter Sethlers date Sabrina Lyles because she knew Mandy liked him. So that's why Mandy and Devon started dating. Amber didn't want Carter dating Mandy."

"That doesn't even make sense."

"It doesn't have to. Amber is crazy."

"Yeah, but...that's psychotic. She doesn't strike me as a psycho."

"But she is. Amber is capable of anything, that's why everyone's scared of her."

Everyone except Tray apparently. Oh, and me.

"And one time," Molly insisted, leaning closer, whispering, "Amber called the police on Mandy's thirteenth birthday party because she didn't invite Amber. They'd had a fight over Bryce. Amber caught her and Bryce kissing in a closet at her own birthday party."

The girl had control issues.

This was how my entire fourth period went.

Normally I sat alone at lunch. So I was more than surprised when I entered the cafeteria and saw my usual table filled. Honey, Bit, Molly, Larkins, and a bunch of the potheads. I glanced at Mandy's table and saw Grant, Bryce, and Devon. No Tray.

Suddenly, I felt his hand wrap around my own. "Come on," he said, pulling me behind him as he walked us back through the hallways.

"Where are we going?" Notice I wasn't protesting, I just wanted to know. It was quite alright with me not to be in that cafeteria. I did see a few disappointed looks when we left.

"We're skipping the rest of the day," he answered, pulling out his keys as we approached his SUV.

This is not the brightest idea in Plan: Stay Out of Trouble. Again, notice that I wasn't protesting.

I climbed into the passenger seat and buckled up.

The drive was quiet when we pulled up to his house.

Instead of heading to his pool-house, Tray grabbed my hand and led me into the kitchen. He threw his keys on the marble counter and opened the fridge. From inside, he asked, "You want some pizza?"

"Not really hungry."

He pulled out a pizza box and a Diet Coke. Placing the can in front of me, he warmed up two slices of pizza for himself.

I grabbed a glass and put some ice in it.

Tray hopped on a counter and ate his pizza.

I drank my pop. All was silent. Both of us just staring at each other.

When he finished, he put his dish away and asked, "Want to watch a movie?"

"Sure." I followed him downstairs, remembering his suggestion Saturday morning. He'd offered to watch a movie that night, guess he hadn't planned on throwing a party.

I was amazed again at the size of the media room. Curling up next to him, I felt his arm wrap around me while he turned the TV on and chose a movie. Tray must've figured I didn't care, because he chose the latest action-filled suspense thriller on his TiVo.

After the second car chase, I yawned and nestled closer against him, feeling his hand slip around my waist.

"Tray," I mumbled tiredly.

"Hmm?" He sounded distracted.

"What are we doing?"

I felt his body stiffen so I rephrased, "I mean, we're skipping school. We're watching a movie. We're not messing around. We're not talking. What are we doing?"

"We're hiding. Thought that was your thing."

"It is." I sat up. "Sometimes."

"Thought I'd hide with you today." He grinned, tracing a finger down my cheek to my lips, where he traced their outline before leaning in for a lingering kiss.

I'm all about not protesting today.

Before the kiss could go further, I pulled away and asked, "Seriously, what's going on?"

"I just don't feel like dealing with Amber and those guys."

"And if they pushed?"

I waited, fully noticing that he paused before answering.

"Then," he shrugged, "I don't know."

"Do they know about your dad and your brother?" I asked suddenly, a thought forming in my head.

"They know about my dad—everyone knows about my dad—but not my brother."

"Why not?"

"Because I don't go around telling people my business. And because he was already in college when we moved here," Tray replied, watching me intently, gauging me.

"So why'd you tell me?"

"Because you understand that stuff," he said simply. "Why do we have to have a fucking conversation about it?"

"Because I want to," I simply said right back. "And because you know a lot of my shit—I should know your shit."

"And what happens when we're done screwing? My stuff goes public?" he asked roughly.

My eyebrows raised at that one. "You see that happening?"

"When we're done with this? Or my life going public?"

"Both."

And that was the crux of it. Tray didn't want to answer that. I could see he didn't want to answer that. So I did it for him.

"I'm not into talking about—what we have going on—that's not me. But...your life won't go public. I can guarantee that."

"And I should just trust you?" he asked shrewdly.

I shrugged. "I think I've already proven you can trust me...with a lot of shit." Which reminded me... "Do you still have the PRS-500?"

"Uh...yeah. Why? You want it back?"

"Yeah." I wanted those codes. Just because I didn't want him to have it, didn't mean I didn't want them. It's why I had Geezer hide everything.

"It's useless anyway. It only showed the building's security codes—I'm sure those have been changed by now."

"I still want it. Geezer wants to study it." It was only a half-lie. Geezer might've wanted to study it, but he'd never asked. No chance in hell I was going to give him the opportunity.

Tray was studying me intently. When wasn't he? But this time I knew he was checking to see if I was lying. So I held firm and was rewarded with a small sigh. "Fine. I'll get it when we leave."

"Thanks."

"The deal was for you to get the PRS-500 for me. We never talked about me giving it back."

"Well, we just did," I stated.

Tray ran a hand down my back and pulled me closer. I knew where this was going, so I put a hand to his chest and pulled back. "Hold on."

"What?"

"You know my shit," I reminded him, not really knowing if it was needed, but... "So I'm just telling you—your stuff goes public, I know my stuff will go public."

"Can we stop talking about the possible consequences if this," pointing to me and him, "ends?"

"Sure." I leaned forward and kissed him, feeling his hand run down my back, and then lifting me up and onto his lap. I complied and turned to straddle him, his hands falling to my thighs, where he caressed them, moving up and down. I melted, my bones turned to liquid as I leaned against him, one of my hands running through his hair. I tilted my head back and sighed, my eyes closed, as he kissed down to my neck and found a spot.

A second later I felt a draft and realized he'd pushed my shirt up and was working it over my arms. I lifted my arms and the shirt was thrown. So I turned to his and soon his landed beside mine.

Meeting his lips again, more urgently, Tray took over and laid me down, with him coming to rest above me.

I loved it.

I grinned, running a hand down his chest, slowly, until my fingers hitched on the inside of his pants, where it was buttoned. I was rewarded with his sharp intake of breath. My fingers flicked the button free and the zipper gave way.

Tray groaned as he swept his hands to my bra and pulled it off, flinging it to the side.

"Fuck," he gasped, resting his forehead against mine.

"What?" I asked, my breathing coming in fast and hard.

"My condoms are in the nightstand."

I swiftly cursed.

"Wait," he said swiftly, standing then disappearing. A second later, grinning in triumph, he waved a condom at me. "Good thing I remembered Bryce left some here."

"Fuck!" I cried out, shoving him away.

"What?"

"I don't want to know where Bryce screwed whoever he screwed," I said hotly, reaching for my bra and shirt.

"Come on, Taryn," Tray reasoned, grabbing my hand and crawling to sit on top of me. "Stop. Come on. I'm sorry, I won't ever utter his name again, not when we're doing this."

"One, that should be a given. And two, only when we're doing this?"

"Oh come on!" Tray cried out, standing and shooting me a glare. "He's my friend. You're—"

"I know," I finally said.

Tray sunk onto the couch beside me. "Taryn, I'm like Bryce. At least I was, before you and me. And I'll probably be like him if you and I—," end, but he didn't want to say the word, "someday in the future." He grinned and then climbed over me.

"You're not like that with me because you wouldn't get away with it," I retorted, folding my arms across my chest. Fully knowing how ridiculous I looked, sulking like a child with Tray straddling me. I even had the pout on my face.

Tray chuckled, grinning down at me. "Yeah, you're right about that. And if I ever did, you'd probably lock me out of my own house and get the cops to arrest me on burglary charges."

He must've seen I was softening because he caught my hands and raised them above my head. Leaning down, his lips a mere centimeter away from mine, he whispered, "But you won't ever do it, because while I'm with you, I won't treat people like that. I fully know how you'd hand me my ass."

I couldn't stop the grin on my face. He swooped in for a kiss, deepening it instantly.

Before long, I was melting all over again, wrapped around him as he slid into me.

CHAPTER ELEVEN

The rest of the day was nice. Tray and I even watched an entire movie. Later, we moved into the pool-house and, of course, spent most of the time fooling around on the couch.

His phone rang a few times—okay—it rang a lot. But Tray put it away after the sixth call. The first few had been the guys, wanting to grab a burger. The last was from Amber. I cringed, hearing her voice on the phone—she wasn't happy.

That was an understatement.

He finally put the phone on silent and left it on the counter. Every now and then we'd hear the voice message alarm, letting us know another person had left a message.

But it went ignored.

We fooled around, watched a movie, swam a bit—we'd started a race, but Tray quit early on. I taunted him as I swam my laps and he cannon-bombed me at different points.

Around ten-thirty that night, I glanced at my phone and realized Mandy had called six times within the past twenty minutes.

Probably wanting to bitch at me. I'd already called home and told Shelley that I was going to Pedlam to check on my friend and that I'd be sleeping at a friend's house tonight.

Tray talked me into staying the night, after all my car was already at school. He might as well just give me a ride there in the morning. I had clothes in my gym locker and he had all the other essentials at his house.

"What?" Tray asked, watching me frown at my phone.

"Mandy called."

"So?" He sat up beside me and grabbed for the phone. "When don't they call? Just ignore it."

"I know," I replied. "But she doesn't call this much; once or twice maybe, not six times in a row."

"So call her," he suggested, "and then once she starts in, hang up."

"Oh and it's so easy," I mocked, shaking my head.

Tray lunged at me, wrapping his arms around me and tossing me back on the couch, him on top of me—his favorite position.

Laughing, I pressed her number on speed-dial as I tried to wrestle my way out of his arms.

"Taryn!" Mandy yelled into the phone. I could hear blaring music in the background.

Holy crap, where the hell was she?

"Where are you?"

"Oh my God, Taryn. We did something really stupid," she scrambled.

"What did you do?" I demanded.

Tray stopped, hearing my tone. He watched as I sat up from him.

"Sasha and Amber went off about you and Tray. How you're just screwing him and that's why you get away with everything you do...and so," she took a deep breath, "Sasha remembered your friend Grayley and how you were so protective of him. And she wanted to get even with you..."

"Yeah?" I encouraged her, a knot of dread forming in my stomach.

"And she remembered that you told her that he hung out at the Seven8, so we asked around and Bryce said the Seven8 was a club in Pedlam...so..."

"You went to the Seven8?!" I cried out, in disbelief.

Oh my God.

"Are you insane?" I added, outraged. "I was joking. I was not serious. The Seven8 is dangerous, Mandy. People go there in masses, girls just don't go there unless they *want* to get assaulted."

"Yeah, well...we kinda figured that out for ourselves."

"Oh, fucking A," I groaned.

I saw Tray moving around the room and realized he was dressing in more formal clothes.

"Can you leave?" I asked, standing also.

"No, um...we're kinda...we're in trouble."

"Oh my God, what kind of trouble?"

"We finally got in and these guys started hitting on Amber and Jasmine. When Bryce tried to step in, they beat him up, Taryn. He can barely walk and he's bleeding everywhere and they won't let us leave."

"Grab one of the bouncers. *Make* them help you."

"We can't move in this place. You don't understand—it's—these guys are keeping us in this corner and no one even knows that they beat Bryce up."

"Are any of the other guys there?"

"Yeah, Grant is here but they won't let him over to us. We haven't seen him since we got here. Amber thinks he got beat up too," she cried out. I could hear a hitch in her voice.

"Oh, fucking hell, I'm coming." I stood up, about to walk out of the room, but Tray caught me and tossed the rest of my clothes at me.

I'd forgotten to finish dressing.

"Hurry. Please," Mandy demanded, hanging up.

Tray had his keys in his hand and waited at the door as I finished dressing.

I swept through the door, darting to his SUV and waited impatiently as he climbed in and backed out of his driveway. When he didn't turn towards the school, I cried out, "What are you doing?"

"You're not going to the Seven8 alone," he stated firmly.

"Jace owns that club. I'll be fine."

"I don't care if God owns that club. You're not going in there alone," he merely said.

I sighed and sat back in my seat, grateful that he was at least speeding down the interstate.

Instead of the normal hour, it only took us forty minutes to get there. Tray parked across the street and I unbuckled my seat belt. "You might want to—" I was about to suggest he stay in the vehicle, but Tray was already out and crossing the street.

As I darted after him, I saw the club's line was around the corner—again. The nightclub was one of the most dangerous clubs around, but for some stupid reason, it was one of the most popular.

Ben was at the front door.

Ben and three other bouncers were manning the front door. Seeing me cross the street, he stepped away from the group. And he folded his arms, an imposing figure, he waited.

"Girl," he murmured, shaking his head, "you shouldn't be here."

"My sister's inside, Ben. She's in trouble."

"Sister?"

"My adopted sister," I clarified. "Is Jace in there?."

"He in a meeting. One that he ain't coming out of. Not even for you, girl."

"Ben!" I cried. "Let us in. I have to help my sister."

"Hold on." He held an arm out, blocking me. "I'll get you some escorts."

A moment later, three burly guys came to the door and Ben lifted his arm up, allowing us entrance—which caused the crowd to swear at us.

I swept inside, uncaring that the escorts weren't even catching up. Tray was right behind me, he had one hand on my elbow and the other through one of my belt-loops. As I stopped just inside the largest area, I could see why Mandy was trapped in a corner. The place was overcrowded to maximum occupancy and probably over the max. If there was a gunshot or a fight, either no one would ever know, or there'd be a riot to the door. More than a handful would probably be trampled to death, trying to get out of the way.

Tray stood right behind me, one arm around my waist, protecting me from the crowd.

"I can't see them," I shouted in his ear frantically. Then I saw Krein—thank God. He was laughing with a guard in front of him, a girl at his side, and two guards behind him.

"Krein!" I screamed over the crowd. It was a fricking miracle that he heard me because he lifted his head, scanning the crowd. A moment later he spotted me, shock on his face before he moved towards us.

Raking his eyes over Tray, measuring him up, Krein grasped my arm and shouted in my ear, "What are you doing here? Jace would freak. Tonight is not the night to be here."

"My sister's in trouble. Some guys won't let her and her friends leave."

"What does your sister look like?"

I pulled out my phone to show him a picture of her.

Krein grabbed my arm and led the way. I tried to see, but I couldn't see anything. There were too many people blocking my view, but I held onto him. A few times he stopped and shoved his way through, one time he grabbed a guy with his arm, neatly twisting him in the other direction as he tried to grab for me.

The place was beyond chaos tonight.

Tray was backing me up, blocking any advances from behind, keeping his fingers inside my belt loop so we wouldn't be separated.

Another time, Tray and Krein both restrained two guys that were fighting. One of them swung at the other and almost fell into me.

Finally, I saw Mandy standing behind a tall, lanky guy with tattoos riddling his body. There were four more, all positioned in a way that kept Mandy and the rest in, but didn't alert anyone watching that they were being held against their will.

"Mandy!" I screamed.

I saw Bryce in the corner, laying on a table. She was right, he was covered in blood and the bruises were already starting to swell.

Fuckers.

I'd never thought Sasha and Amber would be relieved to see me, but then again, they were probably relieved to see Tray and Krein, followed by five guards.

The four guys were quickly hauled off to a side hallway.

I grabbed Mandy in a hug and then turned to follow the guards, just behind where they took the four guys.

We were in the hallway leading to Jace's office, but we were taken to a different area. It was a large open room, with a few bare tables loitering in the middle. At one side there was a bar and a fridge.

I'd never been in there before and it was...scary.

"Tray!" Amber cried out, throwing herself at him.

Mandy couldn't even say anything. She just broke down, sobbing in a puddle.

Gesturing to Bryce, Krein asked me, "You want him taken to a hospital?"

"Uh," I glanced at Tray, who looked him over and said, "Nah. He'll live. My car's outside."

Sasha sat down beside us, shaking. "Tray, thanks for coming."

Krein snorted at her before turning to talk privately with some of the guards.

A moment later, a door opened and Jace entered, stopping short when he saw the crowd.

"What the fuck?" he demanded. He hadn't seen me yet. "Krein! What the hell? I told you no fucking parties. Tonight's not the night. Galverson's here."

Krein smiled tightly and then gestured to me.

Jace's gaze swung in my direction, and froze.

"Taryn," he murmured, seemingly paralyzed.

Just then Tray stepped forward. "We'll take Bryce out."

"Evans," Jace regarded him stiffly.

Tray gave him a tight nod in return, his eyes meeting mine for a second before he put an arm around Bryce and helped him out.

"Krein," I spoke up, "we have another friend in there."

"My brother," Amber spoke up. "Can I go with you?"

Krein waited for Jace's approval.

Jace nodded, jerking a thumb in their direction. "Take her with you, find her brother. And then get all of them out of here."

Amber took one last look at Jace, raking her eyes up and down his body, before following Krein and two other guards.

Sasha was studying Jace intensely.

"What are you doing here?" Jace asked me, looking pissed.

"My sister and her friends were here. They were in trouble." It didn't mean to sound like an accusation, but it came out that way anyway.

Jace took it as one, too. He grimaced slightly, before he replied, "Tonight's the first night of play-offs and there's three conventions in town."

"Who's Galverson?" I asked, my gaze unwaveringly.

Jace's jaw clenched. "No one you need to worry about."

"I can find out," I returned smoothly.

"No. You won't," he said swiftly. "And thanks for beating the shit out of my little brother."

"He asked for it," I shot back.

"He's been...impossible since."

"And you expect me to apologize for that?" Right now, at that moment, it was incredibly hard to remember why I loved Brian. And why so much had been covered up with Jace.

Because right now, at that moment, I was blistering furious.

And Jace knew it.

Handing Mandy to Sasha, I stalked towards him. "I'm thinking you know some stuff because there's a whole lot going on that doesn't add up."

"Taryn," he said warily, "I don't have time for this right now."

I grabbed his arm and whirled him back to me. "What's been going on since I left? Nothing's making sense, Jace. Brian never used to be this psychotic. Geezer's dad is back in town. Grayley's—shit—Grayley looks like he's aged ten years." Then remembering Ben's words, I continued, "And what meeting were you in that you wouldn't leave? Who's Galverson?"

"Taryn," he said sternly, "leave it alone. I mean it."

It stung a little hearing him call me Taryn. Jace never called me Taryn, I've been Terry to him.

"But—"

"You. Will. Leave. This. Alone," he bit out through clenched teeth, his eyes fierce.

"Hey, Jace, we got him. His sister took him outside, Ben's waiting by the back door for Taryn and the rest," Krein called out, walking back in.

Jace whirled and briskly ordered, "Get 'em out."

Pausing, hearing Jace's voice, Krein glanced to me, then back to Jace. His eyebrows arched as he waited. When nothing more was said, he commanded softly, "Alright, Tartar. Let's go."

I stared at his back as he walked away, slamming the side door behind him. The sound echoed.

"Dick," Sasha mumbled from behind me.

Breaking out of my reverie, I turned and saw her helping Mandy.

"Come on," I murmured, leading the way out.

Krein stood uncertainly at the door, holding it open for us.

"Taryn— " he started, but stopped and looked away.

Krein was the joker; he was the badass who played pranks, the guy everyone loved at first sight, but that façade was gone and in its place was the reason why he was Jace's second in command—it was cold and ruthless mixed with regret.

And it hit me. Right then, right there...so much had happened that didn't make sense. My life had been irreversibly changed. And I knew—it didn't make sense.

Nothing made sense anymore.

As I turned and started to walk across the street, I knew. They'd done something. It involved me. It involved Brian. It involved Geezer and Grayley. And it was Jace who had done it.

As the realization started to come clear, I felt the fury build inside. My hands started shaking with each step that took me farther away. Each dull thud my feet made on the pavement.

And I glanced back. Once. I saw Krein still standing there, an arm hanging on the door.

Jace had done something.

And I'd take him down. Because, in that moment, I knew that he had fucked with my life.

We went to Pedlam Hospital. Which was ironic, at least I thought so. While Bryce and Grant were getting checked out, with the rest of the girls too—I slipped up the side stairs, towards Geezer's room. Tray watched me go, so I figured he'd guess where I was. We'd be there awhile anyway. It's the ER, they're always busy.

I waited for a nurse to open the locked door and I caught it just as she turned the corner. Sneaking through, I silently walked down the hallway, seeing Geezer's door was slightly ajar. I could hear the television on, more in the background and he was talking to someone on the phone.

"Dude. I know, but it's not right. Taryn has a right to know. I know, but—just—you promised, man."

The curtain was pulled so he didn't see my shadow enter.

Geezer moaned, "That's not fair. Look, I'm just saying...I won't tell her, alright. Fuck that." He slammed the phone down, swearing swiftly.

Then I stepped around the curtain.

Geezer hadn't seen me. He was staring out the window, replaying whatever conversation had just taken place.

And then he turned his head, and our eyes locked.

He looked paralyzed.

I was furious.

"Taryn—"

I cut him off, coldly, "You're going to tell me. You're going to tell me everything. Right now."

"I can't, Taryn," he began, almost desperately, "I can't...they'll—"

"You're going to tell me because if you don't I'll send your dad straight back to prison."

Geezer cared about three things: getting high, his father, and his friends.

Threatening his life was useless. Geezer didn't care how he went out, as long as he was high when it happened. His dad, however, was another story. He still held out hope that they'd have some relationship, that his dad would love him one day. He knew I'd follow through with my threat without a second thought.

I'd never do the first. It would've been an empty threat, but this one—both of us knew it was the truth.

"If I say anything, they'll kill him, Taryn."

"If you don't tell me, he's dead either way. They'll just get him in prison," I returned evenly.

"Taryn," he begged, tears brimming in his eyes, "I can't. You don't understand—"

"I don't know what, not yet, but I know something's going down. So much doesn't add up, Geezer, and I'm beyond furious. I will figure it out," I promised, my eyes glittering with fury in the moonlight.

Geezer caught in his breath, staring at me, and he weighed his options.

He choked out, "Brian didn't beat me like this because of you. He did it because—"

"Geezer," I reminded him tensely.

"My dad's not working for Brian, not really. He's a drug-runner from Boston. He came into town with a new crew."

"What does that have to do with Brian?"

"Because Brian's working for 'em too."

I tested my theory. "Who's Galverson?" I saw Geezer freeze. His skin turned a chalky pale color. He looked like death warmed over.

"No one," he whispered, looking away.

"Galverson runs the new crew, doesn't he? He's who your father's working for?"

Geezer didn't reply, but he didn't have to. I read his body language, and it was enough.

Jace wasn't at war with anyone. He was working with them.

I walked back out the door and headed to the ER lobby. Seeing Sasha and Mandy curled on one of the couches, I moved to stand in the opposite corner, staring out the window. In the window's reflection I saw Devon and Carter enter the lobby, looking slightly scared, but trying to hide it.

Boys.

Mandy flew into Devon's arms.

Interesting, but I wasn't really surprised. I knew Mandy was going to take him back. It had been an unspoken understanding between everyone in their group.

Carter grinned ruefully before going in search for Tray.

"Devon, I was so scared." Mandy was whimpering again. In that moment I realized how spineless my adopted sister was. I loved her, I had come to love her, but—she was useless in an emergency.

"It's okay, Mands. I'm here. They can't hurt you anymore," Devon was promising, kissing the top of her head, hugging her tightly.

I felt a little sick.

"Like you didn't know they'd get back together," Sasha remarked, coming to stand beside me. She was watching Mandy and Devon.

"I did know," I said softly, grasping the curtain lightly. "I just didn't want to think my sister could settle for someone like him."

Exasperated, Sasha cried out, "You think you're so goddamn better than us."

"No," I said evenly, "I just don't let people walk all over me. There's a difference."

"Settle? You think that's settling?" She gestured to Mandy and Devon. "Devon's one of the nicest guys in school. He's going to Columbia in the fall. He's going to be a doctor. And you think Mandy's settling?"

"Yes," I turned to face her squarely, "because he's weak and she's choosing to let him make her life miserable *most* of the time to feel that prestige...that immediate gratification—*some* of the time."

"You have no idea," she cried out angrily. Her platinum hair flew in the air as she turned on me, her hands coming to rest on her pointed hips.

"I know plenty," I returned stiffly.

Tray and Carter returned to the lobby. Bryce was being led out with Jasmine's arm around him. Grant was supported by his sister.

They turned to go, but Grayley and Brian entered at that moment. It was obvious they were looking for me, because they weren't surprised to see me when their gazes settled on me, standing by the window.

Geezer had tattled.

I know it's second grade, but that's what I thought. Geezer had tattled on me and now I had to deal with the teachers; like I was the one in trouble.

"Taryn," Grayley began first, "you don't know—"

I stared at Brian and said softly, deadly, "I'm going to figure it out."

"Taryn," Brian began softly, taking a step towards me, "you really *don't* know. You can't be asking questions..."

"Like why my best friend," I sent a scathing glare to Grayley, "lied to me and told me my ex-boyfriend beat up Geezer—because of me! You didn't beat him up because of me, it had nothing to do with me."

"It had everything to do with you," Brain insisted, glancing nervously at the front desk. "It still has everything to do with you."

"Why? What are you so goddamn scared that I'll find out? What does Geezer's dad have to do with me?" I didn't care about being quiet, or that I was attracting attention. I wanted to know.

I *had* to know because I knew that it had everything to do with me.

Mandy was confused, but she'd stopped crying. "Taryn? What's going on?"

"Listen," Brian closed the distance between us and reached for my arm, but the second his fingers touched my skin, Tray was beside me.

He didn't say anything, but Brian let go nonetheless and watched Tray warily out of the corner of his eye.

"Taryn, you gotta drop this, okay? Listen to me, really listen to me. If you ever believed that I loved you—you gotta believe that what I'm telling you now is for your own good," Brian pleaded.

He was such a stranger to me in this moment.

I didn't even recognize him anymore. The boy who I fell in love with, the reckless, let's screw the world attitude. An innocent rebel. This boy—man—that was standing in front me, I didn't know.

"I don't know what to believe anymore," I whispered, my eyes finding Grayley's and seeing the torment in them.

Grayley knew too. He'd been lying the entire time.

"Taryn," Grayley began, faltering as I took a step back, "don't...I'm still your best friend. I still—"

"You lied to me," I condemned hoarsely. "You're lying to me right now and you aren't going to stop! I can see that you won't."

"Taryn—" Brian pleaded.

I cut in, yelling, "Shut up! I don't even know who you are anymore. Do you think I like this? That I like realizing that the guy who I wasted five years of my life on isn't real. That everything...everything was a lie."

"It's not a lie. It wasn't a lie," he pressed desperately. "You have to believe that...I didn't even...I didn't even find out until..."

"Shut up!" Grayley hissed, shoving him back.

"But, Gray, it's Taryn. It's—"

"I know, you dumbass! Shut up." Grayley punched him, and realizing what he'd done, he whirled to me, his eyes wide. Panicked.

I had all the answer I needed.

I walked over to Brian and asked him quietly, "Who was the bracelet for?"

The bracelet that I had seen in his room. When I'd broken in to screw with his computer. Brian didn't keep bracelets. He didn't buy them, he didn't even steal them and it had been bothering me.

Brian didn't break into places. That had been my job. The bracelet was an item I would've stole—from a personal account. Someone's private safe. It wasn't a bracelet that was found in a store that could be swiped up with the mere flick of a hand.

That's why it bothered me.

"Who was the bracelet for?" I asked again.

"You," he whispered, glancing nervously at Grayley.

"Where did you get it?" I demanded.

"That's enough!" Grayley cut in, shoving Brian away. "Fine, Taryn! If you want to judge us, tell us to go to hell, fine. We're done listening to your rants. When you realize the mistake you've made, you know where we are. You can come and apologize...and maybe...maybe things will be okay with us." He turned and pushed Brian out the door, the sliding doors shut with a soft swish, just on their heels.

Oh yeah.

I had the answer I needed.

CHAPTER TWELVE

Tray drove the first car, with Carter driving the second, and Devon drove Amber's car. Everyone scattered between the three vehicles. Mandy rode with Devon, Grant and Bryce rode with Carter, and the girls—one guess on who they rode with—in Tray's, with me. Amber ended up riding shotgun with Jasmine and Sasha in the next two seats. I rode in the back, but I was quite okay with that. I would've ridden in Carter's car, but Tray grabbed my elbow at the last second and steered me his way. When we got there, the seats had already been taken, so I climbed in the back.

I didn't join in the conversation, but I didn't sleep either. Instead I stared out the window, replaying everything in my head.

The day had started out good. I'd felt good. Got into a little spat with Amber, realized I'd never like Mandy's friends, and I had a tiny vacation with Tray at his home. Then the night had ended with my world being shattered.

And now I was starting to realize I didn't know what was up or down anymore. Or if I was just turned backwards because everything was coming at me from behind. At breakneck speed.

I was stumbling. And I hated that feeling.

I tuned back into the conversation, and realized Amber was going off about some senior girl, Aidrian Casners—the name was familiar. I think I remember Jasmine refer to her as the 'white-trash' that Tray had slept with at one of his parties.

Huh.

Okay, it bothered me...a little, but I was more focused on my past relationships.

Apparently, according to Amber, Aidrian had dared to wear *her* skirt to school last Friday. Then she had the nerve to hit on Brent Garret—a senior on the basketball team. Guess Amber had staked *her* claim but the white trash didn't heed it.

Maybe she couldn't read invisible signs.

I tuned back out.

Tray pulled into his driveway and everyone filed out. Amber was still chattering, with Sasha adding her two cents. Jasmine was glancing, uneasily at me. Then I saw Mandy, who was holding Devon's hand as they traipsed inside Tray's.

All of the guys immediately zeroed in on the fridge. Bryce and Grant both got fresh icepacks. Carter pulled out some pizzas and Tray emerged from the basement with a twelve pack in hand. He slid a beer to each one of us. Even Amber and Sasha took theirs gratefully. I was half expecting a complaint and a whine for a margarita. But nope. Everyone took a bottle.

I grabbed mine and wandered outside, where I curled up at a patio table.

I felt my phone vibrating and pulled it out.

Jace.

I answered it and then slammed it back shut, fully aware it was a little pathetic, but it was a little something I could do to piss him off. A little something at least.

The next call was Geezer.

I didn't pick up for him either. Instead, I pushed the phone away from me.

I kept hearing his voice. His plea for his father's life. I heard Jace's own words. Walking away meant leaving the bad stuff behind. Go have dinner with my family. Jace seemed a lot more prepared for me to walk away than Brian had.

I grabbed my phone and flipped it open to the contacts. I'd kept Cammy's number because she went through a phase. She'd been determined that Jace had cheated on her with me, that he was in love with me. So she called, every fucking day and night. She'd leave threats, send text messages with the intent to harm and detail of how she was going to enjoy making me hurt.

I kept her number so I knew when not to answer.

If Jace made a deal that involved me, Cammy would be the one to spill.

I dialed her number and heard her answer, a moment later.

"Cammy," I greeted, knowing she knew exactly who was on the other end.

"Taryn," she replied guardedly.

"I have a question for you, Cam."

"Oh really?" she asked sarcastically. "And how may I help you?"

"You answer me, I'll tell you the truth about me and Jace," I offered. She didn't want to know, but I knew she couldn't *not* know.

She'd take the deal.

"What's your question?"

I stood up and paced. "You hang around Jace. A lot more than he realizes. There's been so many times he's told me you weren't there, but you always were and I'm thinking that you have your own little way to get in there—a way that Jace doesn't know about."

"And your point?" she demanded hotly.

I was pissing her off.

"I wanna know if Jace made a deal? It would've been a deal made a long time ago."

"He's made a lot of deals," she said vaguely, but I heard hesitation in her voice. She knew something, but she wasn't sure if she wanted to share.

"It would've been with Galverson."

Cammy was quiet, but I could almost hear her thinking.

"Taryn," she sounded weary, "you shouldn't stick your nose where it doesn't belong."

What the hell?

"Are you trying to be smart?" I asked, harshly. "Just tell me the deal."

Then she spilled the beans.

"Galverson's from the east coast. He brought a crew into town."

"What are they doing here?"

"They're doing shipments. I heard Jace say something about the new storage building, they needed more guards or something. I guess it got broken into."

"What are they storing?"

"I don't know, but do you really have to guess?" she murmured scathingly.

Drugs. But where'd the bracelet come from?

"When did this get set up?" I mused, more to myself than her.

"Galverson showed up four months ago."

A month after I left.

Cammy continued, "But I remember Jace talking to him on the phone last year."

Last year.

I waited for the golden question till the end. I asked, "You hear any deals my name was slipped into?"

Complete silence.

"Cammy," I urged.

"Taryn, seriously, I don't think you know what you're doing."

"You wanna know the truth or not?" I shot back swiftly.

It worked.

Cammy snapped, "Fine. Yes. Last year, Jace said he was making arrangements for you. I don't know what he was talking about or what those arrangements were, but those were his words. It's your turn. You and Jace. What's the truth?"

I lied, "We were telling the truth the whole time, Cammy. We never were together."

"But Brian—"

"I lied. Brian needed something to keep him away, but it was never true."

She sighed, a long sigh of relief.

"Thanks, Taryn," she murmured before hanging up.

I sat down, mentally and physically exhausted, and downed the rest of my beer. I could hear laughter from inside, but I wasn't in the mood to be around anyone. Especially those people.

Then again, who am I to judge? All my friends turned out to be liars and back-stabbers.

I heard Mandy laugh. I hadn't heard her laugh in a long time.

So I stood and went inside, pausing in the doorway, seeing Mandy glowing, wrapped in Devon's arms. Again.

They were all standing around eating pizza. Sasha was off to the side, standing by Amber and Jasmine.

"Taryn, want some pizza?" Carter asked, holding up a slice.

Sasha's eyes darkened in irritation.

I'd been accepted, but she hadn't

"Sure." I grinned back, moving to grab a piece, squeezing in beside Tray. I was surprised when he gave way and instead pulled me against his chest, with me standing right in front of him. He leaned back against the counter, with one hand on his pizza, and the other splayed on my stomach, anchoring me against him.

I was more shocked to see Jasmine give me a small smile before she turned towards Bryce, eating her tiny piece of pizza.

Mandy was laughing again, her arms wrapped around Devon's neck. He was trying to eat, but she wouldn't let him. Both were smiling at the stupid game.

"I don't know about anyone else, but I'm thinking I might skip tomorrow," Grant announced, hoisting himself up on a counter.

"I'm right there with you, buddy," Bryce mumbled, raising an icepack to his bruised face.

"Taryn," Jasmine spoke up, a slight tremble in her voice, like she was scared to talk to me, "is it true that you might talk to Coach Greenly?"

"Who's Coach Greenly?"

"The swim coach," she shrugged self-consciously, "at least that's what Mandy said."

I shrugged. "I don't know. Maybe."

"You swim?" Grant asked curiously.

"Yeah."

"She made junior varsity at Earlington when she was in the seventh grade," Mandy proclaimed proudly, with a smile.

"They trounce us every year," Bryce mumbled around his swollen cheeks. "They're state champs—I have to hear about it every holiday. My cousin goes there, she swims too."

"Mom says that Taryn's good enough. She could maybe even get a scholarship somewhere," Mandy gushed, while I wanted to kill her.

I finished my pizza and leaned fully back, feeling Tray's arm tighten around me, resting on my thigh.

Mandy cleared her throat and asked, the first to brave it, "So, what are you going to do, Taryn?"

I didn't play the dumb game. I knew exactly what she meant, and everyone else did, because everyone waited.

So I answered honestly, "I'm going to find out the truth, and I'm going to make them pay."

That was me being nice because I said it without cursing. Look at me, so grown up.

"So," Carter spoke up, "what are we doing the rest of the night?"

Amber laughed. "I think we should put a movie in."

"I think we should have sex," Carter countered swiftly.

"Hell, the movie can be foreplay," Bryce interjected, cursing a second later when he grinned.

"Bryce!" Amber cried out.

"This is my sister, you guys," Grant mumbled, rolling his eyes.

Amber wrapped her arm around his shoulder and murmured, "Oh, my poor little brother—can't handle that his big sis has sex. Sex! I tell you."

He shoved her away, looking disgusted. "Don't ever say those words together. Ever."

Amber laughed and then shrieked when Carter swept her up in his arms and threw her over his shoulder.

He led the way downstairs.

Mandy and Devon settled on the farthest couch, Mandy curled up in his lap, both looking content.

Carter was already starting a movie by the time the rest of us sat down.

I settled at the end of a second couch when Tray returned from the bathroom. He walked to me, lifted me up, and deposited me in his lap. I barely reacted, but closed my eyes, feeling his arms encircle me and I pillowed my head against his shoulder.

I woke later on and realized Tray was carrying me up the stairs. A little bit later he laid me down on his bed and stripped down to his boxers. I grinned. "Wanna change me?"

Tray knelt over me on the bed and slowly peeled my shirt off. He left my bra on and then undid my pants. Slowly, he slid them down my legs. Smoothing his hands back up my legs, his fingers slid underneath my thong straps and his thumbs rubbed gently against my hipbone before pulling them off.

Then he bent and pressed his mouth there.

I arched my back, suddenly wide awake.

"Tray!" I gasped.

He chuckled, but continued.

When I came, he lifted his head and slid his hands up the side of my body, underneath my bra straps and slid them down. He unclasped my bra and threw it to the side.

I wrapped my legs around him and deftly flipped him over, an old wrestling move. Seeing he was startled, I straddled him and slid my body down his, my mouth lingering on his chest as I moved down.

I bent my head taking him in my mouth, and when he gasped and then arched, I grinned enjoying the torment I was putting him through.

"Fuck," he groaned a little while later.

The fun was over when he tucked me underneath him and reached for the nightstand.

I closed my eyes, my head falling back against the pillow when I felt him cover my body. My legs wrapped around him when I felt him slide into me, and my body moved right along with his.

Both of us were groaning within seconds.

I woke up a few hours later and checked the clock. It was already seven in the morning. I nudged Tray awake and whispered, "I need to go to school."

"'Kay," he mumbled as he rolled over.

I nudged him again. "You have to drive me. My car's there."

Sleepily, he reached for his pants and grabbed his keys inside the pocket. He passed them to me, and yawned. "Park it in the lot."

"Thanks," I said happily as I climbed over him and headed into the shower. Tray had moved all the needed essentials into his bathroom the previous day—it had been our agreement. I'd been scared he wouldn't get around to it, so I made him do it that instant, otherwise I wasn't going to sleep over.

Stepping underneath the shower spray, I was thankful for my foresight.

When I moved back into his room, grimacing at my old clothes, I saw Tray was staring at me. Now wide awake.

"What?" I asked, my hands pausing as I moved to dress.

"You're up early. Why?"

"What are you talking about?"

"What are you planning, Taryn?" he demanded insistently.

"I'm going to school."

"Taryn," he said firmly, standing up, his muscles rippled with his lithe movements, "look, you need to know some stuff before you go off on your little rampage."

"Like what?" I asked, now interested.

"My dad was chief of police. I know all about Galverson."

"What?" That threw me. "How? What do you know?"

"It's not...look...all those people that have been telling you to keep your nose out—they're saying it for a reason."

"What do you know about Galverson?" I couldn't believe his nerve. Now he was joining their ranks?

"Galverson is a heavy hitter."

"You're telling me this now? Why not last night?"

"Because you were pissed last night. You weren't thinking clearly."

"I'm still not."

"You're thinking better." He snorted, raking a hand through his hair. He was tired, he always did that when he was tired. "Look, whatever you dig up on Galverson—come to me before you do anything. Okay."

"Why?" I was dreading his answer, because I knew...

"Just do it."

I finished dressing and moved to leave, but Tray blocked me. "Promise me," he pressed, serious.

"I promise," I said in resignation.

Tray studied my face, searching for the truth. He must not have fully believed me because he added, "It's how Jace and I know each other, the little business deal we worked out. Galverson's the reason my dad's not the chief of police anymore and why he's in South America with my mom. Why we can afford this place."

Fine.

"I promise. Really," I said lightly, genuinely.

That he read as the truth. Tray nodded, kissing me hard and then crawled back in bed.

He looked gorgeous, well, he looked gorgeous when he was awake, but there was an angelic perfection to him when he closed his eyes like that.

I sighed, recognizing the forbidding feeling in my stomach. So I left. Fully content to stay in denial land.

Parking in the lot at school, I went to the locker room and changed into some different clothes. It was just a baggy hoodie and jeans, but it worked. I was comfortable. But I'd kept the tank-top I wore last night on. It smelled of Tray—I know. I'm acting like one of *those* sickening girls.

Everyone noticed the social elite was missing and that I was there. After my fourth yawn, the sound not silenced, my teacher suggested politely, "You are excused, Miss Matthews, to get some coffee."

I blinked, tiredly, and then left, heading straight for the coffee cart. Thank goodness our administration felt sympathetic for the young hard-working plight of the over-achieving student body—which often equated to no sleep.

Juniors and seniors got special privileges—off campus lunches and coffee!

I chose study hall for second period and scoured the internet, bringing up anything I could find on Jace and Galverson—which wasn't a whole lot except arrest notifications.

I made it till fourth period where I slumped into the seat next to Molly.

She was still wearing the pink frames.

"Hi!" She blinked in surprise.

"Hey." I yawned.

"Where is everyone?" she asked, eager for the gossip. "Everyone's gone. Like, they're all skipping."

No, not everyone was missing—just the social elite, which apparently, are the only ones that count.

I pointed out, "*I'm* not skipping."

"Yeah, but," she rolled her eyes before continuing, "you're not...you're one of us. You know what I mean."

"Anyway," I changed the subject, uncaring if it was rude, "you're a science person."

"Hmm?"

"So, are you good with computers, too?"

"Uh—"

"Or do you know anyone who's good with computers? And I'm talking, like, really, really good with computers. Like a hacker?" I whispered.

"A hacker?" Molly squeaked, flushing.

"Yeah," I said dryly, but my eyes were drawn to her neck. "Oh my God!"

"What?" She looked down, flushing again when she realized what I was looking at. "Oh."

"That's a hickey." It sounded like an accusation.

Molly didn't answer, she was too busy blushing. Like a full-out, full-body blush.

"Larkins called." I smiled widely, nodding in approval. "Good for him."

"Please," she mumbled, avoiding my gaze.

It made me smile. Molly she wasn't tainted, like myself. It was nice to have a friend like her.

A friend...hmm...

"It's a good thing. Messing around is fun," I emphasized the word 'fun.' I was starting to realize Molly didn't have that much fun, and I was starting to care about her. I've never cared before.

"It's nothing," she still blushed though, "really. It's not like what you and Tray do."

Which might not always be a good thing, but I stayed quiet.

"So, do you know any hackers?" I asked instead.

"Why?"

"It's for a school project." I refused to feel guilty that I was lying.

"Well," she hesitated, "there's a group of guys that could probably help, but—"

"But what?"

"They're kind of...freaky."

I can handle freaky. "Just tell me who."

The rest of fourth period consisted of lab. Which was boring. But lunch was next and I swooped into the cafeteria, scanning for the tech crowd and spotted them in a far corner, right next to the library—go figure. Molly informed me that they ate right away and then spent the rest of lunch on the computers in the back of the library, you know—where no one went because it was nerd haven.

Molly liked going there too.

Just as I was crossing the cafeteria, I heard the door swing open and conversations halted. Literally. It was like everyone chose that moment to take a collective breath. I turned and saw the social elite—who else could garner that kind of reaction? They must've decided to attend the afternoon. Even the guys had decided to show up and Carter.

I looked back and saw that the techies were finishing up.

Spying an empty seat, I dropped down in the middle of them and asked bluntly, unheeding their startled expressions, "Who's Props?"

Nothing. And because I didn't know if they were suddenly incapable of speech or because he truly wasn't there, I asked again, "Who is Props? My friend said I'd find him here."

The guy next to me cleared his throat and raised his hand cautiously. "Uh...that's me."

He was short and husky, but if he'd clean up a bit he'd be a cutie.

Molly also informed me of this. She'd had a crush on him since seventh.

"You're Props?"

"Uh huh." He gulped.

I smiled and informed him, "We're going to become friends."

The guy looked terrified.

I waited until he finished his food and then I said, "Come with me."

A few moments later, after I told him what I wanted, he frowned and scratched his head, then said, "So you want me to do what?"

"It's a bank account. Okay,"." I said, business-like, pacing behind him in some super-secret tech room. "I want you to get in there and trace all accounts that have tapped in. I need to know where *those* accounts ended up."

"But, that could take days, possibly weeks, for me to even get into the account."

"I have the account numbers," I said quickly, dropping into the chair next to him. "So that part's done. Now you gotta find where all other accounts go. Okay?"

"Um..." The guy still looked horrified.

"What?" I snapped. I was impatient and this guy was not making me calmer.

"It'd help if I knew what exactly you're looking for," he scrambled.

"Why do you need to know that?"

"Because there could be a thousand different traces once I get in there. Anything you can give me would help cut down on some of the leg-work."

"Don't go for anything that's federal. That help?" I raised my eyebrows.

He took a deep breath.

"We're skipping fifth period and you want me to do some *very* illegal stuff—I need to know why," he stammered, looking like he couldn't believe he just said that to me.

"You're going to be skipping more than fifth," I stated.

He didn't move.

"Because there are some people who fucked with me and I need to know why. I'm pretty sure that this is going to lead me to whatever the hell information I need to make sense of why every person in my life is lying to me," I said forcefully.

The guy had a deer-caught-in-the-headlights look and I was fixing to run him over.

I tried a different tactic. "Okay," I muttered, gentling my voice, "what do you want? I can try to get it for you."

He just blinked and then stared at me.

"Really. A friend of mine wanted an invite to a party. I did that. What do you want? Like a computer? I can get that for you," I reasoned. At this rate, I'll try anything. I'd steal anything, if he'd just turn those goddamn fingers to that fucking keyboard.

He still didn't say anything.

Plan C.

"If you don't get to work, I have a car and I will run it over you, then, when you're lying on the ground, I will use my taser on you. Then I'll back up and do it again."

"I want to go on a date with Aidrian Casners," he spit out, his eyes wider than an owl's.

"You want a what?"

"A date. With Aidrian Casners." He seemed to grow more confident each time he said it.

"Who's Aidrian Casners? I don't even know her."

"She's easy to find. She's always out in the parking lot. She's usually wearing a mini-skirt and a halter-top. Yesterday she had on a purple sequined halter top and she wore these sparkling sandals. She has a tattoo on her thigh. It's a unicorn."

"Okay," I cried out, more to get him to shut up. "She sticks out. I got it."

"And?" He waited.

"I'll work on it," I mumbled. "Now get working on my stuff!"

I stayed put until seventh period. Props lived up to his name; I had to give him props. Once he buckled down and actually got to work—he was cursing and sweating up a storm in no time. But I saw the gleam in his eyes. He liked the challenge and this was a challenge for him. I was starting to think he'd never gotten a challenge like this before, or he'd never had an excuse to go looking for this challenge.

Whatever. I was just happy because he was working on it.

"So..." Molly began, waiting for me.

"What?"

"I saw you talking to him." She sounded accusatory.

"Yeah. You told me where he'd be." Did I need to add the 'duh'?

"And?" she asked pointedly.

"And what?"

"Did he ask about me?"

I had to grin. "Who gave you that hickey? Or should I be asking who do you *want* to be giving you a hickey?"

She blushed. So predictable.

"You have to introduce us," she whispered, hunching down over the table as our teacher entered the room.

"You're the one who knows him."

"Well, yeah. But it's not like you'll introduce us, like this is Molly blah blah, blah. You know, just act like we're good friends."

"We are friends."

"We're science lab friends and table-mate friends."

Who said table-mates?

Molly continued, "We're not friend friends."

"You went to a party with me," I reasoned.

"No. I begged you to *invite* me to a party and you got the hottest guy in this school to drive me there, but you and said guy left—very quickly—after you showed up at said party. You were never at the party with me."

"Yes, I was. I saw you drunk. That consists of me being at a party with you." I was starting to enjoy this conversation. Molly could argue and flush at the same time.

"Oh—" she sputtered.

"Alright, alright." I laughed. "Don't worry. He'll be mooning over you in no time." I bit my lip.

"What?" Molly asked, seeing it.

"I just have to do something for him first."

Her eyes bugged out. Almost literally, but, hey, at least she didn't faint. I guess Props was not faint worthy.

"Not that!" I hissed, laughing. "But kinda yeah."

"Oh my—" Now she was flushing with anger. It was really entertaining.

"He wants to go on a date with Aidrian Casners. I told him I'd try to set them up. I think he just wants to lose his virginity to her. Don't worry." I was starting to feel bad for Larkins.

"Don't worry? Do you not understand what 'worry' means? Having the guy of my dreams go on a date with Aidrian Casners is the definition of being worried," she hissed, blushing when she saw Tray look our way. She looked down at the table, and continued, "I'll have no chance after he's gone out with her."

I didn't know if I should comfort her or slap her. I didn't know who Aidrian Casners was, but I was getting the impression that she was not a girl who'd date a computer geek. For real. Molly, on the other hand, could be his first wife.

"Mrs. Maslow," Sasha stuck her hand up, "can you ask Taryn and her freak friend to be quiet?" She turned her heated glare on us. "They're distracting me."

Oh please. I rolled my eyes. She was working on a freaking worksheet and then I realized what she called Molly.

"I think you're the freak friend, Sasha," I said coolly, smirking. I sat back, ready to do battle.

"Miss Matthews, Miss Keeley, if you could please quiet down, it would be greatly appreciated," Mrs. Maslow asked politely, not even looking up from her book.

Great psych teacher. What insight.

Sasha grinned triumphant.

Jasmine raised her hand. "Mrs. Maslow, I was wondering if you'd ask Sasha to stop copying my answers."

Sasha gasped, gaping at her.

I laughed.

Mrs. Maslow lifted her head, more annoyed than interested.

"Miss Klinnleys," she spoke, "is this true?"

Sasha paled, still gaping at Jasmine "No!" she denied heatedly. "Jasmine's copying mine."

"Then why is mine done and yours is only half done?" Jasmine asked innocently. She held her paper up. "See."

"I'm not copying. I swear," Sasha exclaimed emphatically. "I don't know why she said that."

Mrs. Maslow took both of their worksheets and compared them.

"Miss Klinnleys, you may go to the principal's office."

"He's going to talk to you about *appropriate* boundaries," I called after her as she hurried from the room.

"Miss Matthews," Mrs. Maslow said sternly, "it would be beneficial for you if you were to learn your own appropriate boundaries."

"I know. That's what the principal said." I grinned, seeing her own amusement flicker in her eyes. The psych teacher liked me.

When she returned to her desk, I stole a glance to Jasmine and saw her grinning to Mandy—in victory. Then it hit me—Jasmine had just set Sasha up. What a manipulative bitch. I couldn't help but appreciate it. Jasmine was one of the social elite. Sasha was getting too close to Amber. So Jasmine had to send her back down.

CHAPTER THIRTEEN

Psych was psychology. The rest of class passed without event. I mean...what could really top Jasmine's backstab? I couldn't think of anything off the top of my head.

Molly leaned over and whispered, "Are you going to see him again?"

Normally, you'd think she'd be talking about my crush or date or lover (whatever), but no—this was what I liked about Molly, or what I was learning to like about her—the girl's just boy crazy.

Justin Travers.

Then Tray.

Larkins got a shot—who knows...I've got a hunch Larkins won't be going anywhere.

And now Props. I could swear Molly had referred to Travers and Props as the love of her life—both of them. My guess is that it'll be someone new in a few days.

But anyway...no, she wasn't talking about my guy. It was her guy. Her latest interest.

I shrugged. "I gotta take care of something first."

"Call me when you go see Props. I wanna come with."

The girl was a social introvert. She wanted to go to a party just so her mom would have to worry about her—once. But I was learning that she was relentless when it came to boys.

"You one of those girls who constantly has a boyfriend?" I asked, more curious than anything

She flushed—what a shocker. "Why?"

"Because I'm starting to think the only reason we're friends is because I'm your pimp. I'm wondering if you've always been like this?"

"Oh...well...no," she answered self-consciously, glancing down at the table. "It's just...you know these guys. I mean—you don't care, you can go right up to them and talk to them. None of my other friends do that."

"Who are your other friends?" I suddenly realized I talk to this girl in science and psychology. I've yet to see her speak with another student. And somehow...I felt a little guilty at that. Well, *some* guilt.

She shrugged, fiddling with her thumbs.

"Do you have friends?" I asked bluntly, watching her intently.

"I have two other friends and they're..."

"Are they real?" Excuse me for wondering, but she was being so weird right now. Not the blushing bubbly Molly I'd come to know.

"Yes, they're real," she replied, giving me a small glare that seriously lacked vehemence—instead she looked constipated. "They just...they're one of the invisibles here."

"Invisibles," I repeated lamely, not comprehending what she was talking about.

"Like me. I'm....I'm an invisible. At least I was—until I met you."

"You weren't invisible to Larkins," I pointed out. The guy went crazy on me before I became friends with her.

She shrugged. "I know, but Garrett's my neighbor. He doesn't count."

"Oh!" I gave her a wide smile. "He's nice and close. Getting some of that neighborly loving, huh?" I teased, nudging her shoulder.

She blushed and ducked her head—nothing new there.

"You'll have to introduce me to the rest of the Invisibles," I remarked, standing up when the bell rang.

"Really?" Molly asked, startled.

"Yeah. Why not." I shrugged, heading out.

"Um...okay," she murmured, biting her lip self-consciously.

We stopped at my locker. When I opened it, I asked, "What's up with that?"

"With what?"

"You don't want me to meet your friends?"

"It's not that...it's...nothing. It's nothing." She glanced around. "I should...huh...I should get going."

Well that was weird.

"Taryn!" Mandy bounced up to my locker, her blond hair literally bouncing on her shoulders.

"Hey," I murmured.

"So, what'd you think about class?"

"Which one?" I asked dryly.

"Our last class!" She didn't need to add the 'duh,' I could hear it in her voice.

"About Jasmine?"

"Yeah!" Mandy sent me a blinding smile, bleached teeth and all. "We did it for you."

Wait.

"What?" I asked, turning to face my sister. "What do you mean she did it for me?"

"Please." Mandy rolled her eyes, clutching her books tightly. "We've been getting sick and tired of Sasha. She's such a bitch to you."

"And I can take care of myself," I retorted, a little irritated.

"What's gotten into you? I mean, we thought you'd be happy. Sasha's been on your back since last week. Now, her and Amber have suddenly become 'friends.' Please," she said in disgust, "Amber pisses me off sometimes."

"Amber," I stated in disbelief, "you're best friend Amber?"

"You're my sister. Amber shouldn't bring friends in the group who are going dump all over you," she explained matter-of-factly, unaware at how pissed I was getting.

"Excuse me?" I drawled slowly. Mandy looked up at me and her eyes widened in surprise.

"Uh?" She paused, uncertain which way to tread.

"Do me a favor and stop putting me in the middle of your issues with Jasmine and Amber. You and Jasmine pulled that stunt because the two of you didn't like Sasha. Sasha was becoming too buddy-buddy with Amber, and you and Jasmine were threatened. That's why the two of you did what you did. Not because of me. We both know I can take care of myself," I finished tensely.

Fuck that.

"But we did do it for y—"

"No, you didn't!" I cried out, slamming my locker shut, uncaring that we had an audience. "If you were going to do anything for me, it'd be to drop friends like Amber and Jasmine. Jasmine screwed Devon for a year," I ignored her flinch, "a year, Mandy! And Amber knew about it—they all knew about it."

"What?" Mandy gasped.

"But no, instead you're willing to sacrifice having good friends so you can be popular."

"Who knew about it?"

"Take a wild guess!" I shouted. "When you're popular, you gotta expect you'll be the last to know shit. Especially about your cheating boyfriend—who's going to cheat again. And you know it. Every time you're off at some cheerleader camp or student council conference, you're always going to wonder."

"And you have such stellar friends," Mandy retorted, wanting to hurt me.

I fell silent. Oh yeah, I knew exactly how stellar my friends were. Friends who'd lied to me, fucked me over. Yeah, I had great friends.

"Trust me, I am fully aware of how fucked up my friends are," I said hoarsely, turning to storm off. I stopped short, seeing everyone—*everyone*—frozen in place, listening to us. Fuck, I even saw our psych teacher in the hallway, looking at us.

"Miss Matthews," she spoke up, coming to stand in front of us, "I think you and your sister will be meeting with me tomorrow after class."

Oh...shit.

Some of Mandy's friends came up and hugged her, walking away with her, a few of them glaring at me over their shoulders.

Whatever.

I was the one telling the truth. I was just calling it how it is, not putting on some show. With my newfound wisdom, I wasn't about to let anyone get into place to stab me in the back.

Screw that.

Sighing, I turned back to my locker, realizing I forgot to grab my bag with my keys. As I opened the pocket, I saw Tray's keys were still inside. I'd forgotten to give them back. Grabbing them, I pulled my bag out and shut it. I walked down his hallway, seeing a lot of students that I could swear didn't even go to our school; however, I was the new student—one that isolated herself at that.

But they all seemed to know me, judging from their glares or grins.

I saw Tray standing at his open locker, grinning at something Justin Travers and three other guys were telling him.

There they were: the gods of the gods—the popular guys—the ones that every girl had their first crush on—the ones you'd remember after you were married and returned to your hometown...and they'd still give you the butterflies when you saw 'em in a gas station, filling up their newest car with their little kiddies in the back.

Devon, Bryce, and Grant were lounging against a locker a few down from Tray's, but they were listening in on whatever Travers was saying. The other guys—they were the basketball players that had helped vandalize Pedlam—were on the opposite side of the hall, also listening to Travers.

I hesitated, suddenly unsure what to do. I mean, Tray always found me. I'd never singled him out, but he probably needed his keys. For some reason, I was hesitant to approach.

"If you don't move, you're going to get trampled," came a voice from behind me.

I turned and saw a girl with sleek black hair and green eyes, regarding me in annoyance. She was dressed how I used to dress. In fact, her tank top looked like... "You get that from Petros?" I asked, nodding at her top.

Surprised, she replied, "Yeah, you shop there?"

"I used to," I murmured. "I went to Pedlam for a few years."

"Me too," she commented, looking unsure. "I moved here three years ago, but my cousins still go there, so I visit and shop a lot out there."

"Senior?" I asked. We were in the senior hallway, after all. Tray was a god, which was the only reason he was allowed a locker in the senior hallway.

"Yeah, you're not?"

"Junior. You must've moved when I was just starting high school at Pedlam."

"Who were your friends?" she asked, now more interested.

"Brian Lanser. Grayley. Trent Gardner. Liza. Kerri. Geezer."

"Oh," she laughed, "we were in totally different crowds."

"Gentley," I pinpointed.

"Yeah," she chuckled, "take it you're not a fan."

"Gentley and I hate each other," I said matter-of-factly. "Still."

"Oh!" Understanding dawned in her eyes. "You're Taryn Matthews."

"You've heard of me?"

"Oh, honey, everyone in Pedlam and Rawley has heard about you." She laughed. "My name's Crystal Fairs."

"Taryn Matthews," I greeted formally.

We didn't shake on it.

She gestured over my shoulder. "So that's why you're down in Senior Haven. You're Tray Evan's latest girl. Gotta say—he's more of a Gentley than a Brian Lanser, from what I hear about Brian Lanser."

He was not a Gentley. But he wasn't a Brian Lanser either...and she'd just called me his latest girl. Tray Evan's latest girl.

I was a bit uncomfortable with that. Whatever.

"Man, a lot of girls hate you, you know," she mused, grinning at me. "Including me, you should know that." There wasn't much heat behind that statement though.

"Trust me, I'm used to the feeling," I murmured half-heartedly, glancing over to Tray's locker again. He was still talking with the same guys and none of them looked like they were about to move anytime soon.

"Yeah, well, you oughtta head out of here. Casners' going to be coming back from her weekly meeting with our esteemed principal. She's not going to be happy seeing you in her territory."

"Aidrian Casners?" I asked, more alert.

"Yeah..." Crystal frowned, watching me warily. "You say that like you don't know her."

"I got a favor to ask her." I bit my lip. I knew the tight spot Props had placed me in, but...fuck—I needed what he could find for me. So...somehow...I had to befriend this Casners who evidently hated me. What a shocker.

"Matthews, some advice: run," Crystal said bluntly, stepping back.

I turned and saw Aidrian Casners—or a girl who matched Props' and everyone else's description of her. She looked the definition of white trash, but she had attitude. I could tell that. She was grinning up at Tray, almost rubbing her chest against his.

Well, what do you expect? At least she has taste. I wasn't really one to hold it against her, I'd gone for more than a double-dose of seconds.

Now...here's the deal. She had a reputation. Amber hated her, so that made me like her. And I felt some camaraderie for her—she wanted Tray. I could relate. And I needed her to help me out with Props. But the girl was going after someone who I wasn't done with. And I just didn't like seeing what I was witnessing.

Tray wasn't exactly pushing her away, but he wasn't encouraging her either.

I saw her hand snake around his waist and move down. I turned to Crystal and asked, "What does she like? Like, what's she obsessed with?"

"What?" Crystal asked, perplexed.

"What would she do anything for?"

"Uh," she thought a moment, "I don't know. She's pretty crazed about Third Wave. That's a—"

I can do that. I was already walking over when I called out, "Casners."

Aidrian froze. Tray froze. Hell—everyone froze at my voice.

She turned and blinked at me, trying to figure out who I was. After a minute, I saw the recognition in her eyes.

Tray was just watching me, he saw the determination in my eyes.

The rest of the guys moved out of the way.

"So, you're the little tramp that's been warming my spot," she taunted, taking a step towards me.

"Third Wave's at Pedlam in a week." They were playing at the Seven8...made things a bit more sticky, but I could work around it.

She looked a little confused. Obviously, she'd been expecting a battle, but I just grinned at her, waiting for her reply.

"So?" she demanded heatedly, but still confused.

"You want tickets?"

"I have tickets."

"You want front-row tickets?" I sweetened the pot.

"What?"

"I can get you front row seats and back-stage passes," I delivered, waiting. It was too tempting for her not to bite.

Which she did. I grinned, almost feeling all of the pieces slide into place. Everything was working out.

"You can get me that? Why?"

"You gotta do something for me," I stated silkily.

She frowned, glancing at Tray underneath her eyelids.

I stepped closer. "And no, it's got nothing to do with him."

"What is it?"

"I need you to go on a date with someone. Hell, take him with you to the concert."

"Who?" she asked suspiciously.

"Oh no. It don't work that way. You're in or not." I wanted my deal done. I did the negotiations, no one else.

I caught a quick grin flash across Tray's features—he'd seen this side of me before.

Aidrian chewed on it for a moment. Then she said, "Fine."

"Fine," I said firmly.

"Who is it?"

"He'll pick you up with the tickets. Just be ready," I instructed her, and then I raised my hands, Tray's keys hanging from my fingers. "Thought you might want these."

Tray took them, his fingers sliding against mine for a moment.

One hand grabbed one of my belt loops and yanked me against him, he asked, "You coming over tonight?" He bent and nuzzled my neck—I was realizing he loved to do that. One of his hands slid down my back and rested just inside the back of my pants, his palm hot against my skin.

Casners was watching us, so was everyone else.

I was tempted, I really was, but I had work to do.

I sighed, turning to give him a long, deep kiss. "I can't." I pushed him away. "I have work to do. Remember?"

He frowned at that. "Taryn—"

I heard the warning in his voice and I snapped, "Don't even." I didn't care who heard. "They fucked with me—they're going down. Even if I don't get any sleep for a year straight."

I made sure to send a warning sweep over Casners as I finished that statement.

Tray caught my elbow and dragged me away, pulling me into an empty room. He pulled me close against him and warned, "You need to be careful."

I wrenched away from him. "What are you talking about?"

"You're not going after Lanser. You're going after Galverson," he stated.

"So what?"

"So it doesn't matter how good a thief you might be or where you can break into. He won't care, trust me, Taryn," he bit out, gravely serious. "All he'll care about is where you live, who your family is...and he'll go after you, by using them. Just like he went after my family."

"This doesn't have to do with your family or my family. This doesn't even have to do with Galverson. This has to do with Jace and everyone else who's lying to me."

"Why does it matter?" Tray cried out, irritated. "You're not there anymore. You're here. Why does it goddamn matter what they're lying to you about? It might have nothing to do with you, they just might be doing this so you're protected—think about that? It happens, Taryn. It could happen."

"You don't even know—" I shrugged him off.

"No. I don't. But I know Galverson. He's the reason why I'm alone in that house of mine. He's the reason why I don't ever see my brother anymore, I don't even know if he's alive," he shouted.

The shouting managed to rattle me. I blinked, realizing I had only been seeing through my revenge-tinted glasses. That was the perspective I'd adopted since last night, since I made a resolution to find out the truth.

But I saw a different Tray before me. He wasn't giving me the cool, calm, controlled façade everyone else saw. I mean—yes—it was there. If anyone else would've come in, they would have been scared shitless of Evans. But I saw what they didn't. I always had, remembering that I'd seen Tray slip back into his mask when Mandy had sat at our table. She hadn't. She hadn't even noticed anything.

But I was seeing it again.

There was a raw need in him now. And I saw a glimmer of something—something that sent a shiver down my back—just underneath. I saw what Jace had warned me about.

"What are you talking about?" I asked, slightly calmer.

"Nothing. Just," he raked a hand through his hair in frustration, "leave it alone."

"No."

"Taryn," he began again, "I get it. Okay. I get it. You want revenge, you've been hurt. I get it—trust me. But you're going to take on more than you can handle. If you go after Lanser, you're going after Galverson. Galverson's not gonna give a shit what you can steal or what secrets you've got on him. The second you come onto his radar, he's just going to send someone after you."

"I'm not going out to persecute him. I just want to know what they did to me."

"How do you even know they did something?" he asked, losing his patience.

"Because nothing makes sense. It hasn't for a while. Brian's not about stealing bracelets. Geezer's been...he's been off since I left. And Jace—it's like he wanted me to leave. He wasn't...he wasn't trying to get me back for visits or anything. And...he didn't want me to know how Galverson was. Jace never uses that tone with me. Never."

"So what?"

"And because Jace was working a deal a year ago about me. He was 'making arrangements' for me. I need to know what those arrangements were." I clipped out, unmoving.

Tray let out an exasperated groan. "Fuck, Taryn, you're going to get yourself killed!"

"Oh please," I muttered.

"You don't know what you're getting yourself into."

"And you do?"

"Yes!" he yelled, "I do." He caught his words, but he looked at me and said, "My brother was going after him. Galverson was his case. Chance was determined to take Galverson down, but he got to our dad first." He fell silent, drawing in a shuttering breath. "The intersection that Lanser talked to you about—it's *the* intersection in our state—and we're smack in the middle of the drug exportation line. Rawley runs this intersection—it's why Chance knew about Galverson, because he'd run deals through Rawley. Chance went after Galverson's daughter, he used her to tap info on him."

I had a sinking feeling that I would not like what I was about to hear.

Tray continued, "Galverson found out and went after our dad to get at Chance. Chance was a—is—a DEA agent. He's...slightly untouchable, but Galverson doesn't work that way. He tapped our dad. He pulled him into the business, bribed him, got him hooked on coke. Reason why I live in that place is because of money that Galverson sent our way."

Some of it made sense. "Where do you come in?"

Tray laughed bitterly. "I...I was the one who sent my dad away. Chance used me against our dad and Galverson. I got everything, every fucking deal, on tape. Dad thought I idolized him, that I wanted to be just like him, so he took me with him on all the trips. I saw everything. Every fucking deal, every fucking drug-runner there was, every fucking...I saw the girls, I saw the...I saw everything."

"And?"

I didn't want to hear it, but I had to. And I had a feeling that Tray had to say it. I was guessing he hadn't let any of this out—not to anyone.

"And," he took a deep breath, staring off into the distance, "and I took everything I had gathered—wires, videos, photos, everything—and made copies then put 'em in an account. Then I confronted Dad, told him that I had all the evidence I needed to send him away; told him to get the fuck out of my life and that I hated him; told him the next time I saw him I'd kill him."

"So he took your mom to South America with him."

"Yeah," Tray sighed, "and I went to see Galverson next. That's the first time I met Jace. I told him he needed to pull out of Rawley. No business would go through my territory anymore. I just wanted all of them out. I gave him a taste of what I had on him—on all of them—and I told him if anything ever happened to me, the evidence would be sent to the DEA and about seven other law enforcement agencies itching to take him down."

"He let you live." It was a startling revelation, but the proof stood before me.

"Yeah. I was just a kid. Galverson knew that, plus, my dad had become valuable to him. Something happen to me, there'd be a rift between them. And all I wanted was my life back. I didn't really think long-term in the future, you know. I just wanted my dad gone, everything out of sight, which meant Rawley." He chuckled. "I didn't really think what it would do to me."

"What do you mean?"

"I got a reputation because of it. I was known as the owner of Rawley's intersection. Galverson kept his runners away from the intersection, but there were others that didn't listen."

"And you wanted it all gone," I murmured, in my eyes I saw a boy who'd been stripped of everything: his parents, his brother, his sense of safety.

And I remembered how I'd judged him when we first met. I thought he'd had it all: money, family, looks, intelligence. I thought he was lazy, just blessed and advantaged and ready to waste that away.

I'd never been that off before.

"I told you—I know both sides. I know the cops and I know the criminals. So, I'd call up some of dad's old buddies, the ones who lean a bit too much on the opposite side of the law—if you know what I mean—and I sent them after the drug-runners. They always ended up in the hospital. Some of 'em were put in comas. It was a perfect deal. I could ID any drug-runner, I knew who they were working with, and I just told the guys who hated drug dealers, but knew there wasn't anything legal they could do about 'em." He sighed. "Rawley's got the rep for drug dealers to steer clear from here. Even though I don't know some of the new crews. I know the big ones, some of the small guys are probably a lot bigger now, but...that's the thing with drugs. There's always someone new in the business. Lanser was small news back then, but he's progressed to be a full partner with Galverson."

"How do you know he's a full partner?"

"Galverson only meets his partners in person," Tray stated.

"When did this happen?" I asked softly, seeing the battle going on inside of him.

"When I was in the eighth grade," he said hoarsely, his body frozen in place.

I didn't know what to say.

"Tray—" I started, but fell silent.

"It's not really something I want to go through again, Taryn," he said quietly, then he left.

To say that I was off-kilter, was an understatement. Yeah...I knew Jace was in some heavy shit. But—like before...I often placed myself happily in the land of denial. But...holy shit—what Tray had gone through, what I knew Galverson now represented...it put some stuff in perspective.

But I still wanted to know what Jace had done, what he had arranged me. I just...wouldn't bring it up when I'm with Tray. He probably wouldn't ask anyway.

I sighed, a long shattering breath, when I exited the room. Leaving a few minutes after Tray. I glanced down the hallway, most of his crew was gone. He was certainly gone.

And I didn't really want to think about the hell he had gone through...that could be...he'd talked. We'll talk again, but later.

And to tell the truth, I don't know how I was feeling, having all that laid on me. I mean, yeah, I'd laid my shit on him. But...not everything everything. Not like that. But then again—he wasn't going after my demons better left in the closet.

Ugh. And then I had to acknowledge the other feelings. He'd told me...he'd...shared something that went beyond deep and secret—with me. Not anyone else.

I swear, one side of my stomach just dropped in dread...but because I wasn't feeling regret at what he'd shared with me. The fact that he had shared with me, not about what he had shared with me. I felt some old elation mixed in there...and that's what the dread was about.

"Taryn."

I whirled around, grateful for a distraction.

"Molly!" I exclaimed, with a wide smile. Then I saw the two girls behind her. One was skinny, skinny, and more skinny, with pale hair. She wasn't looking at me, but was enraptured with a one-sided conversation with the floor.

It's a talker. Could talk your ear off.

The other girl was about the opposite in every way—she was large, large, and more large. She had jet black hair and looked a little Goth with her make-up, but on second glance I don't think that she was going for the Goth look. I think that was just her natural coloring.

"These are my friends, Angela and Kayden."

"Oh, hey," I said easily. "I like the name."

Kayden was the darker girl. Angela was the pale anorexic. Now, I know it's not nice to label girls this skinny as anorexic, but it's the only word that came to mind.

"Guys, this is Taryn," Molly continued, shuffling her feet awkwardly. She was glancing between me and them.

I stuck my hand out. "Hi."

Finally, both of them looked at me. I think they were a bit shocked that I actually wanted to meet them. And, to tell the truth, I could see why they were known as Invisibles. They made themselves invisible. I never would've noticed 'em if Molly hadn't been talking to me *and* to them.

Angela grinned, one quick grin, and then she was chatting with the floor again. Not really chatting, chatting, but it looked like she was trying to stare it down.

Kayden murmured a soft, "Hi." Then she went back to looking everywhere else again.

Molly gave me another awkward grin, lifting one shoulder helplessly.

"You guys want to go and get something to eat?" I asked, being extremely nice—which was so not me, but I was trying here.

"Hey, bitch!" I turned around and saw Amber walking my way.

Wow. When I turned back around, I was amazed. The Invisibles had scrambled—literally. Even Molly seemed to vanish.

Well, shit, how many arguments was I going to get into today? Did Tray count as one?

"What?" I asked simply. I was getting tired of this.

"What the hell did you say to Mandy?" she demanded, literally seething.

"A whole lot of the same," I murmured, looking for the Invisibles. They were really good at their name. I frowned, checking the other way.

"She's crying hysterically in the girls' locker room. Erin said it's because of you."

"Amber," I started warily, "back off."

"Or what?"

"Oh my God, how many times do we have to go over this? I don't like you. I'm not ever going to like you, but I'm not scared of you either. Whatever you got, try it. Trust me...you'll be fun to take on...and a piece of cake. Until you've got something new to say, just shut up. Please."

"I cannot believe—"

"Mandy's my sister. I love her. But when she asks for my opinion, I'm going to give it to her. And I'm not going to let her pull me into your twisted games. I have enough stuff of my own to worry about."

Amber fell silent. Thank God. I really *was* thanking Him—because she turned and left. Finally.

I looked for the Invisibles again, and after checking out the parking lot I saw them. I couldn't believe it. They were standing underneath a tree in the farthest corner where a picnic table was. Wow. Talk about—a hiding place if you ever wanted to hide from a mass murderer.

As I started over to them, I was also shocked to see Tray's SUV still in the lot, but no Tray. Huh.

"Hey," I called out and saw Molly turn around to me.

"Hi." Her smile looked forced. Guess the whole two groups of friends meeting each other was stressful.

"You okay? You guys want to grab a bite to eat?" I asked, making sure my voice was casual. I had a feeling that if I used anything else, they'd scatter—again—like frightened deer.

"Uh—" Molly murmured, glancing between Angela and Kayden.

"I'll go and grab my car and pull around. How about that?" I suggested, and then I took off before they could say no. To my surprise, they were still there when I drove around. Molly took the front seat, and Angela and Kayden sat stiffly in the back. Kayden looked a little more relaxed though, but not much. Molly was easily the most extroverted of them, and that was saying *a lot*.

"We're going to the diner?" Molly squeaked, flushing when I pulled into the parking lot. It was packed, but it *was* the hang out.

"Yep," I said, a bit more firmly. They couldn't leave without me. I had the keys to the car.

A full minute later, they all climbed out, not a word spoke between the three of them. I led the way, figuring they'd have to stand in the doorway for a good five minutes. But I was surprised. The second we were led to a booth in the back, all three of them hurried around me and squished into it.

Sitting beside Molly—big surprise that Kayden and Angela sat together—I ordered a Diet Coke when the server came over. She gave us a startled look. Don't ask me why—I had no idea.

"So," I commented, staring at Angela and Kayden.

Silence.

Like I'd expected anything else. Ha.

"Um—" Even Molly was coming up with nothing.

I don't know why I was doing this. I don't know why I was sitting—at the diner—with these three in an uncomfortable silence. I was trying to be more than just table-mate and science lab friends with Molly. I actually liked her. And I guess I was willing to do just about anything to keep myself distracted from the things I was so uncertain about in my life: Brian, Jace, Galverson, Tray.

But it wasn't working.

"Do you guys like anyone?" I asked, a bit desperate for conversation.

Angela and Kayden both looked horrified, their eyes wide in alarm, but at least they were looking at me—finally.

"So," I threw a thumb in Molly's direction, "this one's boy crazy. How about you two?"

Still nothing.

"But, I have to tell you, I will only be Molly's pimp. The two of you...good luck, but no pimping. Sorry," I said cheerfully.

I saw a brief smile on Kayden's face, but...in the blink of an eye—it was gone. But hey, at least it was something.

"Hey. You."

Oh please, please, please don't be for me, I prayed. How many verbal lashings does a girl have to go through in a day?

"Scoot in, Taryn."

It was Carter.

I grinned back at him. "Hey." I pushed Molly against the wall as Carter sat on my other side.

He looked around the table, but was quiet.

"So...um," he began, "how's it going?"

Alright, I knew he could be here for one of two things—one, he was send by Tray to make sure I wasn't doing anything stupid, or two, he was here to grill me about Mandy and Devon. Just wanting to beat him to the punch, I said flatly, "I already told Mandy she's an idiot. I had no bearing on her moronic decision to go back to Devon."

"Oh." It wasn't what he was going to say; I saw a flicker of some emotion in his eyes that I couldn't decipher. "Uh...well, yeah. I mean, come on, we all knew it was only a matter of time. It's Mandy and Devon, you know?" I'm sure he meant for it to come out as if he didn't care, be he didn't quite pull it off.

I said lightly, "It used to be you, you know, but I was told on good authority that Amber told you to date Sabrina Lyles because Mandy had a thing for you."

He laughed nervously. "Come on. Mandy's always had a thing for me—me and Tray—if Devon wants her, it's who she's gonna be with. He's like her..."

"Comfortable blanket?" I finished for him dryly.

"Yeah." He chuckled, relaxing. "I like you, Taryn. I really do. We need more of you in our circle."

"I'm not in the circle."

"Oh, yes you most certainly are, he proclaimed heartily. "One, you're with Tray. Two, Mandy's your sister. And three, Amber and Jasmine are terrified of you—and I'm talking 'shit in your pants' terrified of you. I love it. Trust me, that puts you in the circle. Right smack-fucking-dab in the middle. Plus, the guys like you. You don't play those stupid games the rest of the girls do."

"Bryce and Devon like me?" I asked incredulously. I'd torn into both of 'em.

"Well, yeah. They respect you."

I chose to stay silent.

"Anyway, I was wondering what's up with Tray? You two have a fight?" He grinned, flashing one of those godlike charming smiles, at the server who nearly dropped our order. I watched and realized he'd done it without thinking. It had become an automatic instinct—he was a natural born womanizer.

Seriously.

"Why do you ask?" I asked curiously.

"Because he's pissed. I know it's Tray and he's pretty—well—pretty tight-assed about stuff, you know. But something's off with him. The guys want to go to the casino tonight and Tray said he didn't give a shit where we go. That's not Tray. Tray's either up for the casino or he's not. When he says he doesn't give a shit—it means something's off." He drank some of my Diet Coke and continued, "So, what's up with you two?"

"I don't know how it's any of your business," I remarked, grabbing my glass away from him.

"Oh!" His eyes lit up. "So you two did have a fight? Wow. This is...this is a mile-marker—Tray's upset because of a girl."

"You make him sound like he's made of stone or something."

"Last time Tray was upset about a girl was in the seventh grade when Kimberly Farnum moved away...before she gave him a blow job. He was really pissed."

I literally watched the Invisibles shrink further into the booth. I wonder if they knew what a blow job was.

I sighed annoyed. "Thanks, but I can assure you this has nothing to do with blow-jobs. Is he here?"

"Yeah," Carter grabbed my pop again, "we're around the corner. He called and wanted to grab a burger. I just happened to see you 'cause I was heading to the bathroom."

I drank the rest of my Diet Coke.

Carter was watching me, waiting for a response. "So?" he asked expectantly.

I shrugged. "Look...yeah...something went down, but I'm not telling you about it."

"Well, can you go over and get it on with him? I mean, Tray's not any fun when he's like this. You can use my car."

Okay. Seriously? I smacked him in the head.

"Ouch," he murmured, rubbing his head. "What the hell?"

"Want me to smack you again," I dared him.

"Fine." He shrugged, standing up. "But man, Taryn, go and talk to him at least."

"I can't," I said stiffly.

"Why not?"

"Because, I don't know what I'll say, okay? Now leave. It's none of your business." I pointed in the direction of the bathroom.

He rolled his eyes, but he got up and went to the bathroom. I knew he'd probably have something more to say when he came back.

Molly, Angela, and Kayden were watching me—all three of them had their eyes glued to me. Progress!

"What?" I asked.

Of course, Angela and Kayden looked away.

Molly was in awe. "We just sat at the same table as Carter Sethlers. Oh. My. Goodness. Holy. Light. Sockets."

I loved this girl.

"Molly," I murmured, "you could've said hi."

"Right." She was still reveling. "Carter Sethlers sat here. Here. With us. Can you believe it?"

She blinked, realizing it *did* just happen. "I mean—" She flushed, grabbing her drink.

"Trust me, he'll be back. Say hi next time," I said wryly.

Angela squeaked at that, but cowered even farther in her corner.

"Do you guys seriously not talk? Ever?"

"We don't really have anything to say," Kayden spoke up, and I fell back in amazement. She had a thick, almost silky voice; one of those sexy voices that guys go crazy for.

"What do you mean?" I asked, dumbfounded. How can you not have anything to say?

"We're not like you. We're...nobodies," she explained, like it made perfect sense.

Oh no. No fucking way.

"You're not nobody," I said fiercely. "Someone told you that you were a nobody, but you're not. You choose to let them be right or wrong. You're the only one that can decide if you're a nobody or not."

Someone had told me I was a nobody once, and there was no fucking way they were right.

"Taryn," Molly said quietly, from her far corner of the booth. It was only then that I realized how upset I'd gotten.

"I'll be right back," I said, hurriedly, as I slipped out the booth and headed to the bathroom. That word just brought so many memories back to me. I needed to force down all these feelings so I didn't have a break down, at the diner of all places. Breathing heavily, I got a few paper towels and wet my face.

When I got back to the table, feeling like an idiot, I was surprised that Carter was sitting in my place. With Molly, Angela, and Kayden all grinning—blushing—but grinning back at him.

Carter's stock just sky-rocketed with me.

I moved to stand by the table and Carter looked up with a grin. "Hey. Where'd you go?"

"Bathroom." I fixed him with a stare, but we both knew it lacked any heat. He was in good with me now.

He stood and moved to the side. "Why don't you guys come sit with us? We got room. Mitch and the guys just took off."

"Oh, um—" I wanted to say no. I really wanted to say no, but I saw the look in Molly's eyes and I knew she may never have this chance again. It was sad to say, but this might make their entire year. "Sure," I said reluctantly.

Carter grinned, his eyes all-knowing, as he took in my torment. The shithead.

When we walked around the corner, they were in the back corner. Bryce, Grant, and three other guys sat on one side. Tray and two others were on the other side, with three empty chairs at their table. As we neared, the guys looked up and saw us coming. I saw a flash of surprise in Tray's eyes when he saw me.

One of the guys stood up and grabbed two more chairs from a nearby table.

"Hey, Taryn," Bryce and Grant greeted me easily, standing and taking the empty chairs so I could sit by Tray with the rest beside me.

Really. They didn't have to.

I sat down stiffly and smiled to the group. "Guys, this is Molly, Angela, and Kayden. Girls, this is Grant, Bryce, Tray, and—"

Carter took over, "Scotts, Grates, Kinley, Colt, and Derrick." They all grinned in response, but were all a bit taken aback.

"You girls hungry?" Grant offered. "Help yourself." They had at least eight appetizers in the middle of the table, plus individual plates in front of each of them. I really hate how guys can eat. It's a universal curse on women.

I sighed. Angela looked like she was going to pass out. Kayden was biting her lips, both of them, looking everywhere except for at any of the guys, and Molly looked like a lobster, blushing from head to toe.

"They're," I faltered, "shy."

The guys laughed.

"So, why are you with them?" Bryce teased. "Because no one would describe you as shy."

"Fuck off," I said easily, but laughed. "Bryce, you got an idea for the science contest?" We were supposed to do some invention. I had it made—Molly was my partner. It was an easy A for me. "You should hit up Molly for some ideas, she's a science genius, and *my* partner, so don't even think of stealing her."

After looking at me like I'd lost my mind, he turned to Molly and asked, "So, what are you guys doing your project on?"

Molly gave him a tight smile, still blushing, but she managed to get out, "I'm thinking of using a statistical design to find the migrant rotation of Canadian geese in the next three months around level three wetlands."

I was so not participating in that conversation.

The rest of the guys were tuned in—they hunted—they could actually understand what she was talking about. Imagine that, Molly had something in common with these guys.

I felt Tray brush my thigh underneath the table and looked over. He was staring intently at me. He reached for my chair and pulled it closer. Leaning down, he murmured, "Thought you'd be halfway to Pedlam by now."

This is why I wanted to avoid him. I didn't know what to say, because I didn't know what I was even going to do anymore.

I shrugged and signaled for another Diet Coke.

"Taryn," Tray spoke, "are you still—"

"I don't know, okay? I mean, you kinda laid a lot on me, you know?"

"Yeah," he bit out, leaning against the back of his chair, watching me closely.

"What am I supposed to say?"

He shrugged, looking colder than normal—if that was possible.

"I mean, it's not the same situation."

"You're right. You have an easy out. I didn't," he clipped out, sounding and looking even more pissed off than a second ago.

"Oh come on. I have a right to know—"

He stood up abruptly and walked outside, leaving me sitting there, irritated beyond words. I stalked after him, finding him walking to my car.

"Come on, Tray!" I yelled after him and I got even more pissed off—he had my keys. *My* keys in his hands and he was getting behind *my* wheel. I stomped around the car and got into the passenger seat. "What are you doing? This is my car!"

"We're leaving," he replied, gunning my car in reverse.

"I don't really feel like getting in a car accident today," I said tightly. "What about my friends?"

"Those aren't your friends," he shot back. "Those are your charity cases and Carter will give 'em a ride back."

"They are not my charity cases," I said hotly.

"Yes, they are. You feel sorry for them and you're trying to find friends who would never even think of lying to you. Those are your charity cases, you're using them to make yourself feel better."

I slumped in my chair and let my temper simmer, knowing it was going to boil over pretty soon.

CHAPTER FOURTEEN

Tray drove us to school and got into his own vehicle. A second later, he peeled out of the parking lot and I stewed. I knew he wanted me to follow him, but Tray hadn't made that demand.

So, I just sat there, in my car and thought of my options: follow Tray back to his house or go home.

I chose to go home. I needed another shower and a change of clothes. Plus, I could do with some peace and quiet. Tray couldn't get mad at me for going home; he'd be irritated that I didn't follow him, but would be livid if I went to Pedlam.

So I went home. Austin was downstairs and I assume he was hanging out with friends—I could hear other voices, including a few girls. Interesting. I made a mental note to go down and embarrass him later. I couldn't do it now, not when my emotional wiring was so frayed.

"Hey, honey." Shelley bustled around the kitchen.

"Hi," I replied, hopping onto a stool, "what are you doing?"

"Oh, Austin brought a bunch of his friends home. He never acts like it, but it means a lot to him if I prepare some food for them. Gotta do it, all those kids like to eat, you know."

I grinned. "He got a girlfriend down there?"

Shelley sent a radiant wink and a grin my way. "That's my thinking too. Maybe we should 'investigate' later, hmmm?"

"Looks like homemade pizza," I murmured, watching her take a pan out of the oven.

"Oh, hmm mmm. Austin's favorite. Mandy always liked the same. They have the same tastes in a lot of ways. Pizza, lasagna, and now Mandy loves salads. Poor thing." Her eyes lit up. "Oh my gosh, I'm so sorry, Taryn. I forgot to ask how your friend is. The one in the hospital?"

"Uh—" I didn't even know, except that he was a liar. "He's...in rare form again," I replied, with a hint of sarcasm.

"Oh good. I was worried about you, you know. I know that you're having a hard time with moving here from Pedlam. You must have a bunch of good friends back there. I'm sure you miss it."

"Yeah," I said softly, realizing that I did. At times I missed it so much that it was painful. Right now I wished I could just turn my back on it, forget it ever existed, but it was hard.

"Hey, I was thinking," Shelley said brightly. "Why don't you and I go swimming again this evening? You know, after Austin and his friends eat and everything? I thought it would be fun. What do you think?"

"I—" I started, but she interrupted me before I could blow her off.

"Great! Let's plan on heading out in two hours." Then she was at the stairway, calling, "Austin! The pizza's done, guys. Come and get it."

A second later, I had just enough time to step out of the way when Austin and five pubescent boys and three girls rushed upstairs, zeroing in on the pizza in record time.

The girls were slower, looking a bit uncertainly at the pizza. I knew how they were feeling. They wanted it, they were salivating for it, but being skinny meant not eating. *Especially* in front of boys, who were inhaling the food without chewing.

"Hey, your sis is hot, man!" one guy said, his mouth moving around a mouthful of pizza. He nudged Austin. "You never told us that."

The girls were staring at me intently, raking me up and down, checking me out.

"Shut up, dick," Austin retorted, wiping his mouth.

"Austin," Shelley reprimanded, looking stern, but just failing. You could see the way she adored her son.

"Whatever." Austin rolled his eyes. "Mom, where's the pop?"

"Oh. I'll go and grab some. I left them in the car."

"Why don't Austin and all his friends go and get them?" I suggested, staring down one of his friends, seeing a hand reaching out to cop a feel, he was getting perilously close to my ass for his own livelihood.

"Oh, come on!" Austin cried out.

"Go," I ordered. And they went, but Austin flicked me off—it was becoming his favorite gesture—just as they slipped out the door.

I looked at the girls. "Okay. Quick, grab a few pieces and head downstairs. I'll hold 'em off for a while."

Each looked gratefully at me, giving me looks of godlike idolatry as they grabbed their plates and darted downstairs.

"Well," Shelley gave me an appraising look, "I didn't even think of that."

I leaned a hip against the counter. "I'm a girl and I remember what it was like when I was that age."

Pretty soon, the guys bounded back inside, each with a twenty-four pack in their arms. Unloading them on the counter, they each grabbed another piece of pizza. I tapped one of the boxes. "These can go in the pantry, where the pop *always* goes." I gave Austin a pointed glare. The kid was testing the boundaries right now, he knew where they went. I knew he was only acting like this because his friends were here, but Shelley was just letting him get away with it.

Fine. I'll be the bitch.

Grumbling, Austin showed them where to go—half of the guys knew where they went anyway—and when they came back, I saw his hand slowly raising, his finger was inching upwards...

"If that finger touches the air, you're computer's going to mysteriously come down with a virus and all your porn's going to be gone."

The finger stayed in place, and the hand was lowered back to his side, but he still glared at me.

The rest of the little dudes inched away from me. The one who tried to touch my ass suddenly looked like the pizza had gone down the wrong tube.

"Whatever." Austin shrugged, saving face, and then they grabbed the rest of the pizza, some pop, and headed back downstairs.

Shelley was fighting back a grin and burst out laughing the second they were around the corner.

"Oh, dear. I shouldn't be laughing, but I've never seen Austin handled like that. I've never been able to get him to do anything."

I shrugged and went to my own room. It should've been her job, not mine or Mandy's. We weren't the parents.

When I got to my room, I sat at my desk and did homework. I worked for a good hour straight, getting most of everything done, including a paper that's due at the end of the semester in psychology. Mrs. Maslow would be so proud—it was on Pavlov's behavioral conditioning. Ivan and his dogs had nothing on him and those little rats.

"Taryn." Shelley knocked and poked her head through. "You think you'll be ready to go pretty soon?"

I checked my phone, no calls. Thank God.

"Yeah, give me five minutes," I replied, starting to look forward to a good swim.

A moment later we were in the car and Shelley was pulling back out into the road. She was so excited, swimming just cleared her head and she loved that it was something we could do together. And she loved how Austin and I seemed to have bonded. Really. His friends couldn't shut up about me, they thought I was so cool. She'd heard it herself, when she went down to hang out with them and watch a movie. She talked the entire way. I stayed silent.

Holy hell, the water felt great. It felt great to do my own thing again. I spent an hour on the diving boards and two hours doing laps. I felt alive when I pulled myself out.

I saw Shelley at a patio table, talking with a slim, older guy. He looked to be in his thirties, and he didn't look half bad. I saw the shoulders and knew he was a swimmer or had been a swimmer.

"Taryn!" Shelley gushed, extending a hand to me and pulling me to her side. "This is Mr. Greenly. You know, the coach I was telling you about."

"Hi," I said stiffly, feeling uncomfortable. Didn't Shelley know I hated to be hugged by now?

"Prescott saw you on the diving boards. He'd like you to try out for the swim team. Isn't that magnificent?"

"Uh—" I must've looked in pain, because Prescott chuckled.

He murmured, "Coach Greenly." He extended a hand out and shook mine. "You have a lot of talent. If you're interested in getting pushed and training to your potential, come talk to me. My office is in the rec center, just off the pool."

It actually sounded tempting, but I couldn't think about it right now. I had enough on my mind.

On the way home, Shelley was already planning my future: what scholarship I was going to get, what schools I should apply to.

I sighed in relief when I finally managed to escape to my room. I closed the door and quickly laid on my bed, exhaustion seeping into every bone.

I must've fallen asleep, because I woke up to my phone ringing. It was ten at night and the hallway was dark under my door.

Rolling over, I grabbed it—Mandy.

"Hello?" I asked, disoriented.

"Hey, where are you?" she asked.

"At home."

"Mom and Dad home?"

"I dunno. We went swimming and then I fell asleep, but I think everyone's asleep. The hallway's dark and I don't hear anything."

"Thank God." She breathed in relief. "Listen, if Mom and Dad ask, tell them I came home late and left early."

"Are you at Devon's?" I asked, laying my head on my pillow.

There was a moment of silence on the other end before she answered, "Are you going to go off on me if I say yes?"

"No," I muttered. "You already know how I feel."

"Yes, I do," she sounded annoyed, "but this is my decision."

"I know, I know. I'm just looking out for you, you know. We're sisters and all," I mumbled, feeling awkward. All this new family stuff was new to me.

"Okay," she trailed off for a moment, "I thought you'd be at Tray'."

"No. We're...he's not happy with me right now."

"You guys had a fight?"

"I guess you could call it that. I don't know what it was."

"But you're not over there?"

"No."

"And you'd like to be?"

"Yeah."

"But you can't because of whatever it is?" Mandy was just good at this game.

"Yeah."

"You're in a fight," she announced proudly.

"Are you happy about this?" I asked, confused and annoyed.

"Yes! Tray is in a fight, with a girl. A girl. And it's my sister. That's awesome!" she cried out excitedly.

"I cease to understand the significance. All I know is that I can't go over there until I make a decision about something...one that he'll be happy with."

"What was the fight about?" she asked curiously.

"I want to go after my friends. He doesn't want me to." I kept it short and simple. It was the basic gist of it anyway. She didn't need to know all about Galverson and Tray's eighth grade year of hell.

"Oh."

"Oh...what?"

"Nothing. Just, oh," Mandy commented.

I heard a muffling sound on her end and asked, "Is that Devon?"

"Yeah. Amber and Erin are here too. We just ordered some food."

"Who's Erin?"

"A friend of mine. She's on the student council with me," Mandy replied, her voice half-turned from the phone.

"Alright, I'll pass along your lie to Shelley and Kevin." I laughed, hanging up. I got up, brushed my teeth, and changed into my pajamas. I crawled in my bed and curled underneath the covers. I was asleep within moments.

The next morning I had a realization: Shelley and Keven had no clue as to what went on in their own home. None. Mandy didn't come home last night and they didn't even noticed. They didn't care.

To tell the truth, I was surprised they passed the adoption agency's investigation. Kevin was never home. If he wasn't at the hospital, he was off with his golf buddies or at a medical conference. And Shelley was just clueless all around.

I was a bit surprised that their marriage worked. I saw no interaction between them. But I knew there must've been something between them, Shelley went on a lot of the conferences with him. Which is what she was packing for that morning. When I entered the kitchen, I saw three suitcases on the stoop and Shelley was flying from the kitchen, down the basement, back up, and then up to their bedroom. Occasionally she made a side trip to the foyer closet. Then back to do the entire routine again.

It would've been funny if I hadn't realized, at that moment, that I was more a boarder—not paying rent—than a daughter. This is how Mandy and Austin must feel.

"Uh," I spoke up, "Mandy wanted me to let you know that she took off early this morning for school. She needed to do some stuff with student council."

"Oh, okay," Shelley mumbled, distracted. She stopped, suddenly, and turned to me. "You have a good day at school, Taryn. And don't forget to talk to Coach Greenly. He seems like a very nice man." Then she was off again.

Grabbing an apple, I left and saw Austin waiting on the curb with a sullen look on his face.

"Hey, punk. Need a ride?"

He glowered at me for a moment and then stood up slowly, following me to my car. As I pulled out onto the road, I asked, "So, another conference, huh?"

"This one's in Switzerland," he snapped, slumping in his seat. "They're going to be gone for freaking three weeks. It's a month-long conference, that's what Mom said."

"And your dad?"

"He's an asshole," Austin mumbled, looking out his window.

I dropped him off outside the middle school and was surprised when he said, "See you later." No middle finger goodbye this time. We were making progress.

When I got to the high school, I parked in my normal spot. The hallways were crowded, like always, but there was excitement in the air: the football team was leaving for the play-offs that afternoon.

Which meant no Devon for two days.

Which meant Mandy would be annoying as hell for two days.

Which meant...fuck.

First period was exhausting. All the cheerleaders were out—they'd gotten permission to finish their decorations for the pep-rally. The football players were leaving immediately after the pep-rally, which meant we got out of sixth period twenty minutes early. I'd yet to decide if was going to attend or skip. Who wouldn't skip? Seriously.

I actually attended health for second period. No Tray. Molly informed me that he had skipped, along with all the football players.

So needless to say, school passed without event. Every class was full of just normal average students and some of the discussions were actually fun. Interesting to listen to, at least. I got into a debate in history. I knew way more about the Roman Empire than whatever her name was.

Molly told me later that she was our soon-to-be valedictorian.

Imagine that. But I did know more than she did. And the teacher agreed with me.

And...surprise, surprise: sixth period was magically full. It was like everyone that was skipping decided to attend sixth period. And I have no idea why.

Hearing the last bell, everyone filed out and chaos ensued. I swear, half the students took off for the parking lot and the other half went to the auditorium. I was still torn: to skip or not to skip?

"Hey," Molly piped up from behind me.

"Hi." I gave her a lazy grin.

"You going out?" She gestured to the parking lot.

"Uh...I haven't decided if I'm skipping or not."

She looked confused. "Um...the pep rally's in the parking lot."

I shut my locker and replied, "Yeah. I knew that." I'm such a moron.

"Ookay—"

As we both walked down the hallway, I was a bit surprised. The pep rally committee and cheerleaders had outdone themselves. In the middle of the parking lot stood a huge corral and to the side was a livestock trailer filled hay and miniature donkeys.

In the middle of the corral was a stage, with the cheerleaders all standing up and waiting.

"Hey, Rawley!" one of the cheerleaders called out.

The crowd went wild.

As the cheerleaders proceeded to perform their cheer, I saw Tray in the back of the parking lot. He was sitting on the top of his SUV, with a few other guys. I also saw Aidrian Casners standing right below him, smiling up at him. When he looked down, her chest was perfectly displayed for his eyes.

Okay. I guess I never really decided he *wasn't* a bastard so he *really* wasn't letting me down right now.

The cheerleaders finished their cheer and the coach came onto the stage. Speech one was given, speech two (by the football captain, which was the guy that was sitting by Tray) was done, and then the trailer opened and the donkeys were led out.

Even I cracked a smile at that.

The rest of the pep rally consisted of twelve football players riding the donkeys as they attempted to play a game that resembled ultimate frisbee, but with hands. And donkeys.

It was a sight I'd never experienced before and I was suddenly glad that I hadn't skipped.

Molly was giggling the entire time.

I nudged her, pointing to the corner by the picnic tables. "Aren't those your friends over there?"

"Yeah, but they won't come watch this. They'll just stay over there."

"How come?" I asked curiously.

Molly didn't answer, not right away. I asked again, and she said, faltering, "Because Kayden and Angela were made fun of one time during a pep rally."

"What?"

She shrugged, looking uncomfortable. "They got picked by the crowd for a relay and Kayden tripped and broke her nose. Then one of the football players called her Rudolph in the microphone for everyone to hear. You know, because of the blood."

"Oh—" I didn't know what else to say.

"Yeah, then Angela tried to help, but Kayden tripped again and fell on her. Angie Hodgkins called Angela a handicapped elf, said she couldn't walk and hold Rudolph at the same time."

I couldn't believe it. I mean, I knew kids could be assholes, but where were all the teachers?

"The teachers thought it was all a show." Molly explained, no longer giggling.

"I'm sorry," I said sincerely. Molly wasn't saying anything, but she must've had her own share of humiliation. There was a reason the three of them had banded together. Why they were called the Invisibles.

For the first time since I'd been here, I was glad I had come to Rawley. I was happy I met Molly. She wasn't an Invisible anymore and I'd take anyone on that tried to humiliate her again.

"It's in the past," she murmured, her voice cracking. It wasn't in the past. It was one of how many incidents that have happened in the past.

"Why are you friends with me?" I asked honestly, dumbfounded as to why she'd want to be my friend. I was a bitch. It's what I was known for and yet this Invisible had singled me out. She'd talked to me, and she continues to talk to me.

"Because you're not one of them," Molly answered matter-of-factly.

"But—"

She turned and met my gaze, seeing the torment in mine—it must've been there—I was feeling it. Molly spoke truthfully, "You're different. You're...you're one of us but...you're one of them."

Molly continued, "I don't know. I just...knew you wouldn't turn on me like them. You're not like that."

"I'm a bitch."

"Yeah. You're a bitch to *them*. You're a bitch to who deserves it. Not me. Not Angela or Kayden. You're anything *but* a bitch to us." Molly wiped away a tear at the corner of her eye.

I was at a loss for words. My throat suddenly tightened.

Drawing in a shuddering breath, I muttered, "I...I gotta go. See you tomorrow."

When I got to my locker, the hallways were completely empty, which was a good thing. I heaved a sigh of relief. I didn't need to get into anything with anyone.

"Hey." I was tapped from behind.

Turning, I saw Props standing, looking aggrieved. It was the only word I could think of to describe him.

"Hi."

He handed me a flash drive. Gesturing to it, he said, "That's for you. Everything. All trails, all traces, everything. Where each and every account wound up at."

I was surprised. It had been a day. Within twenty-four hours, he had everything I asked for.

"Thanks."

"Yeah, well," he shuffled slightly, stuffing his hands in his pockets, "you get what I wanted?"

"Yeah."

His eyes lit up. "Really?"

"Yeah. You're taking her to a concert at the Seven8 on Friday."

"Oh yeah. Third Wave. They're Aidrian's favorite."

This guy was a littler stalkerish.

"Um...yeah. I told her you'd show up with the tickets on Friday."

"How'd you get her to agree to it, man? I mean, I never thought...you know." He was excited and riding a wave of insomnia no doubt.

"I have to get the tickets first, but be ready Friday. I'll get directions and her phone number—"

"Already have it. I know where she lives too."

"Oh...um...okay."

"The concert starts at eight, so I can pick her up at six-thirty." The dude was all business now. He was gleaming.

"Alright, I'll pass the message." Then off he went, bouncing in the hallway giddily.

Just then a wave of students came back in from outside. The pep rally must've finished because lockers were quickly thrown open and bags were all grabbed. Every football player looked on a mission as they grabbed their stuff and darted back out to the parking lot. Their Greyhound must've been waiting.

I caught a glimpse of Mandy through the crowd. She was bouncing up and down, probably on a high from the pep rally. She threw her arms around Devon and gave him a long kiss.

Then my eyes trailed over their shoulders and met Tray's. He'd been watching me and was walking towards me.

I grabbed my purse and nudged my locker door shut, slipping the flash drive into my front-pocket.

"Hey," Tray greeted, standing a few feet away.

"Hey," I said softly in return. I still didn't know what I was going to say and I was *very* aware of the flash drive in my purse.

"Some of us are going to Rickets' House tonight—early play-offs celebration, but we're all heading out to Crystal Bay right now." Crystal Bay was a local lake that had a small cave which dipped into the cliff overhanging it. On the bottom of the cave was a green-blue pool of water, which literally sparkled when the sun slanted onto it. It was gorgeous and one of my favorite places to swim. I'd gone there once and I was itching to take a dive off the cliff, but when Mandy had taken me, it was too early. That was when I was nice and quiet—before the real Taryn came out.

"Are you asking me if I want to come?"

Tray rolled his eyes. "What the fuck do you think?"

"I don't...I can't. I have to go to Pedlam to get those tickets I promised Casners."

I saw the tension enter his body just at the mere name.

"It's not like that," I reassured him, not really knowing *why* I was reassuring him. "I'm not going for you know. I haven't decided—"

"I don't get why it's such a fucking hard decision! It's a no-brainer Taryn!" Tray stood there, his jaw clenching.

I didn't like him yelling at me and I couldn't stand that he was so angry with me. And I hated to admit that it bothered me so much.

I reached out and slid a finger into the front of his pants and pulled him close. Against his chest, I whispered, "I'm sorry, okay?"

Reluctantly Tray slid his arms around me, one of his palms resting underneath my shirt, just inside the back of my pants. He bent his head next to mine and I felt his breath on my neck.

"Before," I started, "before I would've already been over there, demanding answers, but now...you got in my head, alright? I just have to be the one to make the decision. Me. Not you."

"And I don't understand why it's taking so long," he said roughly, but he pulled me tighter against him, dropping his forehead to my shoulder.

"I don't know why either." I bit my lip, raising my arms around his neck. "But I promised your playmate tickets and those are in Pedlam, so that's where I have to go to get them."

He went rigid again.

I said quickly, "I won't come across Jace or anyone. Promise. I can slip in and out and no one will ever know I was there."

"How long?" he asked harshly. God—he really hated that I was going to Pedlam. Remember the days when he didn't give one shit? Fond memories.

I grinned at my thoughts, but I answered, "Not long. Get in, get out. It shouldn't take long at all."

"I could come with?" he offered.

His offer earned him a deep long kiss. Of which both of us were breathing hard when I whispered against his lips, "Trust me. This is a one-woman job. They won't have any idea I was been there." I took a deep breath. "I could come to Crystal Bay when I'm done."

"You'll have time?"

"When are you going to Rickets' House?"

"Like, ten tonight."

"I'll call when I get back. If you guys are still at Crystal Bay, I'll show up. If not, I'll just come to your place. Shelley and Kevin are heading out for a month-long conference today anyway, so no parents to check in with."

"Fine." He gave me another hard kiss before he left for his locker.

After that, I headed to my car. I made sure I had everything I needed in my trunk and then I was on the road, heading for Pedlam. In the back of my mind, I kept thinking back to when Tray and I were just fuck buddies.

I turned the radio on and let myself get lost in the music. When I got to Pedlam, I circled the block, one down, from the Seven8. There was an apartment ramp, which came up right against where the Seven8's basement ended. I parked in the ramp, and found a small, hidden door that connected the two complexes. I don't even know if Jace knew about it. I found it, accidentally, one time when I was upset with Brian. I'd needed time alone so I went looking for a hiding spot.

I quickly checked to make sure there weren't any added security alarms.

There weren't, so I picked the lock and headed inside. The basement was pitch black—like always.

The nice thing about me—I didn't need light. I've always had excellent night-vision. So I just moved to where the maintenance elevators were and pushed 'em open. Clipping my karabiner to the elevator cable, along with a glick's lock, I hooked my ropes from the karabiner to my waist, and I started climbing up. Sliding the karabiner right along as I inched upwards.

It was a workout and one I hated doing when was on a job, but sometimes there was just no way around it.

So I kept inching upwards. It took about thirty minutes until I came across the sixth floor where the club manager's office was located.

I braced myself between the elevator cables and the doors. Pressing a Listening Ear—it's a very cleverly named device, and there's no sarcasm in that statement—against the doors, I listened to make sure no one was in the hallway. There shouldn't have been anyone there yet. It was around four in the afternoon; the staff wouldn't start heading in for about two more hours.

I gritted my teeth as I pulled open the elevator doors, and slipped through. The doors shut immediately, sliding smoothly back in place. I was exposed in that moment, and I hate it. Stupid Jace didn't want to put venting shafts from the elevator, said it would be too easy for someone to break in. The only nice thing was that this floor was the least populated. Most of the staff either headed up to the private suites or to the conference rooms on the second floor. \Jace told me once that they couldn't put cameras inside the boxes, so they put them up in the hallways instead. That way they had a record of who was going in and out.

I quickly darted down the hallway and picked the lock on the manager's office door. Jace had hired two of them, Noble and Richard. I always had to grin—Richard. It was too easy. I liked to refer to them as Noble Dick. The funnier thing is that they didn't even get along; both were complete opposites. But both were control freaks. Which was why I knew one of them would have copies of backstage passes and some last-minute tickets in their desks. They never trusted the other to take care of that stuff so they acted as if they were the only club manager.

Inside, I quickly rifled through the bottom drawers of Noble's desk first, making sure to put everything back in its place. They weren't there. The second drawer didn't have 'em either. Turning, I caught sight of a pile on his chair. The guy was just messy. Everything was a mess, but I knew Noble knew exactly where everything was.

Looking through the pile, I saw a packet of back-stage passes, banded together with a rubber band. I grabbed two and—a sense of triumph flashed through my body—I saw a file labeled 'Third Wave Tickets.' When I opened the file, I saw a stack of tickets for front row seats.

I grabbed the tickets and the back-stage passes, stuffing them in my little pack that was plastered against my back, and headed back out. Just before I reached the door, I heard voices.

Fuck.

I quickly slipped out the door and ducked into an office further down. Thank God the office was empty. I couldn't be caught in the manager's office. And I really couldn't let them know that I had ever been there.

As I lifted the window, the door suddenly opened and I had just enough time to register that it was Jace's voice.

"Yeah, I'm looking now. Fuck off. I'll get the fucking gun and head down in a minute—"

He must've seen me.

I looked over my shoulder, poised just on the window frame, and saw his cellphone drop to the floor.

He was frozen in place, staring at me.

And then I jumped.

Landing on the patio, three floors down—fuck, that hurt—I rolled to the end and grabbed the under-railing as my body continued to fall towards the ground. Closing my fingers around the metal—damn, it fucking hurt—I could feel my skin tearing away. But I dropped to the ground, seemingly a second later, but my assent was slowed—slightly—by the railings.

I didn't have time to look up, I didn't dare. So I ran, sprinting down the alley and trying to blend in with the crowd on the street.

Gritting my teeth, I quickly wrapped the end of my shirt around my hands, pressing it against the wound as I doubled back. Walking down the parking ramp, I got to my car and climbed inside, quickly starting it and getting out of there. I only took enough time to grab a towel in the back. I tore it in half and wrapped each end around my hands.

As I reached the outskirts of town, I pulled over. I deposited everything in my trunk, swearing at myself—I'd lost my ropes, karabiner, and glick's lock—when I'd had to change my escape route.

First rule of burglary: plan on being caught. That meant: always have an escape route ready. And it meant taking everything with you that you couldn't afford to leave behind, and what couldn't be traced back to you.

The items couldn't be traced to me—not that it mattered. Jace already knew I'd been there. He wouldn't know what I stole though. No, he'd probably think I'd been there looking for secrets or whatever the hell else that he was hiding. Not front row tickets and backstage passes. And that's quite alright. Jace could think whatever he wanted.

But my equipment was expensive. Shit, it was *really* expensive.

I got back in my car, and leaned my head against my seat tiredly. I inspected my hands again, gently prodding to check on the bleeding. It had stopped, but the dried blood glued the towel against my skin. When I'd need to re-bandage, I'd probably open the cuts again.

I started the engine and headed home. I needed to drop my stuff off, disinfect my hands, grab a transparent seal to place over my hands, and then head to Crystal Bay. Complete with my bathing suit. There was no way I was going to pass up a chance to dive off that cliff.

Literally.

CHAPTER FIFTEEN

I'd changed at the house, so I was ready to go when I parked and walked down the steep trail that would open up to a beach as I got further down. Crystal Bay was around a cliff that jutted out, meeting the rocks that the waves crashed into. You had to walk on those rocks, to find the narrow rock-ridge leading into Crystal Bay.

As I braced myself on the rocks and followed it inside, I could hear voices. They echoed off the cliff walls, but grew louder as I drew closer. Ducking inside the cave, I was able to see where the trail led. The light grew dim, but it was still manageable. I grinned, just enjoying the rapids that were leading in and out of the cave, right next to me.

A moment later, I saw the light suddenly explode into brightness. I'd reached Crystal Bay, where an opening in the cliffs above allowed the sun to shine in. I was blinded for a second as my eyes was drawn to the water.

"Taryn!" Mandy called out, shrieking excitedly. "Hey! You made it."

"Yeah." I grinned at her, she was drenched in a white bikini, but she was smiling. She looked happy. "I'm here."

"Great!" She latched onto my arm and I smelled alcohol.

They'd started the play-off festivities early.

"Want a drink? Carter brought a pony-keg."

"Where is it?" I glanced around, seeing a bunch of their friends, but I didn't see Tray or Carter.

"At the top." She pointed up, to the top of the cliff. "You gotta climb up to get some. Carter and Grant were telling us we had to jump to get a cup."

"Seriously?" I couldn't figure the logic. You had to climb up, jump, and climb up again for a cup? It wasn't even worth it. Which was probably the point.

"Yeah, but Erin grabbed a cooler for the girls," Mandy pointed to a corner, "so if you want some, help yourself."

Enough talk. I couldn't hold back anymore.

"I'm going to go look for Tray," I murmured, already moving to climb the trail. It was nice, because the trail wasn't as steep as the one outside. It wrapped around a little, moving inside the cave's walls, but it was slippery. When I got to the top, I remembered why everyone congregated at the bottom. The top was just scary. Scary and rough. It was mostly a hole at the top, surrounded by dense forest. Walking barefoot was not smart.

I hopped around, trying to find the smoothest walkway, with the least amount of pebbles. Finally, I just sucked it up and ran to where the guys were located.

Tray, Grant, Carter, and four other guys were lounging around the pony-keg, each holding a plastic cup.

"Heya, Taryn!" Carter grinned a drunk, lopsided grin at me. He raised a cup. "Want a cup? Gotta jump first."

I rolled my eyes, moving to Tray's side. He slid an arm around my waist and brought me against his chest, his hand resting on my stomach. I grinned at Carter. "It's just a ploy. You just don't like sharing the pony-keg, so you make everyone work for it."

"Ah," he scratched the side of his head, "kinda. Yeah. But you want a cup?"

"No thanks. But I am going to jump." I glanced to the cliff's edge, where the water rushed over it. I couldn't suppress the shiver.

Tray must've felt it, because he asked, "Is that from excitement or—"

"It's all for you, baby," I teased.

"Right," he murmured, chuckling, but I shivered a second later, as he moved again, bringing me in full contact with him.

I slid a hand to his arm and rubbed it absent-mindedly with my thumb. I felt myself melting all over again, but I didn't know if it was from the dive or him. Probably both and if I stayed there any longer, I'd be tempted to push the dive off until later and take Tray into the woods.

I straightened away and murmured, "I'm gonna jump."

Tray stepped back as I walked to the cliff's edge. I've no doubt all the guys were watching, but I didn't care.

My knees were melting as I looked down. I'd remember the sweet ache I felt the last time I'd been to Crystal Bay. I hadn't chanced it then. I'd been more afraid, not from the dive, but from the attention I would've received from Mandy's friends. But that was then. This was now.

I'd taken my gloves off and now they all knew who I was.

"Taryn," Tray called after me.

"What?" I looked over and saw he was walking towards me.

"You want your clothes to get wet?" He gestured to me and I realized I still had my skirt and tank-top on. I'd remembered to take off my flip-flops at the bottom, but I hadn't thought about my clothes.

"Oh." I quickly slipped out of them and handed 'em to Tray. He stuffed both items in his back pocket and I stood there in my black bikini. I heard one of the guys let out a small groan.

I saw the corner of Tray's mouth curve upwards into half a grin. He was watching me closely and he could see the excitement pooling in my eyes. Our eyes held for a moment and then I flashed him a smile.

Then I jumped, arching my arms gracefully, twisting vertically (called a twist group) in the air as I soared. It felt like I was flying. I loved feeling the wind against me and as I neared the bottom, I tucked my head, my arms perfectly straight as I cleanly cut through the water. I swam to the surface, my head breaking the water a moment later.

I couldn't wipe the stupid grin off my face as I swam to the side, nor could I stamp down the flood of adrenalin in my body as I hauled myself out.

"Taryn, that was awesome!" Mandy yelled out, sitting on the ground near the cooler.

"Wow."

"Whoa."

Amber and Sasha rolled their eyes. Okay, I don't know if they did or didn't. I wasn't paying attention, but I imagine they probably did.

"Want a drink now?" she called out, raising her glass.

"Going again," I shot back, and climbed right back up. I didn't pay any attention to the guys as I walked back to the edge, and this time I did a reverse group—I faced the water, but as I jumped I rotated my body backwards as I fell through the air. I brought my arms up for a clean, straight entrance and kicked my legs to send my body soaring back up to the surface.

The truth is that I could've done this the entire afternoon.

After a while, the third dive—another twist group—the guys had stopped watching.

When I knew no one was paying attention anymore, I approached the edge and gently lowered myself to the ground. I put my hands out and raised my body to a handstand and then pushed off. I tucked and then let loose, just before I met the water.

Stealing was my first love. This was easily my second.

And holy hell—if Tray and I end the night together in bed, I'll die happy.

When I raised myself out of the water, I realized my legs were a little weak, so I decided to call a break and found Mandy. I fell to the towel she had placed next to her.

"Taryn, I didn't know you could do that," she greeted me excitedly.

I couldn't form words yet, so I just grinned as I accepted a bottle of water one of the girls handed me.

"You're really good," the water girl said—I think her name was Erin. I just said thanks not wanting to humiliate her by calling her the wrong name.

"Man! Mom said you were good, but Taryn, you should join the team. Like, seriously."

I had to laugh at her words. Like, seriously.

"I could talk to Coach Greenly." This suggestion was made by a girl, her hair in a French braid. I don't swing that way, but I was taken aback by how pretty she was. Her brunette hair literally sparkled and she had the longest eyelashes.

I would've been jealous, but nothing could affect me right now. I was still riding the adrenalin wave.

"Thanks, but I've already met him," I murmured, drinking my water.

"My name's Tristan," she introduced herself, nudging Water Girl aside, she continued, "and this is Erin."

"Hi. Taryn."

"We've seen you around, but you probably don't remember our names," Tristan said easily, confidence oozing from her voice. "I've been in Spain until last week. I go to school over there. My parents don't think Rawley has the best education my family of blue-bloods can achieve."

I couldn't tell if she meant to sound snobbish or sarcastic.

I remained silent.

Mandy giggled. "Tristan can't stand her family."

Okay, the girl was being sarcastic.

I saw Amber and Sasha at the other end of the cave. They were talking with two other girls.

"Where's Jasmine?" I asked, not really believing I had even noticed her absence or that I'd even asked.

"She had detention....Oh! Ah!" Mandy cried out.

"What?"

"We were supposed to go and see Mrs. Maslow, remember? That was today, after school." She actually sounded worried.

I raised my eyebrows. "Are you kidding me? She can yell at us tomorrow, if *she* even remembered."

"Why were you supposed to go see her?" Tristan asked.

"Because we—" Mandy started to say.

I interrupted and said flatly, "We had a shouting match. Our teacher overheard. The end."

"Taryn." Seriously, why does Mandy continue to be shocked with how I say things? She should be used to me by now.

"Oh." Tristan fell silent, eyeing both of us intently.

"What?" I asked, shrugging, finishing my water.

"We could get into a lot of trouble. We should call her."

"Right." I reached for another bottle. "You call her—half-drunk. I know I'm not calling. She was probably just going to make us sit in chairs and look at each other. Really. She's a psych teacher."

"Yeah, but—" Mandy was chewing on her lip.

I said firmly, "Mandy, leave it alone. If she brings it up tomorrow, we'll just tell her we forgot. And we did. Tell her it was the excitement of play-offs and we forgot after the pep rally. Who wouldn't, after watching a game of ultimate Frisbees with donkeys?" I grinned.

Mandy giggled. So did Erin.

Tristan looked perplexed or constipated—I always get the two mixed up.

Suddenly there was a large crash in the water, startling everyone. I even jumped slightly.

The pony-keg must've been empty and the guys had dropped it down. One of the guys ran down the trail and pulled it to the side, lifting it onto the ground. Then, one by one, each of the guys jumped off.

The guy, whoever he was, walked over and handed my clothes to me.

I couldn't stop a grin. Tray had thought about me.

And I couldn't do any more thinking because Carter and Tray ran over and picked Mandy and myself up. Each tossed us into the water. I just laughed, waiting for the water to envelope me, but Mandy shrieked, pretending she was scared and mad.

I rolled my eyes and pulled myself out of the water.

Tray was helping Erin and Tristan pack everything in the cooler, but he was watching me over his shoulder.

Our eyes met and held.

I walked to his side and grabbed my clothes. I slipped the tank-top and the skirt on. The skirt was loose and flowing, so perfect swimming clothing. The tank-top was quickly soaked and hugged my curves. Tray didn't mind, I saw his eyes move up and down my body. I rolled my eyes again—like it wasn't something he hasn't seen before.

Hearing a small cough, I looked over and saw Tristan watching us, glancing between Tray and me. She gave me a weak smile. "We're...huh...we're heading out. You need a ride or anything?"

"I drove," I indicated, feeling Tray grab my elbow when I slipped on my sandals. I didn't need help, we both knew that. It was just an excuse to touch—one we were both grateful for.

The slight touch of his fingers sent shivers down my back and I felt myself melting again. I sighed. I really needed to address how my body responded to the mere proximity of him.

"Tray, when are we meeting at your place?" Erin asked, a slight hoarseness in her voice. She was watching him, almost shyly.

The girl had a crush on him, but then again, I'd heard most of the girls had a thing for him. Like I could really judge, I *was* sleeping with him.

"Ten, sharp," he murmured, his hand splayed openly on my back, walking behind me as I led the way.

Carter led the way out for everyone else, down the trails and around the rocks. When we got to the beach, some of the guys took off—stripping as they dove into the waves. The girls—were being girls—laughing and giggling.

Tristan grumbled and moved up the trail to the cars. Which surprised me. Erin followed along, almost meekly.

Amber and Sasha were waiting for the guys, grinning as they held their clothes up. Then they took off, sprinting for the trail, the guys' clothes still clutched in their hands.

Tray laughed. "Fuck that."

I grinned, moving closer to his side, and he slipped his arm around my waist.

"Taryn." Mandy giggled, stumbling over to my car.

"Yeah?" I asked, opening my car door.

"Are you going home? Or should I get a ride with Tristan and Erin?"

"I'm going to Tray's." I looked up at him as I said the words. I saw the agreement in his eyes.

"Okay, I'll see you tonight then."

"Hey, Mandy, Shelley and Kevin went on a—"

"I know." She waved at me, moving off to Tristan's Rolls-Royce—holy crap. "Mom called and left me a message. Austin's staying at a friend's for the week." Then she climbed inside and Tristan drove off, flicking a wave to us.

"So, you're coming over?" Tray asked, looking over to his vehicle. Two of the guys were already inside, waiting for him.

"I'm hoping," I said ruefully.

I saw the hazel turn to amber in his eyes.

I climbed inside my car shakily, seeing Tray cross to his vehicle.

Starting my car, I was halfway through town when I realized I had nothing to wear. I knew if I went to Tray's that I wouldn't be returning home tonight. So I headed home, to quickly pack a bag before heading over.

When I got to the house, Tristan's car was parked in the driveway. I let myself in and darted up the stairs.

"So, I told my parents that I'm not going back there. No fucking way." That was Tristan, coming from Mandy's bedroom.

"Totally." That must've been Erin. Somehow, her agreeing didn't surprise me.

Mandy giggled. "I could totally stay drunk for the rest of the day. We should do this more often."

"Your sister's pretty impressive," Tristan remarked. "Are her and Tray dating?"

It was silent a moment and then I heard her say, "Well, if you ask Taryn, she'll say no, but yes, they're pretty much a couple."

"Does she know about...?"

About what? I wanted to know now. I'm fully aware that I'm standing in the hallway, shamelessly eavesdropping—the conversation was about me anyway.

"You and Tray?" Mandy asked. "I don't think so. I mean, I don't know what they talk about. They were in a fight the last two days though. Musta made up. Hmmm...I love the making up part."

"Yeah, I heard about you and Devon. He's an ass and has such poor taste. Jasmine. Seriously?"

Alright. I'm on the fence with this girl. She could be cool, but there was something about her that rubbed me the wrong way. She reminded me of a slippery eel...just slippery.

"Shut up, Tristan," Mandy said sharply. "We're over that now."

"Whatever. Just saying. I'm guessing Amber wasn't real helpful, was she?" Tristan laughed, the sound hollow.

"Just because," Mandy started, I could hear the irritation in her voice, "Amber didn't have your back doesn't mean it's the same situation. Devon and Tray are different. Much different."

"You're right. Devon's a puppy compared to Tray," Tristan said amusedly.

That bitch. I made up my mind—I didn't like her.

The bitch was baiting Mandy, purposely. Like she was testing out the territory.

"Hey, Mandy!" I called out, strolling into her bedroom. I paused in the doorway. Mandy was standing in the middle of the room. Erin was on the bed, her knees drawn up to her chest. Tristan was standing over Mandy's vanity table, inspecting her pictures, looking like she owned the place.

"Taryn," Mandy murmured weakly. I could see she was grateful for the interruption.

I saw the appraisal in Tristan's eyes. I didn't know what she was appraising or who, but, fuck, I didn't like it.

I spoke coolly, "Mandy doesn't need Amber to back her up. She's got me now."

Holy shit—I saw the shock flash in Tristan's eyes. She knew full well I'd been standing there, listening to her belittle Mandy. I guess she expected me to come in and throw up a façade that I hadn't been listening. The girl needed to learn—that's not me. At all. I had no patience for those who played games.

"Excuse me?" Tristan asked smoothly.

I looked at Mandy and commented, "I came to grab a bag. Call if you need anything. I'll be at Tray's."

"Okay," Mandy breathed out. She got my message—I'd have her back no matter what, even if I didn't agree with her choice of boyfriend or friends. I was her sister, and that wasn't going to change.

I looked at Tristan one last time and then left. In my room, I quickly grabbed some clothes and packed everything I'd need for a few days. I wasn't going to be getting all dressed up if I was correct in my assumption of what Tray and I would be doing to pass the time. Clothes weren't needed for that activity.

When I got downstairs, Tristan was standing in the kitchen. I heard the television on downstairs, so I assumed Mandy and Erin were there.

"Taryn," Tristan spoke up, straightening from the counter, "I...uh..."

"Yeah?" I asked, letting my bag drop to the ground, waiting to hear what she had to say.

"I think we might've gotten off on the wrong foot," she said uncertainly, shifting on her feet. "I...I'm not around that often," she lifted her shoulder, looking innocently at me," but I consider Mandy one of my best friends. It doesn't help when Amber and Jasmine always have her in their clutches."

"I've seen," I murmured, still cautious of her. She seemed genuine, but there was still something off about the girl.

"Yeah...she told me a long time ago that her parents were going to adopt. They'd been approached by an old friend, I guess, and asked if they'd be interested in adopting," she faltered, clearing her throat. "I just...I'm just a little jealous. I mean, here you are, in Mandy's life. Mandy adores you and I'm jealous because I used to be her best friend."

"Look," I began, feeling uncomfortable, "Mandy's never talked about you, so I don't know anything about you and her being best friends."

"It's not just that," Tristan said insistently, taking a step towards me. "It's Tray too."

I stayed silent.

"He's someone I used to care about. Like, a lot. We were together for a while and I've never gotten over him, I guess."

"I know how it sounds." She chuckled self-consciously. "Here's this girl, coming off all jealous of your life and...I'm not pathetic or psychotic. Really, I'm not. I know you were just being protective of Mandy upstairs. I don't want you and me to get off on the wrong foot. That's all...I'd really like to be your friend. For Mandy's sake."

She's taking time away from me and Tray. In bed.

"Look," I said, all this emotional crap was making me want to run away, "if you're Mandy's friend, just be her friend. From what I've seen, there's not many around who know what that word means. That's all I care about."

"Okay. Yeah. Sure," she said, a bit too eagerly.

"Alright, well," I edged towards the door, "I'll see you guys tonight. You're coming to Rickets' House, right?"

"Yeah," Tristan smiled widely at me looking relieved—from what I had no idea. "Tray's at ten, right?"

"Right." I slipped out the door and was in my car in an instant.

There were a few cars parked outside of Tray's when I pulled up. Great. No sex. However, I brightened, no time for any more emotional conversations. Mainly, the one in which Tray and I disagreed.

I glanced at my hands and saw the cuts were not doing that great. The diving hadn't helped, but it'd been worth it. I grinned, feeling the rush again, the water hitting my body, the air against me.

I stowed my bag in his bedroom first before moving into the main house. Everyone was out on a patio.

Around the table I could see there was a group of guys, Amber, Jasmine, Sasha and two other girls.

No Tray.

"He went to get some drinks," Jasmine commented, seeing my sweeping glance. She gave me a friendly smile and, of course, I was automatically suspicious. "Sit." She patted the empty chair beside her.

I noticed Sasha was glowering at her, but she remained silent.

I chose the empty chair beside Grant, at the end of the table.

Jasmine laughed. "Taryn, you're hilarious, you know that."

Now I was feeling patronized.

The room had grown quiet with an uneasy silence.

Amber broke it and asked, "Is Tristan at Mandy's?"

My, isn't she the curious one?

"Yeah," I murmured coolly, leaning back and trying to relax.

"She's a bitch," Amber announced, grinning as Sasha burst out laughing, "and psychotic."

"She's not that bad," Jasmine argued, look surreptitiously at me. "You're just jealous of her, Ams."

"Jealous? Of what?" Amber swore. "Better watch it, Taryn. Tristan thinks she's the only one Mandy can be friends with. She's going to hate you."

"And she's in love with Tray," Sasha included.

"Oh my God. I'd forgotten that. Tristan thinks that her and Tray have this star-crossed lover thing, like Romeo and Juliet," Amber exclaimed excitedly.

"Maybe she'll kill herself then," Sasha suggested, looking evil.

I rolled my eyes and remarked, "Why do you fucking care so much? This is just unnecessary drama." I stood up. "You, people, are exhausting. Just freaking get over it and live your own damn life."

Walking back through the palace, I heard Tray in the kitchen. He was talking on his phone, his head inside the fridge.

"Yeah, dude. No." He chuckled. "I've got the stuff. We'll be at Rickets' tonight. Yeah, yeah, you can get it then."

He saw me when he stood, one hand holding a bucket of KFC, the other a twelve-pack of beer; his cellphone was tucked between his ear and neck.

"I gotta call you back," he murmured, placing everything on the counter. "Hey."

In that second, looking at him, I realized how tired I really was.

Not just of the senseless drama, but of everything.

I'd been running for so damn long. Running to a better life. And now that I got one, I'd lost the only family I'd ever known.

"You got a deal tonight, huh?" I murmured, hopping up on the counter. Tray came to me and stood between my legs, his hands coming to rest on my thighs.

"Yeah." He breathed out. "That a problem?"

I shrugged and kept quiet.

"It's a problem," he stated, sighing.

I shook my head and rested my forehead on his shoulder. "Like I can talk after all the stuff I've been doing."

Tray moved closer and pulled me into his arms. Then he lifted me up, sliding his hands underneath my legs and moved from the counter. I gasped, but quickly grabbed around his shoulders and neck. He carried me out of the house and into the pool-house. He turned once, to lock the door, and then we walked back to the bedroom, dropping lightly onto the bed.

I sighed. Until this second, I didn't even realize how much I missed its warmth.

He moved in behind me, wrapping one arm around my waist and pulled me tight against him. Nuzzling my neck, his breath caused me to shiver. "So, what's the problem?" he asked.

This was it. Time for *the* conversation.

And I wanted to be anywhere but there...well...maybe not.

"I'll leave it alone," I announced, my voice clear.

"What?" Tray asked, lifting up and rolling me on my back. He gazed down at me in confusion. "What are you talking about?"

"Jace. Galverson. Everything. My guy got some stuff on 'em, but I haven't looked at it yet. I'm not going to," I promised, hoping he read the earnestness in my eyes. "I'm going to leave it alone."

He sat up, pulling me up with him. I rested my back against the headboard. Our legs were intertwined with each other, around the bed sheets.

"Why?" he asked, point-blank.

"Because—" I hedged, sighing.

"Taryn," Tray said firmly.

"Because...I don't know if it's worth it," I finally managed to get out. Holy hell, confessing you're wrong is hard. "Because...everything that happened with you and...you're right. I can't go after Jace without going after Galverson. I'm not that much of a moron. I may do stupid shit, but tangling with a guy like Galverson would be reckless and suicidal."

Tray seemed to be holding his breath as he watched me.

Suddenly, he let it out and whispered, "Thank God."

I let out my own breath that I didn't realize I was holding.

Tray leaned closer and whispered against my lips, "We have some serious making up to do. You weren't here last night."

I grinned and then gasped as he lifted me in the air and strode into the bathroom. Turning on the shower, he grinned. "We both need to clean off." Then his lips were on mine, rough and insistent.

I leaned upwards and wrapped my arms around his neck, jumping and wrapping my legs around his waist. Tray walked us into the shower and pressed me against the wall, his hands sliding forcefully underneath my shirt where he untied my bikini straps. He broke away from me, pulling my bikini top off my arms and threw it over his shoulder. I took that time to grab the ends of my shirt and yank it up and off. Tray did the same, my legs still entwined around his waist. Then he was bending over me, kissing and licking me all over.

My eyes closed, and rolled to the back of my head.

Tray's mouth was back on mine, sweeping inside. Holy fuck. I slid down his length and reached for his pants, my hand swept inside. Tray was making quick work of my skirt, but left my bikini bottoms on.

I managed—finally—to work his button free and slid his zipper down. Then I was back up, my legs around his waist, as I kicked down his pants in the same motion. Tray grabbed me and stepped out of his pants, his mouth entangling with mine, my hands roughly holding him against me.

When I felt his fingers touch me down there, I moaned into his mouth. Tray pulled my bikini bottom down, making enough room for him to slide his fingers into me.

A moment later, I let my head rest against the tiled wall, feeling Tray move downwards as he kept at it.

When it built up, I bit back a groan and then I'd had enough. So had Tray because he set me down and we both stepped out of our remaining clothes. Tray grabbed me and hoisted me in the air, driving inside me almost violently, and I just about screamed.

And I held on tight.

At the last thrust, my body melted. Literally. Tray had to hold me up, but he was a bit unsteady too. We crawled on the bed and wrapped around each other. Tray let out a breath, resting his forehead in the crook of my neck. I grinned against his arm, feeling his muscles twitch slightly at the contact.

"Oh, fuck," he moaned. Then I realized what we'd done.

"It's alright. I'm on the pill."

"You don't have anything," he teased, but underneath the playful voice, I could tell he was serious.

I looked up and met his gaze. "No," I said. "You? You use protection with Aidrian Casners?"

"So you know about her, huh? And yes, of course I did on that one night where I had a lapse of judgment," he remarked dryly.

I knew it was petty, but I had to bring her up. She bothered me. And what bothered me more was that he hadn't pushed her away—both times I saw her boobs dangerously close to him.

"Yeah."

"Rumors are widely wrong. About me, anyways," Tray commented, moving forward to kiss me, lightly, tenderly. He pushed me back and rested half of his body on top of me, a comforting weight. "I'm normally picky about who I sleep with, and Casners was a mistake."

"I'm a bit alarmed that I'm happy with that information." I couldn't help but admit, slightly panicked that I'd even said that out loud. Tray laughed and replied, "It shouldn't. I should be a good thing."

"I'll keep that in mind."

"You get what you needed today?" We both knew he was referring to Pedlam.

I met his eyes, and held them for a moment. Just...reading whatever was in there, trying to get a peek at what was inside.

I read seriousness, a light teasing note, and I read...concern.

"Yeah." I smiled lightly. "I got what I needed."

He traced his hand down my arm and lifted my hand up, his fingers running against the bandages, he asked, "How'd these come about?"

"A quick getaway where I didn't want to answer any questions. Jace walked in and almost caught me, so I had to do some quick thinking. I'm fine." I answered.

"They look like they hurt."

"They did."

"Not anymore?"

"With you and me, like this? I'd be worried if they were hurting." I grinned, kissing him. "They're fine."

"You sure?" Tray wanted to make sure I was okay, which I found endearing.

"Yes," I promised, rolling over and straddling him, "I am sure."

From his vantage point, Tray grinned up at the view. His hands rested on my hips and slid upwards. I closed my eyes, just feeling him.

As his mouth became more exploratory, I sighed. "Maybe we should...the others—"

Tray tucked me underneath him and whispered, "They're not going anywhere." I ceased thinking.

CHAPTER SIXTEEN

Content, I laid there. Tray shifted slightly in the bed and I moaned, "No."

He laughed, but moved to stand up.

I lounged back, pulling the bed sheets to cover me. "We had sex—with your friends just outside."

"Who cares?" he murmured, his voice muffled as he pulled a shirt over his head. "Thought you didn't care about stuff like that."

"I don't, that's the problem. I feel like I should."

He laughed huskily and I grinned, realizing how nice it sounded.

"I gotta head out, it's almost ten."

Fuck, we'd been in here for two hours.

"Rickets' House tonight, huh?" I murmured, more to myself.

Tray asked, "You don't want to go?"

"No, it's just—"

"Gentley will be nice. I'm tired of his shit. If he's not, he'll deal with our crew."

"Then his steroid supply will be cut off."

Tray snorted. "Like that matters to him. Gentley will just go somewhere else."

"You know," I mused, "I don't get it. You're selling steroids to piss your dad off, but your dad's not here anymore."

He shrugged, looking a little sheepish. "I started dealing them when I was pretty young, when my dad *would* have actually gotten pissed about shit like that."

"And you realized how nice the money is?"

"Sort of. It's good to know who's on it, makes making bets a bit easier, if you know what I mean."

"Oh my God. You sell steroids and then you bet on whoever is taking them?"

He grinned. "Sometimes. I don't really need the money, but it passes the time."

"You get a rush from it?" I asked, sitting up, moving to sit beside him.

"I don't know, he murmured. . "I stopped thinking about it a while ago. I just do it, you know?"

"I, on the other hand," I announced, rolling my eyes, "am actually trying not to do anything illegal."

He laughed. "And I pulled you right back in."

"Yeah." I realized it was true, but I said, "I would've stolen something else anyway, eventually. It's the rush. Nothing else like it."

"What about diving? You looked obsessed today."

I smiled, remembering the feeling. Holy fuck, I'd go back, this second, if it was on the table. "Yeah," I commented. "I get it there too."

Standing up, Tray replied, "Well, that's a lot more productive than stealing shit."

Which was true. He walked towards the door.

"Are you coming out?" he asked over his shoulder, a hand on the door handle.

"Pretty soon," I replied, realizing that it required me to get up and get dressed. It required me—moving. The only moving I wanted to do, was my chest rising up and down in a good, deep sleeping motion.

"Alright," he said easily, then slipped through the door. I noticed he'd locked the door from the inside before he pulled it shut.

I was starting to realize, among many other things, how observant and thoughtful he could be. Tray was...surprising and not what the eye met. The guy was gorgeous, that had never been denied. Hell, straight guys probably thought he was gorgeous.

But he was—scarily intelligent. Tray was ahead of me by two moves, at least, and I was just starting to understand that.

Groaning, I moved up and dressed. Finishing a French braid in my hair, I moved to the door and was met with a crowd of people. A party had migrated to Tray's place without us realizing it.

I declined a cup of beer, which was offered to me by a guy manning the keg. Let's hope they only brought one, and not five.

Why would they need a keg before we headed to Rickets' House?

Rooters was at the kitchen table, telling a story to Honey and Bit, who were smiling and nodding politely.

"Hi, Taryn!" Honey exclaimed. "I like your outfit, very cute."

"Thanks." I was wearing loose-fitting, light-weight trousers that weren't too baggy, but were comfortable at the same time, and a sky blue tank top that wrapped around and crisscrossed in the middle of my chest and tied behind my neck.

"Looking good, Matthews." Rooters gave me a whistle. What a moron. But I laughed.

"Is it true? Is Tristan Reynolds here tonight?" Honey asked eagerly.

All this gossip.

I shrugged.

"We heard she got into town last week because she left her boarding school, against her parent's wishes. But she couldn't see any of her friends because her brother made her promise not to let anyone know she was here."

I could care less.

So I lied, "I don't really know anything."

Then I left. I didn't care if it was rude, but seriously, I just couldn't handle the gossip anymore. It seemed like it was all these people did.

"You're still standing, I see."

I stopped in the hallway and saw Crystal Fairs leaning against the stair's spiraled rail.

"Hi." I was surprised—again—I was actually grateful to see her. "Didn't know this was your scene?"

"Aidrian's here. She's entertaining," she said, like it made perfect sense. Crystal added, "You handled her well, by the by. I was impressed."

"Yeah, well, it's a gift," I murmured distractedly as I moved out of the way of people. Holy hell. "What's up with all these people? I didn't think Tray was having a frickin' party before we went to Rickets' House."

"How many you think are going to go to school tomorrow? I'm guessing about a third. I know I'll probably skip the next few days. It's the play-offs. It's like a five-day party...or it should be."

The thought had promise.

Suddenly, Tray materialized at my side and wrapped his arm around my waist. "Ready to go?" he asked.

"No," I answered truthfully. I had no desire to go anywhere with all these people.

Crystal laughed. And her stock went higher.

"Crystal's gonna ride with us," I announced.

Tray shrugged, gesturing to Carter.

Then we heard an ear-splitting whistle. Carter yelled out, "Let's go! Everyone out!"

As the crowd dispersed, Crystal walked by my side and commented, "It's going to be a show when we all show up at that place."

"No doubt. I hope the cops don't follow." Then I remembered—Tray had 'em in his back pocket. Which would account for how he got away with all his steroid business and underage parties.

If I didn't know the whole story, I'd called him an advantaged bastard. Or dick. That was more like me.

It'd started to rain as we drove to Rickets' House and for some reason, it was depressing. Normally, I'm one to grin when it rains. It makes me want to curl up and cuddle, not alone though. It's relaxing and meditative; makes you want to be lazy.

But this time, it was depressing and I don't really know why.

I'd meant to talk with Crystal on the ride to Rickets'. She was a fellow Pedlamite, but maybe that was the problem. She had ties to a place I considered home, a place where I no longer had the bonds that made it home. Those were gone.

Brian...he'd been my rock. He never meant to be, it'd been the furthest thing from his mind the first time we kissed. He was an eighth grade boy, he wanted in my pants. I'm not stupid. It had been the way of so many guys. But Brian was different. There'd been a boyish charm. Yeah, he liked pissing the teachers off—but that was because Jace was already infamous, either hated or loved.

Everyone knew who Jace Lanser was.

Either the teachers hated him or was secretly impressed by him. Most of the girls, even the 'good' girls wanted him.

I could attest to that. I'd decimated a good two dozen trying to worm their way through me.

Brian was a...a puppy wanting to be bad. Because he had an older brother that turned greyhound overnight.

But the funny thing was, it was completely the opposite in their home. Jace was the hated and Brian the adored.

Both brothers, vying for the place each held. Just not in the same spot.

No. Brian thought he could 'pick' me up and he'd be after the next girl. It hadn't happened that way.

We kissed, our first clumsy, disgustingly wet, kiss. It had been outside the elementary school, at their playground. We'd gone over there because no middle school kids would be there. And their teachers always left early.

And the next day, Brian had tried to give me the slip. He sent a note, via Grayley, telling me he thought it'd be better off if we were friends. Just friends.

I retaliated by getting our janitor to change his lock on his locker. And I grinned, in satisfaction, as Brian cursed, trying to get into his locker for a full hour. He'd put such a dent in that locker, the janitor had to change his lock a third time. But before leaving, the janitor had pointed me out.

Brian had been mystified.

We both glared at each other, across the damn hallway, and I taunted him. I told him he better think twice before trying to 'play' me. I thought I was so witty.

And the funny thing is, he'd shown at my locker the next day and walked me to my class. Like nothing had happened. We had our second kiss that day, in the gymnasium, under the bleachers.

But we got caught. So time spent in detention solidified it for us. We were officially a couple, like Bonnie and Clyde.

That's what we liked to think.

But, no, Brian had never sought out to become my rock. It just happened. My foster dad would threaten me, beat me, and I'd just go and sit outside Brian's window. At first he didn't even know, but one time he saw me. After that, I just crawled into his room. If he wasn't there, I'd curl and sleep on his bed. And if he was, we'd hold hands. And kiss, but Brian had become scared of me. So he never pushed. Not really.

And sometimes I got a good foster family.

So I became his rock. During those times when Jace would have a particularly rough fight, I let Brian crawl into my room.

That became the pattern for us.

I knew he was capable of violence. I'd seen it enough time. Never against me, but against his father, and against Jace. That's what they grew up with. Their mom took off a long time ago.

So it was the three of them.

And Jace was right—their dad had turned 'em against each other. Their relationship had been doomed from the beginning. Or so it seemed most of the time. But sometimes, I still saw Brian's idol worship for his big brother. And sometimes I saw the big brother come out of Jace.

They loved each other, but they were just too busy hating each other first.

"Hey," Crystal nudged me with her arm, her voice soft, "you okay?"

I hadn't even realized I was crying.

"Yeah," I murmured, glancing away as I quickly wiped at my tears, "I'm fine."

"Is...?" I knew she wanted to ask about it, but I didn't want to hear it. So I'm sure she got that.

I missed Brian. I missed...the familiarity. I missed hearing him laugh and do his half-groan at the same time. I missed when he'd get angry and the corner of his eyes would squint—just slightly—but then he'd just swear and go back to being happy. I missed...how he could never lie to me. How he'd whisper his love for me. His need for me.

I missed that life.

Brian had been my life.

"You coming?" I was jolted back to reality and realized Tray had the car waiting, dropping off Crystal and Carter at the door. Crystal stood at her door, asking if I was coming in with them.

"Uh, no. I'll walk with Tray," I replied hoarsely.

"Suit yourself," she said lightly, closing the door.

Tray didn't say anything as he parked and shut the vehicle off. Neither of us moved.

I stayed in place, sitting in the back, right behind him, and I cried. I just...cried. They were silent tears, a continuous stream down my face. I couldn't look at Tray so I looked outside.

After awhile, he turned around and held my hand. His simple touch made me cry harder.

Then he moved to the back and held me. He curled me against his chest, with my hands fisting his shirt, and I openly sobbed.

Seemingly exhaustive moments later, I quieted. The well had gone dry.

Tray pressed a kiss to my forehead. He rested his cheek against my forehead and sighed a deep breath, and, for some reason, it calmed me. It strengthened me.

"I'm..." I tried to say.

Tray soothed, "It's about fucking time. Just...cry, alright?"

"I'm good. Really," I whispered, tipping my head back to meet his eyes.

"Sure?"

"Yes." I smiled tenderly and kissed him softly.

"Alright." He sighed. "Ready to go?"

"Ready to go," I assured him, and climbed out of the SUV.

And because no one was around, I reached for his hand, our fingers intertwining as we walked up the drive-way. The smooth slide against each other until they fell into place. Like a key meeting its lock.

It felt good.

But scary.

I brushed away any remaining tears when we got in sight of Rickets' House, and there was no Veronica Teedz wasn't there to welcome us like last time.

Thank God.

There were quite a few people, but none I recognized.

As we entered the house, I tried to loosen my fingers, but Tray simply tightened his grasp so our hands stayed intertwined.

Like before, Tray led the way into the kitchen. He purchased two cups and passed one to me. Then we moved back through. This time I didn't need to separate; I wasn't there for business. So I got to see how many people knew Tray.

Which was a lot. An annoying amount, because he couldn't take two steps without someone rushing over to talk to him or pounding him on the shoulder.

It was fricking irritating.

By the twelfth person—yes—twelve!—I pulled away and remarked, "I'm going to go look for Mandy." I hope to hell no more 'Devon's-cheating-on-me' drama would come up tonight. It shouldn't, the guy wasn't even in the same region as us, but you never know. It's one of the exasperating powers of technology. It didn't limit drama to your location, drama and chaos was widespread.

I don't think Tray even noticed that I'd left. Whatever.

I moved through the first floor, down the hallway, heading towards the patio area. As I weaved around a group leaving, I saw that Crystal, Mandy, and most of the group had taken residence on the patio. I recognized a few students from Pedlam on the opposite corner, but no Gentley and more importantly, no Grayley; therefore, no Brian. At this rate, I didn't know who I wanted to see least—Grayley or Brian. It was a sad day in hell that I'd take being around Gentley over the other two.

A sad day in hell.

"Hey, Taryn," Mandy called out, sitting next to Tristan, who had Erin on the other side of her. Tristan took time out of a conversation with Brent Garrett—Amber's staked claim—to send a smile my way.

Erin waved, then flipped her blonde hair over her shoulder and tuned back into Tristan's conversation.

Crystal stood in the back, in a corner with Aidrian Casners and one other girl—probably another senior.

Aidrian glared at me, but it didn't hold the animosity from before. She was probably still waiting to see if I'd come through with the tickets.

Crystal sent a smile my way, her eyes questioning.

I shrugged and sat beside Mandy.

"Were you guys having sex? Is that why it took you so freaking long to get in here?" Mandy teased, flashing a blinding smile.

"Not exactly," I murmured, stifling a yawn. Seriously—emotional upheaval really took it out of you. You're supposed to sleep after a crying fit. Not party. It's why the phrase says, 'cried myself to sleep.' Not 'cried myself to hang out with drunks.'

I've learned that I'm not good at small talk. So that's why I sat quietly, beside Mandy as she joined in periodically with Tristan's conversation. Note that I called it Tristan's conversation, because it literally was. Brent had his hand on her thigh and he was listening to Tristan. Not Mandy. Not Erin. But neither seemed to care. Tristan would laugh at whatever they said, but she'd turn right back to the basketball player.

This went on for twenty minutes, then I got bored.

Something—maybe the bitch inside of me—was compelled to ask loudly, "Hey, Aidrian."

It was deathly silent.

Aidrian turned her glaring eyes my way, and waited.

"Didn't Amber Lancaster go off on you last week? Something about wearing her skirt? I saw at least two girls wearing my shirt tonight. What kind of psycho does that?"

Mandy sucked in her breath, staring at me in horror. She knew exactly what I had just done. I knew it really wasn't the skirt Amber had been pissed about. It had been over Brent Garrett—the guy who was now salivating all over Tristan.

Her eyes narrowed and Aidrian replied, "A bitch like that does. And it was my skirt." But her eyes had switched to Brent. Everyone heard what wasn't said: 'it was my guy'

Tristan was the only one left clueless, but she was smart enough to realize something in the atmosphere had just changed, because she sat up straighter and looked confused to Erin and Mandy. Both girls avoided her glance.

"Hey, Brent," Aidrian started huskily as she moved just behind him on the couch, "we never did go and get that drink we talked about." She casually touched him on the shoulder.

And then Tristan got it. Well, not my part, but she sent a heated glare at Aidrian. She masked it miraculously when Brent glanced at her, caught in the headlights of both females.

"Uh, yeah, we didn't," he mumbled warily, watching Tristan's reaction.

"Brent," Tristan soothed, sitting closer, "remember that time at Crystal Bay last year, when you tripped and fell into the water." She giggled. "You looked so adorable, but you had that drink all over you."

"Yeah." The guy seemed a little bit scared now, but still interested where this might lead. Just the fact that he's a guy, he was probably thinking: Threesome!

"And remember what else happened that night?" Tristan asked, her voice nails-on-a-chalkboard sweet.

"Uh—" The guy gulped. I could see his Adam's apple bobbing up and down.

I was interested to find out what happened that night.

"Maybe we should do that again sometime," Tristan suggested, looking demure and sexy at the same time.

"Uh," Brent grinned wolfishly, "yeah, I think we should too."

"Brent, honey." Aidrian sent her own seductive smile his way, her fingers moved to his neck and massaged. "Do me a favor? Get me a drink?" She held out her empty cup.

I kind of felt a little sorry for the guy. He didn't know what to do: Tristan or Aidrian.

Oh the life, huh.

"You can get me one too." Tristan answered his dilemma.

"Sure. Sure." His head bobbed up and down, standing up, he murmured, "I'll be right back."

When he left, I saw the two girls turn and glare at each other. Tristan stood up slowly, but Aidrian didn't back down. The only barrier between them was the couch. There was such a contrast between them.

Aidrian looked the equivalent of white trash, but there was an extra flare in her attitude; the way she held herself—strong and tall. She was wearing the stereotypical mini-skirt, the ends frayed, a halter-top that ended just above her midriff, large hoop earrings, fake eyelashes, and glittery lipstick completed her outfit.

Oh no, after a more thorough look, I saw the twinkle in her eyes when she looked at me. She knew what I'd done. She knew full well, but I saw the territorial bitch in her. Tristan was poaching and it was Aidrian's duty to send her packing.

Then there was Tristan. She wore a white, sleek tank top that wrapped itself around her—not the other way around—and crisp white trousers. Rich, stuck-up snob rolled off her. As she stood there on the patio, she looked like the embodiment of class.

Crystal and her friend had taken root behind Aidrian with Erin and Mandy behind Tristan. They looked like they were facing off in a hockey match. The only thing missing was the puck, hockey sticks, the ref, and all the other hockey gear. Never mind.

My work here was done, so I slipped out.

"Hey, girl." An arm found its way around my shoulders and pulled me close to a chest.

Rooters.

"Hey," I replied. "What's up?"

He was standing with Honey, Bit, and Aaron. Just behind them, I saw Helms and Mitch with some girls from Pedlam on their laps. Helms and Mitch looked to be loving it.

"Where'd you come from?"

"Patio."

"Who's out there?"

"No one, it's why I left," I said gracefully, shrugging.

"So, we're thinking of finding some fun Pedlam folks for a game of P & A. What do you say?"

"A card game?"

"Fuck yeah. There's two empty tables. Come on," he said coaxingly, giving my shoulders a squeeze.

What the hell.

"Sure." I replied, but my cup was empty. I held it up and said, "I gotta fill my cup first but, yeah, I'm in.

Honey and Bit smiled widely. I could see the eager looks in their eyes. I liked them, I really did. They were there for Mandy, which would always place 'em in a good spot with me. But they were wannabes.

It made me a bit wary around them. Not because I thought they'd stab me in the back, but because they weren't totally trustworthy. They'd never had to prove that they could be. Yeah, Honey came clean with Bit, but she still slept with Bryce when she knew Bit wanted him.

That didn't show a backbone for trust.

"Great! We're in the corner. Haul your cute ass over when you're done." Rooters gave me one more squeeze before taking off in the opposite direction.

"You want someone to come with?" Honey offered.

"Uh, no. I got it." I gave her a small smile and moved through the crowd.

I didn't run into Tray as I made the trek to the keg. That's what it was too—a trek. People were everywhere and you never knew what to expect when you turned a corner. I was already on guard—Gentley was here somewhere and I was still nervous about running into Brian or Grayley.

I ended up having to circle the entire dance floor to make it to the corner where they set up the card game.

They'd gotten a few more Pedlam students to join the game by the time I got back to them.

Rooters waved me over. "Come on, Taryn. You can sit here." He gestured to the empty seat beside him.

That made me pause. The guy was obviously the leader of this little bunch. Chances of an empty seat next to him were just—stupid and because I'm not a trusting person, I wondered what game he was playing.

I sat anyway. I figured I could handle anything he slung my way.

"Hey, Taryn," Casey Juanke, a student from Pedlam, said. He was from Gentley's crew, but he wasn't that bad of a guy, or at least, I didn't think so.

"Hey, Case," I said easily, picking up the cards Rooter had dealt. "How goes it in Pedlam?"

He shrugged, looking over his hand. "Ah, it goes, you know? Not as much excitement without you and Brian in the hallways."

I grinned at that one. "Hi, Booth," I remarked to another guy that I recognized that was sitting with us. There was a girl with them, but I didn't know who she was.

"This is Caitlyn," Booth introduced her, nudging her with his arm. "She's new so she doesn't know your 'legendary' reputation."

"As what?" I laughed. "School bitch?"

Casey and Booth chuckled. "Maybe."

The game proceeded with a mixture of small talk and banter between the Pedlam students and Rawley students. I was reminded why I always thought Casey was a good guy. He didn't cheat and every taunt he sent out was given in a respectful manner. You knew he was just a good guy. Booth was the quiet one of their little clan. But when he spoke, whatever he had to say was hilarious.

The girl, Caitlyn, was in love with Booth. If I hadn't have gotten the bitch out of me earlier with Aidrian and Tristan—which was totally heartless and manipulative—she would have annoyed me. She was just too quiet and almost worshipped Booth. She's barely spoken two words to me since we met, but she may have just been scared of me. I was okay with that. "Dude, your phone," Booth complained, hitting Casey on his arm.

"Oh." Casey grabbed his cell up and answered, "Yeah, dude...nah, nah...we're playing Prez and Ass in the corner...yeah, you know the one."

"Crisp?" Booth asked.

I froze, my hand in mid-reach to place my two on the pile.

Crispin Gentley.

"Oh, fuck—" Oh yeah, Booth and Casey remembered, a little too late, my relationship with Gentley. I saw their eyes were on me, a look of alarm in both.

I set my card down and leaned back in my chair. Crossing my arms, I asked coolly, "So did he already get his 'package' or does he still have to do that?"

"Uh—" Casey was at a loss for words.

"Maybe you should—" Booth started.

"What?" I snapped, suddenly pissed off. "Run? Hide? Fuck no."

The decision was taken out of our hands anyway. Crispin pushed his way through the crowd, to the table. "Fuck, could you guys pick a fucking table more in the back?" he complained, not even looking at who was at the table.

My eyes were fixated on him, but he was looking over the dance floor.

"Let's go, fuckers." He kicked Casey's seat, but he finally noticed something was off. His eyes trailed over Casey and Booth, then followed their gazes—to me. "Oh," he murmured, straightening up, "it's the Rosette Bitch."

"It's Matthews now," I clipped out, glaring at him with hate filled eyes.

"Whatever, you're still a bitch." Gentley laughed a mocking laugh. "You're not protected tonight. Why? Evans get tired of you? I would, I know that."

"You're just bitter because you never got a taste." I was tired of being twisted into a fucking sex toy. "But then again, why would you? I remember you really liking the confines of that closet."

"Oh, no, you fucking didn't." He laughed harshly.

I stood up. "It's tiring, really. You always have to play the 'slut' card because you're not able to come up with new material, but that's okay. I saw your WAIS-II scores. You're not capable of higher mental functioning. Maybe I should just pat you on the head every time you use the same insult."

So I walked over and patted him on the head.

"That's a good boy. Go for something intelligent this time." I grinned, cockily, but I saw he was seething.

Gentley grasped my arm in a painful grip and yanked me behind him, dragging me away from the table.

"Let go of me, asshole." I was the one seething now, braking my feet, but Gentley didn't even notice. He just pulled me behind him until we were out the door. Once outside, he slammed the door shut, effectively cutting out anyone who'd followed. Which had been everyone. I caught a glimpse of Rooters raising his cellphone, but then Gentley was addressing a few who were lingering on the porch.

"Fuck off," he addressed them very congenially.

They scrambled.

"What are you going to do? Beat me up?" I taunted, but my hand was itching for my taser. That I'd left in my purse, which was in Tray's bedroom.

Gentley glared at me, a good full minute, before he said, "I fucking wish. Trust me."

I did.

Instead I sneered, "What the fuck do you want, Gentley? Pull me out here, make it look like you're putting me 'in my place'? Trust me, I can hit back."

He raked a hand through his hair. "Would you shut the fuck up? You're so damn annoying."

"Oh no, fucker," I began.

Gentley interrupted, "I'm not going to do anything. Fucking A, I can't. If I did, and trust me, I want to, so fucking bad. But I can't. If I did, Evans would have my ass in the hospital and I'd be lucky to walk back out."

"What the hell's going on?" Tray asked, a hint of violence in his tone.

Gentley and I had both been too caught up that we hadn't noticed Tray's approach. He looked to be returning from his vehicle and was regarding us suspiciously. It reminded me of the last time the three of us had been in the same vicinity. Tray had punched him and kicked him out. He looked like he was ready to do it again.

"Do I need to repeat myself?" he demanded, slowly climbing up the porch steps to stand next to me. There was a warning in his eyes as he stared at Gentley intensely.

Gentley held up his hand in a surrender movement. "No, man." He took two steps backward. "Taryn and I were just going to have a talk. That's it, man."

"About what?" Tray clipped out, moving to stand, just slightly, in front of me.

"Look," Gentley tried to assure us, "you and I already did our business. We're good. I was just heading out and I saw Taryn. I thought I might give her a head's up. I got a call that her ex is heading here. It's why I was leaving." He looked at me. "Booth was my ride here, I was coming to get him so we could leave."

Brian was coming. That's all I'd heard.

And of course—just like magic—a car pulled up in front of the house, rap music blaring through its open windows.

Three of the doors opened and guys piled out and leading the pack, was Brian.

When he looked up, he froze, seeing us on the porch, three steps in front of him.

He took in Gentley, then his eyes trailed over Tray and me. They lingered on my hand that I'd unknowingly placed on Tray's back.

I snatched it back, but fisted it, immediately regretting it. Tray turned to look at me and moved back to take in Brian.

The guys behind him, Rice and Hax all shut up when they saw me. Interesting, Hax was one of Jace's guys.

Slowly, the sound echoing, Brian climbed up the steps and stopped, turning to face us. Hax and Rice stayed behind.

Gentley was pushed to the back of the porch, and to the back of my mind. I stepped in front of Tray this time as I faced off against Brian.

"Hey." He nodded to me.

I relaxed slightly at the soft tone of his voice.

"Hey," I breathed out.

He gestured behind me. "You and Ass Face friends now?"

Gentley wisely remained quiet.

"A cold day in hell." I grinned tensely.

"Yeah, that's what I thought." Brian nodded to Rice and Hax. "Go in," he ordered.

They went in. Hax looked at me, lingering a moment before Brian shoved him inside and pulled the door shut behind.

He shrugged his shoulder towards the cars. "You should know, Grayley drove us. He'll be here pretty soon."

"Fine. I'll leave."

"Taryn," Brian groaned—and we'd just entered Drama Land of the Past . "It's not even like that. You have to know that."

"You both lied to me. It's exactly like that," I said firmly.

"Oh for the fucking hell—it's not! There are reasons, Taryn. Very good reasons," he appealed to me. "Come on. There has to be for Geezer—Geezer!—to lie, too. We're trying to protect you—"

"I don't need your protection," I cried out.

"Yeah," Brian said shortly, "you do. You've always needed it."

"Oh please!" I was so pissed, but I was reasonable enough to realize a lot of what I was feeling was from past shit. History that had never been resolved. "You're a moron, Brian!"

"I'm a moron?!" He laughed angrily. "You fucking screwed my brother. That's a moron. You're a *moron* for doing that."

"Oh no," I started, "you screwed Liza and that other girl. You started it."

Neither of us noticed Grayley until he was suddenly in between us and pushing us apart. I blinked, startled that Brian and I had slowly stalked towards each other. We'd been in each other's face, yelling.

I saw Tray and Gentley watching. Gentley looked amused. Tray looked—I didn't want to name what I saw in his hazel eyes.

"Shut the fuck up, both of you!" Grayley shouted. He stood in front of Brian, facing me. "You should leave, Taryn."

"Me? You should leave!"

"Rickets' is our territory. It always has been," he reasoned, watching Tray cautiously.

What the hell? I knew why Gentley tiptoed around Tray, but...Grayley, too? And Brian hadn't said a word to him. This was not the Brian and Grayley I knew.

Contrary to recent events, Grayley was not one to look for a fight; he avoided them at all costs.

But Brian—if a fight was brewing, Brian would be the one to flick the spark.

He loved fighting. He reveled in it.

And Brian was purposely not getting in Tray's face. Yeah, the last time at the hospital—probably wasn't the place to have a fight. But he wasn't moving now, at all, he wasn't even looking at Tray.

Which told me—it all clicked—and I gasped, reeling backwards.

Brian knew about Tray.

Brian was working for Galverson. Geezer had said his dad didn't work for Brian, he worked for the new crew. He 'sorta' didn't work for Brian. So that meant Brian was working for Galverson.

And I'm just stupid for not connecting all the dots until now.

Brian would never work for Jace, but he'd compete with him. And that meant business with Galverson.

And Grayley—Grayley was Brian's brains. Grayley knew...everything.

But, Grayley wasn't one to get involved in the drug business. And whatever else they were running...

I suddenly felt sick to my stomach.

"You're working for Galverson," I whispered hoarsely." My eyes on Brian, I saw him suddenly pale, hearing me.

"Shut up," Grayley hissed.

I continued anyway, "And you got that bracelet from wherever his storage it. You stole it for me."

Grayley rounded on me, shoving Brian away with his back. Grayley grasped my shoulders, his eyes trailing to Tray's over my head. "Taryn. Shut. Up." he said firmly, harshly. "You have to shut up and leave this alone! Leave. It. Alone, for your own goddamn good."

I was still staring, in horror, at Brian.

I saw regret flash in the depths of his eyes. I saw remorse...and...fear.

"Brian—" I managed out, unable to speak.

"Taryn—" He was shoved back by Grayley again.

Suddenly, I felt familiar hands at my back. Tray.

He wrapped an arm around my waist, and stepped beside me. "You can move."

I don't know what look was shared, but Grayley and Brian both instinctually stepped back, after taking one look in Tray's eyes.

"I'm done. We can go," he spoke again and it took a second to realize he was talking to me.

"What?" I choked out.

"We're going. You got everything?"

"Yeah—" I was lost, stumbling. "Uh...my stuff's at your place."

We were already off the porch and heading to his vehicle. I was still in shock. "Oh my God."

When we got to the SUV, Tray walked me to the passenger side and opened the door. I crawled inside and curled up in the seat as Tray got into his side, but he didn't start the engine. He sat and looked at me.

I broke out, "What if they know? What if...they know what Jace did to me? What if...oh God...what did they do to me? What did Jace do?"

Tray remained silent.

"They all lied to me," I cried out. "They all...I hate 'em. I hate 'em. They all—"

"For what it's worth," Tray murmured, watching me steadily, "I don't think they had anything to do with it."

"What? How can you...?"

"Because I'm on the outside looking in, and I know how guys like Lanser and Galverson think," he replied. "They don't share their secrets. Ever. Whatever Lanser did that involved you, it's extremely unlikely that he shared the info with your friends, even his little brother. Guys make it to the top because they keep everything close to their chest."

"I never said anything about—" I started, confused.

"You didn't have to, Taryn. It's written all over your face. When one lie is found out, a person starts wondering what other lies were told and how many of 'em involve you. That's what you're scared of. You're scared that your best friends turned on you, but I don't think that's it. It doesn't make any sense."

I'd fallen silent, shocked at hearing him think out loud. Even in my state, I was a little unsettled at how intelligent Tray is.

"No, my guess is that they found out something and they're trying to protect you against it. I don't think they know how you're involved though."

"But—"

Tray shook his head then continued, "And it might not even have anything to do with you. I mean, yeah—maybe. But you're not exactly a person who just accepts whatever you're told. If you're pissed off, you go after whoever pissed you off. You're a fighter and you're virtually impossible from keeping out of shit." He paused. "Maybe that's it. Maybe they don't want you to find out something, to look for something, that'd land you with Galverson. It all goes to Galverson. It makes sense. Your friends are worried that you'll find out what's going on and you almost already have. You're a thief. You hate not knowing shit, so you find a way to get at it. Which is what you would do if something was going on that you didn't like."

Oh my God. That made perfect sense.

Which meant Brian and Grayley hadn't betrayed me.

"I agree with 'em," he stated, meeting my eyes. "You told me you'd leave it alone."

And I had, I'd already made the decision.

Even I wasn't so out of touch with reality to think I could take on Galverson alone. And Tray was right, Galverson wouldn't go after me. He'd go after Geezer, Brian, and Grayley first, then Mandy, Austin, Shelley, Kevin.

My family.

"I will." I said sincerely. For the first time in awhile, I was scared.

"I will," I said it again, a whisper to myself.

Tray sighed and leaned over, he tucked a strand of hair behind my ear, his fingers lingering on my cheek, then my lips.

I grinned, feeling myself melt. Again—it was inevitable.

I took his finger in my mouth, and licked it, swirling my tongue around it.

Tray groaned in shock.

I laughed. I covered the distance and kissed him deeply. Wanting to forget, wanting to remember who was with me, who I had in my life now. Tray answered me back, our hands in each other's hair, holding each other tight as we tasted each other. Sensually. Needy.

Tray lifted me onto his lap, where he devoured me some more. I devoured right back and melted against him.

"Let's go home," I whispered, not realizing I'd called Rawley home.

Groaning, Tray kissed me a last time before setting me back on my side.

He started the vehicle and pulled out, as we circled to the front of Rickets' House, I saw Brian sitting on the porch. Alone.

There was something I needed to do.

"Wait," I broke out.

Tray braked and looked up at the porch. I saw the understanding in his eyes when he met my gaze.

"Thank you," I mouthed silently, getting out of the vehicle.

Brian was looking at me when I crossed to the porch. He stood up just as I stepped to where he sat.

"Hey," I said softly, remembering the little boy I'd fell in love with. And seeing a faint shadow in the boy before me, merging with the reflection of manhood.

Brian had changed. I knew that, I just hadn't wanted to accept it.

"Hey," he breathed out, absorbing me.

We both knew.

It was time.

"I'm...I'm going to leave it alone. Whatever Jace, whatever arrangements he made for me. I want you to know—I'm leaving it alone." I said first, rushed. I wanted it out there between us. He had to know.

"I didn't beat up Geezer," he spoke, glancing where Tray was parked. "You gotta know that. I don't want you to think I'd do that."

"I know," I murmured. "Now."

"Good." He looked relieved, and he was. I knew him, still. I knew that look. And the knowledge brought a smile to my face.

I still knew him, who stood before me.

A part of my history. But no longer my present.

"Look," he started, "I don't know about that Evans guy, but keep a good twist on his balls. Like you did with me."

That brought a grin to my face.

Brian the poet, he was not.

"I still love you," I announced abruptly.

Brian's eyes whirled to mine, startled, but not surprised.

I added, "I still love you, but— "

"I know." He nodded, shifting in place. "You're in a better place now. Which is good. You deserve it."

"Brian."

"You got a good family. That's a good house you live in now. And there aren't any Lansers in Rawley, that's gotta be a good thing. It just took me awhile to accept it, you know. But I get it now.

"Brian," I murmured, stepping closer, "I loved you. Not Jace."

He grinned, the look stabbing me in the heart. "No, you didn't." He let out a deep breath. "You loved him, you just never did anything about it."

He raised a hand, brushing a tear from my cheek.

"I loved you," I whispered. "Jace was just—"

Brian shook his head. "You loved Jace. I know that—now. I knew it then, I just...didn't want to admit it."

"Brian, don't." I brushed some more tears away. Fucking tears—a nuisance all the damn time. "Don't...okay."

He flicked away his own tear and then pulled me into his arms. Resting his chin on top of my head, he murmured, "I love you too. I'll fucking be here, loving you until I die."

I wrapped my arms around him and sighed. Resting into him, feeling the warmth of his embrace once more. This had been my home—in his arms, for so many years.

He'd been my rock. He'd just never intended to be.

And it all started back when he tried to brush me off in the fourth grade. And I'd 'twisted his balls.' We were Bonnie and Clyde. We thought we ruled our fucking school and town. And we'd been right. We had ruled. But that part of our lives was over.

I pulled away and looked up at him. "Whatever I felt for Jace—it was you. Okay. It was you."

He couldn't say anymore. I saw it.

So I stood on my tiptoes and kissed him one last time—a tender kiss goodbye.

Then I pulled back and walked away from him, leaving the only home I knew behind.

CHAPTER SEVENTEEN

It started to rain again. . And it totally fit my mood.

Tray and I didn't talk as we drove back. It was a good silence, a comfortable silence. And I didn't stop to let myself get scared. I couldn't, not right then. Not after saying goodbye to Brian.

When we pulled into his driveway, it was eerily empty. As we walked into the main house, and into the kitchen, our footsteps on the tile was deafening.

Tray went first to the fridge and pulled out some food. Pizza—what else? As he heated it up, he jumped on the counter and looked at me.

"What?" My voice was hoarse and painful.

He just watched me, without saying a word.

The microwave alarm rang and he jumped back off, putting his pizza on a plate. Grabbing my hand he pulled me out onto the back patio, where I'd found his friends this afternoon when I first arrived.

It was beautiful. Sitting there with the rain coming down on the glass that encased every wall except the open wall that connected to the house. Tray sat and ate while I pulled a chair up beside him and curled my knees against my chest. I sighed, resting my cheek on my knee as I looked sideways to Tray.

"When was the last time you saw your brother?"

Tray frowned slightly, I saw he was a little surprised by my question. "When I told him I wasn't helping him against Dad," he said smoothly."

"What was that like?"

"It was rough," he replied.

"Did you get to say goodbye to him?"

Tray let out a brusque laugh. "Fuck no. Chance beat the shit out of me and then took off after telling me he didn't want anything to do with me. Dad screwed our family up and I was supposed to pick sides. Dad never got along with Chance anyway, even when I was little. I don't remember a lot about their relationship. But I do remember them fighting, all the time."

"What about your mom?"

"Mom was...she was always quiet. Not really all there, you know. I think she was just scared."

"Of your dad?"

"Ah, hell no. Dad wouldn't do a thing to harm her, at least not in the beginning. Towards the end, when Galverson got him hooked on drugs, yeah, she might've been scared then. I don't know. I just think she didn't know what to do with Chance and Dad. They both liked to have us pick sides."

"How old is he?"

"He's my half-brother, from Dad's first marriage. He's fifteen years older than me. So he'd be thirty-two now. He joined the DEA when he was twenty-six." Tray chuckled. "Yeah, Chance always wanted to top whatever Dad did. Drugs were so rampant around here and that was Dad's focus as chief of police; he was successful in cleaning up Rawley and received a lot commendations for it. I think that's why Chance chose the DEA over the FBI or any other agency—so he could outshine Dad."

"What about your dad?" I asked softly. Hearing the bitterness in his voice, I couldn't tell who or what his anger was at specifically—his dad, his mom, his brother, or just the whole situation.

Tray shrugged and sat quietly, staring out at the rain.

"I'm sorry," Tray said hoarsely.

I looked at him in surprise.

He was watching me and gave me a soft grin. "For...I can relate. I'm sorry."

I stood and sat in his lap, straddling him. Tray just watched me, still leaning back in his chair, but his hands came to rest on my thighs.

I slid my hands down his chest and moved to intertwine my fingers with his. I kept them there, feeling the contours of his hands, his fingers, as I watched him, watching me. Without making a conscious decision, I had inched closer to him, bringing him fully against me. Then I slightly rocked my hips.

Tray's eyes had turned amber.

I knew mine were dark with lust, too.

We stayed that way, not moving, but both of us were affected nonetheless. I could hear the rain pounding on the glass in front of us along with our heavy breathing in the room.

"Fuck," he moaned as he slid one of his hands underneath my shirt, gliding it against my skin.

I let my head fall back and closed my eyes, lost in the feeling of his hands on me.

Tray moved to untie my tank top and it slowly fell aside. He sat forward and pressed his mouth to mine—kissing and caressing me lovingly.

I sighed in content.

I tipped his head back and met his lips tenderly.

Tray picked me up, my legs wrapping around his waist, his hands underneath them, he stood and walked into the house. He took us to a room I never knew existed; however, I'd only been inside his parents' room.

This room was gorgeous. That was my only coherent thought before he laid me on the bed and bent to meet my lips once more.

That night we didn't have sex. It was something else, something more.

The combination of the doorbell shrilling and pounding on the door woke us up in the morning.

"The fuck—" Tray cursed, rolling out from beside me. He stood and lifted the curtain. Whatever he saw, he froze. He went absolutely still.

And then I saw what Tray always let simmer just underneath. I gasped, sitting up, when his eyes fall on me. There was a cold ruthlessness in his expression. His whole being looked capable of anything at that moment. He looked powerful.

I quickly sat up. "Who is it?"

"Stay here," he ordered crisply.

I scrambled to the window and looked.

Holy fuck.

There were four cars outside. Each had a guard at the driver and passenger doors, with guns held in open view. At the door stood a middle-aged man, with two guards behind him. Jace was behind the guards looking scary and shut off from all emotion. I'd seen that Jace before too, but he didn't look as powerful as Tray.

I shivered again when I turned and saw him walk to a safe in the closet. He opened it and pulled out a 9mm and a .30 caliber.

"What are you doing?" I asked, now embracing my panic. I couldn't hold it back any longer.

"Get dressed," Tray ordered. "If you hear any gunshots, you run, Taryn. I mean it. They might to want to search the house, see if you're here. There's a hidden tunnel that connects most of the house."

"Why do you have a hidden tunnel?" I asked. I wanted to act like a panicky little girl at the moment, but there's no way in hell I'd do it. I wasn't weak and I wasn't spineless.

"Because my dad was running drugs with Galverson," Tray snapped, swearing when he saw his cellphone was dead. Crossing to the phone, he lifted it and heard a dial-tone. "That's good. We have a dial-tone."

He moved the bed back and underneath it, he peeled back a square piece of carpet that was attached to a panel in the flooring. No one would ever know it was there if they were to walk by it.

"This is where you go, okay. If you hear them searching for you, just climb underneath the bed, and put the panel back in place. They'll never know. Just follow the tunnel until it ends. It'll go down. It curves through the house and then goes underneath the pool and pool-house. It continues until it connects to the street a ways down.

"Have you ever had to use it?" I asked, my eyes entranced.

"Yeah," he hesitated, "once." He pushed the bed back in place.

"Tray, come with me. I don't want you to go down there."

"I have to. They might just be here to 'talk.' If I go missing, everything I have on him surfaces. It's the rules of the game and he knows it. I have so much on him, he'd have to go into hiding for the rest of his life. Plus, drug lords tend to find drug lords. He'd be hunted down and killed."

"Tray," I insisted, grabbing his hand.

I recoiled, feeling the gun instead.

"When Lanser asks if you're here, I'm going to tell him that I dropped you off late last night because you were upset. The plan was that I'd come and pick you up this morning to get your car. Call the houseline in a little bit. If this is what I think it is, you might not have to run."

Oh God.

"Tray," I whispered.

He took one second to kiss me before he left, tucking the 9mm in the back of his pants. It was a little while later when the pounding and doorbell finally stopped.

Tray had opened the door.

I snuck to the door, it was still opened a crack so I could hear everything.

"What the fuck are you doing here?" Tray clipped out, sounding like he could murder someone.

It must've been Galverson, because I heard a relaxed chuckle in response.

"Sal," Jace started.

"Relax, Tray. We're not here to kill you," Galverson soothed, sounding at ease, in control.

"Right, because we do tea and shit like that," Tray said sarcastically.

"Is Taryn here?" Jace asked. "Her car's outside."

I snuck away and scrolled to Tray's name and selected his home line. A second later the phone rang in the house.

"Yeah?" Tray answered, sounding irritated.

"Hey. I'm awake. Can you come pick me up?"

Tray hesitated a second, then answered, "I'll be there in a little bit. If I don't call you back in ten minutes, call the cops." And then he hung up.

I put my phone on silent and crept back to the door.

Galverson was laughing again. It was a creepy laugh, like a perverted psychopath laugh.

"I see why you're Mitchell's favorite."

"Shut the fuck up about him," Tray growled.

"You need to learn to relax. Really," Galverson murmured, shaking his head. "So your little girlfriend's not here, hmmm? That phone call was nicely timed."

"It's ten in the morning. Taryn doesn't sleep in longer than that," Tray merely said.

"He's right. She doesn't," Jace spoke, "and she's not known for being patient."

"Yes," Galverson said heartily, "I hear a lot about this little girlfriend."

"Sal," Jace murmured. I heard the warning in his voice.

What the hell?

"I'm getting tired of this bullshit we're playing, Lanser," Galverson rushed out. You could hear the suppressed anger. "Your little girlfriend was removed for a reason, but she keeps resurfacing. I'm growing tired of it."

"We already went over this. You don't touch Taryn. Ever," Jace bit out, sounding hostile.

"Fine. Fine. But this is why we're here, Tray." He'd put on his cheerful façade again. "I have an understanding that you've become 'close' to this little girl that Jace seems hell-bent on keeping alive."

"You know our previous deal, Galverson. That includes Taryn now," Tray said firmly.

"Now, now. You don't have to raise that gun to me. Just keep it down where it's supposed to be."

"Look," Jace spoke up, taking charge, "keep Taryn away from Pedlam. That's all we want."

Tray let out a short laugh. "Are you serious?"

"I know. Taryn doesn't listen, so...just find a way around her. I got her to Rawley in the first place. Keep her here and we won't have any problems."

And how the fuck did he get me here?

"Look, Taryn told me last night that she's not going to ask any more questions; she's going to leave everything alone," Tray murmured, his voice a little bit more distant.

"Yeah, that's what Brian said, but she broke into the Seven8. So we need to know that whatever she took, she's not going to do anything with it," Jace replied, tense.

Tray remarked, "She stole some tickets to a concert you're having there. That's it. She stole 'em for someone else."

There was a moment of silence. "Are you kidding me?" Jace asked in disbelief.

"Jace," Galverson spoke up, "could this possibly be true?"

"Fuck. Yeah, she does shit like that," Jace cursed.

"It doesn't matter, she's a loose cannon and she has the capability to get inside places I don't want her," Galverson explained in a patronizing tone. "I don't like that. I've already had my balls handed to me by a kid once. I'd prefer that it not happen again." I could hear the barely controlled patience in his voice.

I waited with bated breath for Galverson's next move.

"Keep Taryn away from Pedlam. It's for her own good," Jace ordered.

"I'll keep her out," Tray shot back. He was furious.

"And as long as you do that, we shouldn't have a problem. Should we?" Jace shot back, equally enraged.

The two hated each other. I didn't see that the last time they were in each other's company. They barely acted like they knew each other.

"Fine. We have an understanding," Galverson said soothingly. "Now, Jace, I'd like a moment in private with Tray. It's a family matter."

"Fine," Jace yielded, shutting the door behind him.

"Now, now that it's the two of us, I have a proposition for you, son."

I was surprised Tray hadn't shot him. That was the second time he called him 'son.'

"If it's killing Lanser, I'm in," Tray said easily, but you could hear the violence in his voice.

Galverson chuckled. "Oh, there's a little bit of your father in you. Both of you make me laugh. But, no. It's not about killing a very promising partner of mine. It's about you, Tray."

Tray was quiet. Then he said, "I'm listening."

"You have a multitude of contacts. I was impressed with you when you were younger, but you were too irrational. I feared pushing you, you were too unpredictable then. Now, now you strike me as calmer. More controlled. Smarter about your place in life."

"What do you want?" Tray snapped impatiently.

"You have contacts, Tray. You have a wealth of contacts at your disposal. I know that you've been using them. You know the drug dealers and you know the cops. I'd like to be a part of that wealth of information."

"You want to know what cops'll turn for you," Tray mused.

Dirty cops.

"Yeah," Galverson sounded surprised, "you think I want to get to know clean cops, maybe kill 'em?"

"And you can go to hell," Tray sent his way, sounding assured.

"I've been talking to your father about you. He tells me that you're much smarter than his eldest son. You're classified as a genius. He also thinks you have a thing with authority. You don't like it. In fact, Mitchell tells me that you hate authority, you always have."

Tray was quiet, listening.

"I'd like for you to come work for me. You'd be a first sergeant. You'd work over Jace."

"I'd be his boss?" Tray asked.

"Yes."

"Until he learned everything I know, and then he'd kill me."

"I'm not as stupid as you think I am, Tray, since I let you live so long ago. No, I only let you live because you were

Mitchell's kid. I could stop anything you sent out. I have agents and police in every level of the government. I let you live because you were just a kid. And because you don't buy into this right/wrong bullshit. I saw that you only wanted to be left alone. I saw that and I knew that you'd hold up your end of the deal. I won't kill your father and you won't leak anything on me."

That was news to me.

"You can kill my father all you want. In fact, if I ever see him again, I'll follow out on my threat," Tray said silkily, his voice sending a shiver down my spine."

But it wasn't from fear this time.

"You have another weakness, Galverson," Tray murmured. A second later he continued, "You love your daughter. That's a problem for you."

It was silent again.

"You wouldn't touch her," Galverson replied sounding close to the edge of losing his temper. "You wouldn't dare."

"You underestimated me last time too," Tray said smoothly.

"You, little piece of—no. I know what you're doing. It's that authority thing again, isn't it? Your father was dead-on. You're 'reacting.' He said you do that a lot." He actually laughed. "You're a keeper, that's for sure. But seriously, think about my proposition. I could make you a very wealthy man."

"You already did," Tray said, sounding bored. I knew he was anything but.

"That's true, isn't it. Alright, think about my proposal and get back to me. No time limit." I heard the door open. "And Tray, if you ever think of touching my daughter, I will not hesitate to send my men after your brother."

"I haven't spoken to my family for four years. I could care less what you do to them." Then Tray slammed the door and locked it.

I crawled into bed. And huddled there, my hands trembling. I looked up and met Tray's eyes when he entered the room.

He shut the door and leaned against it. Then slid down, his hands in his hair.

"Fuck," he bit out.

Fuck.

"Tray—" I started, my voice shaking.

"I don't want to talk about it," he cut me off roughly. He stayed in place, on the floor, cradling his head.

"Tray—" I started again. I slipped off the bed and knelt before him. I pulled his hands away and dropped them in shock. His eyes were dilated, a shocking color stood in their normal hazel color.

"What are you...are you on something?"

"No," he pushed me away, "just stay away. I told you I don't want to talk about it." He got up and left, darting out of the house. I heard the patio door slam shut behind him. I moved to a bedroom with windows that overlooked the pool area. Looking through them, I saw the door to the storage building slam shut.

I stayed by the window, just breathing in and out, trying to calm my nerves. But Tray didn't come out.

I waited and no Tray.

After ten minutes, I let out a breath and moved away from the window.

I went downstairs and went to the pool house. When I got onto the patio, I stopped in shock. I could hear pounding sounds coming from the storage shed he ran into.

I wanted to go see, but instead I moved into the pool house. I showered and changed into some new clothes. I pulled my cell charger out of my bag and plugged it in. Then I remembered Tray's phone. I went back into the house, still hearing the sounds, and found his cell in the bedroom. After

I plugged it into its charger in the pool house, I stood uncertainly in the doorway.

He was still in the storage shed.

I finally gave into temptation and moved to the door. There weren't any windows, so I had to open the door to see inside.

Inside was a punching bag, and Tray had stripped down to his waist. He was beating the shit out of that bag. Every now and then, he'd rear back for a hard uppercut. I caught a glimpse of his knuckles. They were bleeding.

I crossed to him, and readied myself for what I was about to do. When I reached out and grabbed his arms from behind, I held on.

"Stop," I spoke, gritting my teeth.

"Get off me," Tray snapped, trying to shrug me off.

I held on.

"Stop it," I bit out again, starting to get pissed.

"Taryn," he warned, "I gave you space when you needed it."

"Yeah, well, that was when we were just screwing each other. We did not screw last night and we haven't been doing that for a while."

"Shut up," he replied harshly.

"Stop it. You're starting to scare me." He wasn't, but I wanted him to stop, so I lied.

"Taryn," Tray cursed at me.

"This is not cathartic. This just makes it worse."

"Says who?" Now he'd turned to infantile arguments.

I shot back, "Says our psych teacher."

I was right and we both knew it.

"Get off me." He finally managed to shove me away, but he didn't go back to trying to murder the bag. He glared at me and stated, "I'm not talking about it. Not yet."

"Fine. But stop that stupid shit. It doesn't help." I gestured to the bag. "And we *are* talking when you calm down."

"I don't want to hear about you saying 'goodbye' to your ex," he threw back.

I wasn't really keen on talking about Brian with him either.

"Fine."

"Fine."

Tray swore, sighed, and then grumbled, "Since when do we talk?"

"Since I'm admitting that we're in an actual relationship. And we are," I said firmly, seeing him roll his eyes. But he didn't argue.

"I'm going to take a shower," Tray remarked, rolling his shoulders.

I went to the kitchen to make some coffee. Hunting around the shelves, in the vicinity of where you would put the coffee pot, I cursed as my eyes fell on the sale-tag that was still on the coffee pot. Who buys a coffee machine and doesn't use it?

When the doorbell rang, I jumped.

When it peeled again, I looked behind me, helpless. Like Tray was going to materialize suddenly. But he didn't. He was still showering, or changing. Not there, which is where I needed him.

After the third time, a hand pounded on the door. I moved to the foyer and paused, still terrified. Who could blame me?

"Come on, come on, come on. I know you're in there." That definitely did not sound like Jace or Galverson.

I blew out a breath of relief and opened the door.

Mandy breezed past me.

Following her into the kitchen, I heard her say, without preamble, "Everyone's skipping today. I couldn't believe it. I thought I'd be a good daughter, you know, like you were the other day, and boy do I regret that now. I actually went to school this morning and had, like, four people in class. Seriously. One of them was your friend Molly what's-her-face. She asked where you were, by the way, and I told her you were probably here. You and Tray left early last night. I saw that Gentley guy and your ex. I figured that was why you guys escaped."

Mandy opened the fridge and pulled out some bagels and cream cheese.

"Where's Tray?"

"Showering."

Wait.

"Does that mean everyone's coming over?" I asked, slightly alarmed.

"Well, yeah." Mandy shrugged, spreading cream cheese on her bagel. "It's what we do, especially when we skip. Duh."

"It's...oh...this isn't a good time."

"What do you mean?" Mandy grabbed the juice next, pouring herself a cup. "You want a cup?"

"No. I want..." I was at a loss for words. I got the feeling Mandy was just the warm-up. In about an hour, this place would be full of people.

When wasn't there?

"Oh," Mandy exclaimed, "Casners is looking for you. She's got a beef with you or something. I would too after what you did last night. Thanks, Tristan was a treat the rest of the night. In between her make-out sessions with Garrett, that is."

I had her tickets. No way was she going to pick a fight with me.

"What are you talking about?" I was tired. I'd been scared shitless this morning, for my life and Tray's, so sue me if I wasn't following along with this conversation.

"You know, her and Tristan. They're, like, mortal enemies, by the way. Good job."

"Oh." That's right.

"Tristan still has no clue, though. No one's had the heart to tell her why Casners went after her last night."

I was having a hard time caring.

"Oh." Should I ask and pretend to care? "What happened?"

"You mean, who did Brent Garrett go home with last night?" Mandy was too energetic this morning. "He went home with Tristan. I just said they were making out the rest of the night. Aidrian Casners hates her. Although I think Tristan was really doing it to get at Amber. Those two cannot stand each other. I've never really figured out why."

"Because Amber thinks Tristan is psychotic and thinks she's the only person you can be best friends with. Oh, and because she thinks her and Tray have a star-crossed lover thing going on," I rambled, stating word for word—or close enough to Amber's statement.

Mandy gaped in shock. "What?"

"It's what I heard." I had officially became part of the gossip mill. Not a subject in the gossip mill, but an actual participant in the mill.

I needed to escape.

"I'll be back. Just...make some coffee," I instructed my sister, hightailing it out of there to the pool house.

Tray was pulling a shirt on when I rushed in and laid on the bed.

"We're a pair, aren't we?" Tray mused, sitting beside me on the bed and bending to grab some shoes.

"Mmmm," I mumbled into his pillow.

Tray didn't reply.

I rolled onto my back and asked, "Why does your place have to be the hang-out when everyone skips? People just show up here. Randomly. Like last night, they had a party when we were in here."

Tray shrugged. "I've lived alone this whole time. I like it when people show up." He flexed his knuckles, hissing in pain.

I sat back on my knees, crawling to sit beside him. I reached for his hands and gently inspected his knuckles. They were still open, raw, and bleeding.

Probably a good metaphor for Tray and me.

He grew still, in pain, as I looked closely at the sores.

"You need to disinfect these," I murmured.

"I have a first-aid kit in the house," he murmured, leaning closer to me.

I looked up and met his gaze. He was looking at me, intensely.

"So we're in a relationship, huh?"

"Yeah," I whispered, studying him, looking for any reaction.

He was doing the same to me.

"Good," he whispered, leaning to kiss me. I grinned against his mouth and kissed him back.

"That means we talk. I'm not in a relationship where we don't talk," I clarified as I pulled away. I meant it, too. Brian and I hadn't always talked out our issues, and I hated it.

"I can do that." He kissed me again.

"We're talking about this morning."

"Do we have to talk about last night?"

"Me and Brian?"

"Yeah." He sounded like he was in pain. He probably was.

"No. Brian and I said goodbye last night. That was it, the end."

"I figured. You kissed him and everything."

"You knew what I was going to do—"

"Yeah, I did." He kissed me again. "It's why I stayed in the car."

"But we're talking about—"

"I know." Tray sighed, pushing me down and laying on top of me. He kissed me. "I know. I know. I know. We'll talk, just not now."

I tipped my head back, enjoying the feel of his lips on my neck. I slid a hand up his back, one of my legs moved to circle his and I slid my foot up and down.

A knock at the door stopped anything else.

Mandy called, "I know what you guys are probably doing, and...stop it. People are showing up and the two of you are becoming rabbits. I don't want my sister to be known as a sex bunny."

"That would make me a playmate," I murmured against Tray's lips.

He grinned. "You definitely look the part." He kissed me again and then sat up. "Can we bandage these? Before more people come over."

"Yeah." I let him help me up. "Lead on, Sir Ass Face." I stood on the bed and jumped on his back, laughing.

Tray stopped. "I thought he was calling Gentley that." His hands coming around my knees, anchoring me in place.

"He was." I grinned, laughing. "I just think it's a funny name. It's like a face on your ass. A nose on your *ass*. And imagine what you would see with your *eyes* on your ass."

"You could kiss my face," Tray retorted.

That brought a smile to my face. "I do."

He knelt and let me off just as we got to the main house.

Entering the kitchen, we saw that it had been raided. And the number of people had multiplied. Mandy was now being kept company by Grant, Amber, and Tristan, the usual crowd minus Devon, Bryce, and Carter.

"Morning," Tray greeted everyone, pulling out the first-aid kit from one of the shelves.

"Dude," Grant breathed out, "what the hell did you do?"

"I beat up a wall," Tray replied, shooting him a cocky grin.

"Seriously—" Tristan started, scooting closer.

"Seriously." Tray stopped her in her place. "It's none of your fucking business." Well, that's settled.

Grant chuckled. "I remember when I used to beat up walls."

"Now you just walk into them." Amber grinned at her brother.

"That's hilarious," Tristan said dryly, rolling her eyes.

Ooh. The embodiment of class from the night before was just replaced by a haughty bitch? I thought I was the only bitch in this crowd.

This was turning into a whole new crowd.

Did this mean...wait...was I the nice one? Oh, fuck no.

"You're hilarious," I shot at her, grabbing the disinfectant and Tray's hand. "Your little show last night."

Tristan glanced at Amber from underneath her eyelids. But Amber saw it. So did I. I grinned. "Isn't that why you hooked up with Garrett? To piss Amber off?" I made my final decision about Tristan: I didn't like her.

"What?" Amber hissed. "You slept with Brent Garrett?"

I half-listened as I bent over Tray's hand and swabbed at the sores. His hand flinched a few times, but he didn't make a sound. I glanced up at him once and saw he had his poker face on.

I quickly finished, bandaging him up swiftly.

When I finished, I rubbed my thumb over them one last time. I looked up and Tray was watching me. A faint grin pulling at the corners of his lips. His plump, luscious lips...

"Taryn," Tristan said.

"Yes," I replied, a little breathless.

"Can I talk to you?"

"No." It was another automatic response. I was still trying to catch my breath. "Why?" I frowned, catching on.

"I want to talk to you about something. In private," she stressed, leading the way into the hallway.

I followed her reluctantly and found myself in a room I hadn't been in before.

Tristan whirled around and shut the door. She crossed her arms and stared at me, looking pissed off.

"What?" I surrendered, slinking onto the seat of one of the couches. It was kind of a...living room. I think this is the third one I've been in.

"What do you have against me?" Tristan asked, demanding.

"What are you talking about?" It was a petty game, but I was willing to play it, with her, at least. It just got her angrier.

"Last night. You sicced Aidrian Casners on me, I know. Erin told me all about Amber, Aidrian, and Brent. And this morning, with Amber just now. Why don't you like me?"

"Because you were a bitch to Mandy yesterday at the house. You were purposely manipulating her. It pissed me off."

She fell silent.

"And because you're just...off. There's something about you. I don't know what it is, but you're just...off."

"You don't like me because something's 'off' with me?" Tristan asked incredulously.

"Yeah." It made perfect sense to me.

"I...that's not fair. It's just not...logical," she cried out.

"You have your logic and I have mine. I'm sticking to mine," I retorted.

Tristan looked flabbergasted. I liked that word—flabbergasted—it's a good word.

I grinned, rocking on my heels. "Anything else?"

"I was hoping we could be friends. Mandy's one of my best friends and I'm transferring to Rawley High next week. I'm going to be around a lot more."

I laughed. "Trust me. I'd be in a shit load of trouble if I had to like all of Mandy's friends."

"I don't think you're taking this seriously," she began stiffly.

I laughed again and rolled my eyes. "What do you want me to take serious? I don't trust you. Generally, people who I don't feel I can trust, end up people I don't like. I'm not going to change my mind. I can handle you being Mandy's friend. Don't worry, I don't like Amber, Jasmine or Devon."

"But, I—" she argued, at a loss for words.

"If you really want to be friends with me, just be nice to Mandy. It'll happen then. Prove me wrong, if it's that important to you."

I left, leaving the confused blue-blood behind me.

In the hallway, I saw Tray poking at some of the plants in the foyer.

"What are you doing?" I asked.

He grabbed my hand and pulled me closer. "I put one of the guns in here. I need to find it and put it back in the safe. Can you distract everyone?"

"Me? I don't talk to those people."

"Just...take 'em downstairs or something. Or you can find the gun and put it back."

I grinned. "Actually, I could, you know. It's one of these mad skills I have." I laughed, savoring the moment with him.

"Shut up," he said harshly, but I heard the laughter in his voice.

"Fine," I murmured, seeing Tristan move into the kitchen, but not before sending a frown our way. "I'll figure out something."

"It won't take long."

"Better not," I murmured, "or I'm likely to kill someone as part of the distraction.

"No killing my friends," he shot back as I left for the kitchen.

I flicked him off behind my back.

CHAPTER EIGHTEEN

I suggested hanging out by the pool and everyone agreed. It worked as a perfect distraction. Turns out the best way to nurse a hang-over is to lounge around in the sun and either drink water or more alcohol. Go figure.

Tray came outside a few minutes later and sat with me, Mandy, Tristan, Erin and Jasmine. We had segregated, somewhat. Mandy, Tristan, Erin, and Jasmine were at my patio table.

The rest sat opposite us, across the pool.

After the Jasmine's incident, Amber and Sasha were inseparable. I was thinking that her plan had backfired. Now she was stuck with Mandy and...me, I guess.

Carter arrived two hours later, complete with a one hundred foot sub.

"Hey, beautiful," Carter greeted, throwing an arm around my shoulders.

"What's this in celebration of?" I asked, grinning back at him. I liked Carter—remember when I slammed the door in his face?

"Uh, it's more of a de-celebration. I have to head back to boarding school. My 'extended' holiday is officially over."

"What?"

"Yeah, but don't worry. I should be getting another 'extended' holiday in a few months. It doesn't take me long to get into trouble there," he reassured me, squeezing my shoulders and steering us away to a corner. "So, let's talk about you and my best friend, who I haven't seen like this since...ever."

"What do you mean?" I grinned lightly, but dreaded what he was going to say next. I had it feeling it was going to turn into some mushy feelings crap that I always run away from. But this was Carter, so I sucked it up and waited for what he was going to say.

"He looks relaxed, Taryn. I don't know what you do." He laughed. "Okay, I know exactly what you do, but any girl can do that too."

I punched him in the chest.

"No, no, I don't need the details. I just want to tell you, as Tray's friend, thank you, for whatever the hell that works between the two of you. He looks good."

Not today. He looked like he was wound tighter than a forty year old virgin who learned masturbation was 'evil.'

"Uh...yeah," I replied, unsure of what I was supposed to say.

It must've appeased Carter, because he nudged me in the shoulder playfully, and then exclaimed, "Tristan! You big slut!" He took off and jumped into her lap. "I heard what you did last night."

"You hear the news?" Mandy asked, she materialized from behind me, a drink in hand.

"You're drinking again?"

"Oh no. This is water. My drunk fest was yesterday. I'm good, thanks," she said dryly. "Did you hear Carter's going back to his school. It sucks."

"Why does he go to boarding school?"

"Because his parents think he can get a better education elsewhere, where all his friends, like Tray, are not. They're not big fans of Tray. Actually, a lot of parents aren't fans of Tray."

"How come?"

Mandy snorted. "Are you serious? Have you looked at Tray? He looks like sex on a stick. Mom and Dad would freak if they found out you're dating him. Wait, you are dating, right? I mean, you're still not in denial? Because it's getting annoying."

"No." I rolled my eyes. "We both know we're in a relationship. Not that it's any of your business."

"I'm going to throw that back at you the next time you're yelling at me about Devon."

Touché.

I argued anyway, "That's different."

"No, no. No, it's not, Taryn." Mandy laughed. "But anyway, Carter and Tray used to be inseparable when they were younger, but...I don't know. Tray went through some phase and he became scary. People either worship Tray or they hate him. Most parents fall in the 'hate' category."

I didn't like this conversation. I shrugged. "They just don't know him."

"No one really knows him," Mandy commented. She paused for a minute, studying Tray. "I mean, I know he likes beer, sex, and pizza. That's about it and I've known him my whole life."

I was uncomfortable.

Mandy burst out laughing. "You're in pain right now, aren't you?" she asked. "You're just hating this." She laughed hysterically.

I didn't get what was so funny.

"I love you, Taryn." She threw her arms around me, hugging me tightly. "I really do. I was a bit worried when we were asked to adopt you, but...man...this is great. You're great. You and me—we're actual sisters. We fight, laugh, cry, but you're there for me, just like a sister should be. You're better than a best friend. Best friends can fight and that's the end of it, but not you and me."

See why I'm so uncomfortable? There is absolutely no point in this conversation. Mandy and I have bonded before, we don't need to do it again. In my opinion, conversations need to have a purpose. They should be limited to these purposes only: 1. To argue; 2. To make plans for the immediate future (stay away from long-term planning, could lead to something more serious); 3. Sex; 4. To inform someone or be informed of something important (I will be the judge on what is considered important). If conversations do not adhere to these requirements, the only exception is if I'm amused (I will also be the only one to judge if it is funny or not).

"Anyway," Mandy continued after her fit of laughter, "I was saying that Carter's parents don't like Tray. I think it's because Tray told 'em to fuck off. The guy hates authority. He used to be awful in the eighth and ninth grade. He was suspended almost every month. They only kept him in school because the superintendent was golf buddies with his dad. Last year he started to get better. He only got suspended every third month or so."

She started laughing again. She had to be drinking; water doesn't have this kind of effect.

Another stipulation: both parties must adhere to the aforementioned stipulation concerning the humor exclusion. I was not amused. According to the rules, this conversation is illegal.

"I just think it's awesome that my sister is dating Tray Evans. Like in a real relationship. This isn't like when he dated Jasmine."

Okay. This conversation needed to be done.

"I have to go to the bathroom."

I veered into the kitchen instead and grabbed some of the magical coffee that appeared out of nowhere.

"Hey." Tray had followed me.

"Let's go back to denying that we're in a relationship."

Tray grinned and hopped onto the island counter, sitting back to listen to me.

I continued, “People suddenly think they can start talking to me about this, you and me. Carter. Mandy. God knows who’s next. I don’t care about what they think. I don’t care about what you used to be like and how you’ve changed. I don’t care that you’re treating me different than you treated Jasmine. I don’t care about any of that, so why do people think they should tell me? Because I should care about that shit? Which, I do not!”

“Just tell ‘em to fuck off. It works for me.” Tray was still grinning, finding my tirade amusing. He lifted a hand to run through his hair.

My eyes fell on his bandages.

“You want me to redress those?” I pointed to his hands.

“Oh. Uh,” he paused to consider it, “nah. They should be good. If I go swimming, then yeah.”

“I suggested swimming. But no one’s swimming.”

“That requires energy.” Tray yawned. “I know I don’t have that much.” He pointed to my hands. “How are your hands?”

I’d forgotten about my cuts. I lifted my hands and looked at them. “They’re better. Not hurting, if that’s what you’re asking.” But I should change their dressings, it’d been awhile.

“You two aren’t doing *it* in the kitchen, are you?” Carter asked, from around the corner. He must’ve been the spokesman, because a smattering of laughs—and giggles—broke out.

It’s only funny when men giggle. Giggling girls: annoying.

Tray retorted, “If we are, you gotta pay to come watch.”

Carter turned the corner, a dollar bill in hand. “Do I know you or what?” He laughed, launching himself up on the counter, landing next to Tray. “So, Taryn, do a dance for me.”

I narrowed my eyes at him.

Tray grew silent, waiting for my reaction.

I smiled, going for sultry, when I moved up next to Carter, sliding my hands along the counter, right beside him. Then I grabbed hold of his pants and yanked him off the counter.

I stepped back as he fell to the floor, landing on his ass.

"That's more entertaining to me." I grinned at him. Tray lifted me up and placed me beside him.

Carter sat there in shocked silence for a moment. "The fuck—" he finally sputtered, glaring at me as he stood up, brushing off his pants.

"You're a moron." Tray chuckled. "When you say moronic stuff, you need to expect to be treated like a moron."

Grant moved back to the sub, which had been left out. He picked up a piece, and remarked, "Man, thanks for the food, Carter. I get sick of Tray's pizza all the time."

"Hey, don't forget KFC," Tray balked weakly.

Grant ignored him. "Too bad you gotta go back to boarding school. You should not go, like your parents would ever know. Aren't they in Europe? Just have Taryn sneak in and steal all your contact info. They wouldn't have a way to get a hold of your parents."

"What?" Carter looked at me, interested.

"No," I said automatically. "No. No."

"You could do that?" Carter asked.

"No. I can't. Not anymore. No."

"That would be awesome. I wouldn't have to go back and my parents wouldn't cut me off."

"I'm not doing anything. No." I shot Tray a pleading look.

He laughed.

"Seriously, Taryn—"

"No, are you not listening to me?! I said no. I'm done."

A very loopy looking Mandy piped up, "I won't let her. So you can hate me. But Taryn's not allowed to do anything illegal...like that."

"Go find a computer genius, promise him whatever he wants and have him do the computer stuff. I don't think you need help breaking into your school's offices. You just need someone to hack into their system."

"I could do that." Carter was thinking pensively. "In fact, I could do that from here. I know some guys that could do it." He took off, darting out to his car.

Tray and Grant were grinning.

"What?"

"He's just going to threaten 'em," Tray answered, laughing. "Carter's not big on public relations. He'll threaten 'em, they'll report him, he'll get in more trouble, and the dudes will get their asses kicked in the end."

"He might get an extended suspension then. He gets what he wants either way," I mused.

Just then Amber, Sasha, and another girl came into the room giggling—see annoying!

"What's going on?" Amber asked pleasantly. She tended to downplay her stuck-up, bitchy, goddess-like persona around the guys.

Sasha was quiet.

"Not much," Mandy answered her.

"We should go to the diner. Or to Sers," Amber suggested, glancing around the group.

"Let's go to Sers and rent a boat," Jasmine added. "That would be a lot of fun."

What the hell is Sers?

But everyone wanted to go to Sers, so the decision was made and everyone left.

Outside, Mandy pulled me towards Tristan's car. "Hold on. I gotta grab my purse," I muttered, darting towards the pool-house.

"Okay. We'll wait," Mandy called after me, moving towards the white Rolls-Royce.

Tray was doing the same when I entered his bedroom. I saw him stuff his wallet in his back pocket.

"What the hell is Sers?" I asked, looking around the room.

"It's a rec center on the lake in town," Tray answered distractedly. I watched him as he searched around the room for something. He lifted up a pillow, but put it back down.

"I plugged your cell in."

"Oh. Thanks." He lifted up a shirt and there it was.

"I did that when you were beating the shit out of that dumbass punching bag," I murmured, looking for my purse.

I looked up, grabbing my purse—which was in the corner—and found him looking at me. "What?" I stopped, slinging my purse over my shoulder, to have it cross my body.

"Nothing." His eyes didn't reflect nothing, but I let it go.

"Okay." I shrugged, moving to the door.

But Tray stopped me, he grabbed my hand and pulled me to him. Bending his head, he kissed me, his hands resting on my hips, holding me firmly against him.

When he lifted his head, he said, "Thanks."

"For what?"

He didn't say anything, but grinned, leading the way out.

I followed him out and headed towards Tristan's car. The backdoor was open with Mandy half sitting outside. "Let's go, Taryn. She's riding with us, Tray."

Tray lazily lifted a hand in response, already heading to his own vehicle.

When I climbed in beside Mandy in the backseat, Tristan sent me a small smile before starting the car. Erin sat in shotgun.

"Mandy, have you talked to Devon lately?" Erin turned and asked. She looked at me, then immediately looked away. I guess I still made her nervous.

He left yesterday. Define 'lately.'

I tuned the conversation out. Mandy had launched into a story about how she drunk-dialed him last night and he was not amused. The guy's getting ready for the play-offs. He probably needed his sleep. I could sympathize with him.

After a short drive to the opposite side of town, we reached Sers. The place was huge, complete with tennis courts, sand volleyball courts, and a diner. The giant rec center sat on the lake with a fifty-foot dock. I could see about twelve boats and a few Skidoo jet-skis anchored to it. On the opposite side of the dock, there were paddle boats pulled up on the beach. The best thing about the place? An Olympic size, indoor pool with three diving boards.

Plus...the place was packed. Mandy was right. Everyone had skipped today and they all seemed to have the same idea.

I saw Larkins at one of the tables with his hacky-sack buddies.

As we walked closer towards the table area, I saw Aidrian Casners and Crystal Fairs at another table. They were surrounded by a bunch of other students.

This was school without the classes and teachers.

Then a thought came to mind, and I looked into the furthest corner and saw Molly, Kayden, and Angela.

"I'll be back," I remarked, veering off in their direction.

Kayden saw me first, sat up straighter and gave me a small grin. It vanished immediately, but it was a grin nonetheless.

"Hey, guys!" I cried out, sitting next to Molly.

"Hi." Molly brightened.

I zeroed in on her neck. "You *are* dating Larkins!" I accused her. "No way are those the same 'love bites' from the party. No way in hell.""

She blushed, ducking her head.

I loved this girl.

"He asked me out last night."

"On a date?" What had they been doing before?

"Yeah. He wants to take me to the play-offs in the cities this weekend."

"That's great!"

"It's...it's for the *entire* weekend," she whispered, looking back up—still blushing.

Wait a minute. "Are you guys skipping school too?"

"No. We were let out. Principal Marshalls said we might as well enjoy the day since everyone else is. We get credit for our classes though."

"Oh," I murmured. "So you don't want to be around Larkins for the entire weekend?"

"Yeah."

"Why?" I was clueless.

"Because," she paused, looking uncomfortable, "things might...you know..."

"Oh." Understanding dawned. "Miss Molly, are you saying that you might be tempted for things to...*progress*?"

"Yeah," she whispered, her body turning an alarming shade of red.

Angela and Kayden were—shockingly—silent. I can't imagine what their advice would be.

"Do you want to...you know?"

She shrugged. "I don't know. I mean it's nice, right? I don't really want to go to college a virgin and I only have one more year before I graduate, to...you know..."

"Practice?" Was that the word? It sounded cold.

"Yeah."

"Molly," I sat up, growing serious, "you can have sex when you want to have sex. I think that you need to be able to talk about sex before you have sex though." She opened her mouth, but I continued, "You need to be able to talk about everything involved in having sex, without blushing."

"There's more than...?" The girl was seriously struggling.

"There's contraception, STDs, positions—'cause there's a lot more than just the missionary position—oral sex...the list goes on and on."

I really think Molly's going to have a heart attack. She was hyperventilating.

I added softly, "Larkins is a great guy. If you don't want it to...progress...just tell him. The guy's crazy about you, he wouldn't want to make you uncomfortable at all. Trust me."

"But you—"

"What about me?"

"You're with Tray Evans. I mean, do you guys...?"

Holy fuck. I was a bit taken aback by this conversation. There was a huge difference between myself and Molly.

"Yeah, we do," I said bluntly.

"Is he, does he...?"

"What?"

"Does he ever...you know," she took a deep breath, "put his hands...down there?"

How far was Larkins going?

"Yes, he does. Do you want Larkins to do that?"

"I don't know...sometimes."

"Do you guys talk before you do that?"

"No!" she was horrified. "Do you?"

"It's different." And it was—I was on a whole other level than Molly. I knew I could tell Tray point-blank that I was uncomfortable with something and he'd stop, no questions asked.

Did Larkins know she didn't want that?

"Larkins might be going there, but he might be thinking it's what you want," I suggested. "You guys should talk. You *need* to talk."

Why the hell was I feeling responsible for this girl and her sex life?

"Sometimes it's...nice."

"Tell him what you want," I said bluntly.

Molly looked a little more appeased and maybe a little bit relieved.

Kayden and Angela looked like they wanted to disappear.

"Alright. I'm going to go," I announced. You could only be socially charitable for so long. And sometimes...talking was too much work. Plus, this conversation did not fall under any of the four requirements or the exception clause.

That was my rationalization and I was sticking to it. I wasn't going to feel guilty about not talking to the rest of the Invisibles.

I marched over to Larkins and grabbed him by the back of his shirt. "Come," I ordered.

As we turned the corner, I asked, "What are you and Molly doing?"

"What are you talking about?" He looked confused, but a seconds later I saw a flicker of awareness in his eyes.

"Do not play with me." I crossed my arms, glaring.

"Fine. We're...this is *embarrassing*."

"Tough," I barked.

"We've been," he looked down, his foot playing with a rock, "I don't know. We get together and do things—"

"Do not push her to have sex with you," I stated fiercely.

"No!" He looked up in terror. "I would never."

"You need to talk to her about what she wants to do." I was relieved. For some unknown goddamn reason, I was irritable and I didn't know why which pissed me off even more.

"How do you...?"

"You ask her what she wants to do, what she likes or doesn't like. She doesn't like your fingers going where they go sometimes."

"Oh God." Larkins blushed, looking like he wanted to die. "Can we not have this conversation? This is seriously—"

"If you can't talk to me about sex, you shouldn't be having it with her," I reasoned. "If you can't talk to me, it's going to be ten times worse with Molly. I'm *making* you talk about it, she's not going to."

"Fine. Can we be done now?" he asked stiffly, looking really uncomfortable.

"Fine."

Larkins ran, an all-out, full on sprint. It made me smile.

"Hey, bitch." I sighed. There goes my good mood. I looked behind me and Aidrian Casners had wandered up, with Crystal and another girl behind her.

What? Were they going to tag-team me?

"Yeah?"

"I know what you pulled last night."

I grinned cockily. "Ah...fond memories." I sighed mockingly.

"I'm going to let you slide on that one—once!" She puffed out her chest. "You got my tickets?"

"I do. Your date will be at your house to pick you up at six-thirty, with the tickets."

She rolled her eyes. "I'm not supposed to *do* anything with him, am I?"

"Yeah."

She froze.

I grinned. "No ditching."

Aidrian relaxed. "Fine," she shrugged, nonchalant, "but, if he don't show with those tickets, expect you and me at war."

"Oh, it's expected." I was amused. Crystal was right—Aidrian was entertaining.

"I see you came in with that slut, Tristan," she commented casually.

"Yeah?" What was she getting at?

"I've always hated her, ever since the fourth grade when she thought she was too good for Rawley. Her and that Amber bitch."

Two of my favorite people. I was warming up to this girl every second.

I saw Crystal was fighting off a grin.

"Yeah," I said, nodding in agreement. Are we having a conversation? An actual conversation? Why?

Have I mentioned I'm not a trusting person?

I might not be trusting, but I'm able to appreciate the humor. And Aidrian Casners, talking to me, a casual, civil convo—was funny. It fit the exception stipulation.

"Amber Lancaster's always thought she was the bomb. Seriously. The girl's a fucking junior, she should stay with the juniors."

"Like you stay with the seniors," I murmured. Umm...she did know Tray was a junior too, right?

"Exactly, Aidrian went off, feeling appreciated, "I mean...she's always been on my back, trying to one-up me. She just thinks she has the right. I should teach her she doesn't have the right to anything. Her brother's pretty hot."

"Good luck with that." I patted her on the arm, finding that more amusing. Crystal had turned away, I saw her shoulders were shaking with restrained laughter. "I'm going to go."

"Oh...sure...yeah." Aidrian came back to earth, realizing she had just confided in me—of all people. She yelled at me when I turned away, "Hey. Tickets. Tomorrow or it's you and me."

I rolled my eyes and resumed walking.

Mandy and the crew had taken residence at a table close to the dock. Tray, Grant, and some other guys were in a boat, looking around.

"What's going on?" I asked, dropping next to my sister.

"The guys are renting a boat. We're waiting."

"We've been waiting forever," Amber complained. "I'm roasting."

"So go get wet," Tristan snapped, sending a glare her way.

"Why don't you?" Amber shot back.

I didn't get the problem.

"Yeah, I'm gonna go," I announced, standing up. I left my clothes and purse with Mandy, who solemnly swore to protect everything before I walked towards the pool in my black bikini.

"Hey, you."

I'm so popular. I just love being popular.

I looked over and saw a guy gesture to me, walking quickly to intercept me. He was covered in tattoos and wore a polo shirt over some trendy faded jeans. His hair was styled into a mohawk.

"Yeah?" I asked when he grew closer to me.

"I want to talk to you." He gestured across the center, to a private corner.

"Why?" I was standing in a bikini, defenseless. Did he think I was stupid?

"It's about your sister. Mandy Matthews, right?" he tossed over his shoulder, all business, already moving ahead of me.

I followed, reluctantly.

When we get to the corner, I asked, "What's this about?"

"Look, your sister owes me five grand."

What?!

"What?!" I cried out, startled. "For what?"

"That's between me and her. But you tell her, that if she doesn't pay, I'm going to cash in my debt."

I was seeing red.

"You push drugs?" I asked cautiously, letting my anger simmer.

"You fucking think I'm going to tell you that?" He grinned, so self-assured.

I didn't like him. In fact, I was quickly starting to hate him.

"Who do you work for?" I asked, ignoring him. "You work for Galverson? Or Jace Lanser? Or someone else? Because I really hope, for your sake, that it's someone else."

He was shocked into silence.

Well, that was all the answer I needed. He was probably a small-time player, but he knew who the big guys were.

"You do know what happens to anyone who pushes drugs in Rawley, right? Or did you just start up?"

"Whatever, bitch..." Ah...the infantile defense mechanism—throwing insults when you had nothing intelligent to say. Nice.

"You need to re-evaluate your position and start spilling. Now," I said firmly.

He didn't say anything.

Fine. It's not like I could assault him so instead, I said, " "I am going to find out who you are. I am going to find out everything there is to know about you. I'm going to know where you sleep, where you eat, who your friends are, and your worst fears. Then I'm going to find out what you're selling my sister, and when I do, I'm going to be bringing war to your front door. Trust me."

"You're a bitch," he snarled, but he was re-thinking his strategy with me. Watching me, he could see the steel resolve in my eyes.

"If you don't want me to destroy you, you better start talking now. And I mean, right now!"

"Holy...jeez...your sister's been coming to me for two years. She's getting a fucking vitamin from me. That's it."

"Vitamin R," I stated.

The guy's eyes widened.

Oh yeah, fucker. I knew what Vitamin R was for.

"What's she doing on Vitamin R?" I demanded coldly.

"I don't fucking know. Ask your sister. But she owes me five grand and she better cash in or—"

"Or what?" I wanted to know. I really wanted to know. Please tell me, asshole, because your life is over. Right now.

"Or—" He'd grown silent, just watching me.

"You better run," I stated, fuming, "and you better run far, because getting whatever Mandy owes you is the least of your problems now."

"You're psychotic," the guy whispered, watching me warily.

"What's your name?"

"Oh no. No fucking way."

"I'm going to find you anyway and I'm going to be more pissed off that it took me longer than it should have."

"Jenkins," he finally spat out, "Mark Jenkins."

The name was familiar, but I couldn't place it.

"Run," I taunted coldly, furious.

He took one last look at me and then left; at first at a casual pace, and then—he ran.

I turned, slowly, and saw my sister laughing and bouncing up and down. She was grinning at whatever Tristan had just said. I watched as she picked up her phone and looked at it. A small frown appeared on her face, but it was gone as quickly as it appeared, her mask firmly in place, looking perfect.

CHAPTER NINETEEN

Tray was still on the dock, thank God, when I got to him. He was sitting behind the steering wheel, grinning at whatever Grant had just said.

I was furious and everyone was a target right now.

Seeing me, one of the guys cleared his throat and nodded in my direction.

Tray glanced behind him, and the laughter halted.

He stood up. "Hey—" he trailed off, his eyes widening at the barely controlled rage written across my face.

"I need your keys." I stuck my hand out, knowing he was going to ask, knowing he saw what was inside of me, but not caring.

"What?"

"I need your keys. Right now." Fucking duh.

"What's going on?" he asked cautiously, reaching for his back pocket.

"Just give me your keys," I repeated. I stamped all of my emotions down so I wouldn't blow up—this was not the time or place.

He held them up slowly. "What's going on?" he asked, studying me intently.

I snatched them up.

"What about our rule?" Tray demanded. He kept a hold of the keys. I tried to yank them away, but he held on to them tightly.

"You said later. With your stuff...you said later," I reminded him, unyielding. "I need that now," I said tightly, wrenching the keys out of his grasp. I immediately turned to leave, walking back down the dock.

"Taryn," he called after me, but I ignored him. I circled around *their* table. I could hear Mandy's laugh, but I didn't dare look at her as I passed.

I quickly crossed to where Tray had parked and got inside. Staring the engine, I peeled out of there. It didn't take long to get to my house. I was braking to a halt moments later outside my house.

I left the keys dangling in the car and ran inside.

Realizing I left my keys at Sers, I ran around to the first floor bathroom window and propped it open. The only sound I could hear was the pounding of my heart.

I hauled my body up and crawled inside.

When my feet touched the floor, I choked back a sob. I stumbled through the doorway and up the stairs. I ran, sprinted to Mandy's room.

In the doorway, her perfect doorway, I froze in place. My horrified gaze took everything in. Everything was labeled and put in its perfect place. Everything.

Her clothes were color-coordinated. Separated from denim for the summer and denim for the winter. Her desk was pristine, actually sparkling when the sunlight caught on it. And her pictures were perfectly aligned.

Then I hauled off and looked through everything. Everything.

I couldn't hear anything. If anyone had walked or rang the doorbell—nothing. My heart was pounding in my eardrums, deafening me. I felt like there was fucking elephant was standing on my chest as I frantically tore into her desk, looking through papers, files. Anything and everything.

I looked in her jewelry box. Her nightstand, a little box that was on there. The dresser drawers. Underneath her bed.

The window frame. I even lifted up her curtain rod and looked inside.

I checked the door, behind the door, just on top of its frame. I checked the venting shafts. Even behind a framed picture that hung on her wall. Behind her posters.

Nothing.

Fucking nothing.

An hour later, still nothing.

I spied her Kleenex box. And I tore it open and in the corner, and found one small bag of Vitamin R.

Fucking uppers.

But she owed five grand—there was no way that this little bag equaled five grand.

I flipped the bed mattress up and saw one of the corners was slightly ripped. Jamming my fingers inside it, I found another little bag.

Then I looked around again, I walked into her bathroom that was connected to her bedroom.

I stood on the toilet and ran my hands along the top of the wall cabinets, the highest to the ceiling, and found a box full of Vitamin R. A whole fucking box stuffed with baggies, all filled with pills. And one by one, I dumped them into the toilet.

It took me an hour. A whole fucking hour.

I told myself to breathe. In and out. Just breathe. But the energy was wrenched from me. I felt like I'd hurdled off the side of a cliff.

When I was done, I stumbled to my bedroom and curled on my bed. My arms wrapped around my knees, curled in the fetal position.

That was how Tray found me. I didn't know how long I laid there like that. Frozen.

"Hey," he said softly, sitting next to me on the bed. I flinched when he tentatively touched me.

"How'd you get here?" I asked. I didn't know what else to say.

"Carter showed up. I had him drop me off here."

"Was Mandy there?"

"Yeah...why?" He frowned, his hand resting on mine.

"Because—"

"Because why?"

"Her drug dealer came up to me and wanted me to pass a message to her for him," I bit out, starting to seethe inside again.

"What?" Tray froze, the small circle his thumb had been moving in stopped. "What did you say?"

"Mark Jenkins. That's his name," I bit out bitterly.

I realized that Tray still hadn't said anything.

I scrambled to a sitting position. "Do you know him?"

"Yeah," he said slowly, not looking at me.

"Do you know who he works for?"

"Yeah."

"Who?"

"No, Taryn. You're not getting involved in it. I'll handle it."

"Fuck that." I got up, standing in front of him. "She's my sister. I do not want my sister on drugs."

"How much did she have?"

"Enough to be dealing 'em herself," I said swiftly. "It took me an hour just to flush 'em all."

"What was she on?"

"An upper."

"Which one?"

"Vitamin R. Methyl—whatever the fuck it is. Ritalin shit," I snapped, raking both my hands through my hair.

"Okay." He stood up and moved to leave.

I grabbed his hand. "Oh no. You're not doing this without me."

"I don't want you involved." Tray tried to shrug me off.

"No!"

"Taryn," he argued, walking down the stairs.

"No!" I shouted, jumping past him to block his way. "I hate drugs. You have no idea how much I hate those things. I really...*really*...detest them."

"I know!" he cried out. "How do you think I feel?"

"Oh," I yelled back, "like steroids are any different!"

Tray grew still and his body went rigid at that. I saw his jaw clench and spasm.

"You and I both know it—they're the same thing," I pressed, uncaring that I was crossing a line.

"They don't have the same effects."

"Bullshit," I swore.

"They're not the same."

"Yes, they are, Tray. And you tap that market...you do it because a part of you likes to get away with it. You do it because it keeps you connected to that life," I goaded, unheeding the warning that flashed in his eyes.

"That's fucking bullshit," he said slowly, dangerously.

"Then prove me wrong and stop selling them."

"Like you're any better," he shot back.

"I'm trying to stop," I yelled. "You're not."

"Well, I'm stopping this Jenkins piece of shit."

"It won't help, not in the long run," I reasoned.

"You don't understand it, Taryn. You have no clue," Tray cried out. "If Rawley doesn't have something going on, then it'll get flooded by something else. It'll be designated as 'open' and that means we'll have so much fucking drugs here, it's not going to matter. So yeah, I keep the steroid business going just so that we're viewed as vulnerable and open. Some dealers aren't that organized, but some are. Some are! They send hunters out. Those guys' main purpose is to find cities that can be infiltrated. I've avoided that so far, but I can't do it forever. But yeah, if steroids help cover us, then fine. Sign me up."

I didn't want to admit it, but it did make a little sense.

"Just," I said, the fight leaving me, "let Jenkins know that he messed up."

It was all he needed to hear, because he was gone as soon as the words left my mouth.

I heard him peel out of the driveway a second later.

I stayed frozen for a moment and then cursed. I was still in my bikini. I had left my purse at Sers, with my cellphone inside. And my car was at Tray's.

I was stranded, in my own home.

As one of my lessons of survival, I learned to stay away from drugs. They were like locusts. They were everywhere, presented as candy. The truth: they were poison.

Drugs had the power to take families away; they just ripped through them and left them in pieces. I've witnessed it many times in families that I've been placed in, but most recently, with Brian.

When he used, I'd bathe him and clean up his vomit. And I took him to rehab. I had to take him four times, until it finally stuck.

I've done a lot of bad stuff, even since I moved in with the Matthews—when I had taken their name.

But there's one thing I want, without a doubt: to stay in this family.

And so that was why I was in Mandy's room, packing her bags.

Three hours later, I heard voices, so I grabbed her bags and took 'em downstairs. This didn't need to be a drawn-out process.

They were in the kitchen, laughing, when I set them at the end of the stairs. I looked up and met Mandy's gaze.

"What are you doing? Those are my bags," Mandy asked, confused, reaching to fill a glass with water.

"Oh! She packed for you," Jasmine murmured, sounding touched. "That's sweet of your sister."

"Taryn, you didn't have to do that. Really. Now I'm going to have to repack whatever you put in there."

I still hadn't said anything, my eyes were flat and void of emotion.

Mandy misunderstood my look. "Seriously, Taryn. The cheerleaders' bus leaves early, but I'll have time to do it tonight."

"Why'd you take off?" Tristan asked, sitting at the kitchen table, curving her legs gracefully underneath her, a glass of ice water in front of her.

"Yeah, no doubt," Mandy remarked, pulling out a Diet Coke. "You left all your stuff with me. It's on the table, by the way. But seriously, you took off and then Tray took off."

"You guys have a fight?" Tristan asked, not sounding sorry.

I took a deep breath and said quietly, somber, "Tell 'em to leave, Mandy."

"What?" She laughed, reaching for a glass.

"Tell your friends to leave. Now."

"Ookay," she joked, "what are you on?"

"Mark Jenkins," I announced, seeing Mandy freeze in place. I added, "Tell 'em to leave."

Her eyes moved from me, to the luggage and then to her friends.

"Tell. Them. To. Leave," I ordered.

"Seriously, you can be such a bitch." Jasmine laughed, sitting opposite Tristan. "It's kind of getting funny."

"Mandy," I barked.

"Uh," she said weakly, "I'll see you guys tomorrow. Why don't you guys—"

"Go?" Tristan finished, looking dismayed. "Are you serious?"

"Yeah, she is," I clipped out, looking at the door pointedly. "Thanks for driving her home."

"Holy shit, you are a real class act," Tristan muttered underneath her breath, standing. Rolling her eyes, she followed everyone else out.

Mandy hesitated in the doorway, before she closed it and looked at me. Her eyes shifted to the bags at my feet.

I kicked 'em and they spilled over.

"These are yours," I exclaimed. "We're leaving for rehab. Right now."

Mandy laughed, shaking her head. "Oh no, oh no, no, no, no. I'm not. I'm not going anywhere."

"You are," I said again firmly, "and you're going tonight."

"No."

"You're addicted. You had enough of it upstairs to sell 'em yourself."

"No," she said again, shaking her head, frozen in place.

"I'm a pro at this, Mandy. I'm not going to listen to your cries, to your begs, or to your pleas. I'm done. I've been there, done that, and I'm not going back. You're going to rehab. Tonight."

My eyes held my promise.

I closed my eyes for a second, flinching as I remembered his voice, begging me not to take him.

"Let's go." I cleared my throat, shaking away the memories.

"I'm not going," Mandy cried out, and I heard the hitch in her voice. She would become hysterical in a second, when the shock wore off and she realized the game was over.

"It's just me right now," I cut off her tirade, "your parents are gone for the next month. Austin won't have to know. So it's just me and this won't go anywhere else, I promise. But you *are* going. I will not listen to anything, any games, any promises, anything. I've heard 'em all, Mandy. I've gone through this before and you're not going to win. You're not going to get out of this. If you run out of here, I'll call the cops."

I had no proof. I'd flushed the evidence, but she didn't know. She didn't need to know.

"I found all of them. In your Kleenex box. Under your mattress. In your bathroom. I found them all. All five grand worth," I bit out, my jaw clenching.

"Do you have any idea?" she started out softly, "any idea what it's like?"

"What? The pressure to be perfect?" I shot back, knowing why she'd gone for them. "To be perfect for your family? Your perfect boyfriend? Your perfect scholarship? Student council. Cheerleading. Keeping friends like Amber and Jasmine. Being one of the most popular girls? No. I don't know what that's like, but I know what it's like it try to be perfect."

I'd taken every excuse she was going to use.

"I used to try to be perfect," I swore, "and it earned me an abusive foster father who'd visit my room at night when I was six."

Mandy paled as my words registered.

"So fuck you. I know what it's like, but I never turned to drugs. Ever."

"I—" Mandy tried.

"No. We're going. There is no debate, no give and take in this. You're going. Now," I said forcefully, grabbing my purse and her keys.

I threw the bags at her. She blindly caught one of them, so I grabbed the other two and her elbow. I led her out the door and into her car. Then I got into the driver's side and started the car.

I locked the doors and pulled out into the street.

And that's when the tears began.

I wiped mine away, as they silently slid down my face. But I kept on driving. My eyes set fiercely on the road.

Mandy bawled. Her hands cradling her face, she rocked, back and forth.

"Oh no. No, no, no, no..." It went on like that for the entire drive. She bawled, and rocked, and bawled some more. And she tried to bargain, she tried to beg, but she saw my face. She remembered what I said, so she started crying some more.

The drive took forty minutes. I took her to where I always took Brian and was greeted by the same front desk clerk, Patricia. She's been here each time I've brought Brian in. She recognized me and gave me soft, sad smile when she saw who was behind me.

Mandy wrapped her arms around herself. She'd grabbed a blanket from in her car, and I carried all her bags inside. I dumped them at the desk, but I didn't say anything. I don't think I could around the lump in my throat.

"Hi, Taryn." She smiled gently, standing up. She gave me the clipboard and pen. "You know the drill."

I nodded, my throat choking.

I shook my head. "She's my sister," I managed to say hoarsely.

"We'll take care of her," she murmured tenderly.

I nodded, my tears blinding me for a moment.

I looked at Mandy and saw that she was worse than me. She looked like a six year old. Raw. Vulnerable. Exposed.

My heart broke into a million pieces for her.

"I'll handle everything," I murmured, more to myself than Mandy.

Mandy just cried some more.

She'd taken a seat, but was rocking back and forth. I stood in front of her, clipboard in my hand.

Pat and two other staff members stood behind her, waiting.

"Mandy," I spoke up, my voice breaking, "you gotta go."

"No," she shook her head, whimpering, "no."

"You have to," I whispered. "You gotta...you gotta face your shit, Mandy. You haven't. You've been hiding, but that's over now. You can make a fresh start now. You can be out of here—" I trailed off, knowing she wasn't even listening. She couldn't. She was still fighting it. Fighting me.

I looked back at Pat, who gave me an encouraging look, a saddened smile.

"We gotta say goodbye," I whispered, my voice hoarse.

"No," Mandy whispered again, to herself.

"Come on. Let's go." I pulled her up and wrapped my arms around her. Slowly, Mandy moved her arms around me, and then she clung to me.

"Don't me make do this, Taryn. Don't make me go in there."

"You have to," I said back, whispering into her hair, "or I'm gone."

Mandy didn't say anything.

"I love you," I whispered, hugging my sister.

Mandy clung tighter.

I saw Pat come up behind Mandy, and she reached for her arms.

But Mandy clung—like Brian had. She screamed, she cried, she begged. And then, finally, she stood and walked with them.

She'd given up. The first part of the fight.

I took a deep breath, knowing what was next, knowing it wasn't over. And I sat down and filled out the paperwork. Making sure they knew the amount of Vitamin R that I found. That this had been the first time Mandy had been confronted. I pulled out our insurance card and wrote everything down. When I handed it over to Pat, my hands were shaking.

"You okay, dear?" she asked kindly.

I shook my head and then I turned and left.

On the car-ride home, I called Tray. When he answered, I asked swiftly, "Where are you?"

"I'm at home. I drove by your place, but it was dark."

"I took Mandy to rehab." I choked on a sob, and stomped it down. "I can't...I'm coming over."

"Okay," Tray murmured and I heard the strength in his voice.

It nearly broke me, but I kept driving.

Almost an hour later, I pulled into his driveway.

When I went inside, all the lights were off. No cars were in the driveway, except Tray's and mine, thank God.

I found Tray sitting in the glass-encased patio, where we'd congregated the night before. He had an open bottle of Jack Daniels in front of him and two shot glasses. He'd been staring outside.

I looked and saw the pool's glistening reflection from the moonlight above. It had been raining last night, but tonight it was clear as day. There was a full moon shining its ray of light down on the water.

Tray didn't look at me, but he pushed out the chair beside him. I bypassed it and curled up in his lap, resting my forehead against his chest as his arms came around me.

We sat there in silence and he held me for a while.

"Jenkins is gone," Tray murmured, holding me tighter, "and his employer is done. I made a few phone calls."

"To your cop buddies?" I asked in a whisper, my forehead burrowing closer in his chest.

He didn't answer. But he didn't need to.

"Thanks," I said softly.

"How's Mandy?"

I looked up at him, sitting up a bit. "She's...not good. She'll hate me for a while. I'm sure I'll be getting hate voice messages from her soon, but I think she's just in shock right now. I told her no one would find out at school."

Tray nodded, watching me intently.

I knew he wouldn't say anything. Just like he knew I wouldn't say anything. Maybe that was why we paired up, we both had secrets—and we both knew how to keep those secrets.

"I'm sorry, fuck, I'm just—" Tray faltered, shaking his head. He rubbed a hand over his jaw and through his hair, not sure of what to say. "If you want to get forgetful drunk, I got the provisions." He gestured to the bottle.

I rested against him again, my back pressed to his chest, and lifted up his hands. I traced my fingers gently over his knuckles, inspecting the bandages. He did the same to me, running his hand tenderly over my cuts.

"This morning," Tray started, I heard a slight hitch in his voice, "I hated seeing Galverson here. The fucker took away my family. I couldn't choose between my dad and Chase, so I pushed all of 'em away. Chance, he was just a dipshit. He hated that I chose Dad's side. And dad...he was so fucking smug, he thought I chose his side. And," he took a deep breath, "I thought about it, I really did. But I heard mom crying one morning. I'd come home early from soccer practice, so she thought no one was around. I heard her when I went to the kitchen, and I found her in their bathroom. She had a fucking razor in her hands and she was filling the tub."

I closed my eyes, seeing it all in my head. Tray, as a child, finding his mother like that.

His voice hardened as he continued, "She was crying about Dad and I realized then that I couldn't go through with it. I couldn't—do what he was doing—so I made the decision. If I couldn't pick, I didn't want anyone of them around. I already had a lot of the taps and stuff for Chance, but I lied to Chance and told him I messed up. That was when he beat the shit out of me. It was the last time I saw him. I was in the seventh grade. It took an entire year to get all the proof I needed."

"You haven't seen Galverson since...?"

"That was the time I used the tunnel, the only time really. I told Dad and Galverson my ultimatum and I hightailed it out of there. I locked 'em in Dad's office and ran for the tunnel. By the time they got out, I was already underneath the pool. I think Dad just forgot about the tunnel, I don't know...maybe he knew and didn't say anything on purpose. He could've. I didn't know if I was going to get shot when I got out on the other side, but I had to go anyways. Live or die, right? Either way, you gotta fight."

It sounded like my motto.

Tray continued, "I saw Galverson this morning and I felt that day, like I was there again. Reliving everything...I half expected my dad to come waltzing in from the library."

"Was Jace there?"

"Yeah, but he was outside. Galverson sent him out by the guards. Fuck, I hid at Carter's for a week after that. Carter never asked, he was just happy that I was around—I never let his dad push him around when I was there."

I grinned, resting my head against his chest. "Mandy told me that most of parents aren't exactly fond of you."

That made him grin. "Shit, they hate me."

I reached for his hand and intertwined our fingers. I studied our hands in the moonlight.

Tray sighed and added, "I stayed a lot at friends' places a lot during that year and freshman year. I was such a shit, too. I was just a punk kid with this giant chip on my shoulder. I'd never talked about it, to anyone. I'm surprised I still have any friends. I was lucky. I think the principal and superintendent felt sorry for me; they just kept suspending me when I'd get in trouble. I should've gotten kicked out a dozen times, maybe more. But they always let me come back. They knew my parents took off, but no one knew why. I don't think they did anyway, I never said anything. You're the first one I've ever told, and it's only because of your own thing with Galverson that I even said anything."

"I'm glad you told me."

"Fuck, Taryn, if he comes after us, I have a contact for witness protection. It's all worked out, but I hate—fucking hate—that I have to have it at all, you know?"

"Yeah," I whispered, letting my legs fall apart, each leg dangling beside him, to the floor.

Tray breathed again as he wrapped his arms around my waist, our hands now intertwined.

"I told Mandy that no one would know, but I lied. They're going to have to call Shelley and Kevin—Mandy's only seventeen."

"She'll be okay," Tray murmured.

"Yeah, but it's going to be a lot of work for her."

"You want a drink?"

"No," I said firmly, my thoughts on Mandy.

"Okay," he said quietly, turning to kiss my cheek. Then he tilted my head back to meet his mouth. It was a kiss meant to comfort me, to show his support.

"I have to talk to her coach tomorrow. They have to know a reason why she's not going to be around. I suppose I'll have to tell the counselor something, too. And, fuck, I have to give Props those tickets."

"Huh?"

"Never mind."

"Play-offs are tomorrow. Carter's planning on leaving in the morning," Tray commented.

"I'm not going." I hadn't planned either way. "Not with what happened and all. Mandy's going to be calling me all day. At least, that's what Brian always did."

"Can you do anything for her?"

"No, not really."

"Maybe you should come with. It'd help take your mind off her and the whole situation."

"I don't know. I just know that I can't take much more. I'm so tired, Tray, of everything. I thought," I let out a deep breath, "I left this all behind. When I get back home, I'll have to clean up her room."

"I saw it. You tore it up, it looked like a bomb had gone off in there."

"I was on a mission. Plus, I know where to look. I am, after all, a thief." I grinned. I was feeling a little better. I didn't know why, or how, but I was better. I turned around and straddled him, both of us remembering our activities last night.

"I can tell Carter to fuck off and come with you. We can take my vehicle, we'd leave whenever you want."

"When's the first game?"

"Three. Most everyone's checking in at the hotel tomorrow afternoon and then heading over to the game."

"A hotel?"

"Yeah, I have a room reserved."

"Were you planning on sharing with Carter and the guys?"

"I was, until two weeks ago." He stared at me pointedly.

"Oh." I grinned.

"Come on," he persuaded, his hazel eyes twinkling with a smidgen of amber. "Mandy's in rehab. Your folk are gone. It'll be fun. It's time to get away."

"Do I have to spend time with Amber, Jasmine, and Tristan?" I rolled my eyes. I'd sign up for rehab myself before I had to spend a weekend with those three.

Tray laughed. "I'm thinking no."

He's right. I really didn't have much else to do, except clean up Mandy's room. Besides, a weekend, in a hotel room, with Tray sounded heavenly. A week ago, I never would've admitted that, let alone think of it.

"Okay." I sighed. "But I have a lot to do in the morning."

"You can get it done. Go in first hour and give your messages. Then pack, clean Mandy's room. We can leave whenever you're done."

"It'd be fun to leave with everyone else."

"Yeah," he agreed. Tray tugged me down to him and I met him half-way, our lips met and we clung to each other. The kiss started out slow and tender, but a spark ignited in me. I clung to him desperately, as I felt the fire explode inside me.

Tray was quick to respond and the kiss deepened, passionate.

Our movements were heated, both desperate to forget everything, the need to be consumed by each other.

Tray stood and walked us to the same bedroom.

By the time he lowered me to the bed, I was already wrenching off his shirt, and his hands were fevered, trying to get mine off. It became a race and we couldn't move fast enough. Finally, he pushed in, a deep slide that left me gasping. He reared up again and again, going deeper each time. I moved in sync with him, both of us a little crazed in the moment.

After we came together, my last thought before I fell asleep was that the world hadn't fallen apart.

CHAPTER TWENTY

Arriving early to school at the ungodly hour of six a.m. is just wrong. What's worse? Glittery, peppy cheerleaders at six in the morning.

Maybe it was because I'd only gotten a few hours of sleep last night, but I was literally dragging. I had a full day ahead of me so I had to start early. I figured I could sleep on the way to the cities since Tray was sleeping in.

"Taryn."

I cringed, but fought the impulse to hurl my coffee at the voice.

"Hey, Taryn!"

My hand gripped harder on my coffee.

"What? I snapped at Tristan's friend, Erin.

"Where's Mandy?"

"Where's your coach?" I asked instead. The coach could say whatever she chose to say, I was only telling my message to those who were necessary. And sadly, I felt her coach was one of those people.

Erin pointed to a woman in her thirties, and you could tell she was athletic. She could've been a personal trainer. She was wearing crisp khaki shorts and a white polo t-shirt. I was relieved to see that she was not wearing glitter.

"What's her name?" I asked Erin.

"Coach Hailey."

I crossed over to her, overhearing her conversation with one of the girls, "We need you to be stronger in our pyramid. You're the flyer, Sasha."

Hearing who was in front of me, I couldn't control an eye-roll.

"I know, Hails. I'll tuck it in, I promise." Sasha actually sounded earnest. Imagine my shock at her attitude. I almost keeled over right there in the parking lot.

Sasha turned around and braked, just before she ran me over, saw who I was and then sneered at me. Ah, that's better.

"Move," I ordered.

"Listen, you little—"

"Sasha," her coach said, and I actually stumbled back a few steps when Sasha shut up and left.

"Cheerleading does have a goddess, and you are her," I stated matter-of-factly as I moved forward.

"Can I help you?" she asked, glancing back to her clipboard.

"Uh, yeah. I'm Mandy's sister."

"*Adopted* sister!" Sasha yelled from behind me.

"Sasha. Bus. Now," Coach Hailey commanded.

I was more than impressed. If this woman was anything other than a cheerleading coach, I'd sign up to be her protégé.

"Uh, yeah," I murmured, "look, Mandy won't be at the game."

That got the coach's attention. Her head snapped up and she asked, "What?"

"She...she had a family emergency and is going to gone for a while."

"Define a while? And please have your definition include 'she'll make be here in five minutes' or 'she'll be meeting us later in time for the championship games'," she barked.

Whoa.

"Uh...the family emergency is not here and she's going to be gone for at least a month."

"No," she stated.

"Excuse me?"

"No."

"I'm not a genie. I can't say 'poof' and Mandy appear magically," I explain, rocking back on my heels, clutching my coffee for strength.

"Mandy's the captain of this team, she leads the count. She's our top flyer and I need her. The squad needs her."

"Well, she's needed somewhere else." I was starting to see why Vitamin R had been tempting to Mandy.

"Listen, I've heard about you, and if this is because of you, wherever she is, undo it. Now. I'll expect to see Mandy at the Dome before the game, okay?" She pushed past me.

I turned and called out, "She won't be there. And no matter how much you're putting this on me, Mandy's *not* coming."

"Listen," she began, turning back to face me.

I got in her face. "No. Because you're not listening to me." I liked teachers, well I respected teachers. I did. But this one...fuck no. "Get over your little trip to Denial Land and deal with it. My sister has an emergency she has to deal with and if you try to get to her, you'll have to go through me."

"Where is she?"

I was silent. I shifted on my feet and crossed my arms, as much as I could with a coffee cup.

"Your name's Taryn, right? Mandy talks about you, a lot. I've heard the other girls talk too. You don't have a great reputation. You're a troublemaker and you're on a spiral ride down. I will not let you take Mandy with you."

That was it.

I crowded her. "Well, right now I'm the only one who's keeping her from hitting rock bottom, so get off my back, *Coach* Hailey."

"I'm calling your parents and setting up a conference for all of us, including the principal and superintendent. You can't speak to a teacher like that."

"Fine by me. When you get a hold of 'em, let 'em know that their family is falling apart. If they were around a little more, Mandy wouldn't be where she is right now."

Fuck. I said way too much. Before I could say anything else I'd regret telling this woman, I turned and swept into the school.

Since it was still way too early, I was faced with a good two hours of nothing before classes started.

This is not a good thing for me. If I get too bored, with too much time on my hands, it's inevitable for me to come up with something that would more than likely get me into trouble. For instance, right now I'm thinking that I could break into the front office and look up Props' locker combination. You know, so I can put the tickets in there now and I wouldn't have to waste time trying to find him later. I would *never* break in without a good reason. Cue the sarcasm.

That's my rationalization and I'm sticking to it.

I was telling myself, don't, don't, don't, .but I found myself circling around the locked office doors. It was a whole lot of dark in there. I knew exactly how to get in there, I knew exactly where the locker combinations were—I saw where they were kept when they issued me my locker. It'd be so easy. A quick slip in, a little measly lock to pick, and voila—the combination I needed.

I jumped a good three inches when my phone rang.

"Yeah?" I snapped out, irritated at the caller for interrupting me and at myself for having weak thoughts.

"Where are you?" Tray asked, sounding half-asleep.

"I'm at school."

"Fuck. Why?"

"I needed to talk to Mandy's coach and I suppose I'll have to say something to the counselor."

"Forget that shit. Tell her on Monday."

It was a good idea. "I can't. I gotta hand over these tickets."

"Slip 'em in the locker."

"They're tickets and backstage passes. They won't fit." Unless I break in the office and find his combination... It was so tempting. Damn this trying to be good.

"Who is this kid?"

"He's a computer geek. His name is Props."

"Props? What kind of stupid-ass name is that?"

"Right. Because while he's actually earned his name, you have friends by the name of Rooters and Helms. Not to mention the very original nickname of using last names instead of first names. Because those aren't lame." I needed to stand up for Props, I kind of liked him. He had potential and he was a good resource for future reference.

"Shut up," Tray moaned.

"I just got bitched out by Mandy's coach, I won't shut up."

"Oh fuck!" Tray started to laugh. The sound was very irritating.

If I wasn't peppy, he couldn't be either.

"Shut up."

"Oh, fuck, this is hilarious."

"What is?" I asked warily.

"The cheerleading coach *is* the counselor."

Oh...fuck.

I hung up on his laughing ass.

I ended up camping out on the picnic tables, set up on the lawn right next to the parking lot. Talking to Tray had helped calm my inner need for an adrenalin rush—he was enough of an adrenalin rush on his own. So, after my second trip for coffee, I got some homework done instead.

The second I saw Props, I was off and hurrying his way. The dude could walk, it was close to a half-sprint. I almost lost him, but I managed to see him swerve into a backroom, somewhere, and I quickly rushed inside.

I was surrounded by computer geek heaven.

There were computers—everywhere—complete with head-sets, cameras, and an actual Lord of the Rings 3D statue in the corner. They liked Aragorn.

"Hey!" I called out.

Props popped his head out from behind a doorway. "Hi!" He was surprised, to say the least, but he looked excited.

I grabbed my bag and dug out the tickets and backstage passes.

Handing them over, I informed him, "These are for you. Show up at six-thirty, sharp. She's expecting you."

"Oh...wow. I mean...oh...oh..."

The guy had gone to Nanaland.

I patted him on the shoulder. "Have fun. Be cool, treat her like shit, and you'll be getting laid by the first set."

Then I left.

When I got home, I was surprised to see Austin in the kitchen.

He grunted in response. Such an eighth grade, brotherly response.

"Hi," I replied a little uncertainly. He seemed normal, but he didn't usually let a whole lot of emotion show. "Have you been upstairs?"

Just then a Pop-Tart jumped out of the toaster, and he grabbed it. "Do you mean, did I see Mandy's trashed room?" he asked.

That'd be a yes. A big fat yes.

When he looked up and met my eyes—he knew. I could see it. Hell, he'd probably always known.

"I took her to rehab last night," I murmured, sitting on a stool waiting for his response.

He shrugged, turning to grab a glass of orange juice.

"How long have you known?"

"It's not the first time, you know. Mom found 'em one time. Mandy gave her a bullshit story, said they were herbal vitamins. They helped her body restore her metabolism, or some shit like that."

"She believed her?" I asked quietly.

"Wouldn't you? Your perfect straight-A daughter on Honor Roll, taking fucking speed?" He shrugged, eating his Pop-Tart. "Of course Mom believed her. Mom'll believe anything, if it sounds somewhat reasonable."

The kid was too smart, way too smart for his own good.

"For what it's worth, it wasn't speed. It was Vitamin R. That's Ritalin."

"Whatever. She's been on 'em forever," he grumbled, stuffing a Lunchable in his backpack.

"Austin," I stopped him as he walked past me for the door, "what are you doing this weekend?" I heard a car engine and I figured his friends were waiting for him.

"I'll be at Dustin's for the next week. Then I'll be at Paul's after that."

"Okay."

He rolled his eyes and left, but stopped in the doorway. He turned halfway around and said, "Look—"

I waited.

"Forget it." He shrugged his shoulders and was off again, the door slamming behind him.

Well. That was refreshing, like always.

It took me an hour to clean Mandy's room, but it was done half-heartedly. I wanted stuff put away so it wasn't such an eye-sore. I knew Mandy would be changing everything anyway when she returned home. It'd have to be perfect and I knew there was no way I'd get it right by her standards.

I was in my room, packing, when my phone rang.

"Hey," I answered, knowing it was Tray.

"I'm ready to go," he announced. He sounded disgustingly, cheerful.

"Wanna drive over and pick me up?"

"Turning down your street." He hung up and a second later I heard a car pull into the driveway.

Then the backdoor opened and I heard footsteps on the stairs and hallway.

When he turned the corner, I had my bag packed.

"Hi." I smiled, relieved that my boyfriend was here to do his boyfriend duty and carry my bags.

Tray raked a hand through his hair, staring at the pile in front of him. "That all?"

"Yep."

Tray groaned, but knelt and picked up my two bags and pillow. He shifted and looked at me. "What else?"

"I got it." I only had my backpack, filled with homework. Never hurt to be prepared for anything, and boredom was something I needed to prepare for. I'm not stupid, I know Tray would want some time with his friends—or in truth—it'd be his friends storming our room, demanding Tray to come out and play.

Tray led the way downstairs, swearing when the bags banged into the walls. After the second picture got knocked off the wall, I turned and held an arm out. "You can't carry two bags? Are you serious?"

"These are not normal bags," he pointed out. "You fucking packed for three months, not three days."

"I'm a girl," I stated, duh. "I am not a boy who needs one pair of pants and two shirts. Girls have different outfits for different events. Hotel, the games, the pool, and parties all equal different outfits. You've screwed how many girls? I'd think you'd be aware of some of these basic, fundamental, facts."

Tray smirked. "No outfits were involved with those girls."

"Shut up," I snapped, grinning.

I held the door open as Tray ducked through and dumped the bags in the back, he carried my pillow to the front. When I climbed inside, I lit up—he'd gotten coffee!

As he drove down the road, I asked, "Where are we meeting?"

"Carter's."

"It's going to be a caravan or something?"

"Probably," he murmured, frowning at the road ahead.

"Do I need to be awake for all this?"

"Uh," he trailed off, not listening to me anymore, "what the fuck?"

Glancing up, I saw a car accident. One car had been completely flipped over and the other consisted of a small square of metal. Literally. Ambulances, police, and firemen were everywhere.

"Go around," I murmured, hunching down in my seat. I reached for my phone and shut it off. For some reason, a sense of foreboding had taken root in my stomach and I couldn't look at the accident. It was an awful feeling and I was confused as to why this accident was making me feel this way.

Tray glanced at me quickly, but he switched down a side-road, bypassing the backed-up traffic.

I reached for the coffee and let the hotness burn my tongue. It took away the uneasiness I was feeling.

"Fuck!" I gasped.

Tray chuckled. "You saw the steam, you felt the cup, you knew it was hot."

"I got three hours of sleep, bitched out by the cheerleading coach, and I waited two hours at school for Props to show up. I'm tired and I'm crabby. Sue me," I muttered, blowing on my coffee.

"Wanna have sex? I can pull over right now."

I bit back a grin and tried to sound exasperated. "Are you kidding me?"

"It's a good tension reliever." Tray glanced at me. His voice was completely serious, but I saw the grin he was fighting back.

I rolled my eyes, giving him a small smile. "That's not funny."

"No, what's funny is you actually thinking about it." He chuckled, facing to the road.

"I was thinking about sleeping. Not having sex in your car."

"It's an SUV."

"It's a car."

"No, it's not. It's an SUV. The dealership guy was very sure about that," Tray argued, grinning.

"You're deliberately trying to piss me off."

"I'm deliberately entertaining myself. You just happen to be an easy target this morning."

"Because of you!"

"You're the one who woke *me* up. I was content to sleep."

"Shut up."

Tray laughed.

"So—" I announced, thinking how I should put this.

"Yeah?" Tray waited.

"Are...are other people going to be riding with us?"

Tray just laughed. "You have *not* made your opinions quiet about my friends. And yet, you needed encouragement to ask that question?"

"Contrary to popular belief, I don't like to always be a bitch."

"Taryn," Tray spoke.

"What?"

"What are you worried about?"

"I don't want Amber, Jasmine, or Tristan riding with us."

"Tristan will for sure have her own car. I swear the girl's identity is attached to that car. So she's not a problem. I'll tell the rest that they need to ride with someone else."

"And what if they insist on riding with you?" I cringed, thinking about that possibility.

"Then I'll tell 'em you're with me and you're crabby. Trust me, they won't want to ride with us."

It was meant to soothe me, and if I were anyone else, I'm sure they would've been insulted. Not me. It made me perk up a little. I liked knowing I had that kind power over girls like them.

"That's good," I murmured, closing my eyes for a moment.

The moment turned into a steadfast sleep, because the next time I opened them, we were at Carter's. I groaned, wanting to be back asleep, but I saw five cars parked in the driveway with a crap load of people ambling around.

"How many are going with us?"

Tray shrugged. "The crew." Then he was out the door, walking lazily to Carter's open trunk where some of the basketball players had congregated.

A few of them nodded in greeting to Tray, two high-fived him, and everyone else either called out greetings or they all looked up and watched.

The bottom line: Tray's appearance was noticed.

I got outside to stretch, but then re-thinking the trip, I decided a last bathroom trip might be wise. As I walked inside Carter's mansion, I heard from the kitchen, "Taryn."

It was Tristan, so I hurried my steps.

"Hey, Taryn." She'd followed me. Don't people realize when they're being ignored? They should learn to realize that.

"Yeah?" I asked, standing in the hallway.

"Sasha called us. She said Mandy didn't show for the bus." Tristan's perfect eyelashes were large and voluminous, and her eyes were concerned. "What happened? Is she alright?"

"She's out of town. There was a family emergency."

"What? Wait!" Tristan grabbed my arm. "What happened?"

"She's out of town for an emergency. It's all you're getting from me." I stated firmly.

"But," she faltered, "I'm her best friend. I should know what happened."

"You should know nothing unless Mandy wants to tell you. If you're her best friend, you'll back off. That's what friends do, they support each other when they're asked for it," I said swiftly, twisting my arm out of her hand.

"What about Amber and Jasmine, do they know?" she asked helplessly.

I turned away and threw over my shoulder, "They're smarter than that. They'll get a 'fuck off' too, if they ask."

I finally found the fricking bathroom. After I used it, I saw Amber and Jasmine talking with Tristan. All three of them looked at me when I emerged from the house, but none of them approached me, thank God. I climbed into Tray's car, seeking refuge and curled up with my pillow and iPod.

Tray climbed in a little later and I opened my eyes, drowsy, when I heard two guys get in the backseat—Helms and Mitch. The two never separated.

I turned my volume up and closed my eyes, snuggling back into my pillow.

The next time I woke up, Tray was slowing to a stop. I sat up, rubbing my face as I saw we were already in the cities, at a stoplight.

I took out my iPod headphones and asked, "Where are we?"

"About ten minutes from the hotel," Tray murmured, watching the traffic ahead.

I checked the back. Helms and Mitch were looking at magazines. When I caught sight of the clock, I realized that we'd been driving for two hours.

"Thanks for driving," I murmured, sitting up in my seat.

Tray didn't reply, but I wasn't expecting one.

Not long after, we pulled into the hotel's entrance ramp. Tray brought the car to the front doors and everyone filed out. Behind us, the rest of the cars either pulled up behind Tray or parked in the lot. Everyone was getting out and grabbing their bags. It'd be mass hysteria inside, considering there were at least twenty of us. Probably more.

I saw Tray grab my bags and I moved to intercept. "I can carry 'em."

"You sure?" he asked, reaching for his own bags.

"Yeah. You can get in first and check in," I replied, nodding to the crowd behind us.

Tray nodded in understanding and went inside. I looked through the glass doors and saw he booted Mitch and Helms to the side, taking their place.

I was proud.

While he was checking us in, I managed to bring everything in—Tray's bags and my own. Then I parked the car on the ramp and circled around to the lobby. Our bags were missing, so I sat back and waited. A minute later the elevator doors opened and I saw Tray.

He held out a key to me. "We're in room 2615."

"What floor?"

"Twenty six." He grinned, leaning against the wall.

I felt stupid.

"How long till we leave for the game?"

"About an hour. Carter's got the room next to ours. A bunch of the guys want to grab some lunch."

I yawned. "What about alcohol?"

"What do you think was in my bags?" Tray murmured, a smirk adorning his features—those hazel eyes, angular cheekbones, those luscious lips...

I murmured, "I could go for something else besides lunch."

The hazel was replaced with his amber coloring. He stood and drew close to me, curving an arm around my waist, he pulled me against him, bending to say softly, "One would think we're just sex-crazed teenagers."

"Hmmm. But we are."

Tray laughed. "I don't classify myself as a teenager anymore." He kissed me and murmured, "Eighth grade. I was a teenager then. I turned adult not long after that."

"Yeah, I know." I sighed, moving with him as he leaned against the wall, his arm still anchored around me. "I don't remember ever being a kid, you know."

"Yeah. I do," he said solemnly, watching me intently. Neither of us moved to close the gap, but we stared at each other. When our floor came, we filed out and down the hallway. Carter was in the hallway, carrying a bucket of ice.

He lit up when he saw us. "Taryn's awake! The day just got fun."

I liked Carter.

He threw an arm around Tray's shoulder, and asked me, "You're going to let your boy party with us tonight, right?" He nodded. "Eh, eh? Play-offs don't come around all that often. Once a year, Taryn. You know what that means...once a year we get to live it up while we can. Oh yeah!"

Tray's partying was up to me? Since when?

I frowned. "What are you asking, Carter?"

"Well, nothing, but Tray was saying you were tired, so if you decide not to partake in the festivities, it doesn't mean Tray can't? Right? Because that would be just—"

"Wrong?" I supplied dryly, seeing the amusement in Tray's eyes.

"Yeah." He grinned, feeling understood.

"Are you calling me a downer?"

"What? No. Just...if you're tired then—" Carter floundered.

I laughed, letting him off the hook. "I'm here to get my mind off stuff. I'm not planning on being a 'downer' and I'm not planning on taking away any of Tray's fun."

But I could still feel that same sense of foreboding from earlier.

I flashed a blinding smile. "How bout we start now? I could go for a shot."

Carter's eyes lit up like a light bulb, you could see how excited he was. When I looked over to Tray, I saw a flash of concern in his eyes, but it vanished when Carter pushed us into his room. On the counter, he already had everything set up. A complete bar without the license.

"What'll you have?" He didn't wait, but quickly poured three shots.

Turning around, he handed them out.

I met Tray's suspicious eyes for a second before I tipped my head back and downed the shot.

"You actually know how to have fun?" I hadn't noticed Jasmine in the corner, but she was laughing.

I had a feeling they'd been 'partying' on the way up when I saw her fall over.

"Have another one, Taryn," Carter suggested, going over to help Jasmine stand up. I saw his hands linger on her waist and hip. Hmm...looked like Carter had already staked his bed-partner for the weekend.

Tray dropped to the bed. I met his gaze in the mirror when I tipped my head back for a second shot.

"Tray." Jasmine laughed, getting tickled by Carter.

"Yeah?" he asked.

"Remember when we were together?"

"Not really," he drawled, falling back on the bed, yawning.

Jasmine giggled, extracting herself from Carter. "Whatever, you're just saying that because Taryn's in here. But really...remember last year when we were here for play-offs?"

"Let me guess," I said dryly, downing a third shot, "you did *it* in the elevator?"

She giggled hysterically, like I'd made a joke. Which I didn't comprehend, neither did Tray, judging from the confusion on his face.

I rolled my eyes and then climbed on top of Tray, purposely slow, sliding my body against his. Hearing his sudden intake of breath, I turned and grinned at Jasmine, tipping my head as Tray started nuzzling my neck. "Yeah. Elevators are so...bad," I said condescendingly, which everyone registered. Jasmine flushed, Carter barked out a laugh, and Tray flipped us over, kissing me more urgently, ignoring the fact we had an audience.

I watched Jasmine. Oh yeah, she was pissed. She was more than pissed, but she turned and grabbed Carter, smashing his mouth to hers as she pressed up against him.

Carter looked like it was his birthday and he turned her against the wall, taking over the kiss.

Tray stopped kissing me, and looked up. I grinned, and turned his face towards them, and he smiled too.

Then I kissed him, one last peck and shoved him slightly. Tray sat up and let me up. We slipped out of the room unnoticed.

I sighed when we got in the room.

Tray bypassed me and dropped on the bed. I stood in front of him, where he grinned. "You gonna do a dance for me?"

"You want sex tonight?" I shot back.

The smile vanished.

I turned to our fridge. "You put some liquor in here?"

I heard him sit up and move to the end of the bed. "What's up with you? You inhaled three shots."

I smiled when I saw he had put a bunch of mini-wine bottles in the fridge. Taking one, I drank it, tipping my head back.

"Taryn," Tray said seriously.

I shrugged. "I'm here to get away from everything, right? I just want to forget."

"And the irony's not lost on you?"

I sighed and stood. "Look...I just...I got a bad feeling, alright...and I don't like feeling it. So fucking sue me."

"It's the same as Mandy taking Vitamin R."

"Oh no. No fucking way is it the same thing."

"It's the same," Tray said firmly, standing up.

"So what?" I cried out. "I can't drink now?"

"No. You can drink—just not when you don't want to feel."

"Oh please," I said, "look at you on your fucking high horse, telling me I can't drink when I want to get rid of this gut-wrenching sense of dread in my stomach."

"Taryn," he murmured.

"No. You telling me you never wanted to forget? To stop feeling like a piece of shit when your family left you?"

"Taryn," he warned.

Well, fuck that. I continued, unheeding the warning in his voice, "Your family left, you pushed 'em away. And you're coming off like you know what's right? Fuck that. I took my sister to rehab. You know what that's like? Or how about the times when—"

Tray left, slamming the door behind him.

"Oh, hell no." I stormed after him, out into the hallway. He wasn't far, some people had stopped him, but I was past caring. "You don't walk away—"

Tray turned and glared, a death glare, but I pressed on, "You don't walk out when the conversation touches on your issues, you can't do that. Not when you're judging my fucking issues—" He'd grabbed my arms and passed by.

"I left before you said something you'll regret," Tray bit out, dragging me back to the room.

When the door shut again, I wrenched my arms away. "Right, because you never say anything that you regret. In fact, you don't say a whole lot, do you? You just hang out up there, on your fucking throne—"

"What do you want?" Tray snapped, shouting. "What do you want me to say? Yeah, I've fucking buried a lot. Do you blame me? I'm not in the same place you are. Boohoo—you fucking took your sister to rehab. So what? She's coming back! She's not out of your life forever, Taryn! You don't have someone holding her life over your head...you don't know anything about my shit!"

I knew tears were rolling down my face, but I just didn't care. I was beyond caring.

I raged back, "Are you kidding me! Are you? You know who your parents are. You know what they looked like, what they liked to eat, what they hated. You know everything about them! You even know they screwed up!! So you get off *your* pity act. My parents didn't want me! They didn't care! Each fucking family I was placed with didn't care. When I was six, I thought that I'd try and be perfect and do anything my new family asked of me, because if I did, *surely* they would want to keep me. What I got was a sick pervert who'd visit my room at night abusing me in ways I'll never get out of my head and his wife who blamed me when she caught him. I was immediately kicked out to the next family. The second I didn't act perfect, I was booted out."

I stopped shouting. Everything just stopped. I stood there, paralyzed as everything I've ever buried surfaced to the forefront of my mind. Things that I buried so far down so I would never have to feel the worst moments of my life. It was like a dam had been broken and I was gasping for air.

Oh God, oh God.

I hadn't realized...I hadn't known...that burying all the memories that I did would explode inside me. It was like my insides wanted out. I let out a gut wrenching sob that came from deep inside me and fell to the ground.

"Oh God—" I choked out, clawing at my clothes, my nails, digging deep into my skin, were drawing blood. I needed to get these memories out of me.

"Taryn," Tray murmured, catching me. "Taryn—" he whispered, holding me tight.

"Tray," I gasped, curling into him, burrowing into him as close to him as I could.

He sat down and held me in his lap, cradling me as I wept.

In that hotel room, with Tray, I grieved for my six year old self. I sobbed remembering all the families that didn't think I was perfect enough for them. I cried for every injustice that had ever been inflicted upon me.

Seventeen years of memories and emotions that I thought were long forgotten and buried poured out of me.

Tray held me the entire night. We missed the game, we missed the parties, the celebration. Tray changed my clothes, kissing my forehead as he slipped the shirt over my head, my shoulder when he worked one arm out, my midriff when he lifted it in the first place. He kissed my thighs when he unzipped my pants and pulled them down. As they passed my knees, he kissed those too. My feet, my toes. He kissed my hands, each finger, when he pulled on my pajama top, my neck as it fitted around it, my stomach as he covered it with fabric. He kissed my toes, pulling my pajama bottoms on, my shins, my knees, my thighs, hips, and lastly just below my waist.

When I was dressed, he quickly changed himself. Turning the light off, he crawled into bed and slipped underneath the covers with me. He wrapped his arms around me, protecting me. Enfolding me.

I broke again.

He kissed my shoulder and whispered, "I've fallen for you."

I sobbed, curling in a fetal position, with Tray pressed behind me.

He whispered again, "I've fallen for the bitch that walked down the hallway and told me to screw myself. I've fallen for the girl who cares so goddamn much about her sister, about her psycho ex, his brother, about anyone who she considers family that she'd do anything for them, including going to jail. I've fallen for the girl who swears at me when she's happy, and who'll fight to the fucking bitter end if it means she'll come out standing."

I never stopped sobbing, feeling his words, feeling it battle the emotions that I was feeling inside.

Tray continued, pressing a kiss to the side of my jaw, "I've fallen for the girl who can tell me to fuck off. Who can have a staring contest with Amber, Jasmine, and whoever else and walk away after they've been reduced to piles. I've fallen for the girl who can bring me to my knees, over and over again, and then press a hand to my cheek and lift me back up."

I couldn't talk, I couldn't think, I couldn't do anything but grieve for my past.

My shoulders were shaking, the sobs were going in and out. I rolled over to look at him and met his eyes through my tear drenched ones. Then finally, for what felt like forever, I let it all go.

Tray cupped my cheek with his hand and he whispered tenderly, “I’ve fallen for a girl who makes me humble.”

I kissed him. A full-out wet, tear-soaked kiss.

I poured everything into it. Everything I couldn’t say.

And that night we made love, for the first time.

CHAPTER TWENTY-ONE

Once you cry it out, and let it all go, you're supposed to feel better, right? I did feel a little better, but something else was brewing. The feeling from yesterday was still with me and it didn't have anything to do with my break down. I just knew something else was going on—I could feel it and it was painful. I didn't know how to fix it.

Tray was asleep beside me, his arms folded around me, his words still in my ears.

I sighed, shivering slightly, but not from the cold. Tray had warmed me, inside and out.

But I shivered nonetheless, because I knew something had gone wrong. Deadly wrong. I knew that it would irrevocably change my life.

I knew it was a dream when I noticed I was with Brian in the woods by the school. He was in front of me, looking at me like he missed me. Why would he miss me? I just saw him the other day. He was trying to tell me something, but I couldn't figure out what he was trying to say. It seemed so surreal. I turned around, and I was back in the hotel bed with Tray. Brian was looking between Tray and me. He looked into my eyes and I saw how much he loved me. He was trying to give me a message. If I could just hear what he was trying to tell me...

"Brian," I whispered, tears in my eyes.

He smiled, a tender, ethereal smile. An immortal smile.

"Brian," I murmured again, confused and scared.

He gave me a smile. Tears were running down my cheeks.

Oh, God. His eyes gave away everything. He was telling me goodbye.

He turned and walked away. Brian was gone.

I jolted awake, tears running down my face. Somehow I knew that my dream was real. I found my phone laying on the bedside table. I had shut it off last night, because I knew Mandy would be calling me at all hours. I didn't think anyone else would need to get a hold of me.

I powered my phone on and saw that I had twenty missed calls since yesterday afternoon—all from Geezer. I really didn't want to call him back. I knew what he was going to tell me, and I didn't want to hear it.

I jumped when my phone rang. I didn't want to answer it, so I just stared at it. Tray woke up immediately. He took one look at me, saw I was awake, and then reached for the phone.

Seconds later, it started ringing again. He answered, "Yeah?"

A moment later, he looked at me and held it out for me to take.

I pressed it to my ear and murmured hoarsely, "Yeah?"

"Taryn."

It was Geezer, but it didn't sound like him.

"Geezer?" I sat up. I needed to know for sure. I had to hear it.

"Oh God, Taryn." He broke down, crying uncontrollably.

"Geezer, what is it?" I was so fucking scared of what he was about to tell me.

"It's Brian."

Brian was gone.

"Oh God—" I broke out, the dam crashed and came tumbling down again.

"He," Geezer paused, trying to get out the rest, "he...Taryn—"

"Charles," hearing his name made him cry even harder, "what happened?"

"He...he was coming to see you. He'd...he said he knew what Jace had done. He was coming to tell you. Oh God, Taryn," he whimpered.

"Charles," I said softly, my heart breaking. I sat up and moved to the edge of the bed. The bed sheet pooled around my waist, as I sat there, phone to my ear, waiting for Geezer to respond.

"I tried calling your cell, but I don't think it's turned on...it was a car accident." It was the car accident we passed, the one that made me feel so uneasy.

I'd turned it off—I didn't want to see how many times Mandy would call. I thought it would be ok.

I didn't say anything. I held my breath. My heart was pounding in my ears.

"He's...Brian...he's..."

He's dead.

I already knew.

"He's dead, Taryn."

I sat there. I couldn't speak and it felt like I couldn't breathe.

Geezer was crying, whimpering like a child, and I just sat there. I didn't have it in me to comfort him. I saw my reflection in the mirror—I was empty of all emotion. I turned it off, just shut it off so I couldn't feel anything. I should know better, last night was the perfect example of what burying your memories and emotions can do to you But I just couldn't feel right now. I wanted to be shut off—from everything .

Tray sat up and took the phone away.

He lifted it to his ear and asked, "Hello?"

I had to hear it all over again.

I heard Geezer tell Tray. And a moment later, after a quick conversation, Tray reached around and replaced the phone.

I sat there.

"Taryn," Tray spoke.

I felt nothing.

"Taryn," he tried again.

Still nothing. Time was frozen as was I.

Then I felt Tray's fingers at my arm. He was pulling me up. And I stood there while he touched me, a cool slide of air hit me and then—I was dressed again.

He'd changed me. While I stood there, staring dumbly, as he knelt before me, his hands at my feet, trying to get my shoes on.

I stared at his back. I saw how large it was, muscular, strong. I saw the muscles bulge, slightly, with every movement he made, every turn he took.

Every reach he made.

He was standing before me, a bag slung over his shoulder. He had all the bags then and he grasped my elbow, pulling me with him. I blinked.

We were on the elevator.

My eyes closed.

We were at the front desk.

I blinked again.

We were in his car and I frowned—not knowing how we'd gotten there. Why we'd gotten there.

Oh that's right—

Brian.

Brian's pastor said all the right things. He told us to remember Brian as he would want to be remembered. How his life had been, to remember his strength and to remember his happiness. We were there to remember Brian. We were there to remember those who had passed on, their memories we'd cherish, to say goodbye, and to gain closure.

Brian was in the front, in a casket, his eyes were closed and he was in a suit. Which was bullshit. Brian would never wear a suit, much less to his own fucking funeral. Brian would want to go out in a t-shirt and torn jeans, frayed at the ends, and he'd want to be barefoot. I'm pretty sure the shiny black shoes he was wearing had never been his.

I was numb inside as I listened to the pastor's nurturing voice, a calm atmosphere surrounding him.

We were there for us, ourselves.

The dead have passed on.

Brian had already left, said his goodbye, I felt it in my heart.

Death is a harsh reality.

Some understand death, embrace it, others fear it.

It's an inevitable stage in life, no one can escape. So all we can do is cherish the life we have remaining.

Embrace those surrounding us, our loved ones and try to live without regrets. Change to become who we want to be when we meet death.

I wanted to meet death head-on. I didn't want it to take me in my sleep. I wanted to see it coming. I wanted to know what was happening.

Brian hadn't been prepared, but then again, Brian was dead. I doubt he cared anymore.

We're supposed to make ourselves spiritually ready. To make right with God. To make right with everyone else, with ourselves. With our souls.

I listened to the pastor. I heard every word, every nuance.

Geezer sat beside me. He looked sober, but from the sheen of tears in his eyes, I knew he'd be smoking the second he could leave. He used it to cover everything: his distress, his despair, his fears.

He held my hand throughout the ceremony.

I looked for Grayley, but he hadn't come.

But it seemed everyone else in Pedlam came. Students from school—I saw Gentley in the back—and even the chief of police—Brian would've thought that was hilarious. But I could only give a sad smile.

And of course, Jace was there, sitting in the front next to his father.

I looked at Brian's father and I saw the life of abuse had worn right through him. He wasn't old, a mere forty-two, but he looked eighty years old. He had tears in his eyes, while he sat stiffly beside Jace.

Their mother had left a long time ago. Brian had once told me she never existed. He'd been ten then. When he was fifteen, he'd confessed that she'd walked out when they were kids.

I looked back at Jace. He sat there, looking straight ahead at Brian as the pastor continued. He looked like he had aged ten years since I last saw him.

And I think I hated him.

Because he was the only one in that fucking church who felt the same as me, but he was so unreachable.

Tray shifted beside me and leaned forward on his elbows.

I looked at him and sighed. I remembered his words: he'd fallen for me.

He'd washed me, fed me, and changed me. He dealt with Mandy's calls when we got back. He made arrangements—for everything. I wasn't able to feel. I'd just...checked out.

And Tray had stepped in my place.

I ran my hand through his hair, feeling its softness, and trailed my fingers down his shoulder, his arm, and reached for his hand.

Tray looked up and gave me a small smile, before kissing my hand. Then he let our hands rest in his lap, where he was tracing my palm with his fingers.

I felt Geezer squeeze my hand again and I heard him draw in his breath. He was pale, trying to hold his emotions back.

I don't know what inspired me, but I leaned over and kissed his cheek. I whispered, "Brian's in a better place now."

Geezer's tear-filled eyes met mine as he listened.

I added, "We're the ones who gotta pick it up. Bri's gone," my voice broke, "But he's better than us."

His tears fell and Geezer didn't even try to brush them away as he squeezed my hand tighter.

I heard the pastor again. He was saying it is not that trouble does not come our way, it is that we can overcome it when it does come our way. And so we lift our prayers up...and God is with us.

I was done crying.

I'd shed my well, but I sighed anyway, knowing I'd be crying if they'd been there.

Tray sat up and drew me against his chest, his arms encircled me, and he kissed my cheek, while continuing to hold my hand.

When we filed out, Tray led the way with Geezer right behind me. We stood off to side, waiting for the processional to leave, for the casket to be raised and carried out.

I hadn't realized who we were standing next to, but I felt someone reach out and touch my arm. Looking back, I saw Gentley with Kimberly.

He nodded to Tray, then looked at me, and murmured, "I'm sorry, Taryn."

He sounded sincere.

Kimberly smiled, a soft, sad smile, and murmured, "I'm sorry too, Taryn." Behind her was Crystal. She nodded to Tray and then hugged me. I was surprised, but I returned the hug.

A feeling of gratefulness came over me.

As we stood there waiting, more and more people came up to me and repeated their sympathies.

I felt like a widower—that my other half died, leaving me bereft—but it wasn't true. I thanked God that I had a chance to say goodbye to Brian—literally and spiritually.

When the casket came out, I watched Jace, in the front end as he passed by.

He turned and met my gaze. His eyes were empty—there was nothing there—no emotion.

But then again, maybe that's what he saw in mine.

As they walked on and around to the cemetery. We all filed along, gathering around as the pastor said another prayer. Brian was joining the earth. His body was here, his soul with God.

Jace stood to the side as the casket was lowered, and then covered with the earth's ground. His aunt and cousin both threw roses in, while Brian's father stood stoically beside his eldest son.

His favorite son in the ground. His favored son in the dirt.

"Hey, Taryn."

I looked up and saw it was Ben, the rest of Jace's guys were behind him.

"We're sorry," he said quietly, giving me a hug, and a kiss on the cheek.

Each one followed suit. Each gave me a hug, then a kiss, giving their sympathy and condolences.

Cammy was at the end.

She'd been crying, her make-up was running down her face. She reached and embraced me. "I'm sorry, Taryn." Then she walked away quickly, hurrying after the guys.

Tray touched my elbow and I saw most everyone had left.

It was over.

We went inside, and I grabbed a rose from one of the flower arrangements—a keepsake—then we went back outside.

Geezer was waiting, glancing uncertainly around. I was reminded that Grayley hadn't come, and it hurt. It really hurt—he should've been here, he should've been a part of this, sitting on the opposite side of Geezer.

"Hey," I murmured, my voice hoarse.

"Hey." He grabbed me in a hug, squeezing my entire body. In my ear, he whispered, "Listen...huh—"

"What?" I asked, standing in his embrace, long after conventional norms.

"Grayley's missing," he choked out, "I wasn't sure about...I didn't know what to say, but...he went to find Brian...and he never came back, if you know what I mean."

When the words registered, my body went cold.

I'd told Brian that I wanted to know what Jace had done, what arrangements he'd made for me. Geezer had told me that Brian had found the answer and had been on his way to see me.

Brian was dead.

Grayley was missing.

And Jace was here.

I looked up, my arms still around Geezer, and I saw Jace standing at his car. He looked like he was waiting—waiting for me.

"Geezer," I said, pulling away. I met his eyes, mine fierce. "Where did he go?"

He looked away, running a hand through his shaggy hair.

"Charles!" I said firmly.

"He," he sighed, stuffing his hands in his pockets, "he...went to Jace's. Brian called me from there. He said he had some information and that he was on his way to find you. He said you needed to know...and then...he never called us back. He was supposed to go and see you, then report back, but he never called. Grayley got antsy and took off to go find him. Then I got a phone call from a friend who works at the hospital; she knew I was close to Brian. She said a chopper went out to Rawley to pick him up. When I got to the hospital, Jace told me he was dead."

I turned away, my arms hugging myself. I was shivering.

"Taryn," Geezer mumbled, "what are you...I mean...what are you going to do?"

"Do?" I asked numbly. .

"Yeah, I mean...we gotta find Grayley, you know? He's my best friend."

"Mine too," I mumbled, my eyes only seeing Jace. His eyes were still blank. "Mine too," I repeated.

Geezer sighed a deep shuttering breath.

"Fuck...," he groaned. "I could go for a joint, like, right now."

"Geezer," I snapped, "stop it! Just stop it!"

Taken aback, looking confused, he asked, "Huh? What?"

"Stop living your life on marijuana. Weed's not going to get you anywhere, you're wasting your life. It's gonna ruin everything for you. So just...stop."

"Yeah, but—"

"No, Geezer. Stop it."

"I can't talk to people unless I'm high," he debated.

"You don't talk to people anyways. You hole up in your house and get high. You're not doing anything. Go back to school—Brian would want you to go back to school."

"Come on—"

"Who do you want Brian to remember?" I asked. "The Geezer who doesn't do anything and just gets high all the time...or do you want to be someone else? Someone Brian would be proud of?"

He glanced away, torn. Pained.

I gentled my voice, "You don't give a shit about your life. But I do. Do it for me, at least until you can do it for yourself later."

He still wouldn't look at me. The topic was too personal, too raw for him, but he'd heard me. It was all I could do for him.

"Taryn," Tray spoke up, his hand touching my elbow, "we should go."

"Okay," I murmured to myself, feeling my feet following behind. As we approached his car, I saw Jace straighten from his. He took a step towards me, hands in his pockets, his tie flapping in the wind over his shoulder.

I saw the intensity in his eyes as our gazes met, but I looked away. I had an awful feeling that Jace had a part in Brian's death and I couldn't face him, not now.

"Taryn—" he started as Tray led me past him.

Tray let go of my elbow and walked to his side of the car. As he unlocked it, I stood there, facing away from Jace.

Standing beside me, he spoke earnestly, "Taryn, look at me."

I didn't acknowledge him. I couldn't. I'd go off and I wasn't going to do that at Brian's funeral.

"Can you please just stop...please?"

"No." I turned to face him. "Brian found something out, didn't he? Something that you did to me and he was going to tell me. And now he's dead. Kind of a coincidence, isn't it?"

Jace paled. "It's not...that's not—"

"Fuck you," I bit out, climbing inside the SUV, I slammed the door.

As Tray left the church, I spoke, quietly, "This isn't about you, it's not about your dad, it's not about Galverson. It's about me and Brian...and whatever Jace is hiding." I looked up and met his gaze.

"I'm going after him," I announced.

Tray didn't say anything, but turned the wheel. He pulled into the nearest parking lot and stopped the engine. Sitting back, he asked, "Do you know what you're getting yourself into?"

"Yes. No. I don't care."

"Taryn, it *is* about Galverson, whether he's your focus or not. Jace is connected to Galverson, so whatever you find—will have Galverson's prints on it too. You'll have both of 'em gunning for you."

"Jace knows what happened to Brian."

"Yeah, probably," Tray murmured, rubbing his jaw, "but it doesn't mean he killed him. It doesn't even mean he found anything out."

"I told Brian that I wanted to know what arrangements Jace had made for me. I told Brian that and then he told Geezer that he found out. He was coming to tell me. He found something out...and now he's dead."

"If it was so dangerous, why'd he leave a trail and tell Geezer that?"

"Grayley's missing," I exclaimed. "He went to find Brian when he didn't call...and now he's missing. Grayley's missing and Brian's dead. I can't sit back anymore."

"Even though it might be you in a casket next?" he asked tiredly.

"Tray—"

"I mean it, Taryn, you go after Galverson and chances are fucking high it'll be your fucking funeral next time. I don't want to go that fucking ceremony."

"My best friend is missing. I can't lose him too," I pleaded.

"Oh come on!" he cried out, pissed.

"You took him on once before. Help me this time. Help me finish him for good,"" I begged.

"Please," I asked again.

"Taryn," he hedged, shaking his head.

"I'm one of the best there is, I can get anywhere, Tray. Anywhere. I went in blind and got into a police station. A fucking police station! I can do that, I can go anywhere with planning. I already have some stuff." At his quick glance, I told him, "I haven't looked at it, not since I decided to leave it alone."

Tray swore.

"Your family's alive," I spoke. It was true, but Tray had already lost them. He'd already lost his family. "Brian's dead." And I lost something similar. "I can't lose Grayley too."

"Fuck...Taryn—"

"Brian's dead," I bit out. "I'm going after him whether you're with me or not."

"Oh—"

I stopped, pleading with my eyes. "You know how to do this. You know how to take him down. You know so much about their fucking world—things that I could never know. Please, Tray, you did it when you were in the fucking eighth grade. You did it when you were a kid. We're not kids anymore."

After a second, I could see his decision flash in his hazel eyes and I grinned. It was time for war.

CHAPTER TWENTY TWO

I was waiting by Props' locker when he arrived to school and I grinned, seeing him pale slightly. His eyes went to the flash drive that was dangling from my fingers. "Heya, Props!" I said cheerfully.

"Hey—" he said uncertainly.

"How was your date?"

He opened his locker and said stiffly, "Fine. What are you doing here?"

"I took a peek at what's on here," I stated, leaning against the next locker. "Guess what? It doesn't make any sense to me. So, seeing how I don't read technical code, I should come to the resident expert. That'd be you."

The guy looked like he was about to pee his pants.

"So, you're going to tell me what's on this," I announced.

"What...what's in it for me?" He hesitated.

"Same deal as before. What do you want? And it better not be a second date with Aidrian Casners."

"Uh—"

Too late—he took too long in answering me—I wanted a 'yes' immediately. I snapped, "You're going to help me or you'll deal with me. And if I'm not scary enough, remember what I said about my car? I *like* running people over with it."

"Fine. Fine. I'll help, jeez. Just..."

"Just what?" I warned.

"Nothing."

"That's what I thought. So, when and where do we get started?"

"Uh," he scratched the back of his head, "how about after school? You could come over to my house—"

"Where I'll have to meet your mom, who will think I'm your girlfriend? I don't think so, you can come to Tray's house. Bring your laptop and whatever techie gadgets you need."

He paled.

I turned and marched off. Not appeased, not fucking at all. I wanted to get at that information ASAP and now I'll have to wait for the entire fucking day.

Swearing, I kicked my locker when it stuck.

"Man, I'm surprised to see you here," Crystal remarked, hugging her books to her chest.

I spared a glance at her, but went back to beating the shit out of my locker.

"You're entitled to some time off, you know? You shouldn't be back at school already. Brian's funeral was yesterday."

"I know when Brian's funeral was!" I snapped, punching my locker. It wouldn't move. Props wouldn't help me right this second. And Brian was still dead.

I was mortified, feeling tears tease at the corners of my eyes.

"Hey, hey, hey." Tray seemed to materialize out of nowhere. He blocked me from the watching audience and Crystal quickly stepped closer, blocking me from her angle.

"Get off," I warned.

Tray rolled his eyes and slammed a fist to my locker, where it opened immediately. He grabbed my books and held them hostage. "You going to calm down?!"

"Give me my goddamn books."

"If you're going to go at it like this, all emotional and shit—we're gonna fail. You have to push it aside, Taryn."

Crystal frowned. We weren't referring to books.

"I don't need—"

"My help?" Tray slipped it, "Because, according to you, you do need my help and I'm telling you—calm the fuck down!"

"My locker wouldn't open." I knew it was a shameless excuse.

"We're not talking about your damn locker and you fucking know it," Tray growled.

"Stop it!" I shoved him away. "Give me a break..."

"You can't afford any breaks, not now." He cursed and drew me with him, down the hallway and into the empty gymnasium.

He sat on a bleacher and murmured, "You took off early."

I didn't respond, but hugged myself. Trying to hold in the blistering rage.

"Taryn," he began, softening his voice slightly, "you have to shut it off. You just have to. Being emotional will end up getting us killed. This isn't some fucking high school prank—this is you and me playing a game that could get us killed. You're right, you do need me on this and this is how it *has* to be."

"But I can't—"

He stood up and said sternly, "You have to or I walk. That's the deal. There's no other way."

I glared at him, hating him in that moment.

Tray grinned at me and pulled me against him. Encircling an arm around my waist, he bent and whispered against my lips, "Why don't we skip and go screw each other's brains out?"

It had some appeal.

"We skipped almost all of last week. I don't think I can afford it."

Tray shrugged. "It's not like you'll get into trouble."

There was that again—the elite—they could fucking get away with whatever the fuck they wanted to. But I'd been included recently, so I could get away with it too. I was such a hypocrite.

Brian's dead. The reminder popped in my head—bringing me back to reality. I'd forgotten, for a few minutes, but I had. I clamped down on the guilt that speared my body.

"I gotta talk to the counselor about Mandy, too," I murmured.

"Fuck that. Your folks should have to do it."

"Yeah," I bit out, "because they're *always* around, aren't they?"

"Come on. Let's go to my place and spend the rest of the day in bed. It'd be good for you."

"So I can enjoy sex when Brian's dead."

Tray pulled away, but not completely. It had worked, partially, but Tray watched me. And I knew he figured it out when the corner of his mouth curved upwards, "Not going to work, baby. I'm not going to 'rescue' you and tell you it's alright and you don't have to feel guilty that you're still living. You know that shit and besides, the guy seemed to love you. He wouldn't want you to go down that route, Taryn."

I knew he was right, but—fuck, fuck, fuck.

"I'm sorry," I slipped out, my hands twisting in my hair. "I'm just...I can't handle this, I can't not do anything, I can't just sit in class, I can't jus—"

Tray slammed his mouth against mine and an explosion erupted inside me. It was what I needed and I met him full-force, drowning in him. My hands wrapped around his neck as I hoisted myself up, my legs wrapped around him and he walked us against the wall. Pressing against me, he licked, sucked, kissed, and caressed my mouth.

"God—" I moaned, raking my hands through his hair, holding him tightly against me.

"Okay, laps around—"

Of course, there had to be a gym class first period. The teacher stopped in shock, students milling around him, trying to see what stopped him.

"Mr. Evans and Miss Matthews!" he reprimanded.

Tray held me in place as he lifted his head lazily and grinned at the teacher. "Hey, Mr. Martson."

"This is not appropriate behavior and the two of you are missing your classes."

I grinned, leaning my forehead into Tray's neck.

"Well, you see, Mr. Martson," Tray began, flashing a charming smile, "this isn't what it looks like."

"It isn't? he asked skeptically.

"No, you see Taryn thought it'd be a good idea to practice her climbing skills."

"On you?" Mr. Martson supplied dryly.

"Yeah, exactly, because you know, I wouldn't let her fall."

"Mr. Evans."

"Yeah?"

"She can *un-climb* off of you now. Then make sure to take a trip to the principal's office. You can resume your 'climbing' there."

"I don't think he'd appreciate that, Mr. Martson," Tray said seriously.

"Out. Now."

Tray let me down and I saw more than a few grins behind the teacher's back.

When we got to the office, Tristan was sitting in the waiting room, looking irritated.

"Hey, guys!" She brightened up, seeing us. "Tray, how are you? I can't believe you guys missed the entire play-offs. Seriously."

He shrugged.

I was bored, pissed, and restless.

"Can it, Tristan," I snapped, pacing.

"You are such a bitch!"

"Please. I'm just callin' it like I see it."

"Right...you know what? I am sick and tired of you. I come back from Spain and all I hear about is how great Mandy's new sister is. She's so fun and free-spirited. She puts Amber and Jasmine in her place—they're right, but what they failed to mention was how you couldn't care one iota about decency. It's called class and you've got none."

I laughed. "What makes you think I care?"

It pissed her off even more. This was putting me in a much better mood.

"Oh my God...I *cannot* believe your nerve. You treat Mandy like shit—"

Oh no, bitch.

"No, you treat Mandy like she's your bitch. Like some little lapdog for you to play with and screw with her mind. You think she's yours, like you have claim over people—which is why you and Amber don't like each other. You're the same, you're both psychotic narcissists." I got in her face.

"If anyone's the—"

"It's you. Trust me," I clipped out, staring her down.

"You waltz into town and think it's yours, but I'll tell you one thing...I've been here a lot longer than you. My family founded this fucking town—"

"Ooh, look at that class. I didn't know blue-bloods knew what swear words were," I taunted, sitting back, watching her stumble over her words.

"Oh my God!" Tristan shrieked. "Can you get over yourself?" She turned to Tray and pleaded, "Tray—"

Tray stood up lazily, and remarked, "Why do you think I'm sleeping with her? Couldn't beat her, so I joined her." He sent me a private grin, his eyes lustful.

"Holy hell! If I knew this school was this entertaining, I'd have been here a long time ago!" Carter exclaimed, standing in the open-doorway. There were more than a few students behind him, shamelessly listening to the entire exchange.

"We're not selling tickets. Shoo, fuckers," I barked.

"I'd pay." Carter held out his wallet.

"Carter, what the hell are you doing here?" Tray asked, moving towards him to punch him in the shoulder.

"Orientation, baby. Orientation." He gestured to Tristan. "Guess that's why she's here too. I'm transferring."

"Let me guess, your files were destroyed in a freak accident." Tray said wryly.

"Something like that." Carter sent me a grin. "Thanks for the idea."

"I'm leaving," I announced, and walked out. This was pointless. If Tristan, her royal fucking highness, hadn't been helped, yet Tray and I shouldn't have to stick around when all we were doing was making out. The principal will probably just throw out some bullshit about appropriate boundaries, and I'd tell him that Tray and I knew exactly how appropriate our boundaries were. Then we'll get detention. Or I'd get detention. This was not what I needed right now. Not when I planned on using every free minute either hunting down Props or threatening Props.

At my locker, Molly proclaimed, "Is it true? Is it true? Is Carter Sethlers going to school here now? I've, like, heard it from eight people."

Who does she talk to? Is there a secret underground of Invisibles that just see and hear everything? Seriously.

"Yes," I bit out, grabbing my second period book now. Tray still had my first period book.

"Oh my God! This is great!"

I said, "You have a boyfriend. Sethlers is off limits."

"Oh." She blushed, how unusual. "Well...yeah, I mean...I spent the weekend with Garrett and it was..."

I couldn't handle another full-body blush, so I asked, impatiently, "Did ya have sex or not?"

I literally thought, for an actual second, that her eyes would pop out of her head.

"Taryn," she whispered, horrified she glanced around, "I...oh gosh...no. We didn't have sex."

"Did you want to?"

"Taryn!"

"Come on. That was the whole reason you were apprehensive about going to the cities for the weekend, right?"

"Yeah, but you don't have to announce it."

"I asked a question. Announcing would be different. I'd use the PA system if I wanted to announce something."

"Hey, bitch!"

I looked up—that *is* my name after all.

Aidrian Casners was pushing her way through the crowd, wearing a frilly pink halter-top over a black leather miniskirt. She had white hoop earrings dangling to her shoulders, which looked like they were about to rip her ears off from the speed she was zooming my way.

I grinned at that thought.

Molly shrieked and melted away. Literally. She had mad Invisible skill.

Crystal was following Aidrian, but I saw the grin she was biting back. She was only there for entertainment. Hell, Aidrian entertained me too.

"What up?" I asked easily, standing to face the firing squad.

"You sent that freak nerd to my house Friday night. I had to baby-sit his ass at Third Wave," she hissed.

I rolled my eyes, then said smoothly, "That freak nerd is going to bank-roll you in one year. Trust me. He could own Third Wave in another ten, max."

That drew her up.

"Really?" Aidrian asked, perplexed. "He's a nerd."

"He's a computer nerd who's going to save my life. So no, he's not a nerd."

"Oh." She was at a loss for words. "I thought...I mean...he's a nerd!"

"He's going to be one of those hot nerds. Hot and rich. Mark my words," I remarked, walking away.

Crystal burst out laughing as I passed her. She fell in line, "I'm in awe of you. I mean, really, truly, madly, deeply. Just awe. Almost idol worship awe."

"She's entertaining," I remarked dryly.

"Hey," she stopped me.

I heard her tone and I knew what was coming.

"No," I spoke first, "it's great that you know what hell my weekend was. It's great that you think I shouldn't be here. But really—I'm fine."

She looked taken aback. "Okay, fine. I just...I just wanted to say that if you ever want to get stark raving drunk, look me up."

I relaxed slightly. "Thanks. I might take you up on that," I said, gentling my tone, but I couldn't erase the impatience I was feeling.

The rest of the morning passed and everyone knew to stay away from me. It might've been announced over the P.A. system. Swear. I'd walk down the hallways and people would scatter, making a path for me.

It might've been the scowl on my face.

"Miss Matthews, you are wanted in the principal's office." Of course, my teacher had to tell me this at the end of class.

"Now? At lunch?"

"It's important."

So off I went. As I traipsed through the hallway, I saw Amber and Jasmine giggling over something. Sasha stood just to the side, glaring at Jasmine's back. Tristan was at her own locker, with her own following already malingering around her. The girl worked fast—she'd be ready to usurp Amber's power in a week.

"Miss Matthews," the receptionist greeted me.

"I got a note."

"Yes, Principal Marshalls is waiting for you in his office right now."

He wasn't alone. I saw Coach Hailey with one empty chair beside her. Guess that had my name on it.

"Miss Matthews, take a seat," Principal Marshalls offered, gesturing to the chair.

As we both sat, he started, "Ms. Hailey tells me that you had a less than professional attitude with her Friday morning."

"Well, yeah. Mandy couldn't go to the game and so I tried telling her that, but she told me I was full of it."

"I did not!" Coach Hailey gasped.

"Yes, you did. You told me you wouldn't accept that Mandy couldn't be there and you'd expect her at the Dome when you arrived. Your exact words. So yeah, I had an attitude because you had one first," I stated matter-of-factly.

Principal Marshalls cleared his throat, sending a beseeching look Hailey's way. "I think the more important matter is your sister. Where is she, Taryn?"

I shrugged.

"I realize you may be scared about 'narcing' on your sister, but this meeting is more about our concern for Mandy. She's been struggling lately, we've all noticed."

"And here she thought she was hiding it so well," I remarked, rolling my eyes.

"Miss Matthews, I don't think you realize how serious this is."

"I do. But it's not my place to send memos for my sister."

I was right and Principal Marshalls knew it. I saw a flash of guilt in his eyes.

"This girl is awful. She has an attitude with everyone. I can't believe you let her stay in our school," Coach Hailey cried out.

"I thought you were a counselor," I shot her way.

"I am." She blinked, the evil robot was reconfiguring what the definition of a counselor was.

"You're not even nice," I pointed out. "Are you sure?"

"Taryn," the principal barked, "you will learn to mind your mouthyou're your manners."

Sounded like the name of a rock band.

I rolled my eyes, but shut up.

"We have two items on the agenda here. One, your sister's disappearance and two, your attitude."

"Ask all my teachers. I don't have an attitude with them."

"Yes, this is why Mr. Martson found you and Tray Evans in an inappropriate position this morning."

See—inappropriate position, inappropriate boundaries—same thing.

I grinned. "It didn't *feel* inappropriate."

"See! Mr. Marshalls, she should be in a boot camp somewhere. There are places that do outdoor therapy, I think Miss Matthews would benefit most from that type of environment."

"Oh come on!" I cried out. "You just don't like me because I didn't take your crap. And Mandy being gone is not my responsibility to explain. When her parents finally show up, it's their job."

Principal Marshalls had been watching the exchange. He said, "I agree—"

With who?

"I agree with Miss Matthews that her sister's absence should be explained by her parents and not her sister. But I agree with Ms. Hailey that your attitude does need dealing with, Taryn." Oh, like the use of my first name is going to scare me. Bite my ass.

He continued his blah, blah, blahing, "I think some consequences should be handed out for your attitude."

"Like I'm the only one with an attitude in this school!" I cried out. "That is so unfair."

"When you transferred here, we were given specific instructions and warnings on your behaviors. You have one of the largest files in school and this is not the first time you've been sent to my office."

Please, that chair was begging to be tipped over.

"And you have an impressive record of skipping classes."

"Like I'm the only one," I retorted.

"Which is why you're primarily here for the prevention of further behaviors," he explained in a tone that was supposed to sound kind, but he sounded like a pompous ass in my opinion.

"She's not even taking you seriously," Coach Hailey remarked, shaking her head. "Boot camp, Peter. It's the only thing that'll get through to her."

And fuck you too.

"Can she not be here?" I asked, glaring. "She's made it abundantly clear what her opinion is. Is there any other reason for her presence?"

Principal Marshalls frowned, but replied, "I agree, Miss Matthews. Ms. Hailey, we've already taken up enough of your time. I'll keep your recommendations in mind and if you could have them typed in a report, it'd be most appreciated."

She was going to argue, but she smiled instead. Like she'd been given a compliment or something. I made a vow, then and there, that I'd find whatever report she was going to type up and I'd shred it. Then I'd find her backups on her computer and trash those. Maybe a bat to her computer would work.

When she left, Principal Marshalls leaned back, considering me. He sighed. "Taryn, you are a mystery to me. Most of these students that walk these hallways make perfect sense to me. I know exactly what's troubling them, how to help them, or how to change them. But you...you were excelling in your classes. Now you're dating Tray Evans, skipping classes, pissing off teachers, and breaking into my office via the venting shaft."

What? I looked up, surprised to see him grinning knowingly at me. He pointed upwards. "Don't think we didn't know who was behind that little prank the other week."

I feigned innocence.

"We just couldn't prove it," he remarked, "But we knew. Principal Corey is a very good friend of mine. I've gotten more than an earful about your juvenile pranks."

They weren't juvenile. And they weren't pranks.

"But that's in the past and now we're dealing with the present."

I readied myself, ready to handle whatever he threw out.

"I've heard rumors that you're a swimmer. Quite good, in fact."

What the hell?

"I think your consequence will be to join the swim team," he announced. "I've already talked to Coach Greenly. He's watched you swim and dive, he said you're given an automatic spot on the varsity team, which is highly unusual here at Rawley, let me tell you. Girls have to compete against each other for varsity spots."

I waited. There had to be a catch.

"My only stipulation is that you do not kicked off the team."

Meaning no skipping practices, no attitude, and no drama with team-members.

"And you can start today," he finished, looking proud.

"What? No! I have something I need to take care of after school," I protested, jumping out of my chair.

"Whatever it is, it can wait. You don't want to get kicked off the team before you even start, do you?"

Oh...fuck!

"Good. Now that that's settled, you can leave, Miss Matthews."

I shut the door behind me. When I got to the hallway, my mind was reeling as I walked to my locker.

Most of the hallway was empty. A few lingered, talking, whatnot, but as I opened my locker, I found myself reaching for my purse. In my wallet, I found the picture I was looking for: me and Brian. We'd gone to the beach that day and we were just being stupid. He was carrying me on his back, my legs were wrapped around his waist and he had turned his head, trying to lick my neck.

I took a deep breath and clipped the picture on my door.

"That your ex?" Tristan asked behind me.

"Yeah," I murmured, my voice lacking heat.

"Look, I'm sorry. I heard about it in fourth period about him. Why you and Tray took off this weekend."

"So what?" I laughed. "Now you're going to be nice to me? Please."

"I'm trying to apologize here. You can cut me some slack."

"Why the fuck would I want to do that?" I asked, more curious than anything else. "You haven't exactly been gracious to me at all."

"I have done nothing *but* be nice to you," Tristan cried out. "But you've judged me based on one time when I was messing with Mandy. You're constantly going after me. If you're not siccing Casners on me, then it's Amber. I can't get a break!"

"And you deserve a break?" I asked in disbelief.

"Yeah. I think I do. I've tried."

"What have you done? If anything, I just don't put up with your passive aggressive shit."

"Look, I'm on the swim team, so I'm just saying we should try to get along."

I didn't even ask how she knew I was joining. The school had a better P.A. system than our actual P.A.

"What do you want from me, Tristan?" I finally asked, resignation settling in my bones.

"I don't know. You're Mandy's sister. I thought it'd be nice if we could be friends, but apparently that's not possible."

"Look." I was really trying here, like—patience of a god trying here, "Maybe...we got off on a wrong foot. And Amber didn't exactly sell you either."

"I can imagine." Tristan rolled her eyes, shifting on her feet. "Look...truce? Start over?'

"Whatever," I mumbled, but it was enough for Tristan.

The rest of the day passed like the morning. People steered clear of me, for the most part.

In seventh period, Molly was almost sullen in psych.

"You can say something. I'm not going to break," I finally said, exasperated.

She blushed. "I'm just...I'm so sorry, Taryn."

"So, who'd you hear it from?"

"Kayden overheard some sophomore talking about it. At first everyone was really mad at you because they all blamed you for not letting Tray go to the play-offs, but then someone said you went to a funeral. And then a freshman heard you and Tray talking in the gymnasium."

I just groaned. The freshman had had front row seats to some inappropriate boundaries. Thank God the teacher had interrupted us. I never thought I'd think that.

Fuck.

I glanced over to Tray and saw him grinning at Carter—he was like a puppy at Petco. Carter was his best friend and I hadn't realized how much till recently. Tray was ecstatic that Carter was at our school again.

No one could tell, but I saw it. There was a little look, a note of excitement on his poker face. His hazel eyes, those...seriously hot hazel-eyes that turned amber when he was...probably shouldn't go there.

"So—" Molly was chewing her lip, looking terrified.

"What? Spit it out."

"Okay? I mean...are you like...I don't know, depressed?"

I rolled my eyes, but answered truthfully, "I handle shit like this by getting angry and getting even."

"Huh?" She was confused. "I thought it was a...it was a car accident, right?"

"Doesn't mean I can't get revenge," I said sweetly, leaning back in my chair.

"You're nice. You wouldn't understand," I said bluntly.

"Yeah, but—" The girl was seriously perplexed.

Enough was enough. I wasn't about to explain myself to an Invisible who recently discovered the fun of making out.

"So you and Larkins, huh?" I mentioned casually, sitting back, and waiting for her to blush. One...two...there is was. I couldn't contain a chuckle.

"Shut up. We're not like that...well—"

"You are. You both had to have the 'sex' talk with me. You are like that."

"We did not." She sighed, blushing at the same time. "Okay—"

"You did. The two of you are a couple. So just fucking admit it."

"Oh my God," she moaned, burrowing her head in her hands. Sorry girl, you can't disappear in the middle of class.

"Did you guys have the 'sex' talk with each other?"

"Shut up. Please," she moaned, her voice muffled by her hands.

I laughed at that, but I pressed on, "Come on. Seriously. Larkins was on strict instructions to have *the* talk. Did he? He better have."

"Do you and Tray have *the* talk?" she asked, her voice still muffled.

"Yeah," I smiled fondly, images of naked Tray in mind, "it usually consists of 'bend over' or 'do you want to screw?'."

"Oh my God," she squeaked, trying to burrow through the desk this time. The Invisible wasn't much of an Invisible right now.

"What's with the act? You were fine asking me questions on Thursday."

"That wasn't about sex," she hissed. "That was about...*other* stuff."

"That *other* stuff is just another form of sex."

She squeaked again which I found damn funny.

"Matthews!" Carter called across the room. "What the hell's so funny?"

Molly groaned loudly and pulled her head from the desk to her lap. Almost—literally—underneath the table.

This made me laugh even more.

"It's annoying," Sasha griped, but it lacked heat.

I gritted my teeth, really, really, really hating that everyone was treating me differently today.

I snapped, the humor vanishing like the slam of a door. "I'm not some fucking fragile china doll. You don't have to treat me like I'm going to break."

Sasha's eyes widened to saucers. She choked back whatever she had been thinking—imagine that, a Hooters platinum blonde *not* having a blonde moment—and sputtered, "Excuse me?"

"Oh, please, Sasha. Since when have you ever sugar-coated your insults?"

"Oh my God. I cannot believe you, Taryn! Excuse me for not going for the jugular—"

"That'd be assuming you've gone there in the past. Trust me, your aims—not even close," I said smoothly. "You're like a guy who can't find the hole."

"Oh!" "Damn!" "Fuck!"

The guys instantly knew what I meant, most of 'em unable to contain their reactions of shock. The girls took a little longer—most of them anyway.

"You're such a bitch!" It's no wonder that Sasha knew the meaning immediately.

I laughed. "And you say that like it's a bad thing."

"Miss Matthews, Miss Klinnleys," the teacher spoke, returning from her errand, "quiet down or you'll both be taking a trip to the principal's office. And, Taryn," her gaze settled on me, "you don't need *another* trip to the principal today."

"How many times you been there today?" Carter asked, leaning forward eagerly.

I didn't answer, but Sasha answered instead, "It'd be her third time. Isn't that, like, a record?"

The teacher must've seen my reaction, because she spoke quickly, loudly, "That's enough. We'll be having quiet time for the rest of the period. You can finish filling out your worksheets."

I threw my books in my locker the second after class. Two students near me jumped in the air, quickly scattering when they saw me scowl.

It didn't help that I saw Tray glance at me in disappointment, and then turn towards his locker. Fucker.

CHAPTER TWENTY THREE

As I stood, looking down below, my reflection looked different. Off.

I wasn't the same—I didn't look the same, I didn't feel the same.

"Miss Matthews!" Coach Greenly called out, making his way across the pool area to me. "I see that you made it to your first practice."

"Uh...yeah."

What I hadn't made it to was letting Tray know that Props would be showing up at his place, ready to start working. He'd pissed me off, and I knew it was irrational, but I hadn't told him to get even. It was pathetic and childish, but it made me feel a little better.

"Good," he clapped me on the shoulder, "swimsuit."

"Not here."

"That's alright, I'm sure one of the girls will let you borrow one."

Great.

Tristan came out of the locker room with a group of five in tow. All of them lined up at one end of the pool and one by one dove in to start warm-up laps.

"You're Taryn, right?" A girl came up beside me. I was guessing she was on the team, since she wore a silver one-piece with her hair pulled into a swim cap.

"Yeah."

"Brady Winters, teammate, or future teammate I guess." She rolled her startling green eyes. "Coach told us this morning you were joining the team."

"That's funny," I remarked dryly, "because I was just told at lunch."

"You need a suit? I have, like, twenty in my locker. Number 812."

"Thanks." I frowned. "I don't know if I've met you before. Senior?"

"Nope, junior. I just don't run in the Holier than Thou Jasmine and Mandy Matthews circle. No offense."

"None taken. Not a big fan of Tristan's myself."

"Believe me, we all know who you get along with and who you don't. You're the biggest thing to come to the school in a long time."

"Winters! Laps!" Coach yelled out.

I read amusement in her green eyes as she turned and called back, "I'm giving them a head-start." She jumped in before he could send a retort back. She had perfect form, and I was surprised to find myself a bit envious.

"Matthews, you joining this team or not?!" Apparently, I wasn't immune to the coach's irritation.

When I came back, swimsuit on, the team had finished their laps and were sitting at some of the patio tables, listening to Coach Greenly. Motioning to me, he remarked, "Get a few laps in and pull up a chair."

Diving in the water felt different today. It didn't give me XX like it usually does. However, after a few laps, I started to feel a little at peace for the first time since I Brian's funeral. After a few laps, I got out and settled in a chair next to Brady.

The team turned out to be a bunch of girls I'd never met. I recognized a few from Tray's parties and the trips to Rickets' House. But there were quite a few who I never would've known if it hadn't been for the team.

Tristan seemed welcomed like a long lost prodigal son. Even the coach doted on her, which was just annoying. Fortunately, only a few girls seemed to idolize her. For the most part, Tristan was more tolerated than anything else. Most of the girls seemed like serious swimmers, not social climbers.

Which was just a breath of fresh air.

Brady caught up with me at the end of practice as we walked out of the locker room. Dressed in street clothes, I was surprised to see that she didn't wear the trendy almost whorish clothes that most girls wore. She was dressed in a loose-fitting t-shirt and worn jeans, flared at the ends.

"So what'd you think of the first day?"

I shrugged. "It felt good to be swimming."

"You're good. Like really good. I'm jealous. I can see why the coach snapped you up so quickly." She sent an easy grin my way, her swim bag over her shoulder.

"You're fast."

"I used to be the fastest swimmer on the team," she remarked, shrugging.

"Who's faster now?"

Brady laughed. "You are."

"What?" Startled, I stopped in the hallway.

"I heard about your dives from the cliff and some of the girls have seen you when you were with your mom. Plus, those laps just now, you weren't even trying and you beat my time. You're the fastest, Taryn."

I was startled, unsure what to say.

"You don't have to say anything." Brady laughed. "I'm just happy you're on the team. You've got a talent that would've been a wasted. Plus, nationals are a sure thing now, thanks to you."

"Thanks." I didn't know what else to say. "Hey, I was wondering, are a lot of the girls seniors this year? I've never seen them around before."

"I'm not the only one who doesn't run in Jasmine and Mandy's circle," Brady answered. "Not all of us are popular sharks like them. We just want to swim and get good grades."

Coming to my locker, I opened it and grabbed my bag and purse. I groaned, seeing three missed calls on my phone.

"Not good?" Brady asked, waiting beside me.

"I was very childish." I sighed, seeing Tray's name on my missed calls list. "I didn't warn someone about something because I was mad."

"Ah." Brady nodded knowingly. "Boyfriend problems?"

"Yeah," I sighed, "he's going to be pissed at me."

"Tray Evans doesn't exactly strike me as an easygoing guy," Brady mused.

At my look of surprise, she explained, "Like I said, everyone knows who you get along with and who you don't. And everyone *especially* knows that you're dating Tray Evans."

"If you're not a fan of Tristan, I'm pretty sure you're not a fan of Tray's either," I commented, walking out into the parking lot.

"Hard to get a read on someone who's larger than life, you know?"

"Yeah," I said quietly, "that's a good description of Tray. Are you dating anyone?"

"I am. His name is Josh Barrons and he's a normal, average student with hopes of getting into Brown to major in psychology."

"You say that like you're apologizing for him," I noted.

"I'm not. But he's no Tray Evans."

I laughed at that. "That's probably a good thing."

"Nah, Josh is Josh. For now. He's my boyfriend, but he's not a Tray Evans in bed, I'm betting."

"That sounds like...a security blanket."

"He is. My personal blankie that I've had for four years," Brady noted.

I jumped, slightly, hearing my phone ring. I'd forgotten how loud the ring was set at.

Brady laughed. "Ah, the demanding, pissed-off boyfriend calls again."

I rolled my eyes, but braced myself as I answered, "Hey."

"You could have fucking warned me!" Tray hissed. I heard loud music in the background.

"Sorry?"

"That kid you were talking about, Props—whatever, he's here. He showed up after school. Thanks for the warning. I had to get rid of Carter and everyone."

"Is he still there?"

"Yeah. And your friend that banged Hooters girl." He cursed, catching himself.

That made me smile. He'd caught onto my nick-name.

"You don't have to call her Hooters girl, I'll have sex with you tonight anyway."

Brady pursed her lips, her eyes dancing in amusement.

"Whatever," Tray groaned, "can you just get your ass here?"

"Yeah, I just got out of swim practice."

"I know. Carter told me."

"How does Carter know I had swim practice?"

"You really want to know?"

"No!"

"Then don't ask. Where are you? Get over here."

He sounded tense.

"Is Props really that hard to handle? You sound like you're at your wits' end."

"It's not him, it's the other guy. What's his name?"

"Trent."

"If I hadn't threatened bodily harm, I swear he would've torn my place apart. Plus, your folks are back in town. They showed up here looking for you, too."

"What?" I froze, my heartbeat suddenly deafening.

"I know. Just get your ass over here. I covered for you. I told 'em you went back to Pedlam to visit some friends because of Brian, but your dad hates me. I think they might've camped out across the street or something."

"Oh God."

"Tell me about it. When you show up, cut through my neighbor's lawn. Just to be sure, alright?"

Swim practice had been a heavenly vacation.

"I'm on my way." I hung up, my mind reeling.

"That did not sound good," Brady murmured, still watching me.

"Uh...it's not. It's not good at all."

"You're not, like pregnant or anything, are you? I know we just met and this could be the beginning of a beautiful friendship, but if you're pregnant, my aunt's a counselor. You can talk to her if you want," Brady offered.

"I almost wish I were pregnant. It'd be a lot easier to deal with," I said tensely. Getting inside my car, I called out through the open window, "I'll see you tomorrow in school."

"Yeah. You can have lunch with us tomorrow, if you want." Brady waved, walking to her car.

I parked around the block and darted through his neighbor's yard. Climbing the wall, I dropped down and was walking past the pool-house when Tray came outside.

The look on his face stopped me in my tracks.

"What's wrong?"

"They've multiplied," he answered, grabbing my hand and dragging me back into the pool-house. In his bedroom, he fell onto the bed and pulled me down beside him.

I laid there, stunned.

Caressing his back softly, I asked, "What's wrong?"

"Gentley's here. That friend of yours is here. Props is working on his computer stuff and your parents showed up."

"I'm sorry your house got ran over," I apologized sincerely. Feeling lame for my pathetic childishness. "I'm sorry I didn't tell you about Props. I didn't know Trent and Gentley were coming over. Wait. Is Gentley here for me?"

"Yeah. I haven't asked and they haven't told me what they're doing here, but they're waiting for you." He pushed himself up, holding himself just above me. "Taryn, talk to me before you do whatever they want you for. Promise me."

"I promise," I said softly, running a thumb over his lips. When I saw a smidgen of amber appear in his hazel orbs, I leaned up and captured his lips with mine. Feeling him sigh, he fell back onto me. As I embraced his weight, he ran a hand down my back and to my legs, curling them around his back.

"We should probably head in," I whispered against his lips.

Instead, Tray dipped his head, deepening the kiss as his hands trailed to my waist and slipped underneath my shirt. I was fast losing the ability to think clearly. It'd been a few days since we'd been together. The funeral, everything, had come crashing down on us at one time.

"Tray," I murmured again, and sighed as I fell back on the pillow with his mouth moving to my neck and trailing downwards.

I sensed the urgency in him as he reared up and stripped off his shirt. Meeting his eyes, I knew neither of us were going anywhere for a while. Whatever was waiting for me would have to wait a little longer.

I sat up and pulled my shirt off. As I fell back, I felt the cool air against my skin, Tray was already pulling my pants off. Quickly we were both naked, our hands fevered, urgent. Gasping, I arched as Tray's mouth moved to my waist and further south. He held my hips captive as he kissed and sucked.

As I came, my breaths coming in shallow gasps, I reached blindly for him and scuttled down, clamping my legs around his waist. Tray met my mouth, curling me underneath him with experienced expertise.

"Taryn," he gasped, reaching for his nightstand.

I held myself back forcibly, as I waited for him to grab a condom, but it was taking everything I had. I wanted him. And I wanted him inside me. Now.

Then, a seemingly hour later, he slid in, stretching me, as he braced himself above me.

We both held on as his thrusts took us closer and then hurdled our bodies over the edge. I melted, again, panting as we both laid there.

It took a moment for the fog to clear and I then remembered who was waiting for us.

"Oh...fuck," I groaned.

Tray laughed into my shoulder, where his mouth was lingering.

"We should head in."

Tray grunted slightly as he lifted himself up again. But he held me trapped on the bed, with his arms on both sides of me. "Taryn, promise me that you'll come to me first with whatever they want."

"I promise."

"I mean it. Those guys don't know what they're doing or who they're going against."

"I will. Promise." I smiled as I saw him look sternly at me. "Now get out of my face before I pull you back down for another round."

Tray grinned, but lifted himself up and off the bed.

We both showered quickly and dressed.

As we entered the main house, we heard shouting from the basement.

"Fuck you, man! I'm telling you we don't need Taryn for this. We should leave before she gets here."

Rounding the corner, I saw Trent shake his head. "Oh hell no, man. We can't do this without Taryn. I'm telling you, we need her."

"And I'm telling you we don't," Gentley shot back.

"You don't need me for what?" I asked, feeling Tray behind me.

Gentley swore, raking a hand through his hair.

"Taryn." Trent looked relieved. "We think we know where Grayley is, but we gotta move now."

"No," Tray spoke up, coming to stand beside me.

"Fuck you, man. This has nothing to do with you."

"This does have to do with me."

"Where do you think Grayley is?" I asked, my heart had started racing at Grayley's name.

"Jace has another warehouse on the eastside. We found it last night, but it's going to be a bitch to get into. We need you for that," Trent explained, watching Tray intensely.

"Why are you here?" I asked Gentley.

"Because Gray's a friend of mine, too." He actually sounded sincere.

"You weren't at the funeral." I turned back to Trent.

"I was trying to find Grayley before we have one for him." He cursed, pacing. I could see why Tray was tense—Trent looked like a caged animal: pissed and hungry. It was a side of Trent that I'd never seen before.

"Where's the warehouse?" I asked.

"Taryn," Tray spoke up, "you promised."

"Where's the warehouse?" I ignored him.

Gentley watched the exchange between us. I knew he was studying us, but he didn't say anything.

Trent looked relieved.

"You'll help?" he asked.

"Of course, but I'm not going in blind. And," I glanced at Tray, "I'll need to run it over with Tray, in private."

Trent cursed. "When the hell do you ever have to run things by a guy? What the hell's happened to you, Taryn? You're like a shadow of the Taryn I know. You've changed. God knows, you'd never be caught dead dating someone like him—"

"And you better remember whose house you're in." Tray said quietly, a clear threat in his words. But it worked because Trent shut up immediately, glaring at us.

"What do you think is going on?" I asked, ignoring everything he just shot at me. That needed to be dealt with at another time, in a more private setting. Grayley was the only thing that mattered to me right now.

Trent hesitated, sharing a look with Gentley.

Tray remarked, poker face firmly in place, "Start talking or you can leave without Taryn's help."

Trent swallowed whatever he was going to say. I saw the words actually come up and have to be forced back down. After composing himself, he said, "It has to do with Jace. Brian's death has to do with Jace." He looked at me then, an apologetic note in those blue eyes. "Brian was coming to you with something about Jace. But he'd been missing for a few days before that. That's when Grayley said he was going to go and find Brian. We found his car on the eastside, about a mile from Jace's warehouse. We think he's in the warehouse."

"How do you know all this?"

"Because things have been wrong in Pedlam since you left," Gentley spoke up now, resigned. He glanced warily to Tray and myself, but continued, "Your psycho ex has been off kilter, Grayley's been acting like a nervous bitch, and your stone-head friend—he's just been more whacked than normal."

"What he's trying to say," Trent sent him a meaningful glare, "is that there's been some shady shit going on at school. I've seen some of Jace's guys in the school parking lot every day. That's not cool. Brian's always been violent, but a month before he died, he was showing up at school black and blue every day. Then Grayley suddenly started acting like he was on drugs or something. Things have just been off. But—"

Gentley stepped in and added, "After you guys broke into our school, things got worse. Security guards were added, like ten at night. Kimberly tried to get into school one night because she left her homework and got ran off by some of the guards. Trent said they're guys that work for your ex's brother."

"That true?" I asked Trent.

"Yeah. I went with her because she was so damn scared to even try. The fucking school is like an army base now. None of it makes sense."

"Taryn," Tray murmured, curling a hand around my wrist, he pulled me into a room. Shutting the door, he said, "What do you know that you haven't told me? I need to know everything."

"We got an entire week?" I joked, in a half-ass attempt. "I know what you know. That Brian was working with Galverson to compete with Jace. Jace and Galverson are running drugs. They built a new storage unit at Jace's club. They're running more than just drugs. And that Jace did something to get me out of Pedlam."

"You sure the new unit is at Jace's club?" Tray asked, frowning.

"What do you mean?"

"They had three guards when we broke in. Serious security. Now they have ten."

Oh God. Cammy said the storage unit had been broke into and they needed more security.

"It's the school," I said, dazed. "It's the school. They rebuilt it when I left. It's why I left. Jace knew I could get in, that's why he didn't want me around Pedlam. He knew I'd get in and find something I wouldn't like."

"It's good cover," Tray remarked, pacing behind me. I could hear him thinking. "But they'd have to have another opening or it'd bring too much attention to their shipments. I'm betting it's underground, but you can get in through the school. That's why they added the extra guards. And we missed it when we went in because we weren't looking. I wonder how far the second warehouse is from the school?"

"You think that might be their opening and it goes all the way to the school?"

"Maybe. Don't you guys have a river that's not far from school?"

"Yeah. Like a mile away."

"I bet that's the opening. They load whatever it is on boats and bring it in from the river. It's a tunnel that goes from the school to the river, but they're storing it underneath the school because it's a perfect cover. Who'd think a school would be a storage unit for drugs and whatever else they're smuggling."

"You're almost scary at how good you are," I noted faintly.

Tray grinned, raking a hand through his hair. "I think like them. Dad trained me that way."

"That's...a little scary."

"And your ex and your two friends have known what's been going on. That's why they lied to you, to really protect you."

"Yeah." I sighed.

Tray pulled me against him, anchoring his arms around my waist. Kissing my forehead, he murmured, "We've got most of it figured out, but we need more. We need to know what's in that second warehouse. We need to know exactly what's in the school and we need to know who Galverson's contracting with because none of this would be happening unless it was really big. He wouldn't chance it, not with what I've got on them. And we'll need proof, stone-cold proof that can't disappear or be killed."

I burrowed closer against his shoulder.

"You still want to do this?" he asked. I felt him holding his breath.

Pulling back, I saw him searching my face. "Brian died, they've got Grayley, and they fucked with my life. I goddamn still want this."

"Okay." He kissed me hard and then let me go. Moving around, he walked back out to the room. "We'll need blueprints. We'll need twenty-four-seven surveillance. I want to know the guard shifts, I want to know the layout, I want to know what's surrounding that warehouse before Taryn goes in. Or she's not going in."

"Who the fuck put you in charge?!" Trent growled.

"I did," I spoke up, coming behind Tray. "I'm not doing anything without Tray's okay."

"Just like—" Trent began, pissed.

But Gentley cut him off. "If we get all that, will you go in?" He was looking at me, gauging my reaction.

"Yeah."

"Okay," he said simply, nodding, "we'll get the stuff for you. I'll have the guys set up tonight to watch 'em."

"The fuck we will," Trent clipped out. "We need to go in now or Grayley may be dead."

"Grayley's my friend too, Trent. But I agree with Evans. I'm not going to send anyone in, even if she's a bitch I could care less about, without knowing exactly what and who she may be running into."

I frowned. Insult or compliment? Whatever. I moved past Tray. "I want in just as much as you, Trent. And I want Grayley alive, but I'm not going in blind. That would be suicide and you know it. Jace wouldn't kill Grayley unless he absolutely had to. Because he knows that I'd go after him and I don't think Jace would want that."

"What's go goddamn special about you?" Gentley asked, frowning. "I don't get it. What can you do that others can't?"

Trent laughed. "Fuck, Crisp, I've seen Taryn get into places that a fucking ghost couldn't. If Jace doesn't want her somewhere, Taryn can get in there. That's why we need her." But not Tray. No one said it, but everyone knew what he was thinking.

Tray stepped forward. "Get out and get that information. It's the fastest way to get what you want. I'd suggest you get started right now."

Gentley looked like he wanted to argue, but he clamped his mouth shut as he yanked Trent behind him, on the way out.

Tray followed, to make sure they actually left, leaving me alone in the basement.

I dropped onto one of the couches, briefly remembering when the room had been occupied with Tray's friends. Tray's and Mandy's. The room seemed different now. Not so light and...easy. Everything was just tense now.

"Hey," Tray said when he came back, "your friend is upstairs if you want to go and check on him."

Holy hell—I'd forgotten about Props.

Standing unsteadily, I asked, "Where is he?"

"I stashed him in my dad's old library. But he's using all of his own equipment."

"Okay." Tray pulled me with him as I followed him in a daze; everything was overwhelming.

The library was huge. It looked half the size of a banquet hall with books lining two complete walls. In one corner was a huge mahogany desk, a fucking Best Buy display behind it. The computer and whatever else (I had no idea) looked all brand new. They probably were. Tray commented once that he doesn't touch a lot of stuff in the house, not since his parents had left.

And I saw Props was hunched over his laptop, a bunch of little gadgets hooked up to his computer with lights blinking rapidly.

"Heya, Props." I greeted.

He straightened, startled. "Hey."

"Forget where you were?" I teased, but I saw he had. That was funny, at least in the sense of everything else going on.

"You owe me, huge!" he exclaimed, wheeling out from his computer. He grabbed up a pile of papers next to him. "I've got names, account numbers, passwords, and a pile of illegal jargon that could get me in the slammer. Holy shit—you owe me big time."

"Well, I'll get ya a hooker," I said easily, straddling a chair next to him. "What do you got?"

"Like I said." I heard the fear in his voice, but it was laced with excitement. The guy was a techno adrenalin junkie. I knew what adrenalin did to a person. He had absolutely no qualms with what he'd just gotten for me. He just liked to voice that he did, it was more socially appropriate. "I've got everything."

As I took the papers, I gasped at what I saw.

Scrambling up, I cried out, "Tray, holy shit!"

Tray moved closer, studying the papers over my shoulders.

"Three Swiss accounts," I said.

"Those are Galverson's aliases," Tray announced as he studied the papers. "Another two in the Cayman's. Jace has four accounts on here, too. Along with—"He froze, standing absolutely still. Déjà vu crashed into my body, remembering the morning when Jace and Galverson had arrived to the house. The Tray I saw that morning was the same I was looking at now. I shivered.

"Along with what?" I asked, holding my breath.

"My dad. And a guy named Carl Broozer."

"Who's Carl Broozer?"

"A kingpin on the West coast." Tray said flatly, his eyes were dead. "Galverson's declared Pedlam as the highway intersection for drug-runs. It makes sense now."

"What are you talking about?"

"Galverson wants my contacts. But he's not worried because he knows I won't say anything—he's got my dad. But this deal must've been set up for at least a few years now. Jace is sitting smack dab on every black-market shipment that's running across the nation. If Galverson's in bed with Broozer and he has contacts in South America—"

I couldn't comprehend whatever Tray was saying. I just knew it was enough to make him go pale at whatever conclusion he came to.

He fixed Props with a piercing stare, causing the kid to yelp before scurrying backwards on his chair. "You got all of this?"

"Yeah." He gulped, the terror was evident in his voice. "Taryn said to follow everything back so I did."

"And you didn't leave any prints? None?"

"No. Hell no. I used a system that I just programmed this fall. It's a ghost tracker. They won't have any idea that I've been in there."

"How do you know?" Tray grilled him.

"Because," he looked like he was reminding himself to breathe, "because I hacked into some FBI databases in September. If they knew I was there, my fail-alarms would've gone off and I'd already be in prison. Trust me, those guys have no idea I was in those accounts."

"Do you know what you did here? It's very important that you know exactly how dangerous this stuff is."

"I know," Props said quietly. "I know, dude. I know that if I talk, I'm dead. I know that."

"And you did it anyway? Why?" Tray asked him, but I answered for him.

"Because he needed permission to do it. He needed a reason to test himself."

I saw that I was right when Props looked relieved.

"He wouldn't have known what he could do if I hadn't asked him," I finished. "Tray, what does this mean?"

"This means that we have enough," he said gravely.

"Enough for what?" But I didn't want to know, not anymore.

"Enough for us to start setting up our plan."

I looked at Props and asked, "What do you want?"

"I don't want anything. Really. I'm good with the date I got and knowing that I'm alive right now."

"Thanks for de-coding this stuff."

"Hey." Tray stopped him, just as he was starting to put all his equipment away.

Props turned and waited. The guy looked like he was about to pee in his pants.

"One word of this and it means you, me, and Taryn could all get killed. You got that?"

The guy couldn't talk. I watched his Adam's apple bobbing up and down.

"He knows," I said quietly for him.

"If I ask, if I give you the go-ahead, do you think you could dump all of this info to the DEA?" Tray asked, staring at him intently; trying to read Prop's reaction.

He was talking about his brother.

"Tray," I murmured, "what are you thinking?"

"I'm just thinking of some options, Taryn. That's all. For now anyway," he answered. Looking back to Props, he pressed, "Would you be able to do that, Props?"

"Any account?"

"No. A specific person's, like if Taryn or I were to go missing."

"Yeah." He was shaking, but he sounded confident. "I could do it."

"Okay. Until then, you stay with your little group of friends. You say nothing. Nothing, you hear me?" We all heard the threat behind Tray's voice.

"Not a word. Nothing. Promise." Props looked like he was about to faint.

"He's got it, Tray. Props, you want some help clearing this stuff up?"

He moved fast, faster than I expected because in a matter of seconds everything was shut down, unplugged, and encased in a bag.

Whoa.

"Guess not," I murmured, half joking.

"We good? I mean, until...you know, until the account stuff?" Props was standing, his bag over his shoulder, asking for permission to leave.

"Yeah, we're good."

And he was off. Seconds later we heard the door slam shut behind him, leaving Tray and I alone.

Tray swore, but moved to his dad's computer. He was scanning all the papers. Moving to sit beside him, I asked, "What are you thinking?"

"We've got accounts. We've got locations of warehouses in here. Schedules. Names of their employers. That kid should be working for the FBI," Tray cursed. He looked scary.

"Hey," I said softly, moving to sit on his lap. I captured his chin in my hand. "What are you thinking?"

"I'm thinking I need to make sure my place isn't bugged."

Oh God.

"You think Galverson would do that?"

"No, I don't. He really does think I'm just some kid who's only interested in saying 'fuck you' to anyone who messes with me. But Jace knows better. Galverson's gotten lazier in his old age and he's been listening to my dad. He really believes that I'll consider working for him. He wouldn't have offered me a job if he wasn't pretty damn sure I would take it."

"This is a bit overwhelming."

"What do you want, Taryn?" Tray searched my face.

"I want...I want to know what Jace did to me and what he did to Brian and where Grayley is." It was a lot, but I wanted to know. "And I want him to pay for hurting Brian."

"And what if he didn't do anything?"

Silence fell between us as we gazed at each other.

"I don't think his accident was an accident," I answered lightly.

"How do you want him to pay? Do you want Galverson to go down with him?"

"Knowing all this stuff, I don't think I can *not* do something with it."

"And if it means that they'll come after us?"

"Then we have to take them all down."

"Okay." Tray kissed me, breathing against my lips. He raked a hand through my hair, holding me firmly in place as he deepened the kiss. "Okay."

I wrapped my arms around him and sank further against him.

"This is what I do." Tray pulled back, breathing deeply. "I look at the entire picture and I figure out our avenues at every possible juncture."

In that moment I remembered Galverson's words. He'd called Tray a genius and in that moment, I knew it was true. Tray was. But he was also a kid whose parents had been taken away from him. And now, I saw that he wanted this too.

"What do you want?" I asked him, my thumb making a lazy circle against his cheek.

"I want, Tray blinked, "I want it over."

"Okay." I kissed him.

"I don't want Gentley and that Trent guy in on this," Tray said firmly. "When they bring their information to us, we take it and you promise that we'll move quickly. But they cannot be there. I don't want them a part of this."

"You don't trust them?"

"No. I just work better alone. Always have."

"You're not working alone this time."

"You and me. That's it."

"Okay."

"Okay."

"It's going to be hard to go to school tomorrow."

"We can't do anything out of the ordinary." Tray shifted, pulling me to lay back against his chest. With my back to his chest, he slid his hands down my thighs, moving to the inside of my legs and coming back up, trailing to the opening at my jeans. Flicking my button open, I gasped as his fingers slid inside.

"Tray," I breathed.

As his fingers went to work, he murmured huskily, "We'll go to school tomorrow. You go to your swim practice and then tomorrow night, maybe we'll have enough info to go into the warehouse."

"And search for Grayley." It was hard to think and speak with what he was doing to me.

"And search for Grayley," he whispered, turning my face around to meet my lips with his as his fingers swept in and out.

Crying out, I let go, all reasoning swept out of my head as his fingers kept thrusting in and out of me.

Whimpering, feeling the crest, I gasped as I spilled over. Tray grinned against my neck where he was nuzzling, feeling my body jerk in response.

A moment later, I murmured tiredly, "I hate that you can do that sometimes."

"I love how I can do that to you," he murmured back, kissing me lightly on the lips. I sighed as I turned and wrapped my arms around his neck. I just sat there as I laid my head against his shoulder, my body completely relaxed as I straddled him.

I might've drifted off for a second because I heard the sound of the keyboard as I came back awake.

I was in the same place, draped all over Tray, sleeping, as he worked around me.

"What are you doing?" I murmured, sleepily. The sex, the swimming, and the adrenalin had taken its toll.

"I'm finishing some of this stuff. Hiding it in some of my own accounts and making copies."

"What are you doing with the copies?"

"I'm going to mail them off to some solid sources. Anything happens to me, the information will go public. No matter what. It's the same system I set up before. And I'm connecting some more of the dots."

"I thought you had all the dots connected." I should really lift my head and look at what he was doing, but his shoulder was a lot more comfortable.

"Most of them, but there are a few I don't have connected yet. That pisses me off because it could be a surprise. A surprise that could get us dead."

I yawned. I really shouldn't have, considering he was talking about my life, but...I felt safe in his arms. In that moment, I knew that Tray would take care of me.

"What do you mean?"

"Like why Jace got you to Rawley or at least out of Pedlam," he murmured, distracted.

"What do you mean?"

"Jace wanted you out of Pedlam, but I don't know if he meant for you to end up in Rawley."

"Does it really matter?"

"Yeah, it could. Any detail like that matters. It's all important."

"You should be a cop or something." I yawned again, my eyelids were fighting to stay open.

Tray must've felt the fight in me, because he ran one hand down my back and soothed, "Get some sleep."

"Do I have to move?" My eyelids were already closed at his permission.

"No, baby. I'll put you in bed when I'm done."

"Okay—" Then I was instantly asleep.

CHAPTER TWENTY FOUR

I woke up and looked at the clock. It was five-thirty in the morning. And Tray wasn't beside me. Getting up, I padded out the door and into the hallway. He'd put me in the same room we'd slept in before. As I circled the stairs, I could hear voices from the library.

What the fuck?

I recognized Carter and Bryce's voice.

"Seriously, dude. Come on," Carter said.

"I can't." Tray replied, sounding exhausted.

"You're up, man. What's the problem?"

"I've got to finish some stuff up before school." I could hear the sleepiness in his voice. And I instantly felt guilty. It must've been seven-thirty or eight when I nodded off to sleep last night. That meant Tray had either catnapped during the night or had stayed up the entire night. While I'd been sleeping like a baby.

Guessing from the waft of coffee I got, I was guessing he'd been up all night.

I slipped inside, but Bryce and Carter didn't notice me right away.

Carter was saying, "School won't care. We can leave now and you'll be back in time to bang Taryn after school."

Thanks.

Tray grinned at that, meeting my eyes, "Sound okay with you?"

"Oh shit!" Carter wheeled around, eyes wide as he saw me.

Bryce tipped his head back and laughed.

"Now I know how you really feel," I only murmured, moving to curl up in the chair next to Tray's.

"Oh God. I'm sorry, Taryn, I didn't mean—" But he just shut up, shaking his head in surrender.

I grinned, resting my cheek against my knees as I pulled them against my chest. "Carter, your simplicity is refreshing at times."

Bryce laughed harder.

Carter looked like he'd blush if he was capable of it. I didn't think he had the capability for it though.

Tray just grinned half-heartedly, as he looked back to the computer's screen.

I wanted to ask how long he'd been up and what he learned, but I didn't want to broach the conversation with Carter and Bryce there. They didn't need to get curious about what would keep Tray up all night, if he wasn't 'banging' me.

"Taryn, we heard you were forced to join the swim team," Bryce commented, the laughter subsiding.

"Yeah," I sighed, "but that's okay."

"Well, then you would appreciate our efforts here." Carter was back, charm and all. "We're trying to persuade Tray to come on a trip with us. The coast is supposed to have some record waves today. How can we miss this chance?"

"I didn't know you guys surfed."

"We don't. Not that much, but we like to *try* every now and then," Bryce said truthfully.

"Whatever. I surf!" Carter declared.

"Yeah and, until recently, you had been going to a boarding school thirty minutes from the coast. We don't live on the coast, it's a good three hour drive. At least," Tray slipped in.

"Come on!" Carter tried again, looking exasperated.

"I'm not going so you might as well as stop wasting your time," Tray murmured, focused on the computer.

I took a sip from his coffee. Holy crap it was strong. Yep, he'd been up all night.

Carter grumbled, muttering something under his breath.

Bryce was watching him, amused.

Carter must've accepted defeat because he turned on me. "Taryn, since we're up, how about you make the morning worth it? Maybe a lap dance, or you could just get naked."

"I already hauled your ass on the floor the last time you suggested this. Want another round?" I delivered smoothly, grinning over Tray's mug.

"Man," he whined, settling further in his chair, "I thought moving here would be more fun than this. This blows so far. Tray won't go surfing. His girl won't strip for us."

Bryce grinned, before hitting Carter on the back of his head. "Cheer up, cousin. You bagged Jasmine on your first day of school. That's gotta be a record."

"Oh yeah." Carter grinned. "Good memories."

"Does that count? It's easy to score with a girl you scored the entire weekend with," Tray remarked, shooting his foot out and kicking Carter off his chair.

"Hey," Carter yelped, glaring at him as he crawled back up, "it counts. The weekend was just a weekend. My first day at school was my first day at school."

"You should go for Tristan." I couldn't help but speak up. "She'd be more of a challenge, wouldn't she?"

"That tight-ass?" Carter laughed. "Hell no. She's rolled so tight a pencil wouldn't get in there."

Bad imagery.

"She slept with Brent Garretts, didn't she?" Bryce asked. "You should go for her, Carter."

"That'd be entertaining for all of us," Tray added as he reached to take his coffee-mug from my hands.

"I don't know. She's kind of—"

"What? Scary?" I laughed, seeing him blanch.

"Yeah. And she's got this scary thing about Tray still. Plus, her and Mandy are best friends."

"Speaking of Mandy," Bryce spoke up, "Taryn, where is Mandy? I called Devon to ask about her, but he won't answer his phone."

Fuck. I'd forgotten about Devon. Well, if Mandy wanted him to know, then she could tell him herself.

"I can't say anything," I said firmly.

"So, it's serious?" Carter asked, suddenly somber.

"I really can't say anything. Sorry."

"But she's, like, alive, right?"

"Yeah. She's fine. Not dying or anything." I made my tone light, just to appease him. I could tell that the guy truly cared about her.

"Maybe I *should* try to bag Tristan. I mean, she's gotta be more interesting than Jaz, right? But then again," Carter mused, the Mandy topic dropped just as quickly as it came up, "Jaz has to be better in bed than Tristan any day."

I hated that I saw all three of the guys sharing a look with each other.

All three of them had been with her.

"You guys make me sick," I announced, crossing my arms over my chest.

Tray laughed as he reached out to rub his hand down my leg. He grabbed my chair and yanked me closer, where he could comfortably rest his hand on my leg.

Bryce just grinned, staying quiet.

"No," Carter exclaimed, "I'll do it. I'm going to bag Tristan."

"This should be interesting." Bryce watched his cousin. "Tristan's not a fan of yours."

"I know. All the more challenging."

"You better get ready for your ass to be handed to you," Bryce warned. "The only guy Tristan's actually ran to was Tray."

"What about Brent Garretts?"

"She slept with him to piss off Amber and Casners."

"You're more on the up and up on the gossip than me, Bryce. I'm impressed." I laughed, loving his look of embarrassment.

"I have lab with Amber." As if that made perfect sense. But it actually did. I kind of felt sorry for Bryce in that moment. I could see him sitting there, helpless, as Amber launched into one of her tirades. One after another.

I caught Tray resting his eyes for a moment, before he yawned again.

"Okay," I announced, "I'm taking the duty of girlfriend serious right now. You two, out. Now."

"What?" Carter whined, but he stood anyway. It was just for show, which I was learning was how Carter mostly was. 75% show, 25% real.

"Yeah, yeah." Bryce stood too and clipped his cousin on the back of his head again. But as they moved down the hallway, I heard Bryce yelp. Carter must've gotten his revenge. And then the door opened and shut.

"You been up all night?" I asked Tray, feeling guilty how well rested I felt.

"On and off. I got some sleep, but there was some stuff still bothering me so I couldn't stay in bed."

"What have you found out?" I asked the question lightly, but I felt my words die in my throat when I saw Tray grow still again. One of those frozen moments, when I knew something serious was going on.

He'd found out something serious. Probably about me, judging by the way he was looking at me. Like he was figuring out how to break the news to me, whatever he had found. And how he knew I wouldn't like it.

"Oh god," I murmured.

"Taryn," he began, moving to face me squarely, "I think...I think Jace arranged your adoption."

What?

He took a deep breath. "You moved to Rawley because you were adopted. So I searched for some local adoption agencies and found one that looked...familiar."

I didn't even know I was holding my breath.

"It's called The Evanson Family Resources and it's sponsored by one of Galverson's aliases."

"How do you know that?"

"I called your friend Props and had him run some of the information for me. He verified what I found out on the internet. The adoption agency was recently funded and it's only had one adoption go through: yours.

"Evanson?"

"Yeah," Tray clipped out, I saw the hardness enter his eyes, "I think my dad was the one behind your adoption. I think Jace went to him and asked him to arrange the adoption. I think he just wanted you out of town and he didn't care where you went. And I think it was my dad who approached your parents. A sizeable chunk of money showed up in your family's account the day your adoption was legalized."

"How much?" I asked, but I didn't want to know. I didn't want to know any of it.

"Ten million."

It was too much. It was a fee. I'd been bought and paid for. I'd been a fucking business deal.

"Oh my God," I said, my voice tiny.

But it was right. Everything clicked.

They adopted a seventeen year old female. They were never home. Mandy had let it slip that they'd been told that they were adopting someone.

"Tristan said an old friend had approached them and asked if they would consider adoption," I murmured, my eyes glazed over. "Mandy told her that."

"I think Mandy got the drugs from your dad. I think your dad was one of my dad's local clients. He mentioned he had a few high rollers in town who liked prescription drugs. It makes sense now." Tray bit out. "I'm sorry, Taryn."

"It always goes back to drugs." I didn't know what I was saying. So much. So much had happened. My life had been turned inside and out, and this was the last straw. "Is it always about drugs and money?!" I cried out.

"You're asking the wrong person."

"I wanted a new life," I said faintly, standing, hugging myself. "I wanted a family. I was determined that I'd do anything for a family. I was going to be perfect. I was going to go to school. Not have sex. Not do...everything that I'd done before. And now...I got that family because of what I was doing before. Because Jace didn't want me to find out all his dirty little secrets."

"Taryn—"

"He bought me a fucking family! I was a fucking business deal!" I screamed.

"Not to Mandy and I'm pretty sure not to Austin. I don't think you were a business deal to them." Tray said firmly.

"Evans and Galverson together. It's how they came up with the name."

"Not real bright, but that's my dad for you."

I didn't know what to think. What to feel. I didn't even know what to believe or who to believe anymore.

"I don't think it was Kevin." I murmured, softly, thinking.

"What?"

"He's always gone on some kind of medical conferences or at the hospital. I don't think it was him at all. It's Shelley." Shelley who couldn't handle disciplining a fourteen year old. Who made Mandy do the dirty work. Either Mandy or me. Oh no. It wasn't Kevin at all—this was all Shelley. And I'd bet anything that she first got the drugs from her doctor husband, but he wasn't around enough to keep the prescriptions filled. So she ran to Tray's dad.

Who knows, maybe they'd had a thing going on. Maybe it was another reason for his mom's suicide attempt.

"I feel sick," I muttered, right before I dashed to the bathroom and actually was sick.

My insides wanted out. Again. Again and again and again.

There weren't any tears. Not after everything. Brian. My breakdown. And now this...I was just sick and more determined.

I wanted everyone to go down.

Jace.

Shelley.

Galverson.

Fucking everyone.

Even Tray's dad, but that was Tray's business. His to handle.

A little shaky, I brushed my teeth and went back to the library a little later when my stomach was calmer.

Tray just looked exhausted.

"You okay?" he asked quietly.

I saw the concern written all over his face and a small part of my world felt right.

"I'll be okay," I promised.

"You're handling it better than I thought."

"I've got nothing left inside of me. I'm done crying and I refuse to be a dry-heaver." I joked, half-assed as I stood in front of the window.

"I'm sorry I had to be the one to tell you that."

"Makes sense," I said. And it did. It all made sense now. Everything. It all ran in one big circle, all circulating around the addiction of drugs.

"You can't go home, you know."

"I know."

"If you do, you can't go off on your parents."

"I know." I wanted to. I really, really wanted to. I was a fucking deal. I meant next to nothing to them. "So what else did you figure out?"

"Jace wanted you out of Pedlam because of the drugs that he and Galverson would have shipping through, from Broozer's business. He knew you'd find out and you wouldn't stand for it. So he arranged for your adoption to get you out of Pedlam."

It was the only thing that could've done it. Jace knew that.

"The plans to remodel the school had gotten approved last fall in a town meeting. That means that either the committee chair is involved or the mayor's fucking involved. Jace was busy. He must own the police force too, to get the river runs flagged through or at least not checked ever. And that second warehouse, it's right smack in the middle of some property that my dad bought six years ago. The warehouse, by default, is owned by my dad."

"Guess your dad's not as inactive in South America as you thought."

Tray looked like he could murder someone. In that moment, that second, I really believed he could've.

"That means I own the building."

I heard it in his voice.

I heard his decision made and I looked back, my breath captive in my throat as I searched his eyes. Trying to figure out what he was really thinking.

"What are you going to do?" I asked hoarsely, not really wanting to know.

Tray grinned. It was a bitter, hardened grin. And it made me want him. In that second I could've taken him down, because I was finding that his ruthlessness was a turn-on for me.

"I'm going to foreclose on some of my properties."

"That'll tip 'em off."

"No. I'm going to have it done when we have everything we need and we can't be touched. That's when I'll sic my lawyers on 'em."

"Your dad gave you power of attorney over everything?"

"Yeah. Over everything, but he probably didn't figure I'd find these out."

"So you actually own the warehouse, but that doesn't help us getting in there."

"No, but it'll make me feel better, knowing that I can take it away from Lanser," Tray bit out, running a hand over his tired face.

"Are you going to make it through school?"

"Yeah, I'll be fine. I probably just won't be able to make sense of a whole lot."

"So what else did you find out?" Again. I didn't know if I wanted to know. Everything he told me made my stomach roll over.

"There's a field that connects the warehouse to the river, which is probably how they get everything into the school. I really think everything's just being stored until the drug-runners can load up for another run. But I'm also pretty sure it's not just drugs, but a whole ton of shit. Brian had a bracelet for you, right? No doubt that was hocked somewhere, waiting to be sold to a highest bidder on the black-market."

"How are they getting everyone in and out of Pedlam without the cops noticing? They can't have every cop on their payroll."

"The conferences," Tray explained. "There are conferences and concerts in Pedlam all the time. And those numbers have actually gone up, so that means more and more people are going through Pedlam. I don't think it's a coincidence that most of those concerts are booked to play at the Seven8 or that most of the conferences are held in a banquet recreation center, which my father also owns."

"And now you own."

"Yeah," he sounded bitter, "I didn't know that I was a fucking landlord."

"If you have power of attorney, how is it that none of these rewards are going to you?"

"Some of them are, I'm sure. My dad was chief of police, but my mom actually had a real-estate business. So a lot of her properties are still thriving and that money goes to my account. I don't check it on a monthly basis. I usually have my accountants check it around tax time, but I'm betting Dad had it worked so that everything filtered through Galverson's accounts first."

"Wow."

"Tell me about it."

"A lot of planning and thinking went into this."

"And we figured it out in the matter of a week. Give or take."

"You figured this out. And you did it all in one night," I breathed, appreciating how intelligent Tray really was. No wonder his brother wanted him on his side. Tray was formidable, either way. As an ally or an enemy. I wouldn't want to go against him, but then again, that's what people say about me, too.

"Yeah, well...you gave me the right motivation."

"Would you rather I didn't? That I wouldn't have done anything, even moved here?"

"No." It was quick and so sure, I never doubted the genuineness. The honesty rang true in his voice.

I found myself melting, a familiar emotion when I was around this boy.

Checking the clock, I saw it was almost seven.

Fucking seven in the morning.

"We have to be at school in an hour and half."

Thank God I'd packed a bag last week, planning on being at Tray's for a while. I was in no mood to slip into my room, dress, and sneak back out. And if I ran into either Shelley or Kevin, I don't think I could keep my fucking composure. But right now, I was good. I was steady. Just wanting to get in, get whatever information we needed, find Grayley, and get out. Ready to take everyone down with us, if need be.

"I'd offer to have sex with you, but I'm afraid I'd fall asleep after and not wake up." Tray joked as he yawned, standing to go into the kitchen.

I followed and hopped on a barstool, watching him refill his mug. As he took a second one out for me, I remarked, "So we're both sans-parents."

Tray grinned at that, sweetening my coffee. I'd like to think I'm one of those hard-asses who only take their coffee black—black and strong. But I'm not. I've got a sweet tooth, hence my addiction to Tray Evans.

The sex was not just sweet, but it melted my pants off. Every time.

I grinned at that thought.

"I'm going to go and shower." Tray set the mug in front of me and headed out the backdoor, to the pool-house.

Checking the clock, I remembered that Brian used to always be up at rehab by this time. Grabbing my cell, I called the main desk. Patricia might still be working. Sometimes she'd do overnights and she always patched me to Brian's room. It was nice being liked by the front desk clerk.

"Hello, Northeast Rehabilitation Center. This is Patricia speaking."

"Pat, it's Taryn."

"Oh, Taryn!" I heard the warmth in her voice. "How are you, dear?"

"I'm good. I was wondering if my sister might be awake?"

"I'll put you through right away. You come and visit, Taryn. I mean it." Then I heard her transfer me.

"Hello?" Mandy was awake, but barely, by the sound of it.

"Hey, sis."

"Taryn?!" she asked sharply, suddenly more awake.

"The one and only, sister dear."

"Holy shit. How are you? Are you okay? Tray called me Saturday morning. I'm so sorry, Taryn."

"I'm...," I hesitated. This was Mandy and I had grown to love her, even if I were just worth a mere ten million to her parents. "I'm getting through it."

"I thought I had it bad, you bringing me, but man—I don't know what I would do if anything happened to Devon."

"And speaking of Devon, does he know where you are?"

"Yeah, I called him. He came to visit Sunday and yesterday."

"Tray said Shelley and Kevin showed up at his house yesterday looking for me."

"Yeah, the counselors called them. I think they're coming out today to see me. Not looking forward to that."

"Austin said your mom found your pills one other time."

"Whatever. Those were more her pills than mine. Dad was there, that's the only reason she even made a big deal about them."

I was right. But my heart just dropped a little at the knowledge.

"But I'm going to say something when they get here. I even talked to my one-on-one counselor about it. Karen said they can't make Mom stay and get into rehab, but she said it's good to have everything out in the open. It jumpstarts the healing process or some shit like that."

I had to grin at that. Mandy. Swearing. I must be rubbing off on her.

"So, you got through the weekend? I know those are the hardest, the first few days."

"Yeah, it sucks, but...I'm here for a reason. Devon broke down crying on Sunday and that just killed me. But I needed to see that, you know. Karen said I need to know how my actions and decisions affect other people. Something about The Impact."

I remembered. The Impact referred to how you hurt others by your decisions and how your decision was a selfish act. Kind of like a ripple effect. I'd heard before when I attended a few sessions with Brian. But later he told me that he got more motivated from watching me leave with Jace. He hated any time I spent with Jace while he was in rehab. It just grated at him.

The Impact had no impact.

"It's good that you saw that."

"Yeah, well...I hope Devon doesn't start sleeping with Jasmine again. That'd be awful."

Oh the weight of her problems. She's in rehab and she's worrying that her boyfriend might cheat on her.

"I think you have more important issues to deal with," I said lightly.

"I know, but still...it'd be just like him to use this as an excuse. He'd probably say something like he couldn't handle the pressure of having his girlfriend in rehab so he slept with Jasmine when he was weak."

"Should've stuck with Carter."

Mandy was silent at that. We both knew Carter wouldn't ever cheat on her, even for all his loud-mouthed reputation. We both knew the real Carter and he's not weak like Devon. But Mandy had chosen and she'd chosen what was more comfortable for her.

"So should I tell Mom and Dad where you're hiding out at? Or keep my mouth shut?"

"Tray told 'em I was in Pedlam. I'd prefer if they believed that." But I didn't want her to feel like she owed me anything.

"Okay, Mom and Dad are fine as long as you're not with Tray. Someone must've told them that you guys are dating for them to ever show up there. I bet that went off well when they heard that. Mom and Dad hate Tray. Especially Mom, but you'd think Dad would hate him more."

"I think they'll forget about it when they get there," I said dryly, reaching for my coffee.

"Yeah. Good point." Mandy yawned on her end.

"I'm going to go, but I'll call you later."

"Okay. Thanks for calling, sis."

"Yeah. Bye."

"Love you."

My phone halted, mid-motion when I heard her. I found myself pulling the phone back to my ear and I said softly, "Love you too."

I did. It's why I did what I did for her.

Hell. I'd even started to love the fourteen year old punk.

School was easier to get through than what I'd thought. Maybe it was because I knew things were in motion. Maybe it was because I knew that my life, and Tray's, would irrevocably be changed. Somehow. Or maybe it was because I wasn't quite ready for what was coming.

I was itching to get inside that warehouse.

But I'd swim after school. That'd help. Hopefully Coach would even have us race today. I had energy to burn. And, of course, none of it had to do with the fact that I'd slept from eight at night till five-thirty in the morning. That's like...nine and a half hours of sleep.

Tray: zero.

I still felt bad about that.

I was surprised, a good surprise, to see that Brady had first and second period with me. Who'da thunk it.

Brady waved me over in first period. Tray looked half dead in second period, but I didn't need to worry. Carter sat beside him and was keeping him awake, by annoying him.

Molly grinned welcomingly as I sat beside her. This was my third or fourth time actually going to XX. I still liked to skip for study hall, but just pretended that I kept forgetting.

Brady slid into a seat at the table behind us with another swimmer, Lexie.

I introduced Molly to them and I thought Molly would die happy. Brady and Lexie immediately enfolded her in their clique.

I glanced over, and saw that Tray was watching me. I smiled, a soft smile and he returned it.

"That's a Tray that I've never seen before," Brady remarked, catching the look we shared.

"What do you mean?"

"He's transformed."

"But he's still hot," Lexie put her two cents in.

"He's like a tamed panther," Molly remarked. Which shocked me. She was talking with two strangers. Getting with Larkins was working, kinda like action therapy or something.

"Kind of, yeah," Brady remarked, frowning slightly at Molly, like she was an enigma to her.

Molly noticed the look and quickly looked to her lap. She was back to being an Invisible.

I nudged her shoulder and commented, "Tray'll like being called a tamed panther. I'll tell him that tonight when we're having sex."

"Oh God." The blush was back. I couldn't go a day at school without at least one from her.

Brady and Lexie grinned, seeing my amusement.

"He'll think I'm calling him a sex panther."

Anchorman was just one of the greats. No way around it.

Brady and Lexie laughed at that.

"Do you have to be so loud and annoying?"

Of course, I couldn't go through one morning without at least one attack by either Amber, Sasha, or now Tristan.

This time, it was Sasha.

"Mr. Hauge," Sasha whined, her voice actually grating against my ears, "can they please work quietly? This isn't social hour."

But before I could blast her right back—and I had the perfect comeback—Tray yawned, and remarked casually, "Just shut up the fuck up, Klinnleys. You're irritating."

And that was all it took. I knew Sasha wouldn't say one word to me for the rest of the year.

The sleeping panther god had spoken.

"Yep," Brady whispered," tamed."

But Sasha had been quieted. Now I only had Amber and Tristan to look forward to.

Note that Tray didn't get reprimanded for swearing in front of the teacher. The panther god was above that rule. But whatever. He was mine.

Third and fourth passed without event. And lunch was a surprise. I sat with Brady and the rest. Molly even came over towards the end when Kayden and Angela had sulked off to the shadows. She was welcomed whole-heartedly, which made me happy. But sad at the same time because it meant Kayden and Angela might be losing a friend. But another Invisible would probably take Molly's place, eventually.

I didn't look for Props, figured he was already on his computer.

Tray sat, sleeping, at the table with the 'popular' crowd: Carter, Amber, Jasmine, Bryce, and Devon. Devon had been watching me throughout lunch, but I had no inclination to go over and talk to him. I'd done my part and had called Mandy. That was enough. I did not need to go make nice to her probably-future-cheating boyfriend.

By seventh period I'd come to the realization that school had become boring. When did school become boring? People either didn't say anything to me, especially after Tray shot down Sasha, but I noticed that this had started the week before. I must've been getting a reputation not to be messed with. Maybe. I don't know, but I realized that either they didn't say anything to me or whatever I said, went. Just like that.

I'd never had that power.

That's what Tray must feel like on a daily basis, for years now.

Wow. It was...just powerful. A control that you couldn't even explain. But it was also boring. No wonder I'd rocked his world.

Swimming helped with the restless energy that I was carrying around. Coach paired us off. Lexie and I raced first. I won. I won every match after that and I saw our coach a bit speechless at times.

I relished the victory over Tristan. I kicked her ass. Which felt so good. And Brady and I were the last match of practice. Everyone had been holding their breaths. Brady and I both consecutively won every match. There were a few others who had won, but it was me and Brady matching up. Everyone knew.

And when the gun went off, I dove in and poured all my fury into my swimming.

Shelley. Kevin. Jace. Galverson. Hell, even Devon. Everything.

And I was surprised when I finished and saw that I was three complete laps ahead of Brady.

The coach had dropped his clipboard.

"Nationals here we come." One of the girls whistled. The rest were still amazed. Speechless.

Tristan looked...constipated. I didn't know what that look was. I couldn't tell if she was angry, jealous, or glad.

"Okay." The coach tried for dignified as he stooped to pick up his clipboard. "That's practice today."

As I left, Brady walking beside me, I saw the rest of the girls take notice. Brady was okay being second. She was okay that I was first, so the rest would be too.

Tray was sitting at my locker, his eyes closed, probably sleeping.

Brady and I paused as we stood there, just in front of him.

"Get up, you dumbass, you're not sleeping." His breathing wasn't deep enough or even enough.

"Doesn't mean I wasn't trying," he remarked, but kept his eyes closed. But he said, as I opened my locker, "Gentley called. They got what we wanted."

I looked up, alarmed, since Brady was still there. Tray hadn't seen her yet.

"Brady, you know Tray?"

Tray opened his eyes at that one and cursed, swiftly standing up.

"I know who Tray Evans is," Brady said lightly, "but I doubt he knows who I am."

"Bannon's girlfriend, right?" Tray held his hand out, "Nice to meet you. You a friend of Taryn's?"

"Yep, I'd like to think so. We're on the swim team together."

"Brady's one of the captains, which says something since she's still a junior," I remarked, grabbing my bag and purse.

Tray nodded, silent.

"It's nice to formally meet you, Tray, although we've met many times in elementary." Which was true, but this was a social introduction. Everyone really knew everyone, when you got down to it. But socially, Brady had just jumped up a level. She needed a proper introduction for that.

"You too. You're number one in class, right?" Tray had surprised her. I could tell because Brady was momentarily speechless, before she replied, "Uh, yeah."

"I'm second," he said swiftly, grinning cockily.

"You are?" I don't think she meant to have such dumbfounded shock in her voice.

"Tray's actually a genius," I remarked, leaning my back against him, feeling his hand come around to rest on my waist, hooking his finger on one of my belt loops. "He just acts dumb most of the time."

Tray chuckled, kissing the side of my face, "You never cared about my intelligence before."

"As long as you keep performing well in bed, I won't ever have to." I grinned. Joking.

"Okay," Brady remarked, nodding, "well, I'll see you tomorrow. I might hit the pool early if you want to join me, Taryn."

"Maybe." But I knew I wouldn't. I'd be lucky if I was even in school tomorrow at all.

When she left, Tray murmured quietly, for my ears only, "Ready to go?"

I met his eyes and we both knew I was—I'd been ready since this entire war had been declared.

I was pretty sure Brady wouldn't have recognized me, if she saw me in that second. But Tray and I, we were in perfect accord.

Both of us were ready to end this. One way or another.

CHAPTER TWENTY FIVE

You'd think that a person, staring across an open valley, knowing the odds of getting across and into the warehouse that stood high above everything else were not good...would feel something. Maybe fear. Maybe trepidation. Maybe hesitation. You'd think, right?

But no. A hell no.

I stood there. I stood standing above that valley, seeing the warehouse below me, and I felt strong. I felt good.

I was ready, maybe too ready.

The guards' just had shift change, there was one every twelve hours on the dot with a break every four hours. The perimeter was easy enough to cross. It'd take me a little while to cover it without attracting too much notice, but it was dark out. That'd help. I was dressed all in black, same material as before. The way it melted around all my curves and had been rewarded with a soft groan from Tray.

Gentley had gotten his hands on the blueprints, I had no idea how he'd managed that. But he had. And Trent vouched for him, otherwise I wouldn't have taken the prints. Of course, both of them had been plenty pissed when Tray informed them they wouldn't be a part of it. I'd thought, for a brief second, that they'd come to blows. Either Trent and Tray. Or Gentley and Tray. If they went at it, I was ready to scram for the safe, and break inside of it to get the gun inside. But apparently Gentley calmed enough to keep in control. He'd held Trent back, but it hadn't saved me from quite a few curses sent my way.

Tray ordered them out at that point.

My big protective boyfriend. Of course, he did have that scary lethal side to him that always helped.

The warehouse was protected by one outer wall made of wire. I'd grabbed some heavy-steel clippers for that. And the walls would be climbed with my hooks and grabs. I didn't want to burden myself with too much and rope, complete with clanky karabiners would not work. Not for this job.

I started off, at a light trot, not fast enough to get noticed but enough to cover the ground efficiently. As I neared the wall, I pulled the clippers out and cut a hole out that was big enough for me to get through. The guards had moved back inside, so I quickly made work of the wall and was standing on the roof in no time.

Tray was right. Whatever was inside wasn't valuable, otherwise it would've been a lot harder to get this close.

Slipping through a vent at the top, I fell lightly to the flooring below. It wasn't too far for a jump and I landed gracefully on my feet, like always. Hugging the wall with my back, I crept down the hallway, quickly finding the guards inside. As I circled around them, nearly invisible to their line of sight, I headed to the basement.

It was an open warehouse inside and when I got to the main room, I was surprised.

It was empty. Completely and utterly empty.

Which sucked ass.

Swearing, I did a walk-about, making sure to cover every single corner, nook, and cranny. Any little thing would help us out. But there was one thing for sure that we got from this trip.

If this warehouse wasn't being used, that meant everything was underneath the school.

And I already knew how to break into that building.

Something caught my eyes, I couldn't tell you what, but I knelt in a far corner. Running my hand over the flooring, I realized something had been lodged just underneath the floor grating. Twisting my finger underneath the grating, I tried to pull the item out. My skin got snagged on the jagged edge, which brought some silent curses to mind, but I managed to maneuver the item out and realized, another surprise, it was a cellphone.

Correction: It was Grayley's cell phone.

Pocketing it, not allowing myself to feel momentary hope, I finished scanning the rest of the room.

A big fat nothing.

Fuck.

So I moved to the next floor and proceeded, until every empty room had been surveyed.

Nothing. So this left me with a dilemma—the two guards in the surveillance room.

Two large, able-bodied guards.

But everything I needed, or could use to get my hands on, sat right before their hands and feet.

So this meant that I either had to get Tray in here for him to do the deed...or I had to take down these two burly guys.

So I did what every proud standing burglar would do.

I grabbed my taser in one hand, a pipe in the other and I headed in.

Surprise was pretty much my only element. As I hit one guy on the back of his head, using every ounce of my body strength behind the pipe, I scrambled and quickly tasered the second guy.

And both went down...after a few more jolts for my own safety.

I downloaded everything I could get my hands on. I remembered everything, everything, that Geezer had taught me. I'm not a computer hacker extraordinaire, apparently not even as much as Tray is or Props or Geezer, but I could hold my own if it came down to it. Bottom line. I could do enough damage, but what I couldn't get...the guards knew I was there. They'd seen me. I was probably on their video surveillance, somewhere, and so I took the pipe and rained free.

The printers went first.

The keyboards bounced up and down, the buttons popped out.

Thump.

The chairs smashed against the walls.

The desks were overturned.

Thump.

The cables were yanked out of the walls and they came crashing down.

The televisions were pulled down, kicked over.

Thump.

And I turned, my chest heaving, my heart beat deafening my ears and I gripped the pipe harder. My knuckles turned white as I gripped it, and I swung, every muscle in my body behind that swing, and I smashed the hell out of every fucking screen that was in that room. One. Two. Fucking six and seven.

Every single one of them.

As the glass sprayed my body, some falling to my hair, it dusted over my body and the ground. But I kept swinging until every damn piece of glass had been shattered.

And then I turned and walked out, a smug smile crossed my face as I left the room. When the door clicked shut, the lights clicked off, like poetry and I was quickly out of the warehouse and moving back over the field, knowing I'd resolved some of my anger behind.

Calmly, I walked up to the car and moved to the front seat.

Tray was in the driver's seat and I saw his eyebrows rise slightly at my appearance. The shattered glass had become a second coating on my body, but it didn't cut. Nothing cut anymore.

Without a single word spoken between us, Tray drove us back to his home.

I gave him the cellphone and the flash drive before I went and showered.

I had turned off. My body was on automatic and my mind was on pause, resting. I don't know, I didn't really give a shit. All I knew was that I was in simmering mode, ever since I decided to trash that fucking room.

An hour later, fully washed, each piece of glass had been swept up and deposited in a plastic bag, I walked into the kitchen and saw Tray lounging on the counter.

"You find anything on the phone?"

"Yeah." He had that look again. The same one he had when he told me I'd been adopted.

"What is it?" I asked, almost bored. But like I said, nothing could cut me anymore.

"He called Brian thirteen times a few days before Brian's car accident."

I just waited.

"And he called the Seven8 three times. He called Geezer once and there was a video."

"A video of what?"

"Of Grayley having a conversation with Jace."

I saw Tray pause.

"Of what?" I bit out.

"They talked about Brian. The video cut just when Grayley accused Jace of killing Brian."

"Where was the video taken?"

"Couldn't tell. It was just a dark room. But...there was an alarm in the back."

"An alarm? A security alarm?"

"No. A bell, like one that goes off at the end of class."

"They were in the school? A school bell?"

"I think so, yeah."

"So that means that Grayley's there—in the school?"

"I don't know, Taryn. I just know that's where he was when he took the video, but the phone was in the second warehouse. An empty warehouse."

"What about the flash drive. Did you find anything?"

"Your friend Props is coming over. He's going to take a look at it, see if he can find anything."

"And until then...what?"

"Until then, we sit and wait."

"We sit and wait?" Are you kidding me? "Jace'll know I was there. I trashed their security room, Tray. What do you think he'll do when he finds out? He's going to come straight here. We can't afford to just sit and wait!"

"And we don't have enough to move on, Taryn. I'm not going into that school unless I know exactly what we're getting ourselves into."

"What was the point of us even going into that warehouse!?" I shrieked. My best friend was missing. My ex-boyfriend was dead and we were just sitting and waiting. Fuck waiting. "I'm going to the Seven8. I'm going to find Jace and make him talk!"

Tray stopped me before I'd gone two steps.

"No, you're not," he said firmly, his hand on my elbow.

I yanked my arm away and took a stand. "You have no idea, Tray!"

He got right in my face. "I have every idea, Taryn!"

"Fuck you!"

"You can check that off the list!"

I hated him. I really, really hated him, but I tried a different way. "We know how to break into that school. I already did it once, I can do it again."

"No."

"Tray."

"No."

"Tray, come on."

Neither of us heard the doorbell because Tray turned and snapped, "I said no, Taryn! We got nothing. I'd hoped for a little more than a fucking empty warehouse, but that's what Jace gave us. He's one step ahead of us. He knows we broke in and didn't get anything. My guess is that it's what he wanted all along. That was the entire purpose of the fucking warehouse, of Grayley's car being ditched and fuck—probably even the cell phone."

"The phone was underneath a floor tile, I don't think it had been strategically placed." I retorted.

"Um...hey guys."

Props had not chosen his timing well because both of us turned and glared at him.

Props gulped and scurried into the library.

"It doesn't matter, Taryn. You're not leaving because I know you'll go to the school and that's not going to happen. Not yet, anyway."

"When?"

"I don't know," he muttered, cursing under his breath.

"They have my best friend." I said quietly. "I don't want to go to his funeral."

"You won't."

"You can't promise me that."

"Then stop making me say shit like that!" Tray snapped. "You were two seconds away from running out. What do you think would happen if you got in that school and you found Grayley?"

"I would've gotten him out."

"No. You would've gotten killed because I can guarantee that he wouldn't be alone. You may be able to do a lot of shit, but some stuff you just can't. That's just how it is, Taryn."

"I am sick and tired of you—"

"What the hell is this?!" Tray shouted. "You're cold before and now you're looking for someone to take it out on? I got picked because I won't let you get yourself killed? Is that what this is about?"

"Shut up."

"You said that you wouldn't make a move without my say-so. I'm not giving it now. I run this show, Taryn. There's a reason why you put me in charge. So just let me do this and I'm saying—now is not the time to go running to Jace for a confrontation. If the car was purposely put there and he wanted that warehouse empty...it's to get you to come to him. That's exactly what he wants and I'm saying no. We go in on our terms, not his."

"Fuck—"

"Hey ho!"

"What the fuck is this? A fucking nightclub?!" I shrieked. Add infantile tantrum to my resume, I'd ceased caring.

But Gentley and Trent walked in, glancing between the two of us.

Whistling softly, Gentley taunted, "Trouble in paradise?"

"Fuck off, Gentley!" I snarled, sending him a heated glare.

"I said I'd call if we had anything," Tray said tensely, standing just behind me.

"I'm not running off so you can back the fuck off," I growled over my shoulder.

Tray ignored me. "We don't have anything, not yet."

"We'll wait," Trent retorted smoothly, jumping on the counter.

"Tray! Yo!" Carter called from the front foyer.

Of all times, this was really the time when I truly, absolutely, with my very last breath, hated that Tray had allowed his house to become the local hangout of the popular crowd. Fuck the circumstances behind the reason.

"Get rid of him. Now." I snapped.

Tray lost it because he turned on me, "You can stop with this bitch attitude any second now because I'm two seconds from locking you in my bedroom."

Carter walked in, with Amber and Tristan—of all people—in tow when I retorted, underneath my breath, "Like it'd keep me in."

Tray clamped a hand on my arm when he turned to greet his friends, "Hey, guys."

"Whoa." Carter came to a halt, seeing Gentley and Trent. "Uh...what's going on?"

"Tea party," Gentley replied sarcastically.

Amber giggled nervously. Tristan paled. But Carter just grinned and let out a whoop, "Sweet! Is it spiked?" He danced over to Tray and threw an arm around his shoulders, "Seriously, dude. What the hell?"

Tray shrugged him off, but he did it so nicely I doubted Carter even realized he'd been shrugged off. "We're just talking. What are you guys doing here?"

"Oh!" Carter brightened. "Well, if you have to force it out of me, you have to force it out of me."

Tristan rolled her eyes.

"But me and Tristan here have a bet. We bet how long it'd take for Amber to get you in bed. Tristan said never, but I have faith in Amber. She knows your old tricks. I give her a good hour, at least."

Trent swore while Gentley laughed.

Tray sucked in his breath while I wrenched my arm free.

As I stalked forward, I said quietly, dangerously, "Are you able to recognize when someone's about to commit murder? Because if you don't, this is what they look like." I pointed to my face. "I'm at the end of my rope to play games with you tonight. So if you still want to be here at this school and not have your mommy and daddy get a call from your old school due to some suspicious break-ins, I'd scurry your ass off. Now."

"Taryn," Tray said quietly.

I proceeded, "If the bet was really to see how quick you could push my lid tonight, whoever bet a fucking second won. My lid's been pushed since last week, so if you want to keep pushing it, go ahead. Just don't come crying to Tray when you get the results full-blast."

"Taryn, that's enough." Tray pushed me back. "Go check on Props. See if he's got anything."

"I'm just getting started," I said smoothly. And it was true. I could go all night. I was in the mood.

"Right now all you're doing is making yourself look like you have PMS. I don't think that's what you want, so go get some results out of Props and then we can talk about moving forward."

"Tray."

"No, Taryn. Props. Light a fucking fire under his ass." Tray shoved me inside and then slammed the door shut.

I turned and saw Props gulping—again—as he took in the look on my face.

"Relax," I murmured, tiredly. The fight had drained out of me when that door slammed shut. "You find anything on that flash drive?"

He still looked nervous, but he said, "Uh, yeah...I mean...just a bunch of videos and stuff."

"What's on the videos?"

"A bunch of guys coming and going. Nothing too interesting."

"Let me see." I leaned over his shoulder and watched as the screen lit up. But what I saw was enough to make me speechless.

Holy. Fucking. Shit.

I saw myself staring at an older version of Tray, walking with a slender female.

They walked in, they walked out. And the rest was of security guards changing shifts.

"So, like I said, not much," Props murmured. "The cameras were wiped every eight hours. So whatever else was on here was wiped clean. It's a loop surveillance. It loops over and over, just recording over whatever was there before unless a new video is inserted. But you got this off the mainframe, so my guess is that this is all there was."

But it was something.

"Make copies and send these to your safe accounts. I don't want anyone else getting this information, you got it?"

Props sighed, but moved to the keyboard.

When I walked back in the kitchen, Amber was going off, "She's such a bitch, Tray! I don't see what you see in her. She just went off on Carter like a homicidal psychopath."

But my cool was back, because I smirked, "Please. Just a homicidal psychopath? I would've hoped for a raging homicidal psychopath, at least."

I didn't miss Tray going rigid when I stepped back in the room. I didn't like it, but I didn't comment on it. It was warranted.

"Hey, Taryn," Carter started, "I, uh...sorry. I didn't mean to press your buttons like that."

"Yes, you did." Duh. "But it's fine. You got me in a rare moment and I let myself go off. It won't happen again."

Carter blinked. There was no other description for his reaction.

Gentley must've been bored because he spoke up, "Can we get some business dealt with tonight? As amusing as this entertainment *is* tonight, Gardner and I didn't come into non-friendly territory for the hell of it."

I remarked, "We didn't get anything."

"But what about the warehouse?"

"What warehouse? What are you guys talking about?" Carter asked. The joys of being blissfully ignorant.

"Empty," Tray clipped out, sighing deeply.

"But—"

"It was empty. Everything was empty."

"So what—" Trent started.

Amber interrupted, "Who's Props?"

Tristan was quiet, wisely. But she was watching everything.

"No one," I said firmly.

Tray sighed, but he affirmed, "No one, Amber."

"What's going on here?" Tristan decided to speak up, none the wiser. But she was alert as she asked, "What's been going on for a while? Because something's been going on. I know that much. Does it have to do with Mandy? Is Mandy okay?"

"She's fine and it has nothing to do with Mandy." I promised.

"Tray, what's up?" Carter tried a different tactic.

"Nothing. You guys should just go, okay?" Tray sounded tired, which he had a right. But, watching him, I knew he'd get a lot more on his plate before the end of the night.

"But—"

"Fucking leave, alright!" Gentley rasped out. "Holy fuck, you people are annoying. He said to leave, so fucking leave."

Amber looked indignant, but Carter read the message when Tray didn't speak up against Gentley. Carter grabbed Amber's arm and led her outside with Tristan trailing behind, but not before sending me a quelling glance.

I turned away.

"What'd you find out, Taryn?" Trent was the one who asked. All three were watching me, but I cut my eyes to Tray. He read the message immediately because he said, "We got an empty warehouse, that's it. So you guys can leave until we find out more. Trust me, we'll be moving on whatever we find but right now—that's nothing. So leave."

Trent was about to argue, but Gentley must've thought better of it because he grabbed Trent's arm and jerked his head to the door.

Trent wearily accepted and followed, reluctantly.

The door closed shut, an echoing sound.

And Tray asked quietly, "So what did you find?"

I looked up and met his gaze. He knew I found something, it was the only reason I would've come back as quickly as I had. But I was reluctant to say it. But I did anyway.

"Your brother's on the video. He's with a girl."

Tray froze.

And then he stormed out to the library.

From the force Tray pushed through the door, Props fell over in his chair, startled. It would've been funny in any other circumstance, but Tray's eyes were riveted on the screen where an enlarged image had been froze in place.

Tray shut down. In that second, I knew he'd shut down. Everything else, even when Galverson had shown up, Tray hadn't shut down. He'd gotten through it, but this time—it scared me.

Tray scared me.

The situation scared me.

"Tray," I whispered hoarsely.

"That's Chance," he said, "and that's Lily."

Chance was with Galverson's daughter. I'd already figured it out.

"Tray, I'm—"

"If you say you're sorry, I will—" But he didn't finish the threat.

"I'm understanding," I only said. It was true. I'd lost Brian. I might lose Grayley and Tray was just reminded, in video animation, what he'd walked away from a long while ago: his family.

"Uh," Props squeaked out, terrified, "I stamped the time for when they went inside and when they left. It was today, at 6:03 p.m. They left exactly twelve minutes later."

Chance was in town. Tray's brother was in Pedlam, a mere four hours before we'd gotten there

And Chance had waltzed in, unannounced, but still allowed. He was either undercover or he was working with Jace.

Fuck.

Chance was known so there was no way he was working undercover.

"Tray," I whispered again, realizing what he'd already figured out the second he saw his brother's image.

"Don't," he clipped out, his jaw clenched, "just don't."

He walked out of the room, his shoulders rigid.

I walked Props out, reassuring him everything was fine and thanked him for his help. As I shut the door behind him, I doubted the guy would ever help us again. He actually had peed his pants, a tiny bit, when Tray turned into scary maniac guy.

I sighed, locking the door and wandered through the house. I shut off all the lights and found Tray in the glass patio, like so many other times. I was starting to realize that was where he went to think.

I sat quietly in the seat beside him and drew my knees to my chest. I sat and waited. I'd wait until morning if need be.

It wasn't long before Tray spoke, in a low monotone voice, "Chance is working with either Lanser or Galverson. I don't know what the alliance is between Lanser and

Galverson anymore, but Chance has to be working with one of them."

"What about your dad?"

"Dad works with Galverson, but he must've joined with Jace for your adoption. It was orchestrated by all of them. Had to be."

"What makes you wonder about their alliance? With Jace and Galverson, I mean?"

"Because Chance hates our dad. He wouldn't work with him, no matter what. So that means that he's working with one side while Dad's working on the other side. I'm betting that they're keeping them separate."

"I thought Chance hated Galverson."

"He did. He does. That hate doesn't ever change."

And Tray would know.

He said again, "If Jace wanted us to go to that warehouse, he wanted us to know that my brother was here. But I don't get why. It's pissing me off."

"Maybe he didn't want us to know."

"Then what were they using that warehouse for?"

"I don't know." And it was true; I wasn't the mastermind, not like Tray or Jace or Galverson.

Tray fell silent, so I said, matter-of-factly, "We don't know what Jace wanted or not. We don't know why your brother is here or why Jace wanted me to be adopted. But what I do know is that Brian died for something. And that something has something to do with Jace and Galverson. And I know that if we don't move quickly, I might be losing another person I consider family. I can't lose one more person."

Tray turned and met my eyes. He said honestly, "I don't know what's going to happen."

I whispered hoarsely, "I don't think we are going to know what's going to happen. But what we know is enough for me."

"Worst case scenario: we get in there and find Grayley dead and we die," Tray spoke, but continued when I flinched, "and best case scenario: we get in there and we get him out, alive."

"But what about taking everyone down?"

"I don't know. I haven't figured that out yet."

That was the crux of it: Tray thought everything out. He had every angle covered, but with this—he couldn't cover every angle because he didn't know how all the pieces fit together.

It was time we figured the puzzle out.

"There's a reason why Jace wanted me gone," I murmured. "I'm good, Tray. I can get in there and I can get out. No one will even know I'm there." It was true. Galverson wanted me gone because of what I could do. It was power, in the skill I'd developed and sharpened over my life—it was powerful.

It was the power to be invisible.

And it made men like Galverson break out in hives.

"Taryn—" Tray whispered, hoarse.

"It's time, Tray."

It was. We both knew it.

CHAPTER TWENTY SIX

It was morning, just before the crack of dawn, and I was sitting with my coffee, just staring out at the window, daring the sun to peak over the horizon. Tray had fallen asleep, he was nestled underneath the covers, looking like my gorgeous protective angel.

I'd fallen in love with him. I had and it didn't scare me anymore. It didn't cause my heart to contract or fall to the pit of my stomach.

I loved that boy behind me, looking all delectable and shit.

He'd told me first. He'd told me he'd fallen, but the 'L' word hadn't been included. That was alright. It was there between us and we both knew it.

And me yelling at him, him yelling back, we both knew it was alright. It was the atmosphere around us. It encased us, a protective shell where it was safe for us to disagree and rage and still know we'd be there for each other.

I'd lost Brian and it didn't cripple me, it didn't paralyze me. And I might lose Grayley and that didn't even freeze me in place. Brian had been my anchor through my life in the past. I'd had been fortunate enough that I got to say goodbye.

I'd gotten more than what Tray had been dealt.

His brother beat the shit out of him after threatening him to choose between him and his father.

He'd been a kid, a fucking kid going through puberty. He was supposed to worry about how many girls liked him, not which family member would be walking out of his life.

But Tray had done what so many could never fathom. He'd stood on his own. He'd decided that he wouldn't bow to either, so he told 'em both to fuck off.

I loved a man like that.

And he was right. Tray wasn't a kid. He'd ceased being a kid long ago. He was a man, he may be in high school, but he's a man nonetheless.

I loved him.

And I loved him even more because he'd be going into that school with me, at my back, ready to handle whatever came at us.

It had been right. Jace had been right. Whatever had been going on, I wouldn't have stood for it. He just messed up and didn't make sure my adoption took me clear away from Pedlam.

The time was right. What Tray and I were about to do was right.

So I found myself standing, in the wake of morning, watching the horizon that was still encased in darkness.

And I felt right, for the first fucking time in my life.

I was meant to do this.

I was meant to be here, with this man, and I had my purpose laid out before me.

"Hey," Tray whispered, moving to stand behind me. He pulled me against his chest as he wrapped his arms around my waist.

I let my head fall against his chest. "Hey," I said softly, still watching the sun.

He dipped to rest his chin in the crook of my neck and shoulder. "You ready?"

"Yeah."

"Let's go," he murmured, before moving to dress.

I turned and dressed in my normal work outfit. The same snug black lycra fabric, complete with everything I needed to break-in. I'd made Tray unearth the PRS-500. The codes were still there and I knew how to override them, but who knew if the same codes were still activated for the warehouse or not. Jace most certainly had them changed, but there was a wireless connection to the PRS-500. So that meant it was possible that only the codes to the school would be changed. All the codes on the device were still active, which meant that the connection was still bridged and working. Bottom line: the codes might've been automatically downloaded to the PRS-500, granting us open access.

Let's hope anyway.

Tray left the room for a minute and I met him in the kitchen.

"So what's the plan again?" I asked for the third time, still not totally believing his choice of accomplices. You'd think Carter, Bryce, Devon, or any one of his friends, but no, .he chose Gentley.

"Gentley's going to be watching the parking lot when you go in. I'll circle around to the river's opening."

"And explain again...him?"

Tray just grinned, but spoke, "Gentley runs that school. He knows who belongs and who doesn't. Plus, he can carry his own. There's a reason why he runs that school and someone else doesn't."

"He's an ass. It's the only reason."

"Then I'd probably have whoever else ran the school to help us. I need someone who can give orders over there and they be followed out. Trust me, he's not a bud, but he'll do."

"He's an ass. I don't like working with asses."

"No," Tray grinned cockily, "but you'll screw 'em."

Gentley would have to do, I guess. But I didn't like it.

Tray sighed. "Just trust me, Taryn. This is my part, what I can do. You'll be doing your job, but I'm telling you that we'll need a third guy on this. Gentley's the best choice, but only because it's his territory."

"It's Jace's territory, not Gentley's."

"No, but Gentley's the acting owner. You know what I mean."

But I was a shit, so I asked even though I fully knew the answer. "And why are we doing this during the day?"

"Less guards and stop playing games."

It hadn't taken us long to devise the plan once we'd decided on actually going through with it. Seeing Chance had been enough to light Tray's fire, but I could tell he was slightly nervous. He'd called Gentley back over and the rest of the night had been spent going over blueprints and coordinating time schedules.

Gentley hadn't been thrilled, but like I'd noticed before—he respected Tray. Or at least he knew who the top dog was, the Alpha male, or whatever. It was all a bunch of nonsense to me. I just needed to know my part, where I was going, and what to do when I found Grayley.

Gentley figured Grayley would be underneath the gymnasium, since the school alarm was slightly louder in that room than the hallways. It made sense. The added echo probably helped us hear the alarm over Grayley's cellphone, but it was still nerve-wracking.

Once in the car, I asked, "Why not Trent? Or Geezer? My friends, not the enemy."

Tray didn't even answer. It would've been the same answer from the first three times I'd asked. Geezer wasn't reliable—he'd probably be stoned or just unable to handle whatever came up. And Trent would do, but Gentley was better. I hated it, I absolutely hated it, but Tray was right. Gentley was the best man for the job, but I needed to whine some more.

When we arrived at our rendezvous spot, my scowl was firmly in place when I saw Gentley was already waiting for us.

He scowled right back, but neither of us spoke. I was a little relieved because our constant insult-exchange had wasted an entire hour of work. Last night, Tray lit into both of us until we stopped and were reluctantly civil to each other.

"Gentley, are you absolutely certain that you'll be left alone in the parking lot all day?"

"Yeah," he shrugged, "I'm sure it's the same at your school, but there's a few of us that can't be bothered, you know."

"Taryn—" Tray had been speaking my name.

"What?"

"Are you ready to go in?"

I noticed Gentley had been checking out my outfit, but it wasn't from lust. I saw the note of surprise in his eyes.

All professional and shit, I said, "Yeah, I just gotta wind this rope quick."

"You got everything?" Tray moved to my side.

"I think so." And I did. I grabbed two small karabiners, a lethal looking knife, my rope, and anything else I could carry on my body that I'd need to break a lock...or if anything came between me and Grayley. He was down there and I was going to get him out. There was no other way around it.

"We go on your count," Tray murmured, for my ears only. Gentley had moved a few feet away, enough to give us a modicum of privacy.

"Tray," I murmured.

"Yeah?"

"Are you—" I would be fine. I knew how to handle myself, how to disappear and reappear, but Tray was coming in from the river. That meant a whole lot more open spaces than I'd have. I could hide in the nook and crannies in the school. But Tray's way was a lot more dangerous, he'd be an easy target for any marksman.

"I'll be fine," he whispered, reassuring me for the umpteenth time. And he had, over and over last night, but it wasn't enough to reassure me.

I really didn't care that he had two guns on his body. Or that his brother had been a DEA agent, and his father the chief of police. I didn't care that he'd been trained, at an early age, to handle himself and any gun he'd come across, or that he could probably out maneuver most SWAT teams.

A sniper's aim was still a sniper's aim.

He kissed my forehead and whispered again, "I'll be fine. I've done this before, just focus on getting in there and finding your friend, alright?"

I grabbed his chin and kissed him hard on the lips.

When we broke apart, I saw that Gentley was watching and he looked annoyed. "Can we get going?"

Tray threw a walkie to him and asked, "You know what to do?"

"Yeah, yeah. Watch the parking lot and if a new crew shows up, I'm supposed to call you."

"Channel eleven-twelve. Taryn and I are both on that channel, but the volume will be on vibrate so you'll have just SOS us or something. Long, short, short, short, long is the code, alright?"

If it had been under any other circumstances, maybe one where we weren't about to enter into a building without knowing if we'd be walking back out, I would've taken Tray down right then and there. The guy was just hot, all authoritarian and lethal. Plus he had a nicely tight body with muscles that contracted even when he breathed. Holy fuck.

"Taryn," he barked my way.

"Yeah." I know, I know. Distracting myself with sex wasn't going to chase away the foreboding feeling that I felt in my stomach. It was the same feeling when we'd driven by that car accident. But holy God, there was no way I'd let that feeling overpower me and keep me from getting inside today.

Suddenly I was overfilled with urgency and adrenalin. I needed to get inside that building. I needed to take that fucker down. Now.

"I'm going in," I announced and was already off, sprinting over the ditches and through the football field.

We'd decided the night before we'd hit the school early, really early, and we'd move in when they probably wouldn't expect it.

I was coming in from the school's backyard. Past the football field, the tennis courts, the swimming pool, the outside volleyball and the basketball courts. Behind the courts, there was a back door that the janitor's used for their own entrance. They usually came and went at their own freedom, so the chances were pretty unlikely that Jace would monitor that door closely. I pulled out the PRS-500 and coded in Geezer's decoder. Thumbing through the various locales and buildings, I found the janitor's door and the security code came up: six, two, three, four.

Entering it on the keypad, the light switched to green and I slipped in.

From a burglar's point of view, it was somewhat of a letdown, but I still had plenty of doors to get through yet.

I knew the camera surveillance had been upped since my last break-in, so the first vent I found, I hoisted myself up and through it. From there it was cake. Kind of, except for the fact that I ran into two small cameras placed in the venting shafts. What moron would want to watch fucking wind blow in a vent? That's right, a psychopath who I used to care about and one time thought I had loved.

Fuck him.

Each camera I came across, I merely bent my head and moved past it. The venting shafts were completely black. I was dressed in black, so only the whites of my eyes could give me away. Problem solved—I didn't look up and kept my nose to the metal as I inched forward.

At one point, the venting shaft inclined so suddenly I had to pull out some grippers to help me crawl up. I hated applying those and the space wasn't the most comfortable, but it was done with the minimal amount of movement. I tentatively moved forward, testing the first gripper to see if they still worked. When the suction cup caught and held, I pulled myself up.

Remembering the blueprints from memory, I counted the distance I'd gone so far from the pedometer I'd slipped on my wrist and saw I should be just above the security room.

This was the tricky part.

We all knew there were security guards. And we all knew they were there twenty-four/seven, so the chances of getting in and out without them knowing would be impossible. So it was my job to handle these guards. Tray would take care of the ones from his end, but it was still unnerving.

I had my taser, but we were hoping to do it a different way.

I pressed the code in my walkie and a second later, the power was shut off.

From below, I could hear the curses from each guard. That's when I made my move and slipped through the vent. They didn't know I was there, but the crackle of my taser was distinct.

"What the fuck?" one guy asked, but I circled around him and then tasered him.

The other two were already heading for the door.

I chased after them and caught one at the door before I was backhanded off the fourth.

Landing with a grunt on the floor, I twisted and aimed for his feet. I didn't have time to get up and make another attempt. He was ready and in a defensive position, so I got him in the leg.

The fucker jumped, but he landed hard.

I quickly grabbed their walkies and taped the button down, neatly tying up their only other method for communication. I knew for damn sure that they hadn't exchanged cell numbers so with the power out and the walkies down, they were alone and for the most part—vulnerable.

Well, I was still invisible, but everyone was now on alert. That'd been expected and put into the plan. Plus, we were hoping the power outage would extend all the way to the river's opening. It'd help Tray and that's what I'd really been thinking of when I passed my vote for this part of the plan.

Now we just needed to be on edge and see if Gentley would pass along his code. Hopefully not. We didn't need any extra crew showing up.

Instead of crawling through the vents, I full-out sprinted to the side door and yanked it open. From there, I ran down every flight of stairs that I found until I found myself approaching the last one. If the blueprints were right, the stairs that I was on should connect to the storage unit underneath.

And in that second, I realized that my priorities had changed. Before, I would've been excited to see whatever was inside. I would've wanted to see other bracelets like the one Brian had stolen for me. I would've wanted to see the vast expanse of drugs, piled up and to the ceiling. But now, I just wanted Grayley, Tray and myself out, safely. That's all I wanted.

I'd lost the edge.

And I didn't even care.

I heard footsteps from the opposite side, so I hoisted myself up and held myself taut against some of the railings above. Two guards exited just below me and climbed the stairs upwards.

They weren't panicked. They weren't loud, but were calm and quiet.

Good.

If they knew they'd been invaded, they'd have been running and cursing.

This was good news.

I dropped back down and moved through the still open door. As I moved down the hallway, in complete darkness, I pressed a code on my walkie. I was asking Tray if he was alright, and he answered back a second later. And he'd added an expletive at the end. It brought a grin to my face.

Some things didn't change, no matter how dangerous and hair-raising the circumstances.

The time had come, I knew it in my bones. The door to the main room now stood before me, but it wasn't the one where we guessed Grayley may be in. We really didn't know what we'd find inside, the blueprints hadn't included the bottom layer. But if they had Grayley, he'd be kept in a small room, off to the end. That meant at the far end of the action. Tray had explained why the significant percentage showed that this is where Grayley would be, but I hadn't cared. I just wanted to know where he'd be and I listened for that location. The rest was just...it was information that Tray speculated on because he had the ability to get inside their heads.

I just hoped he was right.

I moved forward. I pushed back the old, dying, thirst that had once been inside of me for the forbidden discovery and I moved to the last door.

It was bittersweet, but I didn't have time to sit and think about it.

I reached for the doorknob and opened it.

What I saw inside almost made me weep.

Grayley was inside, tied to a bed.

I couldn't speak, but I ran to his side and quickly cut through his bindings.

"What?" he mumbled, sitting up and squinting at me.

"It's me," I whispered.

"Taryn?"

"Yeah. Can you walk?"

"What? What are you doing here?" He was so fucking groggy.

"You gotta wake up and you gotta be okay to run. Not walk, but run. We have to get out of here."

"We can't. I don't know where we are."

"I do," I snapped, the fucking drugs were working miracles on him. "What'd they give you?"

"Nothing. I'm just...Taryn, what are you doing here?"

Oh my God. I yanked him upwards and dragged him to the door.

Grayley dropped to the ground.

"Get up," I snapped again, and this time I slapped him. The fucker needed to get up if he wanted to live.

I could hear my heartbeat in my ears again. I hated that sound. It was so deafening.

I had Grayley. He was alive. It was as if I'd been numb until that second. But now that I had him, I was near panic—Tray was out there.

"We have to go. Now!" I insisted, trying for anything short of shouting.

"Taryn, where are we? Where's Brian?"

He didn't know. My heart stopped for a second. I didn't want to be the one to tell him about Brian.

"We're going. Now!" I don't know if it was the adrenalin, I don't know if Brian was there with us, but suddenly Grayley stood and I had him on my back. I was almost carrying him out the door and down the hallway.

Tray said to meet him halfway. He'd come in from his end and there was supposedly a tunnel that wound up, right underneath the football field. That was our exit. It was an old tunnel on the original blueprints, but the most recent blueprints hadn't shown it. Gentley insisted it was there. There hadn't been any changes around the football field, so it meant the tunnel was there and possibly ignored by Jace. That meant a safe exit for us.

We were almost to the meeting point, I was swiftly counting each step under my breath. Twenty more to go.

Grayley stumbled a few times, but I always managed to lift him back up and keep him going.

Again, I have no idea how it was even possible.

The adrenalin was starting to wear off, but I needed enough to get to Tray. That's all I was focused on right then and there.

Pop!

Gunshot. My heart stopped. Everything went silent. Grayley fell to the ground and I stood. Still.

Pop! Pop!

Two more gunshots. I heard running from up ahead and another burst of gunfire followed.

You know the feeling when you know your fate is sealed. Like when you walk out of a lover's apartment and you stop, mid-hallway, because you know right then and there that the relationship is over? You can't explain it. You don't even understand it, but you feel it. And you know in that split second that everything had changed somehow and you were helpless, but it already happened.

That was how I was feeling. Right then and there that spread through my body. So all I could do was wait, wait for the fucking footsteps to closer to me. I needed to know who it was. And if it wasn't Tray...I grabbed for the gun he'd made me take. I strapped it to my back, wanting to forget I even had it, but he made me take it.

Tray. I let go of the gun and left it there. Still nestled in the small of my back, hidden underneath my clothing.

It was Tray that was running towards me and the world slammed back at me. Everything: the wind, the tunnel, the darkness, and Grayley. He was still on the ground, moaning in pain.

I bent and picked him back up and ran to meet Tray.

"Tray!" I gasped, but I knew he couldn't hear me.

I could see him fumbling against the wall, measuring where the door should've been. And then he was ramming the butt of his gun against the wall, trying to get at our escape route.

I dropped Grayley to the floor and took my own equipment. The end of the knife helped some, but it was our hands and feet that did most of the work.

"Fuck," I gasped, but Tray was quiet. The entire time, he was just focused and silent.

I could see the training he'd undergone in that moment. He flipped the gun in his hand like a kid who'd been given a gun for their first birthday. He turned and aimed it towards the opening where he'd come from.

"Keep working," he commanded tensely, standing poised with the gun aimed, perfectly even.

His hand was calm and steady.

I had another burst of adrenalin because I hammered at that wall, knowing my knuckles and skin were getting cut. I didn't care.

Our livelihood was on the other side. Blood, skin, and pain would gladly be sacrificed to get there.

They were coming, someone was coming. I knew it, but I kept trying. I wailed, I punched, and I kicked. I threw my entire body against the unyielding fucking wall and nothing happened.

Nothing.

Tray faced squarely whoever was coming. He had both guns out now, so I stopped and waited a second.

He didn't say anything.

He didn't order me to keep working, he didn't tell me to stop. Nothing.

And I knew it was over. We'd tried, but we'd failed.

They were here.

I reached behind me, where my gun was still secured, but just held it there. Waiting.

Three guards came around the corner and each took position, their guns pointed right at us.

It was over.

Tray didn't say anything, neither did they.

Grayley spat out some blood.

I waited.

"You disappoint me, son." Galverson stepped out, from the direction where Grayley and I had come. He looked irritatingly unperturbed, like he'd been waiting for this and was just ready at a moment's notice.

I hated him with all of my being in that moment.

Tray said nothing.

Galverson chuckled, a dry laugh, "I had high hopes for you. I thought you could go far in my business."

Tray cocked his gun.

I held my breath.

"Your father told me it was a useless hope that you to come work for me. He said you'd never consider my business proposition, but I needed to try anyway. You're a genius, Tray, but this...this was foolish. You didn't plan. This is why you failed against me."

While he'd been talking, Galverson had circled around us.

"Back the fuck up," Tray bit out, moving to match him step for step.

I was distracted for a moment when Grayley let out a short moan, but I was aware that something was off. Tray was moving away from me. He was my safety net and he was moving away, making me vulnerable.

Galverson moved in and quickly raised his gun and pointed it at me. Straight at my forehead. I couldn't move, and I couldn't disappear. I hated that.

Tray instantly realized his mistake and cursed. Galverson had distracted him, talking about his father and got enough space where I wasn't protected.

"Drop the gun, Tray." He was cold now. The act had been dropped. He was just a cold, murdering, businessman now. He sounded like he was drawing up a business plan.

"You're going to die," Tray promised, the menace was evident and genuine in his tone. He didn't drop the gun. "And you're going to die soon. I promise."

Galverson laughed. "And you'll be the one to do it? Trust me, kid, you don't have the balls. Your father was right about that."

"Is my father here?"

"No, kid. Your pops left a week ago, but he was here. He was here and he left. He's been doing that for four years now." He didn't care, not one iota how his words were cutting Tray up. Tray didn't show it, but I still saw what each word was doing to him.

I hated the asshole even more in that moment.

"I know this is where the bad guy is supposed to gloat and uncover all the nasty little secrets that went down, but,"

Galverson sighed, "I was in the middle of a business-deal and you interrupted it."

Tray moved forward. Slightly.

"Easy kid," Galverson noted, "you might be surprised at who's behind you."

Before Tray could counter his statement, Jace stepped out from behind and pointed a gun at Tray.

Galverson smiled an ugly triumphant smile as he held his gun on me.

I still had one hand on my gun, but was frozen in place.

"Taryn," Jace murmured, sadly, "I told you to stay out."

"Fuck you," I snarled.

Galverson laughed harder, but his hand was steady.

Grayley moaned again from my feet; he'd moved to sit up against the wall.

"She's a spitfire, Jace. I see why you have the hots for her."

Jace just watched me.

Tray was quiet. But not me. "I fucking hate you, Jace. I hate you so goddamn much."

"I know," Jace replied.

"Did you kill Brian? Did you?!" I screamed, but I stayed put.

Jace ignored that and replied, "You were supposed to have a better life. I gave you that life. Why couldn't you just take it?"

"Because when people I love die or vanish, I don't just give up and leave them. What were you going to do with Grayley? He's never hurt you!"

"Oh him," Galverson sniggered, "he was poking around my place. Kinda like you, little birdie. Asking all sorts of questions."

"You're going to die," I repeated Tray's prediction. I just didn't know who would kill him, me or Tray, but one of us would take him down before we did. I'd personally grab his ankle and drag him to hell with me, if I had to.

"Yes, yes. I've had lots of people tell me I'm going to die. Funny how no one seems to follow through." He chuckled, but he stepped forward. I saw the gun raise slightly and braced myself for the inevitable.

I looked up and stared boldly at Galverson, waiting.

Pop!

The world slowed; I felt the world literally drop onto my chest, like a suffocating weight in the atmosphere as I looked around.

It took a second for me to comprehend it, but I was still standing. Tray was still standing. But Galverson, he had fallen with red-velvet blood that poured out of his wound. Shock had been cemented in his eyes as he'd realized what had happened. And who had shot him.

Jace.

Jace stood above his form and he emptied his clip into Galverson's body.

"Jace?" I gasped as I staggered back a bit.

He looked up and met my eyes.

"Jace?" I asked again.

Just then three more shots rained out and the three security guards all dropped to the ground.

Jace nodded behind us. "Your brother, Chance, is out that way. If you go with him, he'll get you out safely."

Tray lingered a moment, his eyes on Galverson's body before he nodded.

"Jace?" I asked again.

"Take her with you. And Grayley." Jace ignored me.

I shook off Tray's hand and stepped forward. I grabbed Jace's arm instead and whirled him to face me. "You asshole!" I seethed and slapped him.

"Taryn, go," he said quietly, "go."

"What was this? What? I don't understand."

I wasn't going anywhere. Tray and Jace both knew it, so he sighed and said quickly, "I've been working with the DEA for six years. Tray's brother was my agent. I tried to keep you out of this, that's why I set up your adoption. Brian found out and I tried to keep him from telling you, that's when Grayley got suspicious. I think Brian told him what was going on. They didn't know I had anything to do with you leaving, but I couldn't protect Grayley. I'm sorry. I planted his phone where I knew you'd find it and I made sure that the videos got Tray's brother. I needed you guys in here sooner than later so that this could all come to an end. But I had nothing to do with Brian's death. You have to know that, Taryn!"

"The DEA?" I echoed, baffled.

"Get her out now!" Jace briskly ordered. "I can't guarantee her safety for that much longer if they find her here. Right now they'll think me and Galverson had a disagreement. I'll take over Galverson's business, they won't even look for you guys. But that's only if you're not seen. Get out!"

Tray nodded and grabbed my arm. He dragged me and carried Grayley out towards the tunnel's opening.

I floundered backwards, but gazed at Jace. He stood above Galverson's body, his gun in his hand, and he watched me right back.

I felt like my world had just been splintered, with little pieces amassing the ground I walked on.

We left Jace behind and I didn't know if that was a good or bad thing. The right or wrong thing.

Gray. Everything was just gray. There was no longer black or white.

I was vaguely aware of Tray's hands at my elbows, but I was lifted onto a boat and deposited on a back seat.

Tray was speaking to someone, his brother. They looked so much alike.

Once upon a time, I knew another pair of brothers.

CHAPTER TWENTY SEVEN

Grayley would be fine. He was dehydrated and a little malnourished, but he'd be just fine after some much needed rest and lots of fluids. He already looked better, hooked up to an IV drip and whatever else the nurse gave him. She named some kind of medication, but I was clueless. I didn't care what they gave him, as long as Grayley would be fine.

Tray's brother had his two co-workers bring us to the hospital. Tray and Chance had reconvened at Tray's home. I figured they had plenty to talk about. Later, one of Chance's co-workers mentioned that Lily—Galverson's daughter—was waiting for Chance at their hotel. I'm sure that was going to be an awkward conversation. I couldn't muster up much sympathy for the girl, but I guess I should've. She just lost her father, right? I should care.

Hell, I didn't know what it was like to have a father anyway.

I sighed as the car was pulled over just outside my home.

One of the agents stayed behind with Grayley. The other picked the short straw and got to chauffeur me around.

Dumb luck for her. Because she was about to see some major fireworks.

Both of Shelley and Kevin's cars were in the driveway.

"You alright?" Her name was Karen, the agent that worked on Chance's team. Or at least that's what Tray had explained to me. I met her eyes in the rear-view mirror. She looked nice, a bit concerned, but mostly just curious.

"I've been through the wringer and don't really have the energy to walk into a second one right now," I replied dully.

"Folks going to be pissed, huh?" Like I said, she was nice. Just nice.

"Karen," I murmured, "you don't know the half of it."

"I can come in with you, if you'd like. Chance told me to make sure you're alright and bring you back to the house. You're my job right now, Miss Matthews."

"It's Taryn."

"Taryn, it is." Karen beamed.

Karen was a bit too peppy for my usual mood, much less what I was in now.

"I'll just go in and pack my bags," I murmured, already out the door and heading up the sidewalk. I could hear yelling even before I opened the door, but the sound was even more abrasive, lambasting me once I actually opened it.

"You will listen to me, young lady!" Kevin shouted, finger pointed in the air. "You will change your attitude or you'll be going right back to that rehab."

"Dad!" Mandy gasped.

Mandy was home. And why didn't that surprise me?

I blinked in as I took in the sight. It was so much of a family meeting that I almost felt left out. Austin sat on the stairs, cradling his head. Shelley sat against the wall, arms folded across her chest. Devon was at the kitchen table, looking a little nervous. And Mandy and Kevin were toe to toe in the kitchen.

"You have brought so much shame on this family and I will not stand for your disrespect, young lady."

"So you're going to ship me off again? Oh wait! You weren't even the one to do it in the first place!"

"No, but I would've. And I won't hesitate to do it this time."

"Kevin," Shelley moaned, "stop, please. I can't handle anymore."

"Please, Mom! You can't handle this?! What a joke. You should be the one in rehab, not me and everyone knows it." Mandy scoffed.

"Amanda!" Shelley exclaimed, self-righteously. "I've never!"

"Never what, Mom? Never had the truth out in the open? Where do you think I got my first dose? Wasn't on the streets, that's for sure. And moving your little stash from the candy machine from underneath your bathroom counter to underneath your mattress didn't work. I still found 'em, Mom," Mandy taunted, and the sight was kind of beautiful.

Ouch.

Shelley looked like she was about to either explode or faint. Either one, would be entertaining.

"You, young lady, need to say goodbye to your boyfriend because it's the last time in a very long time that you'll see him again."

"What?!"

"But—" Devon started, but quieted instantly.

"You can't do that!" Mandy screeched. The honest to God perfect cheerleader mask had fallen from grace. Instead was a living breathing human being.

Thank God.

"I mean it. You are grounded until your father and I figure out what to do with you. That means no boyfriend, no phone, no computer, no television, and no parties." Who knew Shelley had it in her to be stern? And actually parent?

"What about school?"

Points for Mandy—she'd be fighting to go anywhere at this point, even school.

"No school. Not until we decide what to do."

"You mean where to ship me off?" Mandy griped.

Kevin cleared his throat. "Your mother is right. You can say goodbye to Devon and then you need to go to your room for the rest of the night."

"I can't believe you guys! You are such hypocrites! You're always gone. Always! And now you suddenly decide to be my parents?!"

Throw in a foot stomp and you'd have an official temper tantrum.

I loved this Mandy.

"We are not hypocrites and do not speak to your father like that."

"Stop it! Just stop it!" Austin cried out, hurtling to his feet. "This is bullshit. Every fucking word, it's all bullshit."

What did I say before? My mini-me.

"Austin," Shelley gasped, taken aback. Even Kevin had been shocked to silence.

I was so proud of them. A little of me had rubbed off on both of 'em.

"I think it's bullshit that we needed Taryn to man up and do your jobs. She's the one who took Mandy to rehab, she's the one who saw it was a problem and just did something about it. Mom, you don't do shit fir me. And Dad, you're never here to do anything with me. And when you are, you're always in your office. I think it's bullshit!"

Mandy looked over to Devon, but her eyes saw me in the doorway.

"This isn't about Taryn," Kevin started.

"No, it's about you two and you just suck as being parents," Austin retorted. "You don't even know where Taryn is anyway. No wonder she's always gone. Why the hell would she want to be around here when you guys aren't even around?"

Oh boy. Stab me straight in my heart.

"I'm here now, Austin," I spoke up, quietly.

He was a little punk, but in that moment, I saw the little boy in him.

"I'm sorry that I haven't been around," I added.

"And where have you been?" Shelley asked sharply.

I sighed. "I don't think this should be turned around on me."

"You took my daughter to rehab and you disappeared. Mrs. Bates told me that you've been dating that Evans boy. I do not want Tray Evans in your life, Taryn. He is a bad influence and he deserves to be in jail."

Oh, if she only knew.

I said icily, "Right now, I think Tray's the best influence I could have in my life. Especially considering it was his father who sold my adoption to you."

Shelley and Kevin—both froze. Completely still.

"I don't see why you should even make demands as to where I've been considering the fact that you got paid how much? Ten mil, is what I heard. I was an easy enough reward. Got the money and I'm not even around that much for you to deal with me and my 'stealing' ways."

"Who told you that?"

I'd had enough of this. I couldn't squelch the disdain in my voice as I said slowly, "There's a reason why you were paid to adopt me, and it's the same goddamn reason why I was able to figure it out. As far as I'm concerned, I'm done with you as my parents. This family is ridiculous. You have so many problems and I'm thinking I'm the healthiest one here. Mandy and Austin are my brother and sister, no matter what, but you two—no fucking way are you my parents. No fucking way in hell!"

"You need to watch your language," Shelley retorted. I saw the anger spark in her eyes, the rigid set in her shoulders.

But I plowed ahead, not caring, "I'm thinking my language is the least of your concerns. You wanna screw up your daughter and son? Fine, go ahead. Keep using drugs, keep letting your husband leave and avoid everything that goes on here. Just keep pushing your head in your fucking drug pillow and pretend that life's alright. It'll work its way out in the end when someone in this family ends up killing themselves. That'd be a great ending to your fucked up life."

"Shut up," Shelley whispered, "shut up."

"Please, *don't* shut up!" I threw back. "That's *your* problem. You don't say anything and hide. You both hide. Kevin, I'm pretty sure you don't have to go to all those fucking medical conferences."

I saw the relief in Mandy and Austin's eyes. And it was enough, at least for me, to keep going.

"Whatever," I bit out, moving past to the stairs, "I'm just here to pack my bags. I'll be leaving shortly. Mandy, Austin, I'm at Tray's if you need me."

After my bag was packed, the kitchen was still quiet.

Whatever.

I didn't bother to say goodbye when I shut the door.

"Taryn!"

I turned back and saw Austin at the door. He looked uncertain.

"Come on." I gestured to the car and I knew it was the right thing to do. His shoulders seemed to relax, so I threw my arm over his shoulder and murmured, "You can stay at Tray's if you want."

The punk couldn't say anything, but I saw tears in his eyes.

Karen turned in surprise when Austin and I crawled into the back. "Plus one, huh."

"Yep. What can I say? He's a little shit, but he's attached at the hip."

Austin grinned and looked out the window.

I saw one of his hands was trembling slightly, but he tucked it under his leg.

When we got to Tray's I wasn't really surprised to see the driveway packed with cars.

It was mass chaos when we walked in.

Karen quickly vanished down the hallway and I told Austin to hang out while I put my bag in the pool-house.

When I got back to the main house, there were three agents in the kitchen, talking quietly. They shut up the second I entered, but I passed 'em by, in search of Austin and Tray.

I found Austin in a back room. It looked like a smaller media room and he had already hooked up the PlayStation.

"You okay in here?"

"Yeah," Austin mumbled, not meeting my eyes. But that was okay. He was a fourteen year old boy. A lot had happened, but his cool image needed to be protected. He'd earned some 'escape' time.

"I'm going to go find Tray, so if you need something just ask. Okay?"

He shrugged.

Tray was in the library with his brother and two other agents. Karen was talking to Chance in a back corner.

"Hey," I greeted, moving to Tray's side.

"Hey." He sighed, curling an arm around my waist. He pulled me down to his lap.

"How are things here?"

"Jace turned evidence on Galverson and Broozer. Everything's out in the open and the Feds are moving in. Chance told me that they've been monitoring Galverson and have enough with everything that we have on him too."

"He's dead. What good is it to turn evidence on him?"

"Jace will get out and Galverson's entire empire is going to get destroyed. All his men, everything. They'll either scatter and head to the hills, or they'll be prosecuted and sent to prison. It's over. Everything's over. And Broozer will get prosecuted too. Chance said that was why Jace was waiting as long as he did. He wanted to take down Broozer with Galverson."

"What'll happen to Jace?"

"I don't know. Right now, Chance said that he's being protected. But he won't be protected forever. Probably Witness Protection or something."

Jace was going to away.

I tucked that away with everything else. It could be processed later.

"What about your dad?"

Tray shrugged. "He'll probably run and hide."

"So they'll want to prosecute him too?"

"Yeah."

I sighed and burrowed against his shoulder.

I was exhausted, drained, but at the same time, I felt free.

"What about your brother? You and him?"

"I don't know." Tray sounded just as exhausted as I was.

"You and me?"

Tray tucked his chin on my head and held me tighter. "We'll be just fine."

It was enough.

"Austin's here," I murmured, starting to feel drowsy. "And Mandy'll probably show up later. I'm done with Shelley and Kevin."

"You moving in here?"

"I pretty much already did."

Tray grinned against my hair. "Yeah. You kind of did."

"That okay with you?"

"Well, who would turn down all that sex?"

I punched his arm, but it turned into more of a caress.

"Speaking of," I murmured, tilting my head to look up at him, but still against his shoulder.

"Speaking of." He met my gaze. "Let's schedule a nice long orgy tonight."

And I laughed.

Before long, I fell asleep, even with all the bustling around us. But I was sheltered in Tray's arms, safe.

So I dozed.

When I woke up, I found myself in Tray's bed, in the pool-house. God, it felt so comfortable!

I meandered out though, had to. I had a little brother to check on and a phone call to Mandy was needed. Not to mention I should call Geezer and Trent about Grayley. Who even knew what happened to Gentley? Tray probably handled that, he seemed to handle everything else.

The agents were all gone when I got inside, and I saw why a second later.

I'd been sleeping for six hours.

"Hey," Tray called out from behind me.

"Hi." I yawned. "Everyone take off?"

He just grinned. I could hear the TV from downstairs and some laughter.

"Who's downstairs?"

"Carter and the gang." Tray just kept grinning.

"What?" I asked, now suspicious.

"You have any idea how long you've been sleeping?"

"Like six hours or something. I must've been tired." I yawned again, but there was something else. Something was off. I don't know...just a feeling.

"It's Thursday."

So?

Holy shit!

"Oh my God."

"You slept for two fucking days, Taryn." Tray laughed. "You must have to pee."

And I did. I suddenly felt the need right then and there.

I peeled out of there for the bathroom.

Wow, two days. Two entire fucking days. Two days. Two entire fucking days.

Tray had made a sandwich for me when I got back to the kitchen.

"Two days?" I asked weakly, leaning on the counter.

Tray grinned and shook his head. He moved to me and lifted me on the counter. He kept his arms around me, trapping me against him.

"Two days." Huh.

"Two days." He grinned again, leaned in and kissed me.

It felt good. I closed my eyes, feeling his mouth work its magic and I wrapped my arms around him.

"Hmmm," I sighed against his mouth, "can we disappear for another two days?"

Tray answered by deepening the kiss. I opened my mouth for him and his tongue swept in. Holy hell, this guy.

"Oh my God!" Carter screeched from the doorway. "She's alive!"

Tray and I kept kissing, content to ignore him.

"Okay, seriously," Carter remarked, "Room. Now, please, while I still have an appetite *for food*."

"Park it. Please!" That was Mandy and it was enough for me to look up, tearing my mouth away from Tray's, but he wasn't deterred. His lips moved to my neck and those hands were still quite busy.

Hmmm.

"Hey," I said breathlessly.

"Hi," she replied, eyebrows arched, watching Tray's expertise in person.

"You escaped." I noted, trying to hold on and concentrate.

"Yeah."

I wedged an arm between me and Tray and held him at bay while I asked, "How are the parentals? And Austin?"

"The parentals are going to marriage counseling. You and Austin leaving got through to them...I think. And I'm still in the shithouse, but they said I could come over here to see you. Austin and I didn't tell 'em that you've been asleep for two days."

"Yeah...uh—"

"Don't sweat it. Tray said some serious shit went down."

That made me smile. The short stint in rehab did something because I was watching a real human being in front of me. Not the perfect plastic cheerleader who was okay with a cheating boyfriend.

She swore now. Big change.

"Yeah." I laughed, dodging around Tray as he switched maneuvers and pulled me backwards against his chest. He started kissing my neck and slid a hand down my back, between us. When he dipped underneath my waistband, I sucked in a breath.

Mandy just grinned knowingly.

"I'm going to tell the gang downstairs the two of you are a bit...detained. And that you're awake and well."

Tray lifted me in his arms and started to stroll around the room when the doorbell peeled.

He kept walking to the pool house and Mandy called out, "I'll get the door. Don't interrupt your sexing."

Sexing. I grinned against his lips.

Walking into the pool house, Tray pushed me against the wall, sliding a hand underneath my shirt and cupping my breast.

Before long I had my fingers snagged on the inside of his jeans and was working at his zipper.

Hearing a knock at the door, both of us cursed swiftly.

"What?" Tray barked, sighing raggedly, his hand still playing with my breast.

"Uh—" Mandy said, cautious and rightfully fearful of her life.

"What, Mandy?" I called out.

Tray cursed under his breath and I had to kiss him for that.

"Um...you have a visitor...at the door."

"Who is it?" Seriously. I'd gone without sex for almost a good week now. A good hard ride was very much in order right now.

"Uh...you'll want to see this person. Trust me."

Something in her voice had me stepping away from Tray and opening the door.

And it was there—in her eyes. I knew who was going to be at the door before Mandy even spoke.

I opened the door and saw Jace standing there. ...

Jace was here.

"Hey," he murmured, watching me intently.

"Leave. Please." My voice actually cracked, a real godforsaken crack. I was always composed and he could make me do this. Fuck him.

"Taryn—" he trailed off. I saw his eyes look over my shoulders. Looking back, I saw Tray watching us, but he nodded to me and moved back into the kitchen.

"I don't want you here. I can't handle you being here," I whispered. I was being honest. And with Jace, I was always honest. I thought he'd been, too. It was how our relationship he'd been. No lies. No tricks. Just—honesty. But I was wrong.

He sighed, but murmured, "I lied."

"I'm sorry," he added, raking a hand through his hair. His dirty-blonde hair that made so many girls melt for him, literally. "I've been lying for so long that I don't...but you need to know that there's so much that I never lied to you about. It's why—"

"I needed to leave." My adoption, the entire reason why Jace wanted me out. He couldn't lie to me.

Was my heart supposed to break for him?

"Yeah." It was understood between the two of us. We felt what the other couldn't say, we understood their point of view, but it sucked ass because it hurt us—it hurt so much.

I loved Jace and that love had never been given a voice. It had never been given the chance. And he'd ripped that from me. From us.

"What happened to Brian?" I had to know. He connected us, he divided us, and he destroyed us all in the end.

"Brian found out about your adoption and he was coming to tell you. Galverson sent some of his men after him. They staged the accident. I wasn't told until later about it."

"When?" My voice was raw, hoarse, but it was real. And it was desperate. I needed answers.

"Just before the funeral. That's when I called Chance in. I couldn't do it anymore otherwise I'd risk the entire operation. I wanted to murder Sal so fucking bad. You have no idea how hard it was for me not to."

"Oh," I replied bitterly, "I know exactly how hard it was." I'd wanted to murder him.

"I'm sorry. For what it's worth."

I looked up and met his eyes. I saw a grayish tint in their green depths and I knew that I still loved him.

Fuck him, fuck him to fucking hell.

"What are you sorry for?" I asked raggedly.

"For lying to you, for manipulating you, for...I should've stopped Brian. I could've stopped the accident, but I—"

He couldn't have. He was doing a job. One more worthy and honorable than I'd ever know, but he'd lost a brother. While I'd lost my best friend/boyfriend/and security blanket.

We'd both lost Brian and it was an ache we felt in our hearts.

"Maybe." I wasn't letting him off the hook, but I understood that no one can control the future. Not ever.

"Terry," he whispered, ripping his eyes from mine.

"What did you lie to me about?"

"Huh?"

"You said that you lied, but there was a bunch you didn't lie about. So what were the lies?"

"Oh," he sighed tiredly, "just who I am, I guess. Almost everything about me. The Seven8, letting it run drugs, hiding how much I hate drugs, just...I guess everything about me."

"So what didn't you lie about?"

"I cried those nights, you know," he murmured hollowly. "You'd always leave Brian at rehab and it was our date. You and me, comforting each other, but you never noticed that I cried right alongside of you. Those nights nearly broke me."

"What about Ben and Cammy and...everyone?"

"No one knew about me. You were pretty much the only one who might've figured me out. I couldn't risk that, I'm sorry, Terry."

"So you and Cammy...were you really together?" I was not holding my breath. It didn't matter at all to me.

"Yeah, we were. I cared about her." He shrugged, "She just didn't know that I loathed her a little bit every time she snorted some coke."

He chuckled, eyes far-off, "Remember those nights when Brian would have a temper tantrum and you'd hide in my room? I loved those nights."

That was right. It was our little sick joke on Brian. He'd get mad about something and I always threatened to leave the house if he didn't stop acting like a baby. I'd always leave the house, but I never went home. I'd just circle the house and crawl up to Jace's window. He always had it open and ready for me. And every time I'd climb through, he'd just watch me silently and I'd either curl up behind his bed or in his closet. One time I was able to hide under all the covers on his bed. I'd fallen asleep that night and Brian had been furious with me. I woke up the next morning and Jace had been right next to me. That was the first time I felt a tingle from him.

For a week after that whenever Brian would have a tantrum, I actually left the house for mine.

"Yeah," I murmured.

"Fuck, Terry—"

"I know."

"I loved Brian so fucking much and we—"

"I know."

"It wasn't just Dad, you know. Yeah, Dad did his best to brainwash Brian against me, but it was you too. Bri met you first, that was the bottom line and even if I could've taken you away from him...you'd never let me. Because that's who you are."

It was true. I really had loved Brian, but what I felt for Jace was different. Just totally different. And now...it was a bittersweet love.

"I'm sorry," I said hoarsely, "I have no idea what you went through."

"Yeah, you do." Jace grinned sadly. "You just weren't ever given the chance to know your parents. I was, but they didn't want me around."

"I didn't mean that."

"I know."

We both knew.

Brian was gone, buried and at rest. He was happy, finally at peace, and the best version of Brian would've wanted me to say this. So I looked up and spoke, clearly, "I loved you, Jace."

Jace met my eyes quickly, a sheen of tears misting over his beautiful eyes.

I added, "I loved Brian and I loved you, but they were different loves. And I'm sorry that I was never brave enough to choose between them. I think I ripped the two of you apart because I just avoided what everyone knew was there. I'm sorry, Jace."

"I love you too." It wasn't past tense and we both knew it.

Jace lifted a hand and brushed a tear away from my cheek. I hadn't even realized I was crying.

But it broke the dam, that simple soft touch.

Jace drew me against his chest as I sobbed. I let my arms encircle him as I pulled him tighter to me and I felt him bend his forehead to my shoulder. I felt his own tears on my shirt.

He cried right alongside of me.

Jace had made a decision for me a year ago and because of it, everything he'd lived for had been unraveled. And I was in a better place in life. I had a brother and a sister.

I had Tray.

Who would've ever thought it? At first glance a rich, shallow, spoiled boy who had morphed into a man who was capable of what most would shudder from thought.

But right now, this was me and Jace. And we were mourning more than just us.

We both loved Brian. We both had intense, dysfunctional relationships with Brian. But we both loved him and only the other could understand what was ripped out of us from the inside.

Brian had been the rebel innocent that both Jace and myself had never been allowed. And he knew it and he hated it because he wanted what Jace and I had. He didn't want to be innocent, protected. He wanted the respect and power that Jace had carved out and what I demanded from necessity.

But it was all over and done with now. I'd thought before, every time I said goodbye, each of those times had been the last. But I'd always known it wasn't. I still had ties to Brian, I still had ties to Pedlam, and to Jace.

But this really was it.

Jace was leaving.

"What's going to happen now?" I asked, against his shoulder.

His arms tightened around me. "I'll go in Witness Protection and I'll testify when they need me."

"Are you in danger?" Déjà vu. I'd asked that so many other times.

And I felt Jace's cocky answering grin against my hair. "I'm always in danger."

"Shut up."

"On it." He sighed, but still chuckled. He hugged me one last time and murmured, "Don't ever let Evans get away with anything. The guy needs to be held accountable. That's your job now."

"I did it to you and Brian. I can handle my own."

"I know." Jace sighed, pulling back slightly. "But I still really hate the guy."

That was quite alright with me.

I saw his car waiting, Jace saw my eyes trail over his shoulder. So I murmured, huskily, "I love you."

"I know. Me too," he whispered and bent for my lips.

It was the second time I'd kissed him since our cheated night.

It was soft, tender, and loving. It was the Jace that only I knew, no one else.

He pulled away and nodded once, in farewell, and walked to his car. As he climbed into the backseat, something inside of me went with him. Some part of me was sitting in that backseat of his, right alongside of him.

But it was the part that needed to go, because I felt every chapter in my book close.

Who knew closure could be so painful and so refreshing at the same time.

Fucking bittersweet. I hated this feeling. Really, really fucking hate it.

I felt Tray behind me without looking, without any sound.

"Hey," he whispered, sliding an arm around my waist and pulling me against his chest.

"Hi."

He kissed my neck and asked, "Everything alright?"

"It's over." It was the only answer I had. It'd be alright and a part of me already felt it was alright. But for now...I'd closed the last page of that book.

And it just hurt.

But I think it was supposed to.

It's called healing.

EPILOGUE

The water felt refreshing. It always did. And when I surfaced, it was to the sound of the crowd going wild.

Two years now, I'd been the recurring champion at Nationals on the Columbia diving team.

In some ways, Shelley had been right. The scholarships had come in and I'd chosen Columbia. I'd won the first two years and this year I was competing again.

Except Shasta Yoiuen was my competition this year and fuck—she was good. Really good.

She'd beaten me at regionals two months ago, but I knew that I'd just won. I'd just pulled off the best fucking dive of my life. And there was no way in hell that Shasta was going to take that title away from me.

I hadn't gone through hell and back only to be beat by someone like her.

"You fucking have it, girl!" my teammate, Sari, squealed. I loved Sari. Her and I had flocked together our first practice and bonded at a party that night. Of course, she was the incarnation of me in high school, except she slept around a lot more than me. I'd been with three guys my entire life. She'd been with three that first week. But you couldn't help but warm to her jest for life.

She added, "Shasta knows it too. Look at her, she's pissed! No way can she beat that, no fucking way. I love it, man. I love you, you kick ass."

"Good job, Taryn." Coach Mayer patted me on the shoulder. I loved it. He was reserved as hell and I knew the smallest pat shouted volumes.

A second later my scores came up and a deafening roar went around the pool-house.

I'd won. Shasta was a mere shadow compared to my near perfect scores.

Laughing, I ducked around most of my teammates, but a few managed to engulf me in hugs.

My win brought the team to first place.

Everyone on the team had just won a gold medal from Nationals.

Fuck yeah.

I grabbed a towel and pulled my swim-dress over my head before heading to the stands.

Mandy was visiting and Carter couldn't have been happier.

And when I made my way up to them, amidst a sea of well-wishers, I had to wait. The two were disgusting and drowning each other.

"Ahem!" I coughed, not at all subtle.

"Taryn!" Mandy giggled, wiping her mouth. She shoved Carter aside and gave me a tight hug. "I'm so proud of you!"

"I could tell," I said dryly.

"I am." She blushed. "We were just—"

"Carter's happy you're here," I said simply. And he was. It'd taken eight more break-ups due to Devon's cheating, but Carter finally made a stand and the two of them had been together for a year and a half now.

"Taryn, that was awesome. You're a great swimmer." Whatever. Carter came for two reasons. To see girls in their bathing suits and to make-out with Mandy as much as humanly possible.

"Hey, hey." Grayley greeted from behind me, wrapping his arms around me. In my ear, he whispered, "That was fucking hot, Taryn. Really. I'm proud of you."

I blinked the tears away, but his words...got me right there, you know. He was my best friend.

"Geezer will be just as happy as me when I call him," he added.

"Right. Happily stoned," I remarked, sarcastically. Geezer hadn't changed. He still liked the marijuana too much, but...what can you do. He'd probably always be a stoner, but Grayley had mentioned a girl. Maybe Geezer would hold back for the new girlfriend. But I wasn't holding my breath.

"Hey, Taryn. Where's Tray?"

"He was hoping he'd get back in time for the meet, but guess not. Chance wanted him to stick around for some extra meeting. I don't know. He sounded pissed on the phone last night."

"Where's he at?" Mandy asked.

"He flew to some conference with Chance and then they were going to visit their dad. All I know is that he was not having fun."

"Are they still trying to recruit him?"

"Yeah. But Tray wants nothing to do with any of them. DEA, none of them. Ask me, I think Tray kind of gets a kick out of watching Chance's supervisors send their little agents to do surveillance on him. They still think he held back a lot of his contacts when he was working for Galverson and the police force at Rawley."

"Dude, Tray's gotten scarier, if you ask me." Mandy murmured, but firmly encased in Carter's arms.

And he had. But it was a topic no one talked about. Mandy just broke that unspoken rule.

"Oh hey," Grayley murmured, "he's right over there."

And there he was, looking as delectable and fine as shit.

I could see his tattoo underneath the black muscle shirt he had on and it mixed well with the second tattoo he'd gotten between his shoulder blades. It was the Hebrew word for loyalty. And it meant a lot to both of us. I'd been there when he'd gotten it and the sex had been explosive that night.

Mandy was right. Tray had gotten a bit scarier, but I knew most of it was because he was having a hard time dealing with Chance and his father. His dad hadn't ran. He'd been prosecuted and he was in the penitentiary.

It didn't help that some of his father's lawyers were hounding Tray to pay them for his dad's legal services. Tray kept refusing to pay them. He wasn't his father and he didn't own any of his loans. Plus, Chance was always on the phone harping at Tray. Chance was among the legends of government authorities that thought Tray hadn't been completely honest in all the evidence he'd handed over.

And he hadn't been. But would you, considering that you had two drug empires on one side and the government on the other?

Tray kept what he needed to for his life and mine. We called it our life insurance.

And that was something Mandy, Carter, and Grayley weren't privy too. No one was.

I moved away from the group and met Tray on the bottom steps of the bleachers.

"Hey," I whispered, being pulled into his arms.

"Hey," he greeted, kissing me hotly. Almost desperately.

I raked my hands through his hair, twisting them helplessly when the waves of lust engulfed me. He could always do that to me.

"Okay. Public," I panted, pulling away slightly.

"I caught the dive."

I melted and wrapped my arms tighter around his neck. "Really?"

"Really." He grinned and dipped his head again.

"Hmm," I moaned against his mouth, "I'd love to continue this wild orgy that is engraved in writing for tonight, but we have visitors from out of town."

"Mandy will be busy with Carter. Let's escape now."

I grinned, and felt him pull me back for another kiss. I felt like my panties might melt off.

"Seriously," he murmured, burying his head into my neck, "I need some time with you and not them. Mandy'll be fine with Carter. She's coming here anyway next semester. And Grayley goes here, he can see you tomorrow in class."

"I am not looking forward to that semester. Shelley and Kevin are going to be in town a whole lot more."

"Here come the bribes of money, dinners, cars, and lunches," Tray joked.

And it *was* kind of funny. Mandy had cleaned up after a second stint in rehab, but Shelley still refused her problem.

To their chagrin, I'd stayed away. But Shelley and Kevin continuously send me cards and gift packages. They wanted a relationship and would wait when I decided I wanted one too.

It'd been three years. They weren't getting the hint.

But oh well. I was still taking their money and saving it. I thought about buying a plane ticket to see them, ripping it in half, and mailing it to them. Maybe they'd get the idea then.

But Mandy seemed better, probably because she wasn't living there anymore. Austin had turned into the school's bad boy, but that was to be expected. He ran the school almost as well as Tray.

I was proud, like a momma.

My thoughts were distracted again when Tray maneuvered us so that I was between him and the wall. When he dipped his head, I lost conscious ability and surrendered myself.

Like I always have.

And like I always would.

"Taryn, are you going to the party tonight?" Sari exclaimed breathlessly, her gold medal already around her neck. She was fingering it, looking from me to the medal and back again.

Tray neatly hoisted me up and I wrapped my legs and arms around him. As he explored the crook between my neck and shoulder, I grinned lazily to my teammate, "Of course. The team won, it's going to be a raver."

"Fuck yeah. I'm going to get laid." She beamed excitedly, and flushed.

Tray lifted his head and remarked dryly, "I'm trying to get laid right *now*."

Sari rolled her eyes. It'd been like this between them since the first day, three years ago.

Sari wanted to party and Tray wanted his own partying. But for the most part, they got along.

"When aren't you?" she griped, but it was good-natured.

It had better be.

"Can you two stop mauling each other?" Mandy asked, arriving with Carter behind her. I saw Grayley was talking with another teammate of mine across the pool. He'd been after her for a while, about fucking time he got somewhere with her. Not that Grayley had a problem finding girls, it was the opposite, but for some reason...he was holding back with this one.

Kara's nice and all, but she didn't hang out with me and Sari for a reason. She was a good girl.

Maybe that's what he needed. A nice tame girl that would never get him mixed up in a drug-deal gone bad where he's captured and has to recuperate in the hospital for two weeks.

Tray pinched my ass.

"Hey," I cried out.

"Your mind was wandering," he murmured, and looked over to where I'd been watching. "He's a big boy. He'll be fine."

Sari looked over too and harrumphed. "She's a pansy. I don't like her."

Sari and Grayley tried for a good month. That had been freshman year. Ever since then, they'd just been fuck buddies when the need arose. It arose often, for both of them.

"So what's the plan? Are we going out to eat or what?" Mandy asked, Carter tucked her against his side.

"Sari says party, so we party tonight. I don't really care right now. I just want to shower and change." I slid down from Tray, but leaned against him. I noticed Mandy watching him intently.

"Alright. Should we meet up in an hour?" Mandy asked.

"How about two." Tray said briskly.

Carter grinned.

"I'll give you a call later, Taryn." Sari waved off, heading across the pool and a moment later she had subtly maneuvered herself between Kara and Grayley.

I loved that girl.

"I'll do the same and we can grab a bite to eat, okay?" Mandy suggested as Carter was already leading her away.

Tray gestured to the side door, "You need to do anything else? You want me to wait for you?"

"No. I've got everything." And I did. I had my swim dress on and I dangled my car keys in front of him. Everything else was either locked in my car, at home, or in my locker in the pool-house.

The apartment wasn't far away and within a few moments Tray pulled into the driveway.

The house was huge, but not as big as the one he'd had in Rawley. But according to the average college student standards, it was still a fucking palace.

Once we were inside, Tray and I attacked each other. He'd been gone entirely too long.

We fell to the bed and Tray rose above me, staring at me.

"What?" I asked.

His hands were caressing my thighs and working their way inside my bathing suit. I felt his thumb flick against me and gasped. It always worked.

He grinned and slowly bent down to meet my lips, dipping his tongue inside as his thumb slid inside.

I could only hold on as the fever built and a little later, I exploded over the edge.

Fuck.

Then his shirt was off, my dress was pulled off and the swimsuit was quickly thrown on the floor.

Tray was anchored between my legs as he bent to kiss and lick from my lips, down my jaw, and finding my breasts. He suckled one nipple as my legs wrapped around his lean hips.

It was too much.

"Tray," I whimpered, clasping him tighter.

"Pretty soon, baby." And he kept his slow exploration and I was going insane.

"Tray," I said sharply.

He slid his hands down behind me in response and arched my hips to him better for a better angle. And then he slid inside of me, filling me completely.

The first thrust went deep, as they always did, and I arched my body against his. Each thrust took us closer.

Tray grabbed my hands and held them above my head as he bent to suck on my nipples, still thrusting in and out of me.

I almost screamed as I climaxed and Tray shuddered right alongside of me.

A moment later, as we rode the waves out, Tray curled up behind me and tucked his head on my shoulder.

I felt a soft kiss and laced our fingers together.

"I'm glad you're back," I said softly.

"Me too." His voice was slightly muffled as his breath tickled my skin.

"It was hard seeing everyone," I noted.

The trip, seeing his father, and spending time with his brother. I knew that he needed me right now.

"Yeah," he breathed out.

For now, I would leave it alone. Instead, I said, "Mandy's really excited about moving here."

"Carter's excited, too."

I rolled onto my back and met his gaze, both of us adjusting to still stay in each other's arms.

"She's kind of afraid of you." I had to say it. Tray would notice, he's not dumb.

Tray shrugged. "As long as she doesn't try to poison you against me, I don't really care."

"You could be nicer, you know." In some ways, Tray had stopped caring about his reign in Rawley. It was his job, he took it upon himself, to take care of what was his. Rawley was his. But after everything that happened, with Galverson and Jace...he'd become content with only talking to me, Carter, Bryce, and Grant. Amber and Jasmine stopped coming over to the house and after Mandy returned from one of her stints in rehab, she'd stopped considering Tray as a friend.

The publicity had been crazy once everything was out in the open. It was the biggest drug-bust in years and the headlines focused a lot on Tray's family. The media was fascinated with Tray and his family. A father who'd been the police chief turned drug lord. The eldest son a DEA agent. And the youngest son, the one who brought it all to a head.

It hadn't helped that both sons were gorgeous and had the same charismatic 'fuck everyone' attitude.

Tray stopped caring about everyone when everyone became obsessed with him.

Like I said, he'd turned to me and a select few. Most of my teammates and friends couldn't understand why I was with him. They all saw what Mandy now saw. A tough dick capable of being ruthless. Which he was and it's what he showed the world, but they didn't see the other side of Tray.

Tray shrugged. "Mandy and all your other friends are scared of me because they don't understand me. I really don't give a shit to sit and let them analyze me or explain myself to them. It's been almost four years that we've been together. You'd think it'd be enough for them to know that I love you and I make you happy."

"You used to be a friend to her," I only said. .

Tray sighed, and pulled away slightly, but he kept his hand still laced with mine.

"It's just...it's too much, Taryn. I've got Chance on my back, those fucking agents keep tailing me, and I swear I saw one of Lanser's old men watching me yesterday at the conference. I've got enough just trying to survive without having to focus on making your friends like me."

I sighed and moved to straddle him. Tray watched me lazily, his hands automatically resting on my thighs. He moved them up and down. One hand slid to caress my stomach.

I loved it when he did that.

He sat up and moved against the headboard, pulling me with him.

His hand moved to cup my breast, then caressed down against my curves before moving back up to fondle me again.

"You took care of that. You have insurance." I wasn't talking about health insurance.

"Yeah."

"And you're on surveillance because Chance doesn't want anything to happen to you."

The problem was that Tray hated feeling caged and being watched made him feel caged. But it had been like this for three years, and it *was* getting better.

"Yeah."

"So let's go party tonight and you could try to forget about the world on your shoulders. For one night, maybe," I suggested, grinning lightly as he grinned back and tucked me closer against him.

One quick adjustment and he slid inside.

He slowly thrusted upwards, and remarked, "I'd like to start forgetting right now."

Oh...fuck.

I sighed into his mouth and I couldn't help but reflect.

I had survived so much. Life. Brian's death. Jace's separation from my life. And right now, Tray and I were surviving together.

But we were doing pretty damn good.

We had persevered and we were still fucking conquering.

www.tijansbooks.com

34802917R00324

Printed in Great Britain
by Amazon